PONNIYIN SELVAN

BOOK2 : WHIRLWINDS

KALKI R KRISHNAMURTHY

Translated from the Tamil by Pavithra Srinivasan

ZERO DEGREE PUBLISHING

Original in Tamil, Ponniyin Selvan : ©KALKI R KRISHNAMURTHY
English Translation, Ponniyin Selvan : ©Pavithra Srinivasan
First Edition: 2019
By ZERO DEGREE PUBLISHING

ISBN: 978 93 88860 09 3
ZDP Title : 25

ZERO DEGREE PUBLISHING
No.55(7), R Block, 6th Avenue,
Anna Nagar,
Chennai - 600 040

Website: www.zerodegreepublishing.com
E Mail id: zerodegreepublishing@gmail.com
Phone : 98400 65000

Typeset by Vidhya Velayudham
Cover Art by Art Muneeswaran

PONNIYIN SELVAN

PUBLISHERS' NOTE

Writers are the cultural identity, the memory of the aeon, the conscience and the voice of the society. By the sheer magic of their art, they surpass the barriers of language, land and culture. Any country should pride itself on possessing writers – national assets – whose works in translation have the potential to catapult them into international renown.

The Latin American Boom during the 1960s and '70s was a launchpad era that thrust names such as Julio Cortázar, Gabriel García Márquez, Carlos Fuentes, Jorge Luis Borges and Mario Vargas Llosa into the Anglophone literary world where they enjoyed a plausive reception.

Publication of translated nineteenth-century Russian literature fetched Tolstoy and Chekhov iconic status. Due to the availability of and the demand for their works in translation, Haruki Murakami of Japan and Orhan Pamuk of Turkey have become bestselling writers to watch in the present day and age.

What we understand from all of this is that translation and publication are fruitful endeavors that engage national writers and their oeuvres with the world at large and vice versa.

Zero Degree Publishing aims to introduce to the world some of the finest specimens of modern Indian literature, to begin with, we take great pride in introducing Tamil literature in English translation because, as Henry Gratton Doyle said, "It is better to have read a great work of another culture in translation than never to have read it at all."

– Gayathri Ramasubramanian & Ramjee Narasiman
Publishers

Dedication

To Kalki R Krishnamurthy—who first opened my eyes to the wonderful world of history, and guided my first hesitating steps towards the incredible world of historical fiction. From you I learnt my past; through you, I look to my future.

-Pavithra Srinivasan

CONTENTS

Poonguzhali..11

A Muddy Morass..20

Muddled Minds 26

At Midnight...33

All at Sea 40

The Hidden Mandapam 47

"Samudhra Kumari"...58

Demon Island 71

"Here is Ilankai!"...80

Aniruddha Brahmaraayar 86

The Therinja Kaikkola Regiment 94

Guru and Disciple..104

"Ponniyin Selvan" 116

Full Moons Two 123

A Lament in the Night..130

Sundara Chozhar's Delusions 139

"Do the dead ever return?" 150

"Which is the worst of betrayals?" 160

"They've captured the spy!" 167

Two Tigresses 174

The Dungeons..180

Sendhan Amudhan, Incarcerated..188

Nandhini's Nirupam 197

As Wax in Flame 204

Magnificent Maathottam...213

A Bloodthirsty Dagger...218

Through the Jungle..225

The King's Road..233

The Mahout 243

Fast and Furious Battle 252

The Elela Singan Koothu 259

Killi Valavan's Elephant 264

The Statue's Message 271

Anuradhapuram 275

The Throne of Ilankai 286

The True Measure of Worth? 298

Kaveri Amman 306

(He)art Speaks! 312

"Here's Battle!" 322

Mandhiralosanai 329

"Look over there!" 337

Poonguzhali's Dagger 343

"I'm a criminal!" 349

A Rampaging Elephant 361

The Prison Ship 375

Tumultuous Hearts 387

Ghoulish Laughter 400

Death of a Kalapathi 411

The Ship Hunt 417

The Sworn Guardians 423

Whirlwinds 438

The Wrecked Boat 452

Song of a Saviour 462

1

POONGUZHALI

The evening was serene, in its beauty. The sea lay subdued, its exuberance calmed; low waves murmuring along the shores of Kodikkarai. Catamarans and boats bobbed on the waters, making their way towards land; birds fluttered home from sea, at the end of their daily quest for sustenance. Pristine white sands stretched a little away from the water; beyond, dense, thick jungle claimed the landscape, extending for league upon endless league. Not a single branch on these hoary old forest trees swayed; not a leaf stirred. Silence lay upon them, a thick, stifling veil, stretching in all four directions. The sun sank to the horizon, his brilliant red-gold rays dazzling where sky and earth met in their eternal quest for togetherness. A few straggling clouds, failing in a fruitless attempt to hide his glorious light, caught a few stray beams and glowed bright in the evening sky.

A tiny boat bobbed on the sea, close to the shore. Gentle waves rocked the craft like a child's cradle, taking care not to play havoc with the little vessel—which carried a young woman.

And we remember, in an instant, Sendhan Amudhan's ecstatic, almost reverent description of his young cousin. Indeed—this must be Poonguzhali; her luxurious tresses even hold a single petal of the fragrant thaazhampoo, as if to bear out the truth of her name. Long, silky black ringlets flowed from her crown in waves, setting off slender, beautifully moulded shoulders to advantage. The sea scoured its depths and poured out bountiful resources: shells, tiny conches and the like, onto its shores; she had gathered and strung them into a fascinating necklace that now decorated her swan-like neck. Truth be told—they attained a sort of unearthly beauty by ornamenting her, rather than set off her considerable loveliness. But then, what sort of exotic jewel could possibly enhance a face and form that defied description—that was beauty incarnate in every way?

She lay in her boat, majesty limning her every movement, languid, free and enchanting—and then she lifted her voice in song.

Was this why the sea lay like glass, its waves a mirror of tranquility? Was this why the wind died down, tempering its raucous cries to a soothing murmur, in a bid to catch the cadence of her voice? Did every leaf and branch adorning trees in the distant forest silence their endless rustling, just to listen to her lilting melody? Sky and earth pause in their eternal, celestial duty, drunk with the beauty of her exquisite song? And perhaps this was why even the sun tarried a while longer, rather than make for the horizon and sink to the west—just to listen, a little more, to Poonguzhali's voice.

And if they can, so shall we, to verses dipped in honey, wafting upon the gentle sea breeze:

Why anguish, my soul,
When tumbling seas lie smooth?
Why rage, dear heart,

When Lady Earth sleeps, soothed?
Birds of the forest,
Flit homewards, to their nest
Hunters and bowmen
Trudge happy, to their rest
The sky spreads, tranquil,
At ease stay the four worlds,
Yet, beauteous maiden, doe-eyed,
What pains thy heart, why mourn?
Heaving oceans lie still,
Gentle breezes calm,
Yet, sweet maiden
What churns thy heart, what storm?

What storm indeed? What prompted a young woman to sing with such unbearable grief? What was this bittersweet blend of pleasure and pain that overwhelmed her lovely voice? Or perhaps the song itself was fashioned not just with words, but with tears? No one can divine the truth. What we *do* know is that those words and that voice, mingling with the melody, almost break our hearts with their exquisite lament; their grievous sorrow.

Poonguzhali's song faded away. She took hold of the oars, pulled strongly a few times, and beached the shore. She leapt out of the craft nimbly and pulled the boat upon the sands. A few catamarans lay in a heap nearby and she hefted up her craft, making sure it rested against them. Then she leant against her boat, scanning the surroundings.

There! A roaring fire flared on the *mandapam* atop the lighthouse. The flames licked the wood, rising higher with every moment; it would last all night, lighting the beach. *Caution! Do not approach any closer!*—thus would it cry out to vessels scouring the seas. And there was reason enough for such frantic warnings: the shores of Kodikkarai were extremely shallow; the only vessels that could dock here were small

13

ones: catamarans and little boats. Should ships and yachts be so foolish as to approach the shores, they would find themselves aground within moments. Speed would not be of any use either; the vessels would simply splinter and crumble. The fires atop the lighthouse, thus, provided an incredible service to those who plied large ships.

Somewhere in the distance rose a temple spire amongst the dense trees; the home of the deity Kuzhagar, who lived in splendid isolation, guardian to these lonely parts.

Approximately two hundred years ago, the great Saivite saint and Nayanmar, one among the most loyal devotees of Siva Peruman, Sri Sundara Murthy Naayanar arrived at Kodikkarai and chanced upon the deity Kuzhagar, holding His divine and lonely vigil amidst the forest.

"My lord, my soul—who do You guard these forsaken lands; why isolate Yourself on these shores, with none by Your side?" He lamented. "Could You not find another place worthy of Your divine powers? While devotees throng other shrines; where they revere You with great gifts and *bhakthi*, why distance Yourself from them here, in the midst of this dense jungle by the sea? Ah, that my eyes, unfortunate eyes were fated to see this terrible blight—to witness such a sight!"

"Kadithaik kadarkaatru vanthetrak karaimel,
kudithanayale irundhar kutramaamo?
Kodiyen kangal kandana kodik kuzhageer
Adikel umakkaar thunaiyaaga irundheere?
Matham malisoozh maraikaadathan renpaal
Pathar palar paadavirundha parama!
Kothaar pozhilsoozhtharukodik kuzhaga
Ethaar raniye irundhai? Embiraane!"

Two hundred years after the great saint's visit to the shrine, Kodikkarai's guardian deity still stood alone, amidst ancient trees, shrouded by silence. The jungle had grown even denser, if possible; owls and other birds nested in branches, breaking the silence with their mournful hoots. A few huntsmen, almost cadaverous in appearance, were the only ones courageous enough to fashion a few ramshackle dwellings amidst the trees and make the forest their home.

But stay—there *was* a difference. No lighthouse had existed when Sundaramurthy visited Kodikkarai; this imposing structure had been built a few years ago, in the time of Paranthakar the First. A few simple, tile-roof homes had been allotted to the exclusive use of those in the employment of lighthouse maintenance; the priest who performed daily worship in the Kuzhagar Temple also shifted his residence, here.

Poonguzhali gazed around, leaning almost negligently against the boat. The lighthouse, lit gloriously, beckoned; she wondered if she should make her way there. Then, she glanced at the Kuzhagar temple's spire. The *semangalam* pealed at that moment in loud, strident tones and made the decision for her: what was she to accomplish, going home just now? She may as well visit the temple; ask the priest the favour to sing a few Thevaram hymns. Even receive some delicious *prasadham* offerings, and make a meal of it.

To think was to act. Poonguzhali slipped off her post and made her way to the temple. Skipping, dancing, and singing little snatches of song, for such was her temperament at the moment. A herd of deer gamboled across her; sprinting on swift legs along the white sands towards the forest. A little fawn sprang and leapt along with seven or eight of its elders, trying desperately to keep pace. Poonguzhali's heart swelled with exhilaration at the sight. She darted after them in turn, as though trying to capture one. No matter what her speed, though, could anyone ever hope to outrun a deer? The graceful animals evaded her with ease.

A few of them suddenly leapt high, almost seeming to hang in the air for a few moments before they touched down, a good distance away. There, Poonguzhali guessed, lay a quagmire, probably. A muddy hole of death. The bigger deer had managed to cross it without difficulty, but the little fawn was not so fortunate. It tried valiantly to imitate the adults but found that the jump had been too much; its hind legs were stuck fast, in the mud. It tried hard, using what little strength it had to push hard on its forelegs and raise itself, but the treacherous mud was far more powerful. The mother, a beautiful doe, stood by the bank, gazing at its young one with piteous eyes. But there was nothing it could do.

Poonguzhali grasped all these in an instant, and set about gauging where exactly the quagmire came to an end. She ran along the edges, stepping carefully on firm ground that did not give away traitorously, and reached the little fawn trying desperately to pull free. The mother jumped at her approach, clearly frightened out of its wits. Poonguzhali, it seemed, was an expert in communicating with deer; her lips moved, her voice a soft, soothing murmur that calmed the nervous animal at once. Poonguzhali bent and knelt along the edge of the mud pit, reached her hands out to the fawn, grasped it firmly, and began to tug forwards. It stumbled onto firm land; for a few moments, its body shook and shivered in the aftermath of its ordeal. The mother nosed around her child, seeking, perhaps, to reassure it. The next instant, doe and fawn had leapt to their feet and galloped into the forest.

"*Chee*, such ungrateful brutes!" she grumbled. "And yet—not as bad as humans, surely?" She consoled herself, rising and dusting herself off. Then, she continued on her way to the Kuzhagar Temple.

Once past the sandy stretch, she walked along a path almost choked by forest foliage that crested small mounds and dipped unaccountably into pot-holes. This particular jungle, it must be admitted, was rather an anomaly of nature; it boasted no craggy hills abounding with rocks and boulders but only a vast, seemingly unending stretch of sand. The very earth had hardened into mounds through the vagaries of natural forces; bushes and creepers had taken root there, turning them into miniature hillocks. Deep valleys nestled right by said hillocks; this was treacherous terrain with no room to err. We might walk endlessly, caught in the illusion of getting from one place to another—but would find ourselves chalking endless circles, arriving where we started!

Poonguzhali strode swiftly along the path and arrived at the temple within a matter of moments. Outside the shrine and even within the inner walls stood large trees; *konrai* and *panneer* flourished in the temple courtyard, blooming with a hundred fragrant blossoms. She entered the temple whereupon the Battar caught sight of her. His face brightened at once. Few were the visitors to this ancient, lonely shrine; no surprise, then, that he turned to greet her with all the spirit and delight usually accorded to royalty.

He brought her a shell of coconut, the tender kernel intact, and a few temple offerings. "Will you wait here awhile, *Amma*? I shall be along in a moment, once I have locked and made safe the shrine."

Finding your path amidst that dense jungle, especially at night, was an almost impossible feat—but with Poonguzhali at your side, the unfeasible dissolved to naught; there was nothing to fear.

"By all means, *Ayya*," she assented. "Do take your time with your temple duties. I'm in no hurry."

She wandered to the wide passage that ran around the temple and meant for circumambulation, the *praharam*, grabbed hold of a convenient tree branch and heaved herself gracefully onto the *madhil*. A well-proportioned, large statue of the deity Nandi stood where the walls met at right-angles; she leant against it, stretching along the *madhil* with languid ease, and bent her attention towards scraping the coconut with strong teeth.

Twilight was upon the land; darkness seemed to fall with remarkable speed, closing in all four directions. Even as Poonguzhali watched nature's fascinating play, the clip-clop of horse-hooves reached her sharp ears. She turned, gazing at the path with some eagerness. For some reason, the sounds seemed to stir strange memories in her heart; memories of events that swept her away to a dreamland, a land of fantasies.

Something rose her throat—a lump of sorrow that seemed to choke her. Who on earth could be coming? But then, what did it matter? Strange men seemed to wander in and out of this place of late; bound on royal missions, they claimed. Two had even arrived yesterday, and Poonguzhali had felt her stomach turn at the sight of them. They had asked her elder brother to ferry them to Ilankai, showering him with a great many gold coins. *Gold! Ha, who needs their precious money? May the Gods curse those wretched coins, may thunder rain down on it—what could you do with gold and gems in this God-forsaken forest?* And yet, *Annan* and *Anni*, her brother and his wife coveted wealth; they lusted after it. She never could understand their avarice. They were intent on gathering every coin they could find and burying it like treasure.

The hooves sounded nearer, now, and it seemed there was not just one horse, but two. There they were, coming into sight; climbing steadily from a dip in the land on to higher ground. Traveled obviously, for long, and over a great distance; their exhaustion was palpable. Each carried a rider. The first was clearly young; his features were chiseled, open, and his physique, impressive. A proud mien, too—but no matter how excellent his features, could they possibly compare with the sheer beauty and majesty of *that* visage? Why, this one looked almost like a flat-faced owl skulking in a tree-hole, compared to that angelic countenance!

The first traveler, as our readers might have guessed by now, was none other than our old friend, Vallavarayan Vandhiyathevan. The other was the physician's son. Both had traveled without pause from Pazhaiyarai and as befitting those who had covered great distances, looked and felt on the verge of collapse. And yet, once he caught sight of Poonguzhali, leaning nonchalantly upon the temple wall, Vandhiyathevan's eyes brightened perceptibly. The moment he realized that she was subjecting his face to a careful scrutiny, his fatigue vanished; he was almost back to his usual, indefatigable self. He nudged his horse to a stop and stared at her keenly, in turn. Had he known that this fascinating young woman was comparing his face, at that very instant, to an owl in a tree, it is doubtful if he might have felt such complaisance or eagerness. What a wonderful thing it is, to be sure, that one cannot divine the thoughts of others as they wish!

Poonguzhali realized, a little belatedly, that this stranger was staring at her for all he was worth—and that she herself was gnawing at a coconut kernel, at that moment. A sudden twinge of bashfulness made its presence felt; she jumped from the *madhil* to the sandy ground. Then, she began to run along the temple wall.

Vandhiyathevan, watching her, felt an immediate urge to jump down from his horse himself, and take after her in pursuit. He suited action to thoughts, and set off at her heels, full pelt.

As to why he felt these strange impulses—who can divine their reason? All we can conclude is that Poonguzhali simply followed her whim, an instinct that has prompted and pushed humans for tens of thousands of years—and Vandhiyathevan followed his.

Hidden Meanings and Explanations

Kalki's Note:

Today, a thousand years later (that is, when this story was written), Kodikkarai Kuzhagar still stands alone, in isolation!

Translator's Note:

Although surrounded by small houses and the semblance of a small town, Kodikkarai remains as it was, a thousand years ago (in 2003). The Kuzhagar Temple, though much bigger, still stands alone, quiet, and visited by few.

2

A Muddy Morass

Across jungle and muddy hillocks; through trees and bushes; over stones and thorns did Vandhiyathevan pursue the young woman, barely aware of where he was or what he was doing. She appeared in his line of sight one moment; disappeared, the next. And then, just when he despaired of ever glimpsing her again—there she was! Ah, what was that incident in the Ramayanam, when Rama hunted in vain a golden deer that suddenly turned out to be the demon Maareesan in disguise ... a mistake to compare this young lady to a devious demon, though. On the other hand, she did seem to have the fleet-footed swiftness of a deer. *Ammamma*! Her speed had to be seen to be believed, to be sure—but why was he, Vandhiyathevan, pursuing her, over hill and vale? Such madness, running after a young woman ... wasn't this the height of stupidity?

Then, he tried to convince himself otherwise. The more he neared Kodikkarai, the more did memories of Sendhan Amudhan's young cousin wash over his mind—this must be Poonguzhali, then. Her friendship might prove to be of some use to him; he could ask for directions to the lighthouse, at the very least. They'd managed to catch sight of this imposing structure from afar, but finding their way to it hadn't been so easy—especially when they'd descended into the thick forest, and the paths had begun to meander. When it seemed that they'd been wandering in endless circles, Vandhiyathevan managed to glimpse, quite suddenly, Poonguzhali on the temple wall, gnawing at a coconut. All he'd wanted was to ask her directions—but here she was, sprinting across the beach like a hunted golden deer! Perhaps he'd have to give up this ridiculous chase and leave her be—but then, to accept defeat in a race such as this, especially against a girl? Well, *that* didn't sit well with him either—

Ha! They'd finally broken through the forest and reached open space. The sea lay in the distance, clothed in silence—blue, tranquil, and such a vast, vast distance, as far as the eye could see—what a beautiful sight! And there—there was the lighthouse as well, with a roaring fire on top, bright red tongues of flame radiating in all four directions, making a strange, unearthly play with light and shadows.

Wouldn't it be a good idea to leave this mad girl to her own devices and walk towards the lighthouse—no, no, certainly not. Give up the chase here, in open space, where it would be easy to get hold of her? And it wasn't even quite that bad here; his feet didn't plunge into soft sand and render them useless; blades of grass poked themselves up with the sheer grit of survival; the earth had hardened; mud had crusted over in places, under the harsh sun. He could run free, here, without fear of obstacles and get hold of that girl—not that she'd be able to outrun him. And in any case, wasn't she making straight for the sea? No matter what her speed, she'd have to stop when she came to the water's edge, wouldn't she? Or perhaps—would she just plunge into the sea and vanish? What a pity that he hadn't gathered his wits enough to give chase on his horse! He'd have had her within moments in this open space—

Wait—she's hesitating by the water, for some reason. Looking around and ... she's turning right! Just to escape capture at my hands, no doubt; she's making her way towards the dense forest in the distance. If she managed to reach the jungle, he may as well bid farewell to any hope of catching her—and all this running would have been a supremely pointless waste; his legs were beginning to scream for rest, anyway …

And now she seems to have changed her mind again—perhaps she's given up on the forest? She's now twirling in place like a top, and sprinting back. Does she want to return to the lighthouse? Whatever the reason, all he had to do now was take four steps, spring forward, grab hold of her and ask a few pointed questions: *Why do you run from me, my girl?* And if he threw in, *I've brought you a message from your heart's dearest*—ah, wouldn't *that* surprise her? Sendhan Amudhan hadn't really sent her one, true, but what of it? Wouldn't be a moment's work to come up with something on his own—

True to his impulse, Vandhiyathevan gathered all his draining strength and sprang forward with a burst of speed, hoping to catch her mid-flight.

And then, screamed. "*Ayyo!*"

He didn't quite understand what had happened to him, at first. Realization came slowly: his feet were stuck fast in a quagmire. Just them, at first, and then, by degrees, his ankles sank, until he was down almost to his knees!

Adada, the treachery of this place—*how* it had taken him in! It certainly looked safe from the outside, mud hardened on top—but obviously, the mire hadn't quite dried all the way through. Perhaps it never did. Vandhiyathevan had heard of terrible bogs which swallowed goats, cows, horses and elephants, trapping them, and then gobbling them whole, in their slow, traitorous maws, until there was nothing left. Was this mire one of them? So it would seem— even his knees had disappeared, now— was he just going to keep sinking? Until his thighs went in, too? If this bog had a reputation for taking in horses and elephants whole, what chance did *he* have? *Ayyo*, was this to be his fate? His end? All his fantastic dreams and hopes for the future—but wait, there was one way out. The only way, perhaps. This strange gazelle-girl; if only she could find it in her heart to help him—else, he was done for. Well, he had nothing to lose at this point; why not let loose a tremendous yell, and—to think was to act.

"*Ayyo*—I'm dying!" Vandhiyathevan shrieked at the full strength of excellent lungs. "Dying in this deathly morass—won't someone save me?"

It had its effect. Poonguzhali, running in the opposite direction at some distance, stopped. A moment's hesitation and she understood Vandhiyathevan's terrible predicament fully, without a shade of doubt.

The next instant, her attention fastened itself on a boat, settled half in the sand and half in the morass; perhaps it had been in use when the mire had been much deeper, and filled with enough water to paddle about. She leapt into it gracefully, gripped the oars and swung hard, twice. And oh—how wonderful! The boat simply skimmed through the muddy mess like a beautiful swan on water, and reached the other side of the mire, too. Poonguzhali leapt out, anchored herself on solid ground with her feet, reached in and pulled Vandhiyathevan out. *Ammamma*, the power in those slender hands had to be felt to be believed. Why, they would even seem to rival the Thanjai commander Chinna Pazhuvettarayar's, for sheer grip and unyielding strength!

The moment he was on firm land, Vandhiyathevan laughed gaily—even if his legs did shake a little after the ordeal. "You think you've saved me from certain death, do you?" he grinned. "That I wouldn't have made it out on my own?"

"Then why shriek *Ayyo! Ayyo!* for all the world to hear?" demanded Poonguzhali.

"To stop you from running, of course."

"In that case, I'll just push you back in," she took a step back. "And you can display your strength by walking out all by yourself!"

"*Ayyayo!*" Vandhiyathevan leapt back nimbly.

"*Now* what?"

"It isn't that I'm afraid for my life, exactly—just this terrible muddy marsh. Look at the mess it's made already, up to my thighs ..."

A slight smile edged Poonguzhali's lips. "There's the sea, right there," she said, looking him up and down. "You could wash yourself, you know."

"You wouldn't mind going a little ahead and guiding me, would you?"

They began to make their way to said sea, skirting the dangerous morass carefully.

"Why on earth did you take to your heels when you saw me?" Vallavarayan wanted to know. "You didn't think I was some sort of hideous ghost, did you?"

"Not a ghost—just an owl," gurgled Poonguzhali. "That's *exactly* how you look!"

This statement was not quite to Vandhiyathevan's taste, since he rather tended to pride himself on his excellent features. He scowled, feeling a spurt of anger.

"If you really want to know," he murmured. "Owl-face is considerably better than a hideous monkey-face, any day—"

"*What* did you say?"

"Nothing. Just wanted to know why you ran when you saw me."

"Why did you come after me?"

"So I could ask directions to the lighthouse, of course."

"There it is, right there. Where's the need to ask *me* anything?"

"Well, it wasn't that easy, within the forest. But why run like a hare at the sight of me?"

"Because men are horrible, treacherous creatures. I hate them."

"Even Sendhan Amudhan?" came Vandhiyathevan's low voice.

"*Who?*"

"Sendhan Amudhan from Thanjavur, that's who."

"What would you know about him?"

"That he's your beloved lover."

"*What?* What was that?"

"You *are* Poonguzhali, aren't you?"

"Yes, but you said something about Amudhan—that he was my ..."

"Your lover, yes."

Poonguzhali went into peals of merry laughter. "And who told you that?"

"Who but Sendhan Amudhan himself?"

"Thanjavur is quite a distance, after all. That might explain this rather heroic statement."

"Does it?"

"If he'd dared to say it to my face, I'd have flung him headfirst into this very mire!"

"Well, what does that matter? There's an ocean of water to wash away the mess."

"The one you fell in has a reputation for having gobbled up cows, horses—even an elephant or two."

The hairs on Vandhiyathevan's neck rose; his skin prickled in nervous fear as he remembered being mired into the muddy marsh, his legs being pulled down steadily. If this young woman hadn't come along at that instant, by this time, he would have ... he shivered despite himself.

"Anything else from Sendhan Amudhan, about me?" Poonguzhali asked casually.

"He said you were his cousin; his uncle's daughter. That there was no one to rival your beauty, not even in *Devalokham* ..."

"He's been to the abode of Gods and confirmed it in person, has he? What else?"

"That you had a wonderful voice; even the sea stopped its endless clamour and fell silent, just to listen to your song. Is that true?"

"You have a chance to find that out yourself—here's the sea!"

And indeed, they had arrived at the shore.

3

MUDDLED MINDS

Stars winked merrily, in the rapidly darkening sky. A pearly crescent moon sailed amidst them, not unlike a gleaming silver boat in the endless, deep blue ocean.

The wind, however, seemed loath to share the tranquility of celestial bodies; it swept fiercely while the sea thundered and churned, stretching out a thousand silvery-white arms as though to draw those on the shore into its mysterious depths.

"What on earth are you standing about for? Wash the mud off yourself, quick! We'll have to make our way home as soon as we can, or I can bid farewell to all hopes of a meal tonight," sighed Poonguzhali. "My beloved *Anni* is sure to upend the rice-pot and empty it of every last morsel—"

"Is—er—the sea isn't very deep hereabouts, is it?" ventured Vandhiyathevan cautiously.

"Upon my word—I've never even *seen* a coward such as you," she shot back. "There's no fear of that kind here; walk half a *kaadham* into the sea, and you'll find that the water comes up only to your waist. Why else do you think the lighthouse fires burn each every night without fail?"

No matter the reassurances; Vandhiyathevan sloshed into said sea slowly, and with considerable, and very visible reluctance. Eventually, though, he did manage to wash all the swampy mud off his hands and legs, and regain some semblance of cleanliness.

The sight of the Vaidhyar's son trotting up on horseback, leading his own steed by the reins, met his eyes as he clambered back to shore. "*Ayyayo*—the horse—what if it's caught in the bog?"

"Not a chance. Horses are considerably more intelligent than their so-called masters."

"I daresay, but one of them has its master on its back," objected Vandhiyathevan. "And he's dragging my horse along, too—"

"You're right to be afraid, in that case. Run up and warn him, will you?"

"Wait—halt!" screeched Vandhiyathevan as he ran full-tilt against the newcomers. "Stop!"

Poonguzhali came up to them within a few moments. The trio began to make its way towards the lighthouse.

"Why don't you get on your horse?" asked the young woman.

"I'd much rather walk beside you."

Poonguzhali stepped up to the stallion and treated it to a loving caress; the animal shivered as though ecstatic at her touch, and gave a gentle neigh of pleasure.

"It would seem that my horse likes you," put in Vandhiyathevan. "I call that excellent, don't you?"

"How's that a cause for delight?"

"I shall be leaving for Ilankai soon—which means I need a safe haven for my steed; someone I can trust. You'll take care of him, won't you?"

"Why not? Animals like me; they make friends in moments. It's humans that don't."

"Ah, that can't possibly be true. Why, Sendhan Amudhan likes—"

"I must say—I much prefer the company of animals, myself. Can't stand humans."

"What have they done to deserve your undying hatred?"

"Wicked, treacherous creatures. Lies and deceit are all they're capable of!"

"Come, now. Not everyone's that way. Sendhan Amudhan now, is an excellent fellow. So is the Vaidhyar's son; I can vouch for him myself—"

"And you?"

"A good man, of course. It's just that I didn't quite want to blow my own trumpet."

"Why're you both here?"

"The Chakravarthy is ill and abed, don't you know? The court physicians need a great many medicinal herbs for a cure. We were told that this forest possessed quite a few of those rare plants— which brought me and the Vaidhyar's son here hotfoot ..."

"Just a moment ago, you said you were leaving for Ilankai."

"So I did—to bring home the herbs that can't be found, here. The Sanjeevi Malai—the one from which the great lord Hanuman brought those precious herbs—it's still on the island, isn't it?"

"Yes. Which is why thousands there are dropping off like flies from a terrible toxic fever, I suppose."

"Indeed? This is news to me; not even the palace physician, who sent us on this mission, warned us of such an epidemic ..."

"Men! I've never seen creatures that have developed deceit into such an accomplished art form. Two arrived here a couple of days ago and mumbled something of the same sort—but their lies were, at least, somewhat believable ..."

"Who were they, and what did they lie about?"

"Apparently, they'd been sent by some sort of a magician—at any rate, that was their story. The Chakravarthy was desperately in need of tiger's nails and hair from an elephant's tail which could be bound into some sort of *ratchai*, a sacred bracelet and so, a trip to Ilankai was of paramount importance. Now, my brother has taken them in his boat ..."

"Is that how it is, indeed?" murmured Vandhiyathevan. Memories of the sinister *mandhiravadi* Ravidasan came rushing into his mind— not to mention the terrible night in a crumbling *mandapam*, and his hair-raising adventures, within.

Good God, why, why do I get myself into these terrifying situations, he wondered, woefully. *Meeting your enemy face-to-face in battle, testing your mettle against his and distinguishing yourself in the battlefield—now that's the life of a true warrior. What on earth am I doing here, embroiling myself in magic and mystery, caught in a horrifying web of deceit and political plots?*

As for these two men who left for Ilankai a little before me—who might they be? And this girl—how far can I trust her? What if she's one of those wretched conspirators?—no, no, that can't possibly be. She's innocent, this one. Far better to strengthen my bond with her; it might prove useful.

"I'm going to confess the truth, Poonguzhali. My journey to Ilankai has nothing to do with gathering herbs; I lied to you about that. I'm going on an extremely secret mission, and I'd like to share the details —"

"Don't. They say you never ought to entrust secrets to women, don't they? You'd better not reveal anything to me."

"That might be true of ordinary women, but those rules won't apply to you, I'm sure."

"I'm no ordinary woman, am I? And you know this how, exactly? It's hardly been a *naazhigai* since you met me."

"I liked you, Poonguzhali, the moment I caught sight of you on top of that *madhil*. If I may, I'd like to ask you something. You'll tell me the truth, won't you?"

"Ask, and you'll find out."

"Isn't Sendhan Amudhan your beloved? Aren't you going to wed him?"

"What's the point of these questions?"

"He's my friend, and the last thing I want is to go against him in any way. If he isn't your lover …"

"Go on. What's all this hemming and hawing for?"

"Then I've every intention of applying for that post. To tell the truth, Poonguzhali, your opinion of love wasn't quite to my taste, because, my girl, there's nothing more divine in this world — why, even those great saints, Appar, Sundarar and Sambandar have all sung beautiful songs, picturing the lord as their beloved. Tholkaappiyar, Valluvar and other poets who've achieved eternal fame have sung paeans on love. The divinely blessed Kalidasar places romance on a pedestal and worships at its feet while even Krishna Bhagavan fell in love while cavorting with Gopika women in Brindavan …"

"I shall tell you something now, *Ayya*—you'd do well to listen carefully, and meditate upon my words."

"Well?"

"I do like you, yes. I don't quite entertain, for you, the hatred I felt for those rogues who came a couple of days ago."

"Aha! I'm fortunate, indeed."

"But do not *ever* bring up love or romance, again."

"What? But why?"

"Sendhan Amudhan may not be my beloved, but I do have others …"

"*Adada*! You do? How many—and who are they?"

"I shall leave home at midnight, tonight and you shall see them, if you follow me. And—well, you'll know all about them!" Poonguzhali laughed, then—a high, shrill, laugh.

Something deep inside Vandhiyathevan's heart gave an unpleasant twist. *This poor girl*, he mused. *Obviously, she's muddled and disturbed. There wouldn't be much point in asking her help—far better never to mention a word of my mission.*

Walking steadily all this time, they had arrived in the vicinity of the lighthouse, and the dwelling situated close by. A man, old in years, and an equally elderly woman walked out, saw Poonguzhali, the two men by her side and their horses—and gaped in considerable amazement.

"Who are these, my dear?" questioned the old man. "Where on earth did you get hold of them?"

"I didn't, *Appa*," she answered. "It was actually the other way around."

"What does it matter which way it was? I've lost count of the number of times I told you to 'come home before night-fall'—but when have you ever obeyed? You brought two men two days ago—and now here you are again, with two more in tow. What do they want, now?"

"Medicinal herbs for the Chakravarthy, *Appa*."

"She speaks the truth, then, *Ayya*?" the old man turned to Vandhiyathevan.

"Certainly. Here's the royal order." And Vandhiyathevan loosened the cloth at his waist, pulled out an *olai*, and handed it over. Another fell out at the same moment; he stooped in a hurry, stuffing it back into his waist-cloth with some confusion. "Blasted idiot!" he mumbled to himself. "Haven't you learnt a single lesson from your mistake?"

The old man received the leaf and scrutinized it carefully under the light of the roaring fire atop the lighthouse. His face brightened at once. "It is from Ilaiya Piratti herself," he called out to his wife. "These men must be fed—go in, and tell your precious daughter-in-law to save some food. Else, she might tip out the rice-pot and empty it of every last morsel!"

4

At Midnight

Once the night's meal was done, Vandhiyathevan took the old lighthouse-keeper a little aside, and divulged his mission: it was of the utmost importance that he leave for Ilankai as soon as possible. Said old man, Thyaga Vidanga Karaiyar, listened to his speech with some sympathy, but expressed his regret: there really was nothing he could do.

"Once, these very shores were filled with large ships and small craft that jostled for space, nestling cheek for jowl," he mourned. "They have all moved towards Sethukkarai now—to help our armies in Ilankai, of course. I have two boats of my own; my son has sailed in one, with two men who arrived yesterday. I have no idea when he will return. What am I supposed to do?"

"Who were they? Your daughter didn't seem very impressed with them."

"Neither was I. Who were they, and what was their purpose in coming here? No one knew anything—except that they carried Pazhuvettarayar's palm-tree signet ring Not even that would have moved me to force my son into rowing them to Ilankai—but I reckoned without my daughter-in-law," explained the old man "The very image of greed, that woman, and once she heard that they were willing to pay him a whole bag full of gold, she harangued and persuaded him until my son caved in ..."

"Why, whatever's the world coming to, *Ayya?*" marveled Vandhiyathevan. "Here's a young woman who knows nothing about the world, but your son takes his cue from her, and listens to her words of boundless wisdom—!" Then, he seemed to realize how his impulsive words might be interpreted. "I apologize—this concerns your family and is nothing to do with me ..." his voice trailed away.

Remembering, in an opportune moment, what Sendhan Amudhan had revealed about his family all that while ago, Vandhiyathevan recounted, swiftly, his sudden and unforeseen acquaintance with the young man, his mother and his stay at their home that night.

"Aha, that was you, was it? News of you and our adventures has preceded you, *Thambi*. Apparently, men are baying for your blood all over the land—"

"Perhaps—not that I know anything about all that."

"*Now* I understand your haste in wishing to escape to Ilankai."

"You couldn't have misunderstood my urgency more, *Ayya*. My life isn't the only reason I'm in such a hurry—I've been entrusted with a most important *olai*, to be delivered to someone there. You may see it, if you wish—"

"Unnecessary; Ilaiya Piratti's message about you is more than enough. But the thing is—I am unable to help you in any way. What is to be done?"

"You mentioned another boat, didn't you?"

"Yes, but no one to ferry it. If you and your friend would be willing to sail on your own, I shall make arrangements—"

"Neither of us can handle oars. I, in particular, have a healthy fear of the water—in fact, the very mention of the sea ..."

"True indeed; navigation is a terrifying proposition for even experienced sailors. The shore is visible for only a while after setting out; once it vanishes, finding your bearings can be almost impossible—"

"I'm in no position to take my companion with me, either; he shall have to stay here and gather medicinal herbs. You're our only hope, *Ayya*—please do suggest some way out of this predicament."

"There is just one—but I cannot promise you success, alas. Perhaps, if you are very fortunate, you may be able to accomplish something. I advise you to try, at any rate ..."

"What is it that I must do?" pressed Vandhiyathevan. "Tell me, and I shall do my best."

"There is no one around these parts who can surpass Poonguzhali when it comes to sailing and boats. She has been to Ilankai quite a few times as well. Request her, if you wish; I shall put in a word, myself."

"Why not right away? Ask her, won't you?"

"She's stubborn, that one. If she's approached right now and she refuses—she never may agree, and then, your way would be well and truly barred. I shall make sure I ask her tomorrow, when she is in a more mellow mood. You could, too." And Thyaga Vidanga Karaiyar walked slowly towards the lighthouse.

Vandhiyathevan lay down, on the house's *thinnai*; his companion, the Vaidhyar's son, had fallen asleep ages ago. They had traveled long and hard that day, after all; Vallavarayan's eyelids were heavy with fatigue and he fell asleep at once.

***

Abruptly, sleep deserted him.

The sound, of a door opening. Vandhiyathevan's instincts went on alert; he pried open tired eyes, almost gummed together, with some difficulty. A dark shape emerged from within the house, and moved out. Vandhiyathevan trained his eyes through the darkness—undoubtedly, this was a female. The pale, dancing lights of the lighthouse fires fell upon the figure—ah! Poonguzhali—no doubt about it. What was it that she'd said, a while ago? "Follow me at midnight, and I shall reveal my lovers!" *Why, I dismissed it as some sort of joke at my expense but here she is, wandering outside ... where to? Is she really meeting her precious beloved ones at the dead of the night? Always assuming she truly had any, of course—what sort of girl would tell a man something of that kind? Or even challenge him to follow her, at night, to see them? No, something else was afoot here, something mysterious—or perhaps ... whatever the reason, I ought to follow her, mustn't I? Why not? I'd have to talk to her tomorrow; bring her around to my side and get her to ferry me to Ilankai. Following her right now might aid in that mission. She's ripe for danger and might get into a scrape, in which case, I could help—and that might work for the best tomorrow, wouldn't it?*

Vandhiyathevan rose without a sound and crept along Poonghuzhali's path, not even daring to move an inch this way or that. The evening's experience in a bog was startlingly clear in his memory, and he had no inclination for a repeat of that particular performance. No, letting Poonguzhali out of his sight was the recipe for disaster; that mustn't happen.

The landscape lay vast and unbroken for a brief stretch from the lighthouse; it was easy to keep the girl in his sight, and following her footsteps presented no problem. Vandhiyathevan stepped forward briskly, hoping to lessen the distance between them and perhaps, to catch up with her. And yet—the more his speed, the swifter hers; there seemed to be no way of reaching her. For all that, however, Poonguzhali seemed unaware of his presence, behind her.

The jungle took over once they had crossed the barren stretch, and the ground rose and fell in uneven fashion. Poonguzhali chose not to climb over the mound, but skirted it. Both mound and forest ended at a certain point; she skirted this too. Vandhiyathevan hastened forward as much as he dared, reached the place, and craned ahead—thank God! She was still visible.

But the next instant, she had vanished.

What the—*how* could this have happened? What sort of magic or trickery was this? Was there some sort of depression, perhaps? Vandhiyathevan set his sights roughly to where he had last glimpsed Poonguzhali, walked and almost ran intermittently, reached it, and peered into the darkness in all four directions. Had she wandered into three of those, he could not have missed her on any account; he pressed his feet carefully upon the earth and determined that this was no boggy, marshy earth. Well, there was only one other path she could have taken: the one that crested the mound and meandered into the forest.

He peered a little more and his eyes discerned, after some effort, a slender, single trail that bore out his assumption, and wandered through stubbly, hardy bushes. Vandhiyathevan stepped gingerly upon the mound, heart thudding as though it would jump out of his chest. The lighthouse fire's flickering light didn't penetrate these dense areas; the evening's sliver of moon had sunk beneath the sea ages ago. The pale starlight didn't illuminate the path beyond a short distance. Short, scrubby bushes and small trees began to take on vague, horrifying shapes in the darkness; their gloomy shadows grew upon the ground like terrifying apparitions. As leaves upon bushes rustled in the wind, so did their shadows, upon the ground.

Vandhiyathevan's heart skipped a beat each time something moved. What sort of dangers lurked behind those bushes, and within the inky blackness? Poisonous insects, creatures and dangerous predators could spring upon you any moment; perils surrounded you at every turn— from above, the sides and even from behind. *Adada*—what madness was this that had pried him from a safe dwelling and into this forest? *What on earth am I doing here, a perfect target for enemies—and I haven't even my trusty spear on this of all occasions ...*

Wait—what was that rustling sound? That dark, lumpy figure on top of that tree—what was it? And those small, bright pinpoints of light within those bushes, what could they be?

Vandhiyathevan's legs shook almost despite himself. Oh, for God's sake—what was he doing here, at this time of the night? This was beyond ridiculous; time to walk back, down the path and leave—

A voice rose at that very instant. Mournful notes of lament sweeping through him with exquisite sorrow. The voice of a young woman. A heaving, heart-breaking sob—and then, a song:

> *"Why anguish, my soul,*
> *When tumbling seas lie smooth?*
> *Why rage, dear heart,*
> *When Lady Earth sleeps, soothed?"*

Vandhiyathevan gave up all thought of retreat in an instant. He stepped forward, towards the direction of the voice, and climbed steadily up the mound. Soon enough, the summit was visible—and there she was. Poonguzhali. The song had been hers, as she gazed at the stars twinkling in the night sky. They were the only ones listening; the grand members of a celestial audience, presumably.

One of them, of course, was the comet; its magnificent tail spreading across the vast heavens.

The young woman atop the mound, silhouetted in the pale starlight; her forlorn voice; the beautiful song, the velvety night sky, and the comet's mysterious presence almost made Vandhiyathevan forget himself. His legs moved all by themselves, and led him to the top of the mound.

He walked forward to stand in front of Poonguzhali. Behind her, in the distance, glowed the lighthouse fires, painting the land red; the sea spread wide, beyond, the waves forming a sort of silvery line that clearly distinguished land and water …

"So you've found your way here, have you? Not bad at all, considering your homage to Kumbakarnan on the *thinnai* when I left—"

"The sound of the door opening woke me up and there you were, walking swiftly along the path, never even looking back for a moment. *Ammamma*! It was all I could do to follow, keeping you in my sights ..."

"Why did you, then?"

"Well, of all the—! Weren't you the one who asked me to? You haven't forgotten, have you?"

"Did I? And do you remember why?"

"Why ever not? You promised to reveal your lovers. So where are they? Go on, show me."

"Behind you," pointed Poonguzhali. "Look over there!"

5

ALL AT SEA

Vandhiyathevan turned around to have a look … and his intestines seemed to climb up his stomach, thrusting into his chest. Not content with that, they coiled upwards and choked his throat as well.

A thousand shards of lightning struck him all at once; a hundred thousand needles seem to pierce his skin without mercy—throwing his senses into disorder, bewildering him with mindless, stupefying terror.

A vast, unending swathe of pitch black spread out in front of him—but at some places, ten, twenty, no, a hundred tongues of fire seemed to leap out of the very earth. Not a wisp of smoke did they emit; not even light, or the flames that are a natural result of burning logs—these were just simple licks of fire that somehow rose above ground. Some flickered out within moments, while new ones burst at other points.

A huge, terrifying monster with no feature save that of vast, inky darkness. Like Kabandhan the demon, perhaps, with no head, and his mouth opening straight out of his hideous stomach—no, not just one either, but many. And he opened them often and often, releasing sparking tongues of dangerous flame, which flickered out when he closed his lips.

Vandhiyathevan's blood chilled; it seemed to squeeze itself out through every pore of his skin. Never, in all his life had he ever experienced terror such as this—not even in Pazhuvettarayar's horribly dangerous, gloomy subterranean cavern.

"Ha, ha, ha!" Someone laughed eerily behind him, and he turned.

Poonguzhali!

At any other time, her witch-like chortle would have chilled his marrow and sent him spiraling into terror. Now, though, it had the opposite effect: the very fact that here was a human being, a woman of flesh, blood, body and soul, standing right by, offered him something to hold on to, in a moment fraught with peril.

"Did you take a good look at my lovers?" she asked. "These fire-tongued demons are the love of my life. I come here at the dead of every night to enjoy their intimacy."

There isn't a shadow of doubt that this girl is pitifully deranged. By what stretch of imagination could I co-opt her into taking me to Ilankai, Vandhiyathevan wondered. *Is that even possible, at this point?* Even as he was thinking along these lines, something was struggling to edge its way out of his sub-conscious. Some little niggling fact; something about these fire-tongued demons, actually.

"Well? Think your precious Sendhan Amudhan could possibly compare with these magnificent creatures?" Poonghuzhali's voice seemed to reach him from very far away, as though from within the depths of a well—largely because Vandhiyathevan was intently preoccupied with trying to remember something—now what was it—ah, finally! After a great deal of grappling with his recalcitrant memory, here it was …

Sometimes, when lands heavy in sulphur content retained water for extended periods, they tended to become marshy swamps—and displayed this sort of occurrence at night. Sulphur-laden gas would explode out of the ground, resembling flares of fire. This would flicker for a while, sometimes; at others, vanish within moments—*gup, gup*—into the depths of the earth. Simple, ignorant people often stumbled upon these natural phenomena and went rigid with fright; named them fire-tongued demons and lived in fear of these terrible beings ...

Vandhiyathevan had heard elders discuss them; the memory of it all came back to him quite clearly. Intelligence grappled with fear in his heart at that moment—and the former won.

There seemed no point in relating all this to the mentally-challenged girl beside him, though. Sweet-talking her somehow into returning home was of paramount importance, now.

"Your precious lovers aren't going anywhere, my girl. They're sure to be right here tomorrow as well—and you can visit them then," he said, soothingly. "We'll go back, shall we?"

Poonguzhali said nothing. Then, abruptly—she burst into tears, heaving and sobbing.

*Good God, **now** what am I supposed to do?* Vandhiyathevan groaned within himself and lapsed into silence, not really sure of his next course of action.

"Shall we leave now?" he asked again, after a while.

The sobs didn't cease.

By now, Vandhiyathevan was both at his wits' and tether's end. "Do what you will; I'm going home for some much needed sleep," and he began to descend the mound.

Poonghuzhali's tears dried up in an instant. She clambered down the mound, took four or five leaps, and bounded to the ground almost in front of Vandhiyathevan.

He almost ran forward to catch up with her; the two began their trek towards the lighthouse.

Why on earth would I risk getting into a boat with this idiot? As for crossing the ocean—perish the thought! Still, mused Vandhiyathevan, *there doesn't seem to be any other way out. Would it be possible to get on her good side, somehow, and make sure of her cooperation?*

"There's a comet in the sky, these days," Poonguzhali commented. "What's your opinion about it?"

"Nothing. There's a comet in the sky, and that's it."

"They say that such things portend grave misfortune to those on earth, don't they?"

"So it's said, yes."

"You've nothing to say about *that* either?"

"I'm not an expert on astrology. Everyone else says so—and that's all I know."

They walked in silence, for a while.

"The Chakravarthy isn't keeping well, I've heard," Poonguzhali said, after while. "That's true, isn't it?"

This girl mightn't be quite as deranged as I thought, Vandhiyathevan mused, and felt a little spark of confidence light up within him.

"Very much so; I saw him confined to his bed with my own eyes. Neither of his legs have feeling; they're useless, and he can't take a step. Isn't that why I've arrived, to get herbs for his recovery? Would you do me a favour, my girl?"

Poonguzhali did not seem inclined to answer this. "Is it true that the Chakravarthy's days are numbered?" she asked. "And that he'll die soon?"

"That might well happen if you won't deign to help me. Ilankai possesses a very rare medicinal herb, the Sanjeevi, and the Chakravarthy might recover if it's brought to him and ..." Vandhiyathevan put forward his pitch. "Would you ferry me to the island?"

"Say he dies right now," Poonguzhali pondered. "Who will succeed him on the throne?"

Vandhiyathevan almost jumped out of his skin. "What on earth does it matter to us, my girl? Who cares about the succession?"

"We should, shouldn't we?" she retorted. "We're citizens of this *rajyam*, after all."

This girl isn't the idiotic pithukuli I took her for, Vandhiyathevan decided, in some consternation. *I'd better be on my guard around her. There must be some reason for her ridiculous behaviour.*

"Well? Why this deep, dark silence?" Poonguzhali prodded. "Who's going to ascend the throne?"

"Aditha Karikalar has been made the crown prince ... which makes him the rightful successor."

"And Madhuranthakar—doesn't he have any say in the matter? What of his rights?"

"Hasn't he announced that he has no intention of contesting for the throne?"

"That was then—but isn't he supposed to have changed his mind, these days?"

"What of it? The masses must concur, mustn't they?"

"I've heard that he's being supported by many great men, lords and kings ..."

"So did I—but it amazes me that these rumours have managed to reach even *you*."

"What will happen if Sundara Chozhar dies now? At this very moment?"

"The country will erupt in chaos. And that's why your help is urgently needed—to stop such a terrible eventuality."

"Indeed? But what could I possibly do?"

"I mentioned this some time ago—that I have to reach Ilankai as soon as I can, to gather a precious herb ... and you'll have to ferry me across."

"You're begging my favour now, is that it? Aren't you ashamed to ask a mere female, for help?"

"Your father says there's no one else; your brother took across two men yesterday, didn't he?"

"What of it? You've two hands, haven't you? Not to mention your precious friend, as well—"

"But we've no idea about sailing ..."

"It's not exactly a fantastic magician's secret that can't be mastered, is it? Grab the oars, hold them tight, push them in the water and that's it!"

"We need to know our direction, don't we? What if we flounder mid-sea, and—"

"Then drown and die, you idiots! What on earth am *I* supposed to do?"

By this time, they had neared the lighthouse; instinct warned Vandhiyathevan to cry a halt to the conversation then and there. The last thing he wanted was to continue, and confirm Poonguzhali's refusal to the point of no-return. She may have snapped at him about drowning, but something in the way she delivered the retort—something in her voice—made him think that matters were not yet desperate. And that lit a spark of hope, in him.

The second time around, sleep simply would not come to Vandhiyathevan. Vague and disquieting thoughts haunted him; he found it difficult to relax—and eventually managed to do so, only as the fourth *jaamam* began.

Dreams, again.

He and Poonguzhali were seated in a small boat, facing each other, while a sail fluttered above. The sea spread around them in all its vastness; water, water everywhere, while a soft, pleasant breeze sprung up. The boat skimmed along as though floating upon the very wind, while Poonguzhali's radiant face lifted his spirits. There she sat, beauty personified, little ringlets of hair playing about her forehead, and the end of her *seelai* fluttering in the breeze. He forgot his destination and his very purpose; it seemed that *this* was the moment he'd been waiting for; what his soul had pined for, all these years: this boat-ride in Poonguzhali's exotic company. There was just one thing missing, though—now, what was it? Ah, yes, her melodious voice. Hadn't Sendhan Amudhan gone into raptures about it, after all?

"Wouldn't those coral lips of yours part, my dear, and sing a charming song?" he ventured.

"What did you say?" she asked—and smiled. Ah, wasn't that lovely smile worth all the seven worlds?

"I wondered if you mightn't open those luscious lips and sing something."

"And if I did?"

"Why, I'd come close, and upon your beautiful, dimpling cheek—"

Abruptly, she pulled out a sharp little dagger from her waist, and raised it high.

"Careful now," she warned. "Take a step beyond the mast and I'll rip you apart, end to end! The fishes in the ocean are ravenous, you know."

6

THE HIDDEN MANDAPAM

The morning sun's gentle rays, glowing a rosy gold, roused Vandhiyathevan from sleep—but it took him a few moments to shake off his drowsiness, come to himself and take in his surroundings. For one thing, he wasn't sure yet of the heat and light that fell full on his face—was it the sun, or the lighthouse's flames? He scrubbed his eyes, blinked, and forced his mind to think of the happenings of last night: how much of that had been real, and how much the flights of own considerable fancy? Everything was muddled; he couldn't really guess.

The only ones at home were the old man's wife, and his daughter-in-law, who informed him that Thyaga Vidangar had left for the Kuzhagar Temple; delivering flowers for the deity's worship each day was one of his sacred duties.

Vandhiyathevan couldn't quite gather the courage to enquire about Poonghuzhali's whereabouts. He polished off the morning meal they provided, instead, and cast his eyes around, hoping to catch sight of her—to no avail. He walked to the temple but found her father instead, plucking flowers from the trees that grew luxuriously, within the complex. Poonguzhali came by, sometimes, to thread garlands, he informed—but not today.

"She might be chasing deer in the forest, somewhere," the old man volunteered. "Or wandering along the seashore—I could not say. Look for her if you can and ask, why don't you?" He shrugged. Then, he looked at Vandhiyathevan, warning in his eyes. "Careful, though. She's a wretch, the girl. I would be very cautious if I were you; do not entertain the wrong sort of ideas. Forget approaching her as a woman—and if you are one of those who have read epic romances and think to entice her through flowery speeches dripping with *sringara rasam*—don't. She will turn into a furious Badrakali in an instant and then, well, your life will not be yours."

The previous night's dream flitted across Vandhiyathevan's memory; his skin prickled almost despite himself.

Then, he plunged into the forest, in a bid to look for her. Where, though, in this vastness? He lost heart within awhile; it was all he could do to peer into the gloom. Now, he simply wanted to get out of the looming, stifling stillness. He did, and began to walk along the seashore, but a long trek bore no fruit; Poonguzhali was nowhere to be seen. Well, she was bound to return home for her mid-day meal, wasn't she, he mused. He'd simply have to get hold of her then.

Something occurred to him just at that moment, and he stopped. The sea lay just ahead, a vast body of water, calm and soothing. The waves were few, and the sudden desire to pitch in and splash around to his heart's content was overwhelming. Even more important: the sea was shallow around these parts, he'd heard; why, Poonguzhali herself had confirmed it just the evening before. There was no reason to hesitate on the shore, was there? Then too, he'd have to get rid of this silly dread of the ocean at some point: traveling on boats had now become a necessity and you couldn't do that if you shivered in mortal fear of the sea, could you? No, he'd have to overcome it, somehow.

Vandhiyathevan unwound the cloth coiled around his waist, removed his dagger, laid them down on the sandy shore, and waded into the sea. Slowly. Step, by hesitant step, as carefully as he could, placing each foot firmly into the sand. After plunging along a good distance, though, he found that the sea didn't come up to more than his knee; tiny waves splattered against his body, and even then, the water rose no more than waist level. "Well, what a wonderful ocean, to be sure," muttered Vandhiyathevan, half-amused. "Looks like I can't even squat down for a wash," and he went in even further.

Oh, good heavens, he wondered suddenly. *There's absolutely no depth and I've waded in a long way from land—what if the sea just rose, right now? What if the waves grew and battered against me, and—*

Worried, Vandhiyathevan turned to look at the shore.

Well, I've certainly come a lot further than I intended, but the sea isn't going to misbehave as much as that, he consoled himself. *And—oh, wait, there's Poonguzhali! I must clamber back and get hold of her. Use all the strength of my considerable conversational powers and ask her, once again ... why, it looks like she's seen me as well—that's probably why she's come here, in fact. She's walking in my direction, certainly—and ... is she making some sort of sign? What, though?*

Oh—wait—oh, oh, what on earth is she doing? What's she looking at, on the ground? What's she picking up? Why, that's my waist-cloth, and—don't, don't pick that up, woman—that's mine, don't you hear? No, she can't—this blasted sea and its roaring waves ...!

Wait—she's heard my voice—and she's saying something as well—That's mine, Poonguzhali, don't touch it—

Don't you ever listen to what you're told? How dare you simply walk away with things as though they were yours—stop, woman, stop!

Vandhiyathevan began to splash towards the shore. Poonguzhali turned once, caught sight of him—and began to run, in her turn. In the direction opposite her home, and the lighthouse!

Why, that stupid wretch—assuming that she was a wretch—what if she's just an insane idiot? And if so, how am I to wrest my waistcloth from her hands ...?

Having stumbled at least twice in the sea and swallowed a mouthful of salty water, Vandhiyathevan more or less fell onto shore and managed to make his way up it. Then, he began to pursue the girl in earnest. The more he ran, the greater her speed.

In the distance sprinted a group of fifty or sixty deer. *Ah, what a beautiful sight, to be sure—those deer, practically bounding across the sands in ones and twos—this young woman is no less as she leaps and springs along the ground; she's every bit as beautiful as those graceful animals.* There was something to be said of girls such as these, free spirits who lived a wild, untrammeled life—not that he could voice these thoughts in her presence, of course. No, that would be the end of everything. Hadn't the old man warned him enough? ... Still, why was this wretched girl running helter-skelter into the forest? The *nerve* of her—how was he to ever run her to earth if she disappeared into the forest—and there she was, within the forest now—and that *did* it! Oh, was there ever an idiot, a *moudeekan* such as him? Whoever heard of a garland surviving the wretched fingers of a monkey? That's how terrible everything was, now ...

Vandhiyathevan entered the forest in his turn, and ran here and there. Worried and flustered beyond measure, he didn't see where he was going, pushing bushes and plants about and acquiring a considerable number of scratches and bruises from thorns. "Poonguzhali!" he called out, for a while. "*Poonguzhali!*" Then, his brain seemed to give up on rational thinking. "Dear tree, have you seen her?" he asked plaintively, stumbling around. "You haven't spied Poonguzhali hereabouts, have you, beloved crow?"

At this rate, I'm going to go completely insane, he mused—when something fell from a tree.

Why, his precious waistcloth! He practically pounced on it and unrolled it carefully, to check the contents. Yes—*olai* and gold coins, everything was safe.

"Your money is intact, I gather?" came a voice from above. Vandhiyathevan craned his neck. Poonguzhali it was—perched on a branch.

The run had taken its toll on him and he glared up at her, perspiring with exhaustion and nervous tension. "I've never seen or heard of a mad monkey such as you!"

"Well, I've never come across an owl like you, either," Poonguzhali retorted. "You and your big round eyes—*Ammamma*, the way you stared!"

"Why would you lead me on a wild goose chase? If it's money you want—"

"*Chee*! Why would I want to touch your precious gold?"

"Why run all the way here with this, then?"

"You wouldn't have entered the forest if I hadn't, would you? Just trudged back home."

"And if I had?"

"Get up here, and you'll see."

"See what?"

"Ten or fifteen soldiers on horseback—swords and spears, glinting in the sun!"

Her expression seemed to confirm the veracity of her statement, but Vandhiyathevan wished to know for himself in any case, and began to climb the tree. Before he did so, however, he coiled the waistcloth once again, and secured it around his waist. Poonguzhali may have dropped it by mistake—and hatched another plot to try and wrest it from him. Who knew, after all?

He clambered to the top, finally, and peered at the lighthouse in the distance.

Poonguzhali was right. Ten or fifteen cavalrymen *were* grouped there, holding aloft swords and spears. He wondered who they might be? But that was obvious, of course—who else but Pazhuvettarayars' men, in pursuit of him? It now looked like Poonguzhali had saved him from imprisonment—a great deal of danger, at the very least. Why, though? What was her purpose? There were a few other issues as well that were murky ...

They clambered down.

"You've helped me escape a terribly gruesome fate, Poonguzhali," Vandhiyathevan expressed his gratitude. "Thank you very, very much."

"Liar. What do men know of gratitude, anyway?"

"Don't class me with others—I'm not the same."

"*That* you certainly aren't. You're in a class all by yourself, aren't you?"

"May I ask something, my girl?"

"You may—but I won't guarantee an answer."

"Why did you wish to save me? What's the reason for your sudden compassion?"

Silence. Her rather stunned expression made it obvious that she hadn't expected the question. Then, she seemed to regain her equilibrium. "I've always had a soft spot for idiots, I suppose," she volunteered, finally.

"Excellent. How did you know that those men were here for me, though?"

"One look at your stupid face and I knew you were escaping someone—or something. I guessed it yesterday—and confirmed it this morning, through the kind efforts of your friend, the physician's son."

"What on earth did *he* blab to you?"

"He woke up this morning and came to me straightaway, saying that he wished to look for herbs in the forest. I promised to point them out, and brought him here. And then he began to make love to me—and I said that you'd managed to do that before him—"

"*What* did you say?"

"Patience—just listen. I said that you'd started petitioning for a place in my heart—and that was when he began to blurt out his suspicions about you. All along the way here, he'd been having his own doubts—that you'd committed some grave treachery and were escaping royal guards—and that they were in hot pursuit. He knew that straightaway, apparently. *Don't fall for the charms of that cut-throat traitor*, he said. *Marry me!*

"*You're going a little too fast for me*, I protested. Didn't we have to ask our parents and elders, first?

"Here's what your precious friend said, then: *Let's follow ancient Thamizh traditions and perform kalavu manam: consummate our marriage right away!*" She paused. "Wonderful, isn't he?"

"That wretched bastard!" Vandhiyathevan exclaimed. "*Sandaalan!*"

"Just then, we heard horse-hooves, and I asked your friend to climb up a tree and see what he could—you know, I can't help laughing whenever I think of how his legs shook when he peered through the branches," Poonguzhali gurgled.

"Jokes apart—what happened next?"

"He scrambled down the tree. *See, I was right, wasn't I?* he asked. *Royal guards have smoked him out even here, and have arrived to arrest him!*

"*In that case, they're likely to arrest you as well, considering you are his companion*, I suggested. *You'd better run and hide somewhere, hadn't you?* He agreed that he certainly did, and left my side. And then, something happened—something I'd entirely expected, of course ..."

"What? What happened as you'd expected?"

"After having sworn to me that he'd conceal himself, he walked straight towards the soldiers on horses, and promptly had himself arrested."

"*Ayyo*—the poor idiot ..."

"How wonderfully sympathetic. For my part, I'd advise you to save your pity."

"You would? Why?"

"Listen to the rest, and you'll see. He marched up to them and they stared at him, astonished. They glanced at each other, and whispered amongst themselves. *Who are you all?* asked our man. *We're hunters,* said they. *We're here in search of deer,* explained one of them. *Not deer, you haven't,* said our man. *What's more—I know what you're really after.* Their surprise knew no bounds, and they prodded him even more. *You've come for Vandhiyathevan,* said our man. *And I know where he is. Will you let me go free if I lead you to him?* They agreed, and he took them all to my home ..."

"That rat—the bastard! *Sandaalan!*"

"I came in search of you once they'd all gone, and there you were in the sea, enjoying a leisurely bath ..."

"You could've told me all this then and there, couldn't you? Why snatch my belongings and run away?"

"Would you have taken to your heels quite so quickly, if I hadn't? What if you'd decided to confront those soldiers in a manly fashion and grapple with them in a grand fight? You mightn't even have credited me with telling the truth. And by the time I'd explained everything, those men would've likely caught sight of you ..."

To think that I branded this girl a lunatic, Vandhiyathevan rued himself. *Ah, what foolishness!* He felt a prickle of shame. *I'll have to put all my trust into her—I've no hope of making it to Ilankai without her help. All the trouble I've gone to thus far, would have been in vain, and I might even be imprisoned by Pazhuvettarayar's men, once again.*

"You've no idea of the immense help you've been to me, my girl. And now—you're the only one who can assist me to accomplish the rest ..."

"What do you expect me to do?"

"You've seen my precious friend, haven't you—and know exactly what that devil is capable of? Now you know that there's absolutely no point in trusting him. I'm afraid you'll have to be the one to ferry me to Ilankai."

Poonguzhali was silent.

"I'm no rogue—you know and trust me, I hope. I must get to Ilankai somehow and as soon as I can, my girl, on a most important mission. You must help me accomplish this—"

"And if I did?" She looked up at him. "What would you give me?"

Bashfulness crept into her face, for probably the first time since he'd met her. Her cheeks dimpled, and her exquisitely lovely countenance seemed to glow with even more beauty, if that were possible. She looked radiant.

She'd asked him quite the same question in his nightmare the night before, Vandhiyathevan remembered. His lips twitched with the overwhelming desire to give the same answer—but he bit his tongue hard, and stopped himself with considerable force of mind. "If you will render me this assistance, my girl, I shall never forget it. Not till my last breath. I shall be grateful to you all my life. There doesn't seem to be any way I can repay your enormous service—but if there's something you wish me to do, then, by all means, I will."

Poonguzhali grew thoughtful, seemingly weighing her options. Must she reveal what she truly wanted—or not?

"If there's something you require from me—some assistance—tell me, and I'll be happy to aid you."

"Is that true? Do you really mean that?"

"I swear it. *Sathiyam!*"

"In that case, I shall ask you when the time is right. You won't forget this, will you?"

"No, never. I shall be waiting for the day I can repay my debt."

Poonguzhali sank into thought again. "Fair enough," she said, finally.

"Come with me. I'm taking you to a hidey-hole within this forest. You'll have to stay there until night falls, and there's probably no chance of food. You'll likely starve."

"Never fear. Your kind sister-in-law very grudgingly offered me some *pazhaiya soru*, last meal's rice, and I devoured a great big heap of it just to infuriate her. I shan't need anything until tonight ..."

"I'm not sure there'll be anything to eat, even then. I'll try and bring you some food if I can. Now, remember: you'll have to obey my instructions and stay where I tell you, until nightfall. I shall return once it's dark, and make some sort of sound. You've heard the nightingale's song, right? Cuckoo, cuckoo ...?"

"Certainly I have. And even I hadn't, I shall be sure to recognize your voice."

"You're to come out only when you've heard my call. We'll have to get into the boat and begin our journey within a *jaamam* of nightfall."

"I shall wait for the nightingale's song."

Poonguzhali led Vandhiyathevan to a sandy mound in the middle of the forest, the far side of which sported a luxurious growth of bushes and trees. She pulled aside some of these deftly, with the ease of long practice, and slipped into a depression of sorts, through a tree. Vandhiyathevan followed her, to see the lip of an old, crumbling *mandapam*. Closer scrutiny revealed two large pillars, visible in the dark shadows. So effectively was the moldering edifice screened by vines, creepers and tree branches that it was well nigh invisible from any direction.

"A leopard once made this *mandapam* its lair; I live here now," Poonguzhali explained casually. "This is my home away from home— my own, special retreat. I come here whenever I get tired of human beings and wish to escape their presence. There's a pot in the corner with drinking-water. Stay here all day. Don't peep out no matter what you hear: voices, horse-hooves, or any uproar around these parts. Don't climb the top of this *mandapam*—don't even look out."

"You're asking me to stay here after night-fall too?" Vandhiyathevan demanded. "What if some sort of wild animal—say, a tiger or leopard finds its way here?"

"Cats like those don't come in here these days. Foxes and the stray wild boar might sneak in, though—and you're not nervous about those, are you?"

"Not at all, but what if they happen to fall upon me in the dark? I don't have my spear with me—I left it at home."

"Here, take hold of this, then," Poonguzhali picked up a weapon that lay on the grimy floor of the *mandapam*. A strange piece indeed, this one: it had sharp, sturdy thorns, almost like miniature swords on either side; thorns that were stronger even than iron. Lord Indra's celestial weapon, the *Vajrayudham*, might have been a splendid specimen like this one, perhaps!

"This is like no weapon I've ever seen," he murmured, looking it over. "What's it made of?"

"A fish's tail," Poonguzhali answered. "This was what I used to kill the leopard that lived here, when it sprang upon me."

7

"Samudhra Kumari"

As it turned out, Vandhiyathevan didn't find it very difficult to while away the daylight hours: half he spent in sleep; the rest, he mused pleasantly over the conundrum that was Poonguzhali.

What a strange girl, to be sure. Such a pleasing, beautiful name; everything that was supple, elegant and charming—and then there was her character ... hard, and utterly ruthless. Wait, was she truly quite that cruel? No, there was some sweetness in her character as well. But then—just look at the way she described her leopard kill. So matter-of-fact, as though it was all in a day's work!

And yet, why did she act and speak as though in a rage, sometimes? There was just a hint of madness in her that seemed, well, unnatural. There ought to be some reason—some depressing incident, perhaps, that had warped her mind. Or had it been a pleasant interlude, after all? Who knew? A woman could be a perfectly unreasonable lunatic regardless of pleasant or unpleasant incidents in her life—or perhaps this one was just a freak of nature, and her character had been shaped thus from birth. Not that he'd seen any such, well, abnormalities in her parents; perfectly ordinary, rather subdued characters, weren't they? Lunatic natures apart— why was she so concerned about him, anyway? Why save him through the skin of her teeth from those Pazhuvoor men? *And she's promised to ferry me to Ilankai as well ... is there something else at work here? Has she an ulterior motive underneath all these caring impulses? No—couldn't be. And yet— why has she changed her mind? What sort of repayment does she expect for her assistance? She's promised to tell me later—I wonder what it might turn out to be ...*

All this time, as he pored lazily over these thoughts, a part of his mind couldn't help but realize that Poonguzhali had certainly been right about one aspect: the forest did abound with unheard of commotion and upheaval. Horse-hooves pounded; men raised voices; small jungle creatures scurried here and there, terrified by the activity while birds screeched their alarm. But there were moments of complete calm as well, when the forest grew still.

It didn't take much for Vandhiyathevan to comprehend that the pandemonium was on his account—and all, the direct result of the treachery of the physician's son.

What a prize idiot! Just hours after meeting Poonguzhali, he's decided that he's fallen in love with her. Ha, a likely circumstance, that. Why, it was almost laughable—like a tiny little pond, reeking of scum and filth, desperate to join hands with the glorious, magnificent Vadavamukagni! Or a squeaking rat daring to marry a ferocious, magnificent lioness. And yet— wasn't it wonderful, the way the girl had used this perfect specimen of stupidity? The way she'd taken advantage of his seething, impotent lust? Hadn't she roused a storm of jealousy in his heart within moments? Why, she'd turned him into a treacherous bastard within the space of half a *naazhigai*. Ah, there was a great deal to be said of the power women harnessed within themselves ...

One thing he'd had to admit to himself, loath as he was to do so. *You'd preened yourself over your clever strategies, hadn't you, Vandhiyatheva,* he told himself, wryly. *Thought you were wonderful, didn't you, with your tricks and slippery tactics—no one could beat you at sleight of hand. But you've met your match here, in this uncivilized, wild girl, roaming the forests! Ah, her ruse to drag you away from the sea, towards this concealed mandapam— words couldn't do justice to her lightning swift thoughts and reflexes! What do you think would've happened, lad, if she hadn't? You'd have been arrested by the Pazhuvoor men, of course, and your precious, important mission would've hung in tatters ...*

No, he really couldn't afford to be quite so careless or unguarded, any more.

The sun sank, a fiery ball in the western sea. And in Kodikkarai, this is a splendid feat of nature, not to be missed—for, the shore, which runs south for a while, suddenly turns and goes almost straight west. A visitor to these parts, therefore, can stand atop a mound and gaze over a magnificent vista: the sea spreading out in the east, south and west! During certain months, it is even possible to witness both the sun and the moon—one rising with dazzling splendour in the east, and the other setting with a radiant glow to the west—turning the seas into a heaving mass of molten gold. Vandhiyathevan felt an almost overwhelming desire to climb atop the *mandapam* and witness these sights—but managed to exert his self-control and decided against it.

Darkness fell and in the forest, its approach seemed swifter as it closed around in all four directions. In the *mandapam*, already swathed in gloom, it was even worse, as everything turned pitch black. Unable to bear the stifling darkness any more, Vandhiyathevan ventured out, clambered atop the sandy mound that covered the *mandapam* and peered around. The lighthouse flames burned bright in the distance, while stars twinkled in the night sky, bright as diamonds. The forest abounded in sound once again—this time, of eerie night creatures. There was a great deal of difference, Vandhiyathevan realized, between the jungle clamour of day, and that of night. The screeches and whispers and murmurs during the latter seemed, somehow, so much more unnatural: your heart raced with fear, and your flesh prickled with sheer terror. You could see a tiger in broad daylight and not feel a stab of panic. And yet—the slightest movement of a rat darting through the bushes at night was enough to set pulses racing with terror!

Cukkoo, cukkoo … ah! The nightingale's musical call fell on Vandhiyathevan's ears like the welcome rush of divine song, and he began to make his way towards it. There—Poonguzhali had arrived. *Don't make a sound*, she signed, and he realized that the shore was very close.

A boat lay on the sands, primed for journey; the mast, sail were in complete readiness and a rope, used to bind them together lay coiled neatly within. The small vessel had two protruding sticks as well, and a large wooden plank was fitted onto them.

Vandhiyathevan hastened forward, in a bid to help her push the boat into the water.

Keep your hands to yourself, Poonguzhali signed. She maneuvered the boat with considerable deftness and eased it along the shore; it slid into sea without a sound.

Vandhiyathevan came forward again, to try and climb in; Poonguzhali stopped him. "Hush—wait a moment." Her voice was very low. "You can get in once we've gone a little further." And she began to wade through the water, dragging the boat along.

Vallavarayan pushed it as well, with the creditable intention of helping her—but it seemed to have the opposite effect: the boat came to a standstill.

"Why don't you keep your hands to yourself and just come along?" she chided him.

They went past the shore, where waves beat upon the sands. "We're safe to get in now," Poonguzhali announced finally, and clambered in first. Vandhiyathevan made haste to do so as well, upon which, the boat began to rock—so wildly, in fact, that it almost seemed as if he'd fall overboard. He managed to hold on, somehow, and righted himself. His heart did pound madly at the narrow escape, though.

"We can talk now, can't we?" he asked.

"Of course," she said, nonchalant. "If you've gotten over your attack of the trembles, that is."

"Trembles? What attack? That's just nonsense. I'm fine."

"If you say so."

"Don't we have to do something about raising the sail?"

"We might become visible to the people on shore, if we did. That'd make it easy for them to capture us."

"And what if they did? I'd smash my fists into their faces, wouldn't I?" Vandhiyathevan announced, grandiosely. "There's absolutely no need for you to be afraid, my girl," and he embarked on a long and considerably embellished account of his various courageous feats.

"The wind's against us, right now; raising the sail might take us right back to the shore," Poonguzhali explained, finally. "It might change after midnight; that's when the sail is likely to be of use."

"Oh well, in *that* case—" Vandhiyathevan made a grand gesture of acceptance. "You do seem to know what you're doing. Excellent. No wonder your father suggested that I choose you to ferry me."

"My father? Who're you talking about?"

"Thyaga Vidanga Karaiyar, of course. The lighthouse-keeper?"

"I suppose he is—but only on land. Once I descend into the sea, though—"

"Even your father's different, eh?"

"Why, certainly. He's the Lord of the Oceans; Samudhra Raja. Did you know that I've another name—Samudhra Kumari? Daughter of the Oceans? Hasn't anyone ever told you?"

"I'm afraid not. Strange name though, isn't it?"

"The Chakravarthy's younger son is called *Ponniyin Selvan*, isn't he? A beloved title, isn't it? Mine's the same, too."

Vandhiyathevan's fingers felt along the cloth tied around his body, almost subconsciously.

"Everything's safe, I take it?" asked Poonguzhali, who had noticed the gesture.

"What? What do you mean?"

"That thing you've bound up so preciously within your waistcloth, of course."

Vandhiyathevan almost jumped out of his skin. He stared at her, startled. The tiniest seed of suspicion began to germinate, deep within him.

Poonguzhali, however, didn't seem to find anything amiss; she was handling the oars strongly as she carried on a conversation; the boat cleaved easily through the water.

"When will we reach Ilankai, do you think?" Vandhiyathevan asked her.

"When dawn breaks—if there're two of us paddling, that is. And the wind has to do its part too."

"Then let me help, why don't you? I'm not the kind of man who'd let you do all the work."

He gripped the oar beside him, plunged it into the water, and tried to paddle, but ah—this looked a lot easier than it actually was. Handling oars was certainly no mean task; it required a great deal of strength. Under his incompetent hands, the craft simply swung around in an arc—*virrr*—and shuddered to a stop.

"Why, what's this? Why won't the boat move *now*? It seemed fine when *you* used the oars."

"I'm Samudhra Kumari, aren't I? Now, just sit in your place and keep still. I've sworn to take you to Ilankai somehow, and I'll make sure I keep my word. There—will that do?"

Vandhiyathevan subsided, abashed. Only a little, though, and for a very brief moment. Soon, he began to look around in earnest; the sticks and plank tied to the boat caught his attention.

"What're these for?"

"For balance; so the boat doesn't rock too much."

"Oh, good grief—is there anything even worse than the rocking *now*? I'm getting giddy here—isn't it flinging itself about enough?"

"You think *this* is choppy? You ought to go out in a boat during the months of Aippasi-Kaarthigai, when *vaadai* winds blow—that'll show you *turbulence!*"

From the shore, the sea seemed a calm, tranquil place, almost like a silver sheet that covered a vast surface up to the horizon; *on* it, however, Vandhiyathevan realized that the opposite was true. The surface was continuously being broken by waves—small, foamless waves that swung the boat up and down, up and down, like a cradle.

"What happens to this plank if there's a gale?"

"Depends on the gale. Stiff winds don't do much damage as a rule; the plank holds on. But if there's a really big wind—like a storm, perhaps, or even a cyclone—the boat might capsize and we'll have to be careful not to untie the plank from the boat. It's the only thing that might help us hold on and survive, in the water."

"*Ayyo!* Is that even possible—for the boat to capsize?"

"Severe whirlwinds can toss and splinter even huge ships to pieces; what of our tiny vessel, then?"

"What's—what are whirlwinds?"

"Don't tell me you don't know what *those* are. Well, it happens when winds from one direction collide with winds from another. We have *kondal* winds here, during the months of Thai and Maasi—those are perfectly harmless, and you can take a boat from Kodikkarai to Ilankai with ease. Make it there and back within the night. Vaikaasi month, though, you have the *Chozhaga* winds, and it gets a bit difficult to get to Ilankai, then. We're now in between the *Chozhaga* and *Vaadai* season. Wind and wind might collide sometimes and gales would whip the sea, like when you beat milk for curds. Waves the height of mountains rise on the surface, and there are enormous troughs that gape open like deep valleys, and the water whirls and swirls around them—*kara kara*—and God help us if the boat ever happens to get caught in a churning whirlpool like that, because that'd be the end of us. *Arokara!*"

Terror seized Vandhiyathevan abruptly—and suspicion too, at that very moment. "*Ayyo!*" He yelled. "I'm not going—not going—take me back to shore!"

"What are you blathering on about? Shut up. Close your eyes if you're that afraid. Or better still, sleep."

The germ of suspicion had taken frightening root now; every one of his worst doubts was being proven right. "You—you *evil* woman— devil—you're trying to drown me here—that's why you're taking me out to sea—if I fall asleep, that'll make your job easier!"

"Good God, what madness is this?"

"I'm not—I'm not mad—stop the boat—stop it! Or I'll jump into the sea!"

"Do, by all means—but before you jump, kindly give me the *olai* meant for Ponniyin Selvan!"

"Oh—*oh*! What do you know about that?"

"I opened the waistcloth you hold onto so carefully at all times— that's how. You didn't really think I'd ferry just anyone from Kodikkarai, did you? Without knowing their identity or destination? Of course I did, this morning, sitting atop the tree—and I read that precious *olai*—"

"Witch—and I've come all the way here—trusting you—are you going to turn around the boat, or not?" Commonsense seemed to hang in tatters; a sudden burst of insane fury seized him, almost overpowering

Vandhiyathevan. "Turn the boat," he screamed, casting all semblance of normalcy to the winds. "Turn the boat—*turn it!*"

"I really do think Kundhavai Piratti committed a grave error of judgment," Poonguzhali said, almost conversationally. "Imagine trusting someone like you, with neither wit nor presence of mind, to accomplish a mission as important as this one! Where did *her* wits go begging?"

"Ha—you know even that now, do you? You know who gave me the *olai*? You're wicked—evil all through! Will you turn the boat? Or I warn you, I'll jump!"

"Go right ahead," was Poonghuzhali's jovial answer.

Sanity had taken complete leave of Vandhiyathevan. Poonghuzhali's words were the final straw; he lost his head.

And jumped into the ocean.

Somewhere, in the back of his mind—the one that retained useful information—was the reassuring thought that the sea was very shallow around these parts; he was in no danger. That was until he actually did fall into the sea, wallowed in the water—and found that his feet didn't strike sand. There was no ocean floor here—they'd managed to come to open sea, by this time. The ocean here was deep. Very deep.

Realization struck. He screamed. Long and loud, with the full pitch of his lungs.

By this time, he'd learned to swim—or something like it, anyway. His inherent fear of the water remained, however, and terror paralyzed his limbs, sapping his strength, leaving him helpless. A river or pond was different; the shores or banks were always visible and you could take heart from that. There was hope of rescue, there. But this—this was the sea! Water, water and nothing but water everywhere, in all four directions. The ocean wasn't especially choppy, but there *were* small waves which raised him up one moment, and flung him into a crevasse the next.

"*Ahhh!*" He screamed when he came up once; the boat was clearly visible. It vanished from his gaze, however, when he went down. The sea closed in around him; all he could see was a dark, gloomy wall of water. His tongue lost the ability to move; he couldn't even scream. The third time a wave threw him up, it seemed that the boat had moved even farther away.

That was it, then. He was going to die right here. In this vast ocean.

His mind seemed to give up.

This is going to be my watery grave, he thought. *Not just for me, but my waistcloth and the olai bound up in it as well!*

Kundhavai's face swam in front of his mind's eye, at that moment. *What have you done?* Her eyes seemed to ask, brimming with reproach.

Ah, the fantasies I cherished! All those marvelous castles in the air ... why, I hoped to restore the magnificent Vaanar clan to its glory some day— that I might ascend a gleaming, richly decorated throne, set with precious gems, with Ilaiya Piratti at my side, a vision of beauty! And now—all that's gone. Ruined! Because of this wretched, wretched girl—no, not a girl; she's the devil incarnate; a demon who paraded in the guise of a woman! A spy of those evil Pazhuvettarayars — no, no, a devoted servant of that beautiful witch, Nandhini, probably. I may not survive this blasted ocean, but if I ever manage to get my hands on this demon-girl ... Chee! Why waste my last moments on earth thinking murderous thoughts? I may as well meditate on the divine, that I may attain a better fate ... Umapathi! Parameswara! Lord of Pazhani! Perumale—You Who guard the world, resting upon the Milky Way ...! Princess Kundhavai—forgive me, for I'm dying, without having completed the task with which you entrusted me—wait, there's that boat again! Ah, if only I could wrap my hands around that demon-girl's throat ...!

It couldn't be said that Vandhiyathevan's dramatic plunge in to the ocean ruffled Poonguzhali much. Not at first, anyway. She sat in the boat for a while after he vanished, rather negligent, to be honest, confident that he would flounder for a while, gulp a few mouthfuls of sea-water and then, eventually, clamber into the boat, somehow. *It won't hurt him to stew in his juices a little*, she grinned, and even rowed a bit, so the distance between him and the boat widened.

She realized her mistake soon enough.

The man can't swim well at all, she thought, and her heart sank. *And he's terrified. All those unearthly "Ahhhs!" and "Ohhhs!" aren't fake; he really is floundering. No, he's not doing this just to rattle me. He's going to start swallowing sea-water soon, at this rate, and sink even more quickly—and worse, his body would be practically impossible to find. Che che, what an idiot I've been—I started this as a joke, just to tease him and now it looks like it will end in disaster—I ought to have kept my stupid mouth shut until we reached shore, at least—certainly not given away the fact I knew his precious secret. Now I've likely ruined everything. And yet—who would've thought the ruffian would do something this insane? A man like him to be terrified of the water—well, it was beyond anything, wasn't it? How could I have anticipated this?*

The next time Vandhiyathevan was thrown up by the waves and appeared in her line of sight, she took action, and began to row the boat in his direction; in moments, she was almost by his side. "Get in!" she called out. "Come on, now!"

Vandhiyathevan, however, seemed lost to the world. He didn't seem capable of hearing her words or even if he did, it was doubtful if he possessed the strength to actually swim over, and get into the boat. All his faculties, especially sight and hearing, seemed to have been completely suspended—except for one: screaming. He could and did raise one hand above the choppy water, raised his head, and gave vent to a shrill, inhuman yell. "*Aaaahhh!*"

That, Poonguzhali realized swiftly, was the cry of a man who had given up all hope of being rescued; of even making it out of this desperate situation alive. The broken, terrified scream of a man who knew himself to be forsaken. The *pirai* moon's pale beams fell on his face as he raised it from the water, and she caught a glimpse, for a brief moment: there was no doubt that this was the face of a man who'd taken leave of sanity. Sheer numb terror had twisted his features and his eyes blazed with mindless panic. There was no point in expecting him to climb into the boat of his own volition. *I'll have to drag him in myself,* she thought. *How wonderful of you to have brought all this upon yourself, my girl. There's a lot of merit to the saying, Females lack foresight …*

To think was to act.

Poonguzhali did several things in short order, within the next few moments: she untied the rope coiled within the boat to raise the sail, tied it firmly to the plank secured to the boat, and fastened the other end to her own waist. Then, she plunged neatly into the ocean, swam with deft strokes towards Vandhiyathevan, approached him close enough to reach out with her hands—and stopped.

Vandhiyathevan had seen her—and his eyes blazed with sheer, unadulterated, murderous rage.

Poonguzhali's thoughts raced at the speed of lightning; experience had taught her exactly what people such as this, numb with the exhaustion of battling waves and about to drown, could do. They tended to clutch the neck or shoulders of those who came to their rescue; panic blinded their minds and they usually ended up preventing their would-be rescuers from dragging them ashore. The instinct for survival gave them the strength of an elephant, and they gripped their saviours so tightly that the latter were in danger of drowning, themselves. Even competent swimmers couldn't free themselves, or swim away; both ending up at the bottom of the ocean!

Poonguzhali knew all this, of course, and came to a decision within moments. She treaded water, approaching Vandhiyathevan, battling for his life, just a little closer. By now, she was near his head. Using just one hand to swim, she curved the fingers of the other into a fist, and reared back. Gathering all her strength, she brought her fist towards his face.

The punch exploded between Vandhiyathevan's nose and forehead.

Years of rowing across choppy seas had strengthened her hands incredibly; her fist smashed into his face like *Vajrayudham*—and his head seemed to splinter into a thousand pieces. His eyes fractured into ten thousand painful fragments; each piece seemed to dazzle and blind him like a hundred thousand jagged shards of lightning. Samudhra Kumari's terrifying face appeared on each splintered piece, deafening him with a series of terrifying cackles: *Ha, ha, ha, ha …!* Just like the demon she was. His ear-drums seemed to rupture into a bloody mess as the laughter amplified and almost drove him to madness—like a thousand, ten thousand, no, a hundred thousand murderous ghosts, out for his soul!

Then—nothing.

His sight failed; so did his hearing. He lost consciousness.

There was nothing now, but darkness. Inky, pitch-blackness …

… and an endless, stifling silence.

8

DEMON ISLAND

A celestial being she might be, but it would seem that sometimes, Vaanamaadevi, Goddess of the Sky, was quite as witless as human beings. Men let the Supreme Being, Paranjyothi, Lord of the Cosmos slip out of the sky of their hearts and search for Him endlessly among gloomy, dank temple corridors, lighting a hundred thousand lamps in sanctums in a vain bid to catch some glimpse of the divine.

So, too, does the Sky Goddess, rivaling insignificant humans practically every day: she lets slip her beloved, the Night, into the arms of the scheming ocean, and then begins to worry that he is lost to her forever. Vaanamaadevi is as foolish as they come, apparently, for she lights a lamp that shines with the brilliance of hundred thousand! And that is not all: she hunts for her lover all night with millions of tiny lights that never extinguish! Small wonder that she forgoes respite and spends endless hours awake, brooding over her loss.

The first sight that met Vandhiyathevan when he awoke, was an array of thousands of brilliant, flickering little lights that seemed to fill his vision. What temple was this, he marveled, that boasted so many lamps, anyway? And then, his senses seemed to right themselves; these weren't lights, he realized, but stars, twinkling in the night sky. He was lying on his back in the boat, and a rope was tied securely around his waist, around his wet clothes.

A pleasant breeze blew, soothing his mind and body immeasurably. The gentle murmur of the sea, now considerably tranquil, seemed to resound like a deeply spiritual "Om," and calmed his tumultuous mind. And in the midst of all this rose a gentle, sweet song—a song that seemed strangely familiar. Now, where had he heard it before?

> *"Heaving oceans lie still,*
> *Gentle breezes calm,*
> *Yet, sweet maiden*
> *What churns thy heart, what storm?*
> *Why anguish, my soul,*
> *When tumbling seas lie smooth?"*

Ah, to be sure—that strange girl—the wild-spirited Poonguzhali! He raised himself just a little, and looked across. Ah yes, there she was, rowing with all her strength and singing that sad little song.

And, like a bolt of lightning that illuminates everything in a moment, the previous night's happenings flashed across his memory all at once. Well, everything, that is, until his own terrifying flounder in the sea and Poonguzhali plunging in, swimming towards him. Nothing after that, though. She'd probably rescued him from the ocean, bundled him into the boat and bound him to the planks across the craft for good measure, so he wouldn't tip overboard during another turbulent episode. And she'd actually taken care to tie the rope above the cloth around his waist—so it wouldn't chafe against his skin.

Vandhiyathevan checked his waistcloth, tied above his lower garments once again, and had the satisfaction of knowing that both *olai* and coins were safe.

Ah, what a terrible error of judgment to have ever suspected this girl of ulterior motives! Had she truly wished to kill me, she needn't have rescued me at all. And the trouble to which she must have gone, trying to heave my dead weight into the boat—especially since I couldn't help myself at all! How did she even manage it, I wonder? What a wonderful woman!

Oh, she's getting up—why? She's seen me awake and is now coming towards me to ... what on earth is she going to do? Chee, no, this isn't right. She's doing something else—aha! She's going to raise the sail and tie it to the mast. What a difficult task—and all alone too—

"Poonguzhali—Poonguzhali!"

"Finally awake, are you?"

"Untie me—let me help you."

"I'll thank you to just stay in your place and not do a thing. That's more than enough. And if you want to get out of the rope—go right ahead. The knots are easy. You don't need my help. But don't jump into the sea again, will you?"

Vandhiyathevan followed her instructions and rid himself of his bonds. Meanwhile, Poonguzhali raised the mast all by herself, unfurled the sail and secured it deftly, whereupon the boat almost leaped forward, practically whirring through the water.

"Samudhra Kumari?"

"Yes?"

"I'm thirsty."

"Considering all the sea-water you've swallowed, not surprising, is it?"

She picked up a makeshift water-bottle, a *surai-kudukkai*, and came close. "I even brought you some food—but that became a casualty of your magnificent adventure overboard. Thank heavens for drinking-water, at least." She flipped open the flimsy pith lid, and handed it to him; Vandhiyathevan gulped down the water.

Thirst slaked, he cleared his throat with some embarrassment. "I, ah, clearly made a mistake, about you. And I'm sorry."

"Forget it. We're strangers, each going their way once dawn breaks. Who cares?"

"What time is it now?"

"Find out," said Poonguzhali. "There—look at the Saptharishi constellation, above you."

Vandhiyathevan craned his head to gaze at the horizon, in the northern sky. The Seven Sages *had* changed position, it seemed, since the time he boarded the craft; they'd shifted in a semi-circle. Ah, the star of Arundhati, now—how close it was, to Vasishtar! A truly pious wife, always by the side of her beloved husband, as legends praised. But the Dhruva star, on the other hand, hadn't changed position. It never did. For aeons it had stayed in place without shifting so much as an inch, where the skies and sea met, lighting the way for seamen and navigators, showing them the right direction. The Dhruva star—now, who'd spoken about it, recently? Comparing someone to it—ah, yes, the Kudandhai astrologer, of course. And the person he'd been speaking of: Prince Arulmozhi Varmar, whom he'd likened to the pole star. *Good God, am I truly about to have the opportunity of meeting the prince? Is that going to happen through the kind offices of this young woman?*

By now, Poonguzhali had returned to her place.

"Know the time? We're halfway through the third *jaamam*, now. The wind's changed," she announced. "We'll be at Naaga Theevu by daybreak."

"What?" Vandhiyathevan was startled. "What do you mean—Snake Island?"

"Why, yes. There are a great many islands clustering around northern Ilankai, and this is one of them. It's got an advantage too—it's the only one from where you can travel into Ilankai on land without having to cross the sea, again ..."

"What're *you* going to do? Once you've set me down at Ilankai, that is?"

"How's that your concern?"

"Well—you've done me this incredible service, haven't you? Aren't I supposed to repay you, somehow? You mentioned that you'd ask me something in return for your help, after all."

"I've changed my mind. I'm not going to ask anything. You're an ingrate."

She was entirely justified, Vandhiyathevan knew, in her accusations. His fingers felt around his middle again, making sure the waistcloth and its contents were safe. "Samudhra Kumari," he began. "I know I made a terrible mistake when I suspected you, early last night. Won't you forgive me?"

"Very well; forget it. Now, you'll have to think about your next course of action. What're you going to do, once you reach Ilankai? How will you learn the prince's location?"

"The good God helped me cross this ocean; he'll show me a way, I'm sure."

"Your faith is remarkable. Do you really believe that He interests Himself in the affairs of petty humans?"

"I'm afraid I've never immersed myself into philosophical soul-searching. I've a habit of praying whenever I find myself in difficulty or danger, and He's helped me out, so far. He did send you to row me to Ilankai, didn't He?"

"A little less of your conceited rambling, if you please. I'd no intention of helping *you* out; God didn't appear miraculously in my dreams and command me to ferry you, either—"

"No? Why did you go to all the trouble of saving me, then? Why're you rowing me to this island, now?"

"That's no concern of yours, so don't bother asking."

Vandhiyathevan subsided into silence, rather thoughtful. A somewhat startling, and not unpleasant idea took root, in his arrogant mind—had this naïve girl been captivated by his considerable good looks—his courageous mien, wondrously sculpted features—and fallen for him? Then he changed his mind. Her behaviour and speech weren't of a woman madly in love with him. No, there was something else at work here; some other reason for her actions—well, he'd simply have to wheedle it out of her, somehow.

"I'll have to admit," he drawled. "I *am* worried about something ..."

"Worried? *You*? About what?"

"Ilankai is full of dense forests and mountains, I've heard."

"More than half the island is so, yes."

"And—what about wild animals? I've heard there're plenty of those too."

"Wild elephants do roam in huge herds in the forests. Sometimes, they venture out, as well."

"I've heard that the people of Ilankai are uncivilized savages."

"That's a complete lie."

"Very well; it must be true, if you say so. And now, I'm supposed to find Prince Arulmozhi Varmar in this terrible, fearsome jungle."

"Didn't you say just now that that wouldn't be too difficult?"

"So I did. What complications could possibly arise in trying to find the blazing sun?"

"But you think differently, now? Why?"

"Grey clouds might blot out the sun—or he could have slipped underneath the ocean."

"No fluffy cloud or petty sea could possibly conceal this particular sun—and if they tried, Ponniyin Selvar's presence would light up the clouds and dazzle the very oceans!"

Ah, the radiance that fairly transforms this young woman's face at the mere mention of the prince's name! Like scores of Chozha subjects, she reveres him as God, Vandhiyathevan mused. *I wonder what sort of divine power Arulmozhi Varmar possesses that turns people into such willing devotees?* Aloud, he asked: "You think, then, that it wouldn't be too difficult to find him on this island?"

"All you have to do is enquire the whereabouts of the Chozha armies—and you'll be able to run the prince to earth."

"But Chozha forces have spread out over half the island, I've heard."

"So have I. From Maathottam to Pulasthya city, or that's what I managed to learn."

"You see? I'm not sure it's such an easy task—the good God knows where exactly he's camped. I could trudge along all the forest paths I find, but those wouldn't lead me to him, and it would likely take ages! I *have* to take this *olai* to him as soon as possible—you've seen it; you understand the urgency of my mission, don't you?"

Samudhra Kumari vouchsafed no response to this, but sank into silence.

"If I knew where the prince was, I needn't wander all over the island," Vandhiyathevan's voice was persuasive. "I could reach him without loss of time."

"Well, there's a way," Poonguzhali volunteered.

"Ah, I *thought* you might find one."

"I said I'd set you down at Naaga Theevu in the morning, didn't I?"

"Yes?"

"Well, there's an island called Boodha Theevu, right beside."

"Demon Island—that sounds terrifying!"

"There's no reason to be. It used to be called Bodha Theevu—the story goes that this was where Buddha Bhagavan descended first, upon his journey through the skies. He made his seat under an *arasu* tree, and began to preach the tenets of Buddhism, and that's how it got its name."

"And then it was twisted into Boodha Theevu, I presume."

"Exactly. Of course, a lot of people grew terrified at the mere mention of the name, just like you; no one goes there now. Only those who aren't afraid of demons."

"Brave spirits like you, I suppose. After all, you're not afraid of even fire-tongued demons, are you? Now, what was it that you were about to say, about Boodha Theevu?"

"If you'd wait a *naazhigai* on its shore, I could make enquiries and tell you Ponniyin Selvar's location in Ilankai."

"You would? Make enquiries of whom?"

"The demon on the island, of course."

"And you'll introduce me as well, wouldn't you?"

"No, never. You're not to follow me inland. Promise that you'll stay right here on the shore, and keep an eye on the boat. I shall get you the information you need."

"Fair enough," Vallavarayan agreed.

A pleasant breeze ruffled his hair, lulling his tired body and mind. The boat practically leaped through the water, spurred on by the sail, cleaving through the ocean. The sea soothed, with its deep, low, thrum.

Vandhiyathevan's eyes seemed to close all by themselves. He slipped away, gently, from wakefulness to sleep.

తా

Hidden Meanings and Explanations

Surai Kudukkai

Bottles made of the preserved shell of bottle-gourds and used in ancient and medieval times to carry drinking-water.

Saptharishi Constellation

The *Saptharishis* refer to the seven *rishis* or sages of Ancient India: Vasishtar; Marichi; Pulasthyar; Pulahar; Atri; Angiras and Kratu. In their honour, a constellation consisting of seven stars is known as the Seven Sages. Another star, found in close proximity to the star that is Vasishtar was promptly named Arundhati, after his wife. The west knows the Saptharishi Mandalam as the Big Dipper or Ursa Major, and Vasishtar-Arundhati as the Mizar Double.

9

"HERE IS ILANKAI"

The sight that met Vandhiyathevan's eyes when next he awoke, was enough to astound him.

The sun rose in a dazzling fireball in the east, fiery rays blazing the sky; the sea glinted and gleamed at the horizon, a mass of molten gold. Udhayakumari, Lady of the Dawn, ushered in a new day, radiant in her glittering halcyon attire. A beautiful island, rich and green as precious *maragatham*, loomed from the sea in front of him, in the direction of the boat, clothed, it seemed to his fanciful eyes, in an exquisite sea-garment. To his right, another island, similarly green and lush, came to view. It wasn't quite obvious if these were surrounded by the sea on all sides, or it was all just one long stretch of land. Peering between the two land masses, he glimpsed a few more of the same, draped in varying, pleasing shades of green. Lying in his place in the boat, he cast his eyes around in wonderment, fairly dazzled by nature's loveliness, wrapping him in all seven colours of the rainbow and seven thousand variations; all the colours of the universe, it seemed, in those fresh, morning hours. It didn't seem real, in fact; so divine was the scene, the air, and even the islands. It must be the work of an extraordinarily creative artist, a celestial genius who decided that he would stun humans with his talent. *Let me show you what heaven really looks like*, he'd probably said, and set out to paint a divinely exquisite picture.

"This isn't really *sorgam*, you know," a voice filtered down into his blissful mind, disrupting his appreciation of nature in her element. "Just Ilankai."

Vandhiyathevan shook himself out of his reverie. "Well, it *is* true that I wondered if we'd wandered into heaven, for a moment," he admitted.

"Not exactly heaven—but almost like it," Poonguzhali answered. "A celestial land that demons clothed as humans have been trying, with all their might, to turn into hell for years."

"Who're these demons you speak of?"

"People like you—with nothing but war on their minds."

"Does this comprehensive list include Ponniyin Selvar?"

"Why're you bringing him up?"

"You said you'd enquire about him, didn't you?"

"I said I'd find out his whereabouts—certainly not enquire about whether he's man, demon or *deva*."

The boat was approaching the islands swiftly; soon, the deep, all-pervasive thrum of the ocean was interspersed with the murmur of waves beating upon the shore.

"Well? What's your pleasure?" asked Poonguzhali. "The island straight ahead is Boodha Theevu; the one to the right is Naaga Theevu. Where do you want me to go? Snake Island? I can set you down there; you'll find your way to the prince, won't you?"

"I'd much rather get down at Boodha Theevu, thank you. I might be delayed a little, but it would be best if I knew my destination at the very least."

"Fair enough. You've sworn me an oath, remember."

The boat beached the sands of the little island; Poonguzhali leapt out, threw a warning to Vandhiyathevan to take care of her little craft and as he stood watching her, walked swiftly through the dense, green foliage and vanished into the trees.

He pondered for a while upon the mystery of Bodha Theevu somehow getting mauled by peoples' tongues into Boodha Theevu; then his thoughts circled around the horrifying *boodham* that may or may not dwell within the island, and its characteristics. Then he wondered about Poonguzhali and her behaviour: what might be the mysterious secret that dwelt deep within this peculiar girl-woman?

Poonguzhali returned within a *naazhigai* as promised, got into the boat, and invited Vandhiyathevan to climb in as well. They began to move towards Naaga Theevu.

"Did you manage to learn what you wanted?" Vandhiyathevan broached the subject.

"Chief Minister Aniruddha Brahmaraayar is on a visit to Maathottam, it seems, to seek an audience with Ponniyin Selvar; likely, the prince arrived there yesterday. As for how long he'll remain in the city—that's more than I can say," Poonguzhali informed him. "You could find out when you reach Maathottam yourself."

"How far away is it, do you think?"

"Five or six *kaadhams*, perhaps—and the terrain's thickly forested, I might add. And no, they're nothing like the jungles of Kodikkarai; don't make the mistake of thinking you can get through that easily. You'll find that the trees pierce the very skies and sometimes, it's dark even during noon, when the sun's at its highest. Elephants and other wild animals infest the forests, so you'll have to be on your toes."

Vallavarayan heaved a deep sigh. "If only I had a clever young woman like you to guide me through those treacherous paths—"

"What's the point of you, then? Give me the *olai*, and I shall deliver it myself to—no, no what am I saying? I'm a lunatic—I shall never be able to do this ... well, you're the one who's accepted Ilaiya Piratti's commission, aren't you? You'll have to complete this task yourself."

"Very well, and so I will. I shan't give it up—not for anyone, no matter how hard they beg and plead. This mission is mine, and mine alone. Besides, you've helped so much—and that's more than enough."

Closer, closer to Naaga Theevu, by the moment; Poonguzhali's hands handled the oars with practiced efficiency, but her expression made it very obvious that her thoughts were elsewhere, flitting in a fantasyland of her own.

"Samudhra Kumari?" Vandhiyathevan's low voice shook her out of reverie; she returned to earth with a thud.

"What is it? Why did you call me?"

"You mentioned that you expected something in return for your assistance, didn't you? Now would be the best time to tell me how I can repay my debt—land is approaching even as we speak."

Far from returning a vehement protest, Poonguzhali remained silent, as though weighing her options.

Vandhiyathevan's spirits rose. "Your assistance in my mission has been invaluable; you've performed a great service not just for me, but the whole of Chozha *samrajyam*—to the emperor of these vast lands, in fact," he explained, earnestly. "I shan't rest easy unless I find a way of repaying you."

"You mean everything you say, I hope? You're not one of those sweet-talking rogues who get away with pretty speeches and mean absolutely nothing, are you?"

"As the Samudhra Rajan is my witness, I swear to you that I shall honour my words."

"Just words on water, you mean."

"I call upon Akaasa Vaani, Bhooma Devi, all the deities who guard the eight directions, and the sun and moon, to bear witness to my pledge—I shall honour it. There, now."

"Fair enough—but you'll have to understand: I've no faith in your pledges or oaths. D'you think I place the slightest dependence on men keeping their word? Those who lie at the slightest pretext aren't going to honour some silly little promise. But you—I thought you were a good man, the moment I set eyes on you. That's why I shall tell you—"

"First impressions are the best; you needn't change yours at all."

"Once you've met Ponniyin Selvar, delivered your precious *olai*, thrashed out every single thing you ought to discuss and talked yourselves to the last breath—when he's alone and, well, not up to his neck in work and is in a mellow frame of mind—ask him, *Do you remember Samudhra Kumari?* And if he says he does, then tell him that I was the one who ferried you to Ilankai."

Poonguzhali, my little innocent! So this is your ambition; the deepest desire of your heart, is it? But, my girl—how can a little sparrow ever hope to seek the company of the mighty Garudan, lord of the skies? Is such a thing even possible? Even more important—are you really in a position to wish for this? Such aspirations will lead nowhere …

Aloud, his rely was nonchalant. "Why, what a convoluted conversation for something so simple—for a moment, I thought you were about to ask for something impossible. Certainly, I shall tell the prince about you—in fact, I shall, even if he doesn't bring up the subject at all—"

"*Ayyayo*, don't! If he doesn't bring it up—"

"Then *I* certainly shall."

"And tell him what, exactly?"

"Everything that happened, of course. *Your Highness*, I shall begin, *great prince, Ponniyin Selvare! You do remember Samudhra Kumari, don't you? And if you don't, kindly dredge her from the recesses of your consciousness, now. For it was she who dragged me from the Pazhuvettarayar's wretched rogues; she who ferried me, single-handed, to Ilankai! When I floundered in the heaving sea, gasping for breath, unable to swim, she pulled me into the boat, to safety! Had it not been for her, your highness, I wouldn't be standing in front of you, large as life and twice as healthy—not to mention bringing you the olai, as well.* There—will that do?"

Poonguzhali seemed to consider his eloquent speech. "So far, so good," she conceded. "But there it must stop. Don't add anything and for goodness's sake, don't tell him that I asked you to remind him!"

"*Cheche*, certainly not. What am I, a complete idiot?"

"And if the prince should return an answer—well, you must tell me his words, exactly. No more, and no less."

"How do I meet you again?"

"I couldn't think of anything easier; I'm either in Kodikkarai or Boodha Theevu. Or if not in those places, paddling in a boat somewhere in between."

"Shall I stop at Boodha Theevu on my way home? Will you be there?"

"On no account are you to enter the island; that would be a disaster, and I've warned you of it. You may check the beach for my boat—and if you find it, make some sort of sound. You remember my call last night, don't you? Like a nightingale? Can you do something like that?"

"Not like a nightingale, perhaps, but there's something else I can imitate," Vandhiyathevan assured her. "Listen to this ..." He closed his mouth with his palm and gave vent to a loud, hoarse croak: the harsh, completely unmusical, ghastly cry of a peacock.

Poonguzhali went into a peal of laughter.

The boat approached Naaga Theevu and beached the shore; they clambered out of the boat. Vandhiyathevan took his leave while Poonguzhali got back in and reversed the craft with expert hands. He took a few steps and turned to look at her, a gleam of expectation in his eyes. Would she change her mind about leaving? What if she said she'd like to accompany him, after all? That would be wonderful, wouldn't it? He didn't mind acknowledging to himself that he rather hoped she would.

But no—Poonguzhali didn't seem to notice him at all. Her expressive face showed that she'd long ceased to inhabit the earth, and was wandering in some marvelous dreamland of her own.

10

ANIRUDDHA BRAHMARAAYAR

We must interrupt this tale briefly, for a grievous error has been committed: one of our oldest acquaintances, Azhwarkkadiyaan Nambi, has been rather neglected for a while and our invaluable readers deserve an apology—well, perhaps Nambi himself requires a little more than just an apology; some desperate groveling at his feet would not be amiss. As to why—that is patently obvious: Nambi is in a towering rage at this precise moment.

His fearsome top-knot flies about, tossed wildly by the untamed winds of Rameswaram's seashore; his trusty staff, never pliant at any time, swings even more above his head. An unruly horde of Aadhi Saivars and Veera Saivars have surrounded him, and as they seem intent on causing him grave bodily harm, we are, understandably, rather worried about the Nambi's fate. And yet—there is still hope: Azhwarkkadiyaan's Narasimha Avataram, the very image of the lion-man incarnation of Thirumaal, and the speed of the staff swinging valiantly in his strong hands, serve to soothe us inexorably.

The day he eavesdropped on the conversation between Kundhavai and Vandhiyathevan had been his last, in Pazhaiyarai. He started out that very day, traveling faster than wind and even thought, towards the south. Nowhere along the way did he pause to snatch the chance of an argument with a Saivite to uphold the merits of the Vaishnavite sect; he even ignored several promising squabbles with quite extraordinary strength of mind, that they might not prove a distraction to his mission. After a brief halt in Madurai, wherein he learnt certain of the details he wished, he began his journey further south.

The day Vandhiyathevan disembarked in Ilankai courtesy of Poonguzhali and her trusty boat saw Azhwarkkadiyaan arrive in Rameswaram, in the evening.

The moment he set foot on that sacred land, however, it was as though a dam had burst within his heart; all his devotion, his unquestioned faith in the holy Vaishnavite sect overflowed the confines of his mind— and the various batches of Veera Saiva devotees milling everywhere did nothing to staunch the flood. If anything, their presence had the opposite effect: theirs were most important duties, consisting of shepherding, for immersion, various clueless pilgrims towards the several sacred wells or *theerthams* that dotted the place liberally; making sure they could worship the deity within the shrines and informing devotees, at great length, about the spiritual and religious history behind said shrines and wells—which meant that a fresh set of pilgrims brought every Saivite out in a roaring, teeming, pretentious welter of eager explanations, intent on simply taking over the devotees.

They did it to Azhwarkkadiyaan, now.

"Come, come, *Appane*, plunge into these holy wells and cleanse yourself of these terrible, blasphemous signs, these Vaishnavite profanities off your body!" one exclaimed, in a self-righteous voice. "This is the site of Rama's redemption, after all—this is where his *Brahmahathi* sin evaporated, don't you know? You may now follow his example and purify yourself, body and soul, by washing away these *naamams*!"

"There are sixty-four wells here: the Rama *theertham*, Lakshmana *theertham*, Anjaneya *theertham*, the Sugriva *theertham* and many others," another, cut in. "Each of those after whom these are named, immersed themselves in their sacred waters and washed away their heinous sins. You may come with me to the Anjaneya *theertham*, my man—and I shall make sure those wretched Vaishnavite symbols are rubbed off your skin; I shall perform the specific *sankalpam* that will rinse away—"

"Don't listen to them, *Appane*," barged in a third priest. "I shall take you straight to where Rama rid himself of his *Brahmahathi dhosham*— the sin incurred for killing a Brahmin—by sculpting in sand a sivalingam with his own hands, on the seashore ..."

"*Stop!*" Azhwarkkadiyaan stared at them all, eyes practically spitting sparks of fury. "Stop your nonsense this instant, all of you! Take yourselves off and wash your tongues first in all these precious *theerthams*—that you may cleanse yourselves of all *your* sins!"

"Ah—you believe we may have incurred a sin by uttering the names of Rama and Lakshmana, do you? Not at all; be assured, my man— know that this famed temple site, this *kshethram* is called Rameswaram: where Rama purified Himself by worshipping Easwaran, the most divine Siva Peruman Himself," explained a staunch Saiva Battar, quite seriously. "And so, you see, even the name lost its sin, by its very association with our lord!"

"With all due disrespect to your most ridiculous, ignorant selves—it doesn't look like you know the first thing about the name of this divine shrine, or its significance!"

"And you do? Enlighten us, then."

"With all my pleasure. It was your precious Sivan, you see, who was plagued by the dreaded *Brahmahathi dhosham* on account of having plucked one of Brahma's heads—and when he set foot in a place visited by Rama Himself, Thirumaal's most complete incarnation ... well, Sivan's own sins were washed away in an instant! And Rameswaram was named thus, because He worshipped Rama here— and that, *moodasikamani* Battars, is the true religious history of this place. Now you know."

"Why, you little—who are *you*, that dares to call *us* ignorant nincompoops?" One particularly enraged priest let loose his ire. "What makes you such an arrogant idiot—a horn on your head?"

"Hardly that, my stupid Battar—but this staff in my hands! As for who I am—why, certainly I shall do my best to banish your ignorance, and inform you of my precise identity: I am Azhwarkkadiyaan, the servant of those who serve at the divine feet of Nammazhwar who was born on this earth in Thirukurugoor, to bless all humanity with the Thamizh Vedas, most sacred of hymns! And I serve another purpose; I use my staff, my *kaithadi*, to great effect and drive away the ills of ignorance, which makes me a *kaithadiyaan* too!" And he brandished his staff to great effect.

"Great servant who serves the servants of the Azhwars," began a priest, irate. "I find the purpose of your top-knot puzzling; why not shave it all off? That way, the inside and outside of your head would be the same," he chortled.

"Ah, my dear Battars, it was indeed my intention to discard my knot in this sacred place—how fortuitous that you've reminded me!"

"*Adei*, send for a barber this instant, from the Naavidhar Street!" crowed an enthusiastic Battar. "And tell him to sharpen his knife—might as pull out all the hair from this one's skull, roots and all—"

"A barber's a waste of time, I tell you," another priest butted in. "Why bother with his services when *we* can perform his offices just as well? Anyone have a good, sharp knife?"

"Pray wait, wait just a moment, kind priests—allow me to relate a little story of my own: once, you see, I wasn't quite so bald; my head was full of thick, luxuriant hair. That was before I took a sacred oath: you see, I pledged to pull out a hair every time I broke a Saivite head. And now, as is obvious even to you, I've lost more than three-quarters of my glorious tresses; it's my intention to complete my vow and immerse myself in this ocean, in celebration," Azhwarkkadiyaan announced gleefully. "Well? Why don't you all line up, so I can begin?"

"*Adede*—witness the mouth on this Vaishnavite upstart!" exclaimed a shocked Saiva Battar.

"Break all our heads, would you?" another sprang forward wrathfully. "Would you even dare? Go on, try it—"

"Trust me, good men, I make no empty promises," Azhwarkkadiyaan began to swivel his staff about his head with some speed. "Not for nothing have I pulled out more than three-quarters of my hair, you know."

"Get him!"—"Bind him up!"—"Off with his head!"—"Grab that stick of his!" Outraged and furious might be the many yells and shrieks from all sides, but no one dared approach Azhwarkkadiyaan, and that was the truth.

And then, a sound arose—a sonorous shout that stopped them all in their tracks and attracted attention.

"Make way! Make way for the Mahamanya Chief Minister of Sundara Chozhar, Emperor of the Three Worlds; make way for Aniruddha Brahmaadhi Raajar! *Paraak—Paraak!*"

Stunned silence descended on the gathering, but no one seemed more astonished than Azhwarkkadiyaan himself as he tucked his recalcitrant staff under his arm, and stared at the approaching spectacle.

The site of their heated squabble had been a corner of the Rameswaram temple wall; past it lay the sea, a vast, imposing sight. And what an impressive tableau it presented, to be sure: large, hefty ships; smaller craft, yachts, boats, canoes and even petty vessels such as *vallams* and *vathais* dotted the surface liberally, crowding as far as the eye could see. Masts bearing huge sails that fluttered in the stiff wind littered the sea in such profusion that they blotted out the water, the skies and even the little clusters of islands that loomed beyond.

The Chozha Empire's renowned Chief Minister Aniruddha Brahmaraayar was now making his splendid, majestic way to shore in a boat, following the stentorian shout of his usher, not to mention the impressive armed guards before, and behind his regal person. The quarrel on shore caught his attention; so did Azhwarkkadiyaan himself, now standing with his staff in his crook, the very picture of innocence. The Brahmaraayar made a sign; the Vaishnavite folded his arms with utmost deference and scurried down to the water's edge.

"Such antics on the seashore, Thirumalai," the Chief Minister's suave voice was laden with reproach. "What are all these street-theatrics in aid of?"

"As to that, Great Teacher—what else can it all be, but a divine charade of the glorious Kanna Bhagavan Himself? Isn't He the one who initiates every spark of illusion, of deception and even the very theatrics you now speak of—but stay, I can scarcely believe this: is the sight that meets my vision real? Or, perhaps my eyes are playing cruel tricks on me? I'm not dreaming, am I? Or is all this just Maya ...?"

"Never did I think to see the day when you might denounce the whole universe as a magnificent illusion, Thirumalai. I'd believed you to be a staunch Vaishnavite; when did *you* convert to Maya and begin to propound its treatises?"

"Ah, great Guru, when you, the greatest Vaishnavite ever known, can convert to Saivism, why may I not discard the precepts of Vaishnavism? I may as well amend my name, now that my faith has changed: do you think Sri Sankara Bhagavadhpadhacharya's most devout *Adiyaan*, servant, might suit?"

"Wait, Thirumalai—you go a little too fast for me. Where and how did you come by the knowledge that I had become a Saivite?"

"The signs that decorate your blessed person tell their own tale."

"These—! Ah, Thirumalai, you haven't changed the slightest; still the same as in your early days, jumping to conclusions based solely on appearances—why this uproar, pray, that I've chosen to wear sandalwood paste flat on my forehead, rather than upright?"

"I am, respected Guru, a most uninformed idiot, as has been established by now. I look to you to banish the darkness of my ignorance, Great One; teach me that which matters and that which doesn't—and guide me onto the path of righteousness."

"I shall guide you all you want; make sure to seek an audience at my seat. Look, over there—do you see a tiny island, in the sea? It boasts a *mandapam*; you may come to me there."

"As you wish, Guruve, but—" Azhwarkkadiyaan pointed to the Veera Saiva Battars at a little distance, who took a collective step forward at this. "What if these quarrelsome Saivars won't let me?"

"This insolent Vaishnavite—ah, most illustrious *Brahmaadhi raajare*, Great One—he declares that he will break open our heads!" One of them was swift to lay his complaint. "He deserves to be flogged—punished severely—!" The rest took advantage of the Minister's presence in similar fashion, and strode forward with loud, raucous voices.

"Rest assured that I shall deliver his just desserts," Aniruddhar promised. "You may all leave, now."

The assembled priests, though mollified slightly, didn't seem very delighted at this assurance. "Couldn't we possibly punish him ourselves?" demanded one vigorous Saivite, mightily disappointed with this turn of events. "Couldn't we shave off his wretched top-knot, rub away those blasphemous *urdhva* signs off his body, dump him in a well and scrub him clean—" he went on with imaginative penalties, carried away by his own eloquence.

"*What was that?*" Azhwarkkadiyaan fairly growled, eyes burning with righteous wrath.

"My very pious priestly gems," began Aniruddha Brahmaraayar, in a honeyed voice. "As you can see, this one's a great deal too arrogant and unruly for the likes of you. Leave him to me, and I shall deal with him summarily." He turned to his personal entourage, seated behind him in the boat, and signed to eight of them. "Make sure that this man is brought to my dwelling."

The soft command worked like magic; eight men leapt out instantly and surrounded Azhwarkkadiyaan in a matter of moments.

The boat moved on; so did Azhwarkkadiyaan, well ensconced within a ring of eight warriors.

The Veera Saiva Battars dispersed as well, the arrogant exploits of the Vaishnavite foremost on their minds and tongues.

11

The Therinja Kaikkola Regiment

Chief Minister Aniruddha Brahmaraayar had chosen to hold court in an old *mandapam* situated in a tiny island off the much larger ones that dotted the Rameswaram coast; here he granted audience in state, surrounded by the paraphernalia that was judged indispensable for the administration of a government. Accountants; clerks; *thirumandhira olai* officials charged with documenting official events; personal entourages; guards and a score of others stood in their places, ready to carry out the *mandhiri*'s every command.

And one of the first—as soon as Aniruddhar disembarked from his boat, entered his court and took his ornate seat—was to ask for those who sought an audience with him.

The first to arrive was a group of five men; all looked affluent, the mantle of prosperity settled firmly about their ample shoulders. In keeping with their status, they presented a necklace set with nine kinds of dazzling precious stones on an embellished plate, which Aniruddhar received with courtesy. "Make an official entry, if you please," he said, as he handed the expensive gift to the waiting clerk. "This precious contribution must be kept aside for Sembian Maadevi's temple renovations."

"Pray, introduce yourselves," invited the Minister, of the men.

"We represent the *Nana Desa Thisaiyaayirathu Ainnutruvar*," said one of them, promptly.

"I am pleased to welcome you, here. How goes your trade in Pandiya Nadu? All well, I presume?"

"It prospers each day, and goes exceedingly well."

"And the people of those lands? What are their sentiments?"

"They say that never have they ever known such a benign rule as that of the Chozhas; not even under their own kings, the Pandiyas. They are especially impressed, *Ayya*, with the valour of Prince Arulmozhi Varmar and his great feats in battle, for you see, all that has transpired in Ilankai has spread far and wide among these people—"

"And what about trade and commerce with the countries of the Southeast? Do your ships ply well, and frequently?"

"Emperor Sundara Chozhar's reign has been most beneficial; we have no cause for complaint and suffered no loss to our businesses. Every one of our ships sent last year returned safe; not one was damaged or lost."

"No danger from pirates on sea, I hope?"

"Not this last year, no; ever since Chozha forces decimated them near the islands of Manakkavaram, our ships have naught to fear in the South Seas."

"Excellent; now, what developments, if any, regarding my *olai*?"

"Your commands have been carried out in their entirety. A thousand sacks of rice; five hundred sacks of corn and a hundred sacks of *thuvaramparuppu* have been assembled here, in Rameswaram; all that needs to be done is for them to be transported to Ilankai."

"Could that not be done in your own vessels?"

"We will, should you so command. We wish, also, to know when the war in Eezham might come to an end."

"Ah, who could divine any such thing? Your *varthaga sabhai* possesses an astrologer, doesn't it? Why not ask him and let me know his conclusions?"

"An astrologer we possess, but as for his pronouncements and conclusions, *Mahamanthri* … why, we hardly dare believe them, ourselves."

"Don't you? But what earth-shattering predictions has he made?"

"That Prince Arulmozhi Varmar will encounter nothing but victory no matter where he goes; that ships bearing the Chozha emblem will scour the high seas with pride during his rule, triumphing in far-flung lands beyond the oceans; that the tiger-flag will flutter gloriously in kingdoms that lie thousands of leagues away …"

"Well, good for you, then, for your affairs will prosper."

"Indeed; he prophesies that our sea-trade and commerce will swell and flourish more than ever."

"Excellent news; and so it shall be, with the divine Sri Ranganathar's grace. You shall have to send food supplies such as this one each month to Ilankai, for as long as the war shall last. Now, you may take your leave."

"As you wish; so we shall."

Once the Great Five Hundred's representatives had shown themselves, out, a guard appeared, and bowed low. "The Senathipathis of the *Therinja Kaikkola* Regiment await your pleasure."

"Allow them in," Chief Minister Aniruddha Brahmaraayar granted permission.

Three men marched in, the very epitome of majesty. Their faces shone with the fervour of battle, and their very mien proclaimed that

Veeralakshmi, Goddess of Courage resided in their hearts. Brave warriors, each one of them, possessing an *anjaanenjam*—hearts that never faltered no matter what the catastrophe.

"The *Sundara Chozha Therinja Kaikkola* Regiment, I presume?" began Aniruddhar.

"Yes, *Ayya*—but to call ourselves thus is embarrassing, to tell the truth."

"How so?"

"Here we are, gorging ourselves on the emperor's food, and yet we've done nothing but sit around without a thing to do for the last six months."

"How many arms does your regiment possess? What are your numbers?"

"Three massive arms; these men accompanying me are the commanders of the Left and Right Arms, while I am in charge of the Middle or the *Naduvirkai* Division. Each of us commands around two thousand soldiers—and all have been doing nothing but dining on fine food and sleeping off the daylight hours. So much that we—well, I think we are in danger of forgetting combat, completely."

"And your petition?"

"Permission to leave for Eezham; we wish to join the army under the command of Prince Arulmozhi Varmar, *Maathanda Nayakar* of the Ilankai forces!"

"Very well. I shall seek the Chakravarthy's approval when I am next in Thanjai, and let you know."

"But, great Brahmaraayar ... what if the war should end by then?"

"Of that, you need entertain no fear; I am sure hostilities will not cease quite so soon on that island."

"Is that so? Are the men of Eezham such accomplished warriors—? Why, send us there and we shall make sure they know and fear the strength of our arms; our valour ...!"

"Ah, well do I know that you will stun them with the strength of not just one, but all three of your Arms—am I not aware of your battle prowess, the superb strategy of your massive forces once they enter the field? The *Naduvirkai* division cleaves through enemy hordes and attacks in the centre, while the *Idangai* and *Valangai* divisions fall upon the left and right flanks of foes, resulting in their consummate decimation—"

"Indeed; thus did we destroy the Pandiya *sainyam* and the Chera hordes."

"In battle proper, yes, fighting according to the rules of honourable combat. Such victories are possible only because your enemy is clearly visible, and willing to meet you face to face. Isn't that the only way you can show them what your Arms—one or three—are capable of?"

"Have the warriors of Ilankai become exponents of the black arts or turned into *asuras*, like Raavanan's demon hordes? Surely they haven't become experts in magic? Do they conceal themselves within the clouds and fight without honour?"

"They have disappeared, yes, like the very *maayaavis*—but no, they do not fight. Their location would be revealed in an instant if they did, wouldn't it? No one can discover where Ilankai's Mahindan or his so-called trusty warriors lie hid; they have managed to do an excellent job of secreting themselves in that island's jungles and mountains. As a result, good men, our forces have seen no combat for at least six months—now, pray tell me: what would be the purpose of sending you all there?"

"We must beg you to do so, *Mahamanthri*; no matter where Mahindan and his precious men hide, within forests, hills or the heavens themselves—we shall find them, drag them out of their petty holes and throw them at the prince's feet. And if we do not—well, we shall change our title to the *Slaves of the Vellalars Regiment*—and that will be a fitting punishment for having failed in our duty!"

"*Pray* do not swear an oath to that effect! Who on this *jambuthveebam* does not know of the *Therinja Kaikkolar's* extraordinary courage and valour in battle? Rest assured that I shall petition the Chakravarthy, and convey his orders as soon as I can. I must ask you to be patient until that time; do your best, great men, towards putting down rebellions in Pandiya Nadu and maintaining peace amongst her harried people—"

"There are no more enemies to be routed there, *Mahamanthri*; the people are greatly relieved that war has ended, at last, and happy to go about their lawful occasions, engaging in agriculture, trade or various other crafts and businesses as it suits them. The Pandiyas have been decimated—"

"Now there, I am afraid, you may have erred; members of the royal family have most certainly *not* been completely routed out. There are still those who lay claim to their throne and equally, those who care deeply about restoring their rights and therefore engage in various nefarious conspiracies ..."

"Aha, those rogues! Where are these plotters and schemers? Let us know, at once!"

"Certainly—when the time is right. As you know, Ilankai still harbours some of the Pandiyas' greatest inheritance: their ancient crown, studded with precious gems, the invaluable necklace gifted by the celestial Indra and the diamond encrusted sword. Somewhere, we suspect, in the wilds of Rohanam, deep within those hills, they lie—and until they are recovered, I fear that Pandiya hostilities may never quite die down."

"All that needs to be done, in other words, is to recover their royal heirlooms; set Prince Arulmozhi Varmar upon the Madurai throne, crown him the king, hand him the scepter and their sacred sword! Ah, that the day should arrive, soon—"

"*I beg your pardon*—what is this that you say?"

"Only the one great desire of all the people of Chozha Nadu, and the army."

"These, great warriors, are matters of state and bound by protocol; they lie beyond our purview and we need not discuss them. I shall share some news with you, however, that is bound to delight you—"

"Our attention is all yours, *Mahamanthri.*"

"Cease labouring under the delusion that war might effectively be over, with Eezham; there will most certainly be others. Once Prince Arulmozhi Varmar resolves the conflict in Ilankai, he has elaborate plans to set off on a massive *digvijayam*, a tour of triumph, in all four directions; a thousand ships shall embark, filled to the brim with soldiers, towards Manakkavaram. Mappappaalam, Mayirudingam, Kadaaram, Ilaamuri Dhesam, Sri Vijayam, Saavagam, Putpagam and many others; he shall engage them in a war—ah, such a war that has not been seen nor heard, in history, and win these lands and their people. The great warrior plans a splendid expedition to the south, towards the Munneerppazhandheevu which number twelve thousand and then, on towards the west, where he will march against Keralam, Kudamalai and Kollam, which shall accept his supremacy; the heads of their kings at his feet. Our prince shall cast his eyes next towards the north, and once he journeys with his huge forces upon the kingdoms of Vengi, Kalingam, Rattapaadi, Sakkarakkottam, Angam, Vangam, Kosalam, Vidheham, Koorjaram, Paanchaalam—ah, there is no doubt that they will embrace defeat and acknowledge his suzerainty as well, and our prince is destined to fly the tiger-flag atop the Imayam, just as his illustrious forefather, Karikal Valavan once did. These, gallant Senathipathis, are just some of the many plans our *Maathanda Nayakar* of the Southern Chozha Forces has charted for the future; there will be no dearth of opportunities for lion-hearted men, or those whose blood thrums in their veins, shrieking for battle; neither will be there be any lack of instances in which to prove their considerable daring. Therefore, you and the members of the *Therinja Kaikkola* Regiment must be patient for just a while—you have a great many wars to look forward to, not to mention rampant bloodshed."

"Long life to Emperor Sundara Chozha Chakravarthy!" chanted the three commanders, their voices piercing the very roof. "May the Gods grant a long and illustrious life to Prince Arulmozhi Varmar! Long live *Mahamanthri* Aniruddhar!" Then, one of them stepped forward. "We have another petition, *Ayya*. You know, doubtless, that we are styled the *Sundara Chozha Therinja Kaikkola* Regiment."

"So I do."

"It is also common knowledge that should the need arise, we are pledged to protect the Emperor with our lives; that is an oath we have sworn with our own hands, awash in the blood of our wretched enemies."

"As you say."

"You must be aware that we are bound to the Emperor and only to him; we neither accept nor approve of another's authority."

"That is as it should be, and certainly no less than what I expect of you."

"Once, we were a part of the Pazhuvettarayar's massive army and, well—we do not wish anyone to question our loyalties on that score."

"Ah, what is this that you say? How does the question of loyalty arise?"

"A great many rumours have drifted to us ... about certain mysterious events in Thanjavur."

"I strongly suggest you let them drift away again; there is no cause for you to repeat, let alone lend credence to them."

"The Velaars of Kodumbalur might, perhaps seize this chance to raise suspicion against us—"

"They will not; no one will believe them should they make such an attempt."

"The human body is not long for this world; a mere transient shell ..."

"Therefore, true warriors have no cause to fear death."

"The Emperor of the Three Worlds himself, some day ..."

"Must ascend to the divine feet of God, yes."

"The Chakravarthy is severely indisposed, we hear ..."

"Witness the comet shining bright, in the night sky."

"If such a calamity should indeed befall us—then our soldiers wish to join the personal regiment of Prince Arulmozhi Varmar, and become known as his *agapparivaaram*."

"You are honour-bound, I might remind you, to serve only the Emperor; that is your sworn duty."

"And yours, *Mahamanthri*, is to take us into your confidence; deliver us the Emperor's commands. Accept this sacred responsibility—else permit us at least, to journey to Thanjai and seek an audience with the Chakravarthy!"

"I am afraid I cannot recommend that course of action; your arrival in Thanjai will lead to a great deal of confusion and unnecessary upheaval. I shall take it upon myself to meet the Emperor and submit your petition; you may rest easy on that score."

"We already do, now that we have entrusted our fates into your hands. Allow us to take your leave."

The commanders of the *Therinja Kaikkola* Regiment departed within moments.

"I wonder what *aakarshana sakthi*, what wonderfully divine power Ponniyin Selvar possesses," murmured Aniruddha Brahmaraayar to himself. "… that turns sane, normal men into such willing slaves within the space of just one meeting?"

In a much louder voice, he issued his next command: "Now, that Vaishnavite ruffian … bring him before me!"

꧁

Kalki's Notes:

Nana Desa Thisaiyaayirathu Ainnutruvar : This group, with a truly impressive name, was a reputed Merchant Guild enjoying trade and commerce with countries overseas, under the Chozha Empire.

Sundara Chozha Therinja Kaikkola Padai : Today (written circa 1950) the *Kaikkola* people might stumble through life as weavers in Thamizh Nadu without even proper facilities—but they were a renowned warrior clan during the heydays of the Chozha Empire. It was the Emperor's prerogative to pick and choose the best among them and form his own elite regiment: the *Agapparivaarap Padai*. These personalized forces were known as the *Therinja Kaikkola Padai* and the usual practice was to add the names of the Emperors they served, to the regiment's name.

12

GURU AND DISCIPLE

We would like, at this juncture, to reveal details of a research connected with Thamizh Nadu's history, to the esteemed readers following this story.

There is a pretty little village, Anbil by name, in the Lalgudi Taluk of Thiruchirappalli Jilla or district; North-Indian experts have translated this name as Premapuri. Approximately forty-five years ago, a Vellalar began to dig up the foundations of his old, crumbling home in an effort to re-build and refurbish it. And then, something happened: he stumbled upon an interesting artifact in the rubble. A collection of copper-plates with words etched into them, bound by a large ring running through holes at one end. The Vellalar kept his find at home for a while, these huge plates that needed more than two men to lift them. It was at this time that Sri R S L Lakshmana Chettiar arrived in the village to renovate the temple; the Vellalar handed the plates to him. Sri Lakshmana Chettiar, who suspected that they might contain valuable historical information, promptly delivered them to Maha Mahopathyaaya Swaminatha Iyer who, in turn, understood their value and surrendered them to Sri T A Gopinatha Rao, MA, a noted epigraphist. The astonishment and amazed delight of Sri Gopinatha Rao on receipt of these plates had to be seen to be believed; he was as delighted as if he had been given an extraordinary cache—for these heavy copper-plates were, indeed, a treasure trove: they contained vital details of the ancient Chozha dynasty.

These *cheppu pattayams* were full of information about the grant of ten *velis* of land by Sundara Chozha Chakravarthy, four years after his ascension to the throne, to his *"Maniya Manthri,"* Anbil Aniruddha Brahmaraayar. Aside from inscribing details of the imperial lineage up to the time of Sundara Chozhar, Madhava Battar, the royal scribe, had also made sure to describe Aniruddha Bramaraayar's no less impeccable Vaishnavite lineage and the great service rendered by his parents, grandfather and even great grandfather, at the renowned temple of Srirangam.

Information on the Chozha dynasty contained in the Anbil copper-plates agreed, in large part, with that found in the Anaimangalam and Thiruvaalangadu copper-plates, thus confirming their historical accuracy; in addition, the Anbil plates offered a few details hitherto unknown, and therefore gained unprecedented importance and fame, in the annals of Thamizh Nadu's historical research.

We desire our readers to continue reading this story, armed with the knowledge that Aniruddha Brahmaraayar was a minister of much renown in the Chozha Empire with *cheppu pattayams* extolling his service and knowledge.

***

Azhwarkkadiyaan entered the *mandapam* where *Maniya Manthri* Aniruddha Brahmaraayar reclined in state; performed a solemn circumambulation around the minister thrice; prostrated before the great man, and rose. *"Om Hreem, Hraam Vashattu!"* His four chants reverberated around the hall. "I must request you to give me leave, Great Teacher," he bowed, finally.

"What *is* all this in aid of, Thirumalai?" An amused smile played upon Aniruddhar's face. "Why this elaborate plea for farewell, pray?"

"There is reason enough, Great One—for this measly servant, this *daasan*, is about to immerse himself in the ocean and divest himself of all aspirations towards being a true follower of the divine Sri Vaishnava traditions, not to mention his name, Azhwarkkadiyaan, servant of the servants who worship Thirumaal, and also—much as I shudder to utter the words—the great good fortune of serving at your feet, for I intend to embrace the Veera Saiva Kalamuga traditions. I shall take up a skull in my hands and wander this earth, chanting the holy *manthram, Om Hreem Hraam Vashattu*! I shall grow my tresses long and bind them into a *jadamagudam*, a very crown of hair, not to mention other accoutrements such as a bushy beard and moustache, and make sure to break the skull of every Vaishnavite I come across …!"

"Stop, *Appane, stop*, in the name of all that is holy—would you subject my skull to the same fate?"

"Does this mean that you are, in actual fact, an adherent of the gloriously sacred Vaishnava traditions, *Guruve*?"

"Why would you even question that fact, Thirumalai? Who did you think I was?"

"Who are you? Now *that*, Great One, is what I cannot quite understand; indeed, I entertain grave doubts about your identity … kindly enlighten me: are you indeed the great grandson of the illustrious Anbil Ananthaazhwar Swamigal who considered it a privilege to spend all his life in divine contemplation and the worship of the illustrious Lord Sri Ranganathar, engaged in penance on an island nestled between two rivers as He guards the cosmos?"

"I am, *Appane*."

"And are you, in fact, the noble grandson of Anbil Aniruddha

Bhattacharyar, who took it upon himself to spread the holy word of Sriman Narayanan in all four directions, that it might resonate around the world?"

"Indeed I am; I was named after that great saint, to tell the truth."

"And you *are* the sainted son of Narayana Bhattacharyar who overwhelmed scores of Vaishnavite devotees by singing the beautiful, chaste Thamizh hymns of Azhwars in a manner that would melt even the hardest of hearts?"

"Yes, my good man, I am!"

"And are you also not the son of the great lady, the very queen of women, *mangaiyarkkarasi* who served the lord by lighting *nundha* lamps in the golden abode of Sri Ranganathar, and soothed the hunger-pangs of His numerous devotees by giving away food on silver platters?"

"I would certainly entertain no doubts on that score."

"Then—then—do my eyes deceive me? What is this sight that meets my vision? Ah, what are these words that fall upon my two ears?"

"Pray explain what you mean by these convoluted exclamations, Thirumalai. What has happened to make you entertain grave suspicions about the performance of your faculties?"

"I heard with my own ears reports to the effect that you entered the precincts of the Sivan temple here, and performed the ritual *archanai* and *abishekam*, in worship."

"Your ears have not deceived you."

"My eyes tell me the truth as well, I suppose, for I see your sacred person liberally adorned with the signs of visit to a Saivite shrine."

"Indeed."

"But are you not my teacher, the great one who taught me that Sriman Narayanan is the God among Gods in this wretched *kaliyugam*; that the sacred hymns of Azhwars are akin to the holy Vedas themselves, and that the only path towards *motcham*, eternal salvation, was to chant the name of Hari and sing His praises with a heart full of joy?"

"So I did. What of it?"

"If you, my esteemed Guru, will not practice what you preach, then what is to be the fate of your lowly disciple?"

"Ah, you refer to my visiting the Sivan temple for a *dharisanam*, worship, don't you?"

"Enlighten me as to which deity you glimpsed there, *Guruve*."

"Who else but the divine Narayanamurthi, pray?"

"But—doesn't the Sivan temple possess the form of a *lingam*? At least, that is what I have heard. Wasn't that why the Veera Saivars surrounded me in such profusion, and mocked me so mercilessly?"

"Misinformed child, is it true that you bear the name of our pious Sadagopa Adiyaarkadiyaan, who chose to be incarnated on earth in the blessed Thirunagari?"

"There can be no doubt on that score."

"I shall ask you to take the trouble of remembering one of the illustrious Nammazhwar's precious gems, then—and if you cannot, I shall do it for you:

"Lingathitta puraanatheerum

Samanarum Saakkiyarum

Valinthu vaadhu seiveergalum matru nun

Dheivamumaagi ninraane ...!"

Thus has Sadagopar spoken; why, then, do you find fault with me for witnessing the divine form of Narayanamurthi, within a *lingam*?"

"Ah, words fail me when I think of his supreme erudition— imagine, he's actually lumping *lingam*-worshipers with the Samanars and Saakkiyars! Now, if that isn't genius, what else is?"

"Really, Thirumalai, I wonder when you'll give up this deplorable inclination for sarcasm. Our Sadagopar has more to say; now, listen:

"Neeraai, Nilanaai, Theeyaai Kaalaai,

Neduvaanaai

Seeraar Sudargal irandaai Sivanai

Ayanaai …"

And this, this supreme force that is everything on earth, from water, to earth, to even Sivan and Ayan himself, is none other than Thirumaal! Now, open your ears and mind, Thirumalai—and listen well:

"Muniye Naanmugane Mukkannappaa!

En pollaak

Kanivaaith thamaraikkann karumaanikkame

En kalva!

Thaniyen aaruyire enthalai misaiyai

Vanthittu …"

You see, Thirumalai? *Mukkannappaa*, the Three-Eyed One! And Sadagopar exhorts Him to bend His divine gaze upon him, and place His feet on his brow—such is his prayer! And here you are, objecting to my visiting a Sivan temple …!"

"I beg your pardon, Gurudeva—please excuse my ignorant ramblings and accept my humblest apologies! Clearly, I haven't made the effort to take Nammazhwar's lessons to heart; I've wasted the choicest years of my life in petty quarrels and strife, not to mention casting aspersions upon your noble self. Pray grant me a boon, Great One."

"Make your petition first, and I shall see about granting it."

"I wish to retire to Thirukurugoor, *Guruve*, where I shall apply myself towards collecting every one of Sadagopar's thousand beautiful hymns. Later, I plan to travel extensively all over the length and breadth of the country and spread his divine message …"

"Why this sudden urge to spend your life in contemplation of the divine?"

"I broke my journey at the Veera Narayana shrine on my return from Vada Vengadam, and sang a few Azhwar *pasurams*; one of those who serve the deity, a certain Easwara Battar listened with tears coursing down his cheeks—"

"A great man, that one; a true servant of the lord."

"His young son stood by as well, and I was amazed to see the glow that suffused his young face as he listened to the divine *pasurams*—ah, like a radiant full moon in the night sky! When I was done, he came up and asked if I knew any more, in a sweet, innocent voice, untainted by the whims of the world … and I found that I could not utter the word *No*, without feeling a twinge of embarrassment. I must admit that the thought of surrendering myself, this dog, to the service of the Almighty occurred even then—and today, that resolve was strengthened …"

"Has not the Geethacharyar, Author of the Bhagavad Geetha, Krishna Bhagavan himself laid down the cardinal rule that one should always practice *swadharma*—one's own sacred duty—as prescribed by their birth and the scriptures?"

"Yes, *Guruve*."

"Great saints will incarnate themselves in this world to gather the hymns of Azhwars and spread their sacred message; much the same way, great men will be born to parse these songs for their wonderful Vedhic messages, translate them into the languages of the North, and take them to people all over Bharatha Kandam. You and I, Thirumalai, have chosen royal service as our *swadharma*; surely you have not forgotten the solemn oaths we swore, pledging ourselves body, mind and soul to Chozha emperors …?"

"I haven't, *Guruve*, but I must admit that I've been reconsidering that decision. It's been eating away at my heart, especially when I chanced to overhear certain things that have been whispered about you—"

"Indeed? Elaborate, if you will."

"They say that you've given up your faith on account of the Chakravarthy's magnificent gift of ten *velis*, not to mention the fact that it's been recorded on copper-plates. And that you've abandoned your religious principles, your caste *dharma*, and traveled aboard a ship ..."

"Ah, the jealous ramblings of a foolish multitude—! You need not regard those, for it is quite clear that they wish our people to remain frogs in a well. I shall neither deny the Chakravarthy's bequest, nor that it has been inscribed in copper-plates, but surely you are aware that I became minister to the Sundara Chozhar, four years prior to these events?"

Azhwarkkadiyaan stayed silent.

"Do you even know when our friendship began, Thirumalai? We studied under the same teacher, learning chaste Thamizh and Vadamozhi. Mathematics, Astrology, Theology, Philosophy ... we studied all these too. At that time, there was no question of him ascending the throne; neither he nor I even considered that possibility. Who would have thought that both Rajadithyar and Kandaradhithar would embrace death and Arinjayar would become king in their place, or that even he would die, so soon after ascension, which would lead to Sundara Chozhar's succession? He had more than an inkling of the enormous obstacles he might face once he came to power, for he made me swear that I would aid him by taking the post of minister; else, he would renounce the throne, for he was quite sure he would never be able to bear the burden of a crown by himself. I swore that I would assist him as best as I could, and I have managed to carry out my duties faithfully until this day. Surely you know all this, Thirumalai?"

"I do, Gurudeva—but no one else does, it seems. Such as those who wander the cities and the whole country, engaged in rumour-mongering—"

"Those who traipse the streets trading ridiculous rumours do not matter; you need not worry about them. I shall admit: I have myself, on occasion, entertained doubts about giving up the Acharya traditions and entering royal service—but not for the past two days. Thirumalai, you do know my real purpose in coming to Rameswaram, don't you? Not to worship in Sivan temples—but travel to Maathottam?"

"I suspected as much, Gurudeva."

"And you were right. Ah, Maathottam has not changed at all since the days Sundaramurthy and Sambandar set sight on it long ago, on the banks of the Paalaavi River, and sang ecstatically of its beauty!"

> *"Vandupannseyyum Maamalarpozhil*
> *Manjai nadamidu Maathottam*
> *Thondar naadorun thuthiseya*
> *Arulsei Kedheechura madhudhaane!"*

Flower gardens overwhelmed with bees that seek the nectar of countless blooms … witness the beauty of Sambandar's verses, Thirumalai! Some of our wonderful scholars here are true examples of stupid frogs in wells; they claim that Sambandar did not really visit Maathottam, but planted his sainted feet in Rameswaram and simply leaned over to look at it. You need not regard those idiotic assumptions—"

"Then—did you visit the city just to experience and delight in its wonderful natural beauty, *Swami?*"

"Not really; I merely brought up the subject as I intend to send *you* there. No, my purpose in journeying to Maathottam was to visit Arulmozhi Varmar …"

"And—did you indeed meet him, Gurudeva?" For the first time in the conversation, the slightest touch of excitement and anticipation coloured Azhwarkkadiyaan's voice.

"Aha, the very mention of the prince excites you, does it, Thirumalai? Even you wish to know about him, don't you? Yes, I did meet him; spoke to him. I managed to learn, in person, the exact truth of the extraordinary reports I had been receiving from Ilankai. Listen, Thirumalai! King Mahindan seems to have been in possession of an impressive army—but now, nothing is left of it; the hordes have vanished like dewdrops in bright sunshine! Mahindan's army contained quite a few soldiers from the Pandiya and Chera countries, but once news reached them that the Chozha forces were being commanded by our prince, they dropped arms, deserted the Ilankai forces and joined our own! How could Mahindan wage war, pray? He fled the battlefield for the hill-country of Rohanam, where he stays hidden. Which is why our men have no one to fight, as of now."

"Why, then—it appears that the *ilango* has no further need of remaining there; why doesn't he come home with his armies? That would put an end to all these endless bureaucratic arguments about sending food for our men, too—"

"That could be done, yes—but Arulmozhi Varmar does not really favour such a plan of action; neither do I, for that matter. The moment he returns, Mahindan will poke his puny head out of the mountains and hostilities will erupt all over again. What would be the point of it all, pray? The rulers and people of Ilankai must clasp hands with us in friendship—or the tiger-flag flutters high in those lands, signaling complete Chozha authority. Our prince is now working towards both ends, to tell the truth. Do you know what our warriors are engaged in at this very moment, in Eezham? The last few battles have almost completely decimated the ancient city of Anuradhapuram; all its wonderful Buddha Viharams, temples, *Thaadhu garbha* towers are practically falling to ruin. At our prince's command, his men are working towards renovating, and setting the city to rights."

"Well, here's a pretty tale, if you will. I wonder if he has decided to abandon the Saivite and Vaishnavite faiths and join the Saakkiya sect? You would encourage it too, no doubt."

"You and I, Thirumalai, do not really matter; neither do our opinions. We are mere subjects and can engage in petty quarrels about the superiority of our faiths until the end of time; a king, however, has a duty towards his people and must ensure that he supports the growth of all the faiths in his land. Fortunately for him, the prince seems to have stumbled onto this truth without the promptings of others and now that he has found the right opportunity, is making excellent use of it. Listen, Thirumalai: I have heard stories of the *chakra* and conch lines, symbols of Thirumaal that mark his hand; doubtless, you have, too. Not that I ever felt the inclination to ask to see them. Those stories might be true for all I know, or they may not. But of one thing I am sure, and I shall declare it now: if there is anyone capable of ruling all this earth, becoming an *ekachakraadhipathi* and exercising his influence single-handedly over this great land—it is Prince Arulmozhi Varmar. Some are born with such greatness, you know. You saw the *Kaikkola* Regiment Commanders and merchant chiefs just now in this very hall, didn't you? I am sure you listened to their speeches as well. Ah, how magnanimous, how fluid they are in their demands, when it comes to the prince? Foregoing the one condition that rules them: money …

I chanced upon an ascetic on the summit of the Podhigai Hills some days ago; omniscient, blessed with the gift of prophesy. Did you know what he said? *There comes a time for the elephant; and there comes one for the cat, too.* And this is the time of the Southern lands, their time to flourish. For millennia, powerful emperors, great saints, lion-hearted warriors and awe-inspiring poets have all emerged from the North—but those lands are due for enormous upheaval; indeed, an eclipse will shut out the warmth of their success for a set of rogues, a swarm of ruffians, a scourge will sweep over the Imayam mountains and wreck havoc on the North; they will reduce temples to dust, and smash our idols into pieces. Our culture and traditions, our *sanadhana dharma* will be in danger of being destroyed—and it is the South that will become the bastion of our values; the one last refuge that will safeguard our Vedhas, temples, and our way of living. Great kings, emperors among emperors will rise and come to power, their splendour spreading in all four directions. Illustrious saints, noble scholars and pious devotees shall be incarnated here—such were the prophecies of the ascetic, and I, for one, have begun to believe in his words, Thirumalai."

"You've been busily engaged in building fantastic castles in the air, *Swami*—but there are powerful forces at work that might wreck the entire foundation of this empire into rubble! Had you seen what I saw, and heard what I heard, Gurudeva, there would be no place for such complacence; you would be quivering in your seat, in fact, rocked by the conspiracies that threaten the Chozha *samrajyam* ...!"

"My mistake; I seem to have forgotten—all this enthusiasm has clouded my intellect, and I haven't even listened to the account of your travels. Tell me all you know—you may be frank; no matter how terrible the news, I shall hear it."

"Here and now, *Swami*? Is that your command? For, the tales I bring— Vayu Bhagavan, lord of the winds would shiver and shake; the king of the oceans would be shocked into stunned silence; birds in the air would freeze mid-flight, curl their wings and fall to the ground; Aakasavaani and Bhooma Devi would shriek in terror," Azhwarkkadiyaan went on. "Do you really wish me to unfold them here?"

"In that case, come with me," commanded Aniruddha Brahmaraayar. "This island possesses a subterranean cavern that will not allow even a wisp of air. Let us go there at once, and you shall tell me all you know."

13

"Ponniyin Selvan"

Another momentous event was happening elsewhere, even as Vandhiyathevan disembarked at Naaga Theevu, setting off towards Maathottam while Azhwarkkadiyaan and Aniruddha Brahmaraayar grew embroiled in the politics of an enormous *samrajyam*: Kundhavai Devi and Vanathi, the Kodumbalur princess, were seated in the *ambari* of an elaborately decorated royal elephant, taking ponderous but majestic steps towards Thanjavur.

Ilaiya Piratti had decided, some time since, that she wouldn't visit the capital. There were several reasons behind her resolve, not the least of which was the fact that Thanjai did not possess regal residences enough for royal visitors. She would have to dwell in the Chakravarthy's principal complex, lumped with other royal ladies, for the rest of the palaces were occupied by the Pazhuvettarayars and various other high-ranking officials. Pazhaiyarai offered a great deal of freedom to women such as herself; she could leave and enter home as and when she pleased. In Thanjai, however, the circumstances would be vastly different: she would have to bow to the Pazhuvettarayars' commands every moment; her movement within the palaces would be visited with constraint. Ilaiya Piratti had never much relished a life that was so full of restrictions; she did not foresee any enjoyment now, either.

There were other reasons as well. The young queen of Pazhuvoor— the empire resounded with tales of her arrogance; Ilaiya Piratti found herself grimacing with dislike at the very mention of her behaviour. The Chakravarthy seemed to wish the ladies of his family at Pazhaiyarai as well; to Kundhavai, it had seemed a good decision to stay where she was. She ignored the promptings of her heart in steadfast fashion, stifling the urge to visit her ailing father and care for him the way only a beloved daughter could.

Meeting Vandhiyathevan, however, had wrought a change; she found herself subjected to a rather severe turmoil. The empire seemed to be crumbling around her, almost in danger of falling to ruin under the vicious attacks of conspirators and devious plots while here she was, paddling in elegant boats on ponds, spending her days in song and dance among flower gardens and beautiful creepers! Her older brother was in Thondai Nadu, while her beloved *thambi* was in Ilankai; she it was, now burdened with the responsibility of wading into royal matters in their absence. After all, hadn't Aditha Karikalan been pressing for reports on affairs in the capital a long time now, through trusted envoys? How could she oblige him if she stayed in Pazhaiyarai?

Vandhiyathevan's tidings had been terrifying, to tell the truth. Until then, the only thing that had displeased Ilaiya Piratti was that the Pazhuvettarayars exercised a control that went above and beyond their authority—but now, they seemed to be casting their eyes on the very throne! And they'd made sure to somehow inveigle Kandaradhithar's poor son, Kundhavai's *chithappa* into their wretched schemes, not to mention many of Chozha Nadu's so-called loyal officials and chieftains. Who knew what might happen next? What mightn't these villains stoop to, seized by greed, and possessed by incredible avarice? Her dear father

Sundara Chozhar's very life might be at stake—there was nothing to ensure his safety in the capital. If the worst did come to worst and neither of the Chakravarthy's sons was by his side, what could be more convenient than to set Madhuranthakan on the Chozha throne? They would stop at nothing to achieve their ends, and even should they be overcome by some scruple, that wicked witch Nandhini would teach them outrageous means to accomplish their devious plots; she would urge them on, should they hesitate. All the more reason why Kundhavai must stay by her father's side, in Thanjai. She could keep an eye on things; see how deep the rot had set in, so to speak. Not to mention ensuring his safety, as well.

After all, why were they so intent on setting frail Madhuranthakan onto the throne? Spurred by altruistic motives, were they? Or consumed by the need to do their best by the empire, to abide by the tenets of fairness and justice? No, not at all! He would simply serve as a figurehead; a convenient puppet whom they could pull apart as they wished, thus allowing them to rule in his stead. And then—then—Nandhini's hands would hold the reins to this vast empire; *she* would wield the highest authority and everyone would have to bow to her. The women of the palace would have to fold their hands in deference in her presence, and—*chee*! What a horrible picture, what a terrible fate! Not on her life would she ever allow such a situation to come to pass—not as long as she had any say in the matter. *Let's see*, she swore. *Let's see just how far that witch will go, what sort of games she will play ...*

Not that she was going to have an easy time of it in Thanjai, she mused, ruefully. Her parents would wonder why she chose to give up a comparatively comfortable life in Pazhaiyarai, and traveled all the way here; she would have to bid sweet farewell to the independence she had been used to. Someone was sure to bring up the subject of her marriage and she would hate it. Nandhini would undoubtedly cross her path a few times; she, Kundhavai, would not be able to bear her arrogance ... but no, this wasn't the time to worry about inconsequential things when the wellbeing of an entire empire was at stake. Her father's life, from what she could understand, was in danger too. Kundhavai's place was in Thanjai at this very moment.

But there was another reason—far, far more compelling than any of the others she'd listed to herself, so far. Vandhiyathevan. Any news of his whereabouts, his fate, would be welcome to her, for reports of the Pazhuvettarayars sending men to Kodikkarai in his pursuit, had reached her.

Would such an enterprising man, so full of clever tricks and ruses up his sleeve, allow himself to be caught? In the face of such an eventuality, surely he'd have to be brought to Thanjavur—in which case her presence in the capital would do much to aid his cause. It would be no easy thing to condemn Aditha Karikalan's envoy; they would have to pin some sort of crime on him; that explained why he had been accused of trying to stab Sambuvaraiyar's son. This was a complete fabrication, no doubt—but there lay the rub; Vandhiyathevan's innocence would have to be proven beyond doubt. She ought to speak to Kandamaran herself; perhaps that would shed some light on the truth ...

While Kundhavai bent her considerable intelligence towards the conspiracies looming over the empire, and found her heart trapped in a quagmire of problems that seemed almost insurmountable—her companion, Vanathi was in quite a different frame of mind. Always guileless and less intrigued by complex issues, her heart, pristine and innocent, dwelt with admirable simplicity on one, and only one question: when would Prince Arulmozhi Varmar return from Ilankai?

"You did say that you'd written an *olai* asking him to return at once, didn't you, *Akka*?" she asked, now. "Where would he arrive, do you think—Pazhaiyarai? Or Thanjavur?"

Her concern was immense, of course, and entirely understandable: what if the prince should come to the former while they themselves had gone to the latter?

Kundhavai, who had well and truly lost herself in puzzling cogitations, turned to her. "What did you say?" she asked, abstracted. "Were you speaking of Ponniyin Selvan?"

"Of course, *Akka*. And I've wanted to ask you—you've referred to him so quite a few times now, but never mentioned why. You've been putting it off for ages! You'll tell me now, won't you? Thanjavur is so far away, and this wretched elephant seems to be moving at the pace of a tortoise!"

"If this wretched elephant, as you so unkindly stigmatize it, went any faster, you and I would be pitched to the ground, *ambari* and all. Let me tell you something, my girl, about what went on in the Thakkolam war, shall I—"

"I'd rather you explained the nickname *Ponniyin Selvan, Akka.*"

"You're not going to let me be, are you? *Kalli*—you little wretch! Very well, I may as well oblige you." And Kundhavai Piratti began her tale.

Sundara Chozha Chakravarthy had been blessed with an idyllic family life, the first few years of his kingship; many were the occasions during which he paddled along the river in a boat, surrounded by his loving family, bending an indulgent gaze at their boisterous laughter and engaging pranks. Their exuberance mingled with the mellifluous music of Paanars and the soothing strains of the *veena*, competing with even the roaring waters of the Kaveri. Someone would pipe up with a joke or a ridiculous mime, and the burst of accompanying laugher drowned out even the tumble and rumble of the river.

The adults would congregate in a corner of the boat sometimes, engaging in amusing banter while the youngsters gathered in another, romping in play. There were moments when these classifications were completely forgotten and everyone would mingle with joy and lose themselves in amusing occupations.

It was during one of these exciting excursions when the Chakravarthy, his queens and the children were gliding along the river in an elegant royal craft, that a voice rose in sudden panic. "Where's the child? Where's Arulmozhi?" It belonged to Kundhavai. Arulmozhi was not more than five years old at that time; Kundhavai, seven. Sundara Chozhar's youngest was the darling of every member of the royal family but there was none, perhaps, who showered him with affection more than his sister—and she was the first to notice that the little boy was no longer on the boat. She gave the alarm at once; the family was almost paralyzed with horror. The royal entourage nearly turned the vessel upside down in search of Arulmozhi — but there was only so much space on a boat, after all, and no little boy to be found. Kundhavai and Adhithan shrieked with terror; the queens wrung their hands, worried beyond measure, while the royal ladies and companions babbled their confusion and concern. Some of the boatmen dove promptly into the river; Sundara Chozhar did so, himself. There seemed little point to these measures, however, for who knew where the child was now? The current was fast and furious; the waters could have carried the frail body anywhere. For that matter—who even knew *when* Arulmozhi had fallen overboard? Men thrashed through the waters aimlessly, with no hope or direction; but there was nothing. By now, the situation aboard the boat had worsened; several queens and their companions swooned, but there was no one to spare them a glance. Those who did retain their consciousness raised their voices in mournful lament; "*Ayyo! Ayyo!*" Their grief-filled cries overpowered even the tumultuous waters of the Kaveri; birds on the trees that lined the banks fell silent, overwhelmed by their heartache.

And then—a miraculous sight met their eyes.

At a little distance from the boat, right in the middle of the river, rose a figure: that of a woman, holding aloft a child in both hands. The lower half of her body was submerged under water; her golden, radiant face, bosom and raised arms were all that were visible, and a good deal of those was concealed by the child she held. Sundara Chozhar, who had caught sight of her just like everyone else, practically cleaved through the water, reached her, and took his son. The boat had almost moved abreast him by this time, and those within gladly received the boy; they assisted the over-wrought father aboard, as well. The moment the emperor reached safety, however, he lost consciousness; the royal entourage swung into overdrive, trying to revive him, and caring for the rescued prince. But what of the fate of the woman, his rescuer? No one knew. What had she looked like? Could anyone describe her? This too, drew a blank; no one had registered her features. Nor did she accost the royal family, claiming to be the prince's saviour. In the end, a consensus was reached: it was Mother Kaveri herself who had taken human form and saved Arulmozhi Varmar; a special *poojai* would be performed in her honour each year, on this day.

And Arulmozhi, beloved of the royals until this time, now became the beloved of River Ponni as well: *Ponniyin Selvan*, her cherished son. Those of the family who knew this incident, began to refer to him as such.

14

FULL MOONS TWO

The city of Thanjai was well nigh bursting at the seams with exhilaration. And why not? Wasn't their beloved princess, who hadn't visited the capital in ever so long, arriving that very day, having experienced a change of heart? And wouldn't every Chozha citizen worth the title rejoice over it? For, there was no one in the empire who hadn't heard of the princess's manifold charms; her exquisite beauty, intelligence, compassion and numerous sterling qualities; not a day went by when someone or the other didn't bring up her name on account of some occasion or the other. Almost all of Thanjai had been in uproar for a while over rumours that Kundhavai Devi might visit the city during the auspicious Navarathri festivities and stay at the royal palace; confirmation that she would arrive today had raised their expectations to fever-pitch, and a not inconsiderable crowd had gathered at the city gates. And just as an ecstatic ocean raises foamy waves to welcome the full moon, so did the sea of people in Thanjai raise a resounding, overwhelming roar, in hourly expectation of their honoured guest.

And much to their delight, their very own lustrous orb, a radiant *poorna chandran* did rise—in fact, the good citizens of the capital were treated to the rare sight of two exquisite countenances, blessed with the beauty of a pearly moon, at the very same moment.

The city gates were flung open with a crash as Kundhavai Devi and her entourage neared the fort; a magnificent royal retinue poured out in full force to welcome the long-awaited princess, of which the Pazhuvettarayar brothers formed the advance guard—and not just them either, for a pearl-encrusted palanquin inlaid with ivory-work, followed them. The screens shrouding the occupant rustled and moved apart—to reveal the *sundhara madhivadhanam*, the charming countenance of the Pazhuvoor Ilaiya Rani, Nandhini Devi.

Kundhavai descended from her royal elephant; Nandhini did the same, from her palanquin. The latter seized her chance at once, walking swiftly to the forefront and paying her respects to Kundhavai; the princess smiled slightly, accepting the compliment that was her due.

Chozha citizens, who now had the heaven-sent opportunity to drink in the famed beauty of these exquisitely lovely women at the same time, nearly lost their heads with enthusiasm; their delight overflowed the banks of self-imposed propriety. Such was the combined effect the two women had, on the general populace.

Nature had certainly done her best to endow them richly: Nandhini's skin glowed with a golden radiance; Kundhavai was the proud possessor of a delicate rose-leaf complexion. The Pazhuvoor queen's face rivaled that of a full moon, almost perfectly round, while the princess's divine countenance was slightly oval, the work of a highly talented celestial sculptor. Nandhini's large, dark eyes, laced with the faintest rose-red lines, the beautiful *sevvari*, fluttered like those of an effervescent honeybee; Kundhavai's limpid, blue-black orbs reached almost to her ears, and were as exquisitely shaped as *neelothpalam* flowers. The young queen's pert nose was just a smidge flat, fashioned as though of ivory itself; the Chozha princess possessed a sculpted nose full of character, rather like a beautiful *panneer* bud. Full and soft were Nandhini's lips, red, red, as though the bearers of sweet nectar while Kundhavai's own were just a shade thinner, rather like the honey-bedewed, delicate petals of a pomegranate blossom, a *maadhulai mottu*. The former wore her lustrous hair in an elaborate bun, decorated to resemble a magnificent flower-bouquet; the latter had chosen a much more regal style, her luxurious tresses worn high on her head, made to resemble a crown—for was she not the Queen of Beauty, indeed?

It could not be said that everyone assembled at this momentous occasion was capable of isolating and appreciating each aspect of these two women, their considerable beauty or their various embellishments—but it did not require any extraordinary degree of intelligence to understand that though their style and attire may be markedly different, Rani and Piratti were both exquisite in their own way, and were certainly without equal in loveliness.

It must be acknowledged that hitherto, Nandhini had rather fallen short, in the eyes of the citizens of Thanjai: they had fostered a vague loathing and dissatisfaction for the young Pazhuvoor queen and all her works. Kundhavai Piratti, on the other hand, commanded their allegiance, almost akin to a deity. It pleased them beyond all bounds, therefore, that the Ilaiya Rani had put herself to the trouble of arriving at the city gates and welcoming Ilaiya Piratti in person.

The vastly uncritical general public may have been lost in appreciation of the royal ladies; the objects of their appreciation, however, were engaged in a charged conversation that resembled shards of jagged lightning smashing into each other:

"Welcome, Devi, welcome!" Nandhini opened her gambit in honeyed tones. "Ah, we were lost in grief—perhaps Ilaiya Piratti had abandoned all thoughts of us!—but today, it's clear that your grace and compassion are without equal."

"But how can that be, my dear Rani?" Kundhavai's tone matched the young queen's, perfectly. "Distance does not equate a bad memory, does it? For that matter, you haven't visited Pazhaiyarai either, but can your error be misconstrued as forgetfulness?"

"Bees are drawn to honeyed flowers, after all; they merely obey their instinct. Beautiful Pazhaiyarai may command all the visitors she chooses—but Thanjai is a different matter altogether, for who will volunteer to visit an ugly city?"

"But what's this that you say? To call Thanjaipuri, ugly … pray—how can that be?" wondered Ilaiya Piratti, with well-simulated surprise. "When it's common knowledge too, that the very epitome of beauty lies imprisoned within these walls—"

"Some such rumour did fall on my ears as well—that the Chakravarthy has been incarcerated within this fort. The time for all such worry has ended, however: aren't you, his daughter, here, to rescue him from a terrible fate?" Lightning flashed and sparked for a moment, in Nandhini's gleaming eyes.

"Here's a pretty tale! No power on earth can even dare think of locking up the Chakravarthy—not even Indra, lord of the Devas!" retorted Kundhavai. "That wasn't what I meant; I was referring, in fact, to Nandhini Devi, the very image of exquisite beauty—"

"Well may you say so, Devi—and I must ask you to repeat your kind remark in *his* hearing, for the Lord of Pazhuvoor treats me little better than a prisoner. Now, if you would only intercede on my behalf and—"

"But what good would *my* recommendations do, pray? The prison that binds you is no ordinary one but that of love, isn't it? Especially, when—"

"Indeed, when it's a man getting on in years, there's no escape at all, is there? I've heard of terrible dungeons here; even those locked into those cells might have a hope of freedom, but in my case—"

"—there's no hope of escaping *those* bars, I'm sorry to say—considering that you've chosen these handcuffs and walked into your own prison, incarcerated of your own free will—but then, virtuous women who claim Seetha, Nalayini and Savithri as their idols, won't even try to bid for freedom—why, what's the commotion over there?" Kundhavai peered into the distance.

Truth be told, an intense uproar seemed to have erupted amongst a group of women standing a little away from the fortress gates. Kundhavai and Nandhini approached them but not even proximity helped to understand the reason for their shrill shouts, as everyone chose to scream at the tops of their voices all at once. A few moments passed before any sense could be made of their outcry and finally, their grievance, nay, request, was clear: having gleaned information that Ilaiya Piratti would be present for the Navarathri celebrations, they wished to pay their respects at the palace often and thus, wished to have the various restrictions and rules that bound entry into the fort, relaxed, for this period.

"Pray, speak to your husband or your brother-in-law and kindly make arrangements for granting their request, Rani; surely there's no reason to fear these defenseless women? The Chozha *samrajyam* isn't likely to come to any harm at their hands," said Kundhavai. "After all, haven't the Pazhuvoor brothers extended their considerable authority in all four directions, right to the seashore?"

"But why stop with the seashore, Princess?" Nandhini's tones were dulcet. "Their power and authority extend a far greater distance—why, even beyond the seas. You are certain to receive confirmation of this fact very soon, you know." Her knowing smile almost cleaved Kundhavai's heart in two. Her mind spun furiously, trying to divine the meaning those malicious words. *What—what could the witch possibly mean?*

By this time, Nandhini had made a sign to Periya Pazhuvettarayar, conveying the petition submitted by the gathered women and Ilaiya Piratti's own wishes.

"Who may gainsay the princess's slightest fancy?" was all that Periya Pazhuvettarayar would vouchsafe.

This being the signal for the end of their impromptu meeting, the whole convoy made its way into the fort, accompanied by the lusty cheers of the surrounding crowds.

For the next few days, Thanjai and outlying areas were seized by a frisson of endless excitement and delight; Kundhavai Devi's visit happened to coincide perfectly with the Festival of Nine Nights and Periya Pazhuvettarayar kept his word: people thronged into the city and exited all hours of the day and night as and when they wished. The fortress gates were thrown wide open; various festivities, song, dance and theatrical performances were in full swing, both within the palace and without, all of which commanded an eager public in large numbers.

Two radiant full moons often rose to grace these occasions and the gatherings leapt up in turn, akin to the proverbial oceans roaring enthusiastic approval.

The world outside might be the very epitome of festive cheer—but deep within the hearts of those very same moon Goddesses ... ah, that was a different matter altogether. There, it was all sound and fury as volcanoes erupted, spewing fire and molten lava, destroying every bit of happiness. The Pazhuvoor Ilaiya Rani and Pazhaiyarai Ilaiya Piratti were engaged in constant warfare; their weapons were sharp, prickly words coated with the poison of hatred, and looks calculated to pierce even the hardiest armour; in such manner did those exquisitely beautiful women clash endlessly in battle. Sparks flew as sharp swords clashed during these hostilities; spears, carefully honed to dangerous edges crashed furiously into each other like raging firestorms. Two shards of jagged lightning cut across each other in the dark night sky, quivering in the aftermath of their blows; two ferocious tigresses flew at each other, grappling with their bodies and trying to gouge out each others' eyes; two dangerously beautiful cobras twined around each other, spreading their hoods, flicking their thin, red forked tongues in a desperate bid to tear into the other.

There seemed no end to this curious battle; both won and lost at different times, experiencing the giddy rapture of a hard-won victory or the sharp, excruciating sting of defeat.

One simple soul, however, saw no cause to participate in the outside world's festivities, nor try to understand the war raging between these two *chandramathis*, two fiercely independent personalities. Vanathi, the Kodumbalur princess, barely found time to speak even a few words with Ilaiya Piratti, these days. She tagged along with her "elder sister" wherever the latter went, it was true, but her attention never lingered on what was happening right under her nose. Instead, she created a magnificent imaginary world for herself, and reveled in it, night and day.

15

A Lament in the Night

Song and art flourished during those centuries in Chozha Nadu; dance and drama were not to be left out either and prospered in their turn. Naturally, so did artists, who were nurtured and patronized with much generosity by Thanjai. A staunch devotee of Sivan who lived in those times, Karuvur Thevar by name, has this to say when he sings the praises of *inji soozh* Thanjai, or Thanjai, surrounded by towering walls:

Minnedum puruvaththu ila mayilanaiyaar
Vilangal seya naadagasaalai
Innadam payilum inji soozh Thanjai

True to his words, theatre had grown and prospered in the Chozha capital as evidenced by the presence of a great many halls; the best among them was ensconced in the most prestigious location of all: the Chakravarthy's own palace.

Thanjai played gracious host to talented dramatists who excelled at visualizing, and writing and executing many wondrous new plays. Thus far, their predecessors had always veered towards mythological fables. For some time, however, the capital's imaginative storytellers had been expending their efforts towards another subject: valorous tales of glorious warriors, as well as those who had accomplished courageous deeds a little before their time. And which dynasty better than the Chozhas, for the sheer number of heroes it had produced over generations? Thus Karikala Chozhar, Vijayalayar, Paranthaka Thevar and many other illustrious kings formed the subject of their creative genius, their exploits evolving into dramatic and thereby, spirited performances.

The Navarathri festivities included three uproarious days of plays celebrating the valour of noble Chozha kings, staged within the royal palace; enthusiastic citizens gathered by the thousands in the moonlit terrace opposite the artfully decorated stage, and enjoyed the performances immensely. A separate space, set apart by its beautiful pearl-encrusted pillars and blue silk *vidhanam* or awning, was meant for the royal ladies; queens, princesses and their personal companions watched the proceedings, sure of privacy within the guarded enclosure. And during all such performances, Nandhini made sure to seat herself as close as possible to Kundhavai Devi. Not many appreciated this behaviour, but there was nothing they could do except grumble amongst themselves about her incredible conceit—for who could afford to alienate powerful Pazhuvettarayar and his lovely wife? When Ilaiya Piratti herself made sure to suffer that arrogant one's advances and welcome her company, what recourse was left to other, lesser women?

Of the three plays staged on Chozha rulers, the last, based on Paranthaka Thevar, was easily the most popular. And it was on that day, during that play, that a seachange, a rustle of emotions, made itself visible amongst the watching audience and thereafter, grew at a furious pace.

Thus far, it had been Sundara Chozhar's grandfather, Kopparakesari Paranthakar who had been revered most amongst those who had had the felicity of ruling the Chozha kingdom. His long, forty-six year reign had seen the borders of his dominions expand beyond comprehension; his rule extended from Eezham to the fertile banks of the Tungabhadra. A great many wars were waged and victory was always his; Paranthakar earned the grand title, *The Kopparakesari Who Conquered Madurai and Eezham*, to his satisfaction. His deeds were not confined to war alone; he gifted the hoary Chidambaram temple with a golden roof and garnered enormous praise. His last days, however, were not quite in the same vein as his golden years; consecutive defeats on the battle front meant that Chozha borders shrank again.

Not all those setbacks could dim his glory, though. Kannara Devan's vast army crashed down from the Rettai Mandalam or Rashtrakuta kingdom in the north like a massive ocean wave; a colossal, decisive battle was fought in Thakkolam. The Chozha forces were commanded by Paranthakar's firstborn, a warrior the likes of which *Bharatha Kandam* had never seen: Rajadithyar. Under his capable generalship, Kannara Devan's huge hordes were forced into retreat—but not before Rajadithyar sacrificed himself, embracing death upon his elephant. His devoted men carried home his arrow-ridden body in state; they laid it in the palace, where Emperor Paranthakar and his queens lost themselves in sorrow, shedding tears over the brave son who had laid down his life for his land and ascended to a warrior's heaven. Just then, a voice boomed out from behind the curtains: "Grieve not; grieve not, for Prince Rajadithyar is not lost forever; he lives on in the heart of each Chozha citizen!" And with that comforting pronouncement, the performance came to a close.

The audience, captivated by the brave feats of the previous generation, enjoyed every moment of the play with joyous exclamations and crows of delight. But the chief cause of the murmurs that swept through the crowds at various intervals was this: two men had assisted Paranthaka Chakravarthy immensely, during the course of his momentous battles and wars: the Kodumbalur king, and the lord of Pazhuvoor. Both boasted intimate, familial connections with the royals; women from each family had married into the Chozha dynasty, and all their resources and men often went to the aid of Paranthakar. Such was the intimacy of their bond that most were hard put to decide which was the right hand, and which the left. As for Emperor Paranthakar himself, the ruler made sure that he treated both kings equally, for who could distinguish between two eyes, and designate one better than the other? The present-day Pazhuvoor lords' *periya thanthai*, or their father's elder brother had been Paranthakar's contemporary; Pazhuvettarayar Kandan Amudhanaar had been his name. His Kodumbalur counterpart was Vanathi's grandfather and the father of Kodumbalur Siriya Velaar, the man who gave his life in Chozha service in Eezham.

The dramatists responsible for the play and the artists themselves had taken great care not to praise or defame either of the two kings, or to show overt favour to one or the other; they had rehearsed constantly with this creditable aim, ensuring that the fame and valour of both were exhibited well. In particular did they draw attention to the fact that Emperor Paranthakar had never treated one above the other, but had dispensed his favours with no bias.

And yet, judging by the reactions of the watching public—it was obvious that such an impartial outlook was very far from their minds. Some of them, it seemed, were supporters of one faction, while others favoured another. A section of the audience erupted in cheers when the play depicted the Kodumbalur commander perform a feat of valour; another roared with approval when a Pazhuvoor soldier stepped onto the stage. What began as a rather subdued affair with muted applause soon blazed into a roaring inferno. Ecstatic cries of "*Naavalo Naaval!*" exploded from the gathering, shattering the air in all four directions.

Whatever the feelings of other members of the royal party, the cheers and applause pleased Kundhavai Piratti greatly, and she felt no qualms revealing her approval. "Look, Vanathi, my girl," she would exclaim, whenever the Kodumbalur clan gained prominence. "Your people are coming to the fore!" Her innocent companion, always ready to be pleased, would look appropriately delighted, and express her exhilaration. "Wonderful, Rani!" Kundhavai would exult to Nandhini when the Pazhuvoor men exerted themselves to prove their valour. "Now *yours* are the stronger!"

It seemed, though, that the Ilaiya Rani was not quite as pleased as the Kodumbalur princess at these comments, if her expression was anything to go by. To have this clannish rivalry bandied about in public to the enjoyment of idiotic commoners who yelled and screamed, not to mention encouraged by Ilaiya Piratti, was not exactly to Nandhini's taste. And then, to have herself, Nandhini, ranged alongside that cowering, drooping *girl*, Vanathi—the subject of Kundhavai's mocking comments! Many were the moments when she wondered if she should rise and walk away—but to do so would be to make a mountain out of a molehill; to admit defeat. And that would never do. And so, the young queen of Pazhuvoor bit her pretty lips, and stayed in her place.

Not that Kundhavai herself hadn't noticed this by-play. One look at Nandhini's beautiful face, and she could read every single expression perfectly. So far, she had understood every one of the Ilaiya Rani's thoughts, except for one—and it puzzled Ilaiya Piratti exceedingly.

The instances in the play when the Pandiya King faced a crushing defeat; fell at the feet of the Ilankai king, begging for asylum; abandoned his crown and famed necklace of precious gems in Eezham once it was obvious that no help would be forthcoming; made an ignominious escape to the Chera country—every one of these scenes drew wholesale approval from the audience members ... but Nandhini? Her face reflected unbearable pain. Kundhavai puzzled over this surprising reaction, speculating about the reason behind it. Wondering if conversation would serve, perhaps, to shed some light on this conundrum, she opened a promising gambit. "What a pity that the Chakravarthy could not share in this delightful experience and watch this wonderful play with us! After all, hasn't he accomplished everything that his illustrious grandfather did, in his time as well? Ah, if only *Appa* were to recover ... "

"And why wouldn't he, now that his beloved daughter's here to take care of him?" Nandhini's voice stopped short of being a retort. "Once the herbs from Ilankai have arrived, his recovery should be nothing short of miraculous."

"What's this about herbs from Ilankai?" enquired Kundhavai.

"*How* like you to ask such a question! You wouldn't know anything, I presume? Hasn't the Pazhaiyarai physician sent a man to gather medicinal herbs from that island? Weren't *you* the one to send another, to assist him?" And Nandhini turned her large eyes upon Kundhavai, directing a limpid gaze at the princess. "Are all those reports a lie?"

Kundhavai bit her lips. Pearly white and dainty indeed were her teeth, like an orderly row of jasmine buds—but teeth are teeth, after all, and her lips protested the painful treatment. Fortunately, a loud cry of "*Naavalo Naaval!*" rose from the public at the moment, deluging the question, and saved her the trouble of answering it.

***

With a last, heartfelt pronouncement that Sundara Chozhar's health, handsome countenance, life and rule may last long, the play came to an end; the audience, pleasantly exhausted after an uproarious evening, practically sang and danced back to their respective homes. The consorts of various lesser kings left as well, followed by their dutiful entourages. Later, Empress Vaanamaadevi left for the shrine of Durgaiyamman, the Chozha dynasty's much revered guardian deity, in company of her royal companions.

Malayaman's daughter held many fasts and performed a great many rituals in a spiritual bid to aid Sundara Chozhar's recovery; one of these involved frequent pilgrimages to the Durgaiyamman shrine. The nine nights of Navarathri were an especially auspicious time and the Goddess's temple was inundated with rites meant to augment the occasion. Sacrifices were offered for the Chakravarthy's good health. The Queen visited the shrine each night faithfully, and returned only after the *ardha jaama poojai*, or midnight worship came to an end; many elderly royal ladies accompanied her.

It was not the custom to encourage young women to enter the Goddess's precincts; the temple priests frequently fell under the spell of the divine and drove themselves into nightmare-inducing frenzied dances, often recounting old legends that told of ancient curses. Maidens were unused to such things, and were usually not allowed to witness such happenings.

Kundhavai Piratti, however, was a different matter altogether: who in their right minds would ever dare to warn her about the "dangers of seeing horrible sights," and forbid her from going anywhere she pleased? The princess accompanied the royal mothers to the Durgai shrine each night, and paid her respects at Devi's feet—and Vanathi, her devoted companion, was often left to her own devices during these times, alone in the palace.

The Kodumbalur princess was brimming with happiness, the night of the play on Paranthaka Thevar; her ancestors' great and valorous deeds, enacted so well on the stage, had filled her with pride—and on its heels had followed thoughts of Eezham, of course. Memories of her father who had lost his life there rose without pause and so did those of the prince, now on that very island, straining every nerve for revenge. Sleep simply would not come; she could not even close her eyes. Perhaps her revved up mind might get some rest if she could discuss the play with Ilaiya Piratti, once that damsel returned from the temple—but certainly not before then.

Well—why not stroll along the palace's upper balconies, instead of twisting and turning in vain upon her bed? The whole of beautiful Thanjai would be spread out, a magical vista, underneath the edifice from that height—she might even be able to spot the Durgai shrine if she looked hard enough.

She rose with alacrity at the thought. Vanathi might be very new to this palace, but surely it wouldn't be that difficult to get to the upper balconies and terraces? There were any number of corridors after all, supported by pillars and enough *thoonga vilakku* lamps to light the heavens, weren't there?

She began her journey. The paths seemed to meander endlessly; many of the lamps that had burnt so brightly in the early evening had blown themselves out; a few were flickering, casting a smoky halo around their niches. Maids and other women in royal service sat or leant against pillars in nooks and crannies, deep in sleep; Vanathi hadn't the heart to disturb them and went on, valiantly trying to find her own way. On and on and on … how much more would she have to walk? Would these corridors never end?

Abruptly, a voice reached her. Feeble, low, and filled with grief. Vanathi's skin prickled with goose-pimples; her body shivered. Her feet stopped, paralyzed.

There—there it was again!

"Is there no one to help me?"

Ah—wasn't that that Chakravarthy's voice? Good heavens, what had happened? What danger threatened him? Was it his illness, perhaps—or, something else? But oh, the queen and most of the royal mothers had left for the temple! Still, there must be someone by his side—surely they wouldn't leave him entirely by himself? All the same, it wouldn't hurt to go and see …

Vanathi forced her considerably wobbly legs a few steps forward. The voice seemed to float from somewhere below and the path ended there, as well. She peered down.

A vast, spacious *mandapam* spread out beneath her interested gaze. Ah, wasn't this the Chakravarthy's sleeping chamber? Yes indeed, for there was the Emperor himself, lying upon his bed. All alone too. And he was mumbling something in an endless stream. *Let me listen to his words …*

"Adi paavi—you wretched, wretched creature! Yes, it is true—I did kill you! I didn't mean to, but I was the cause of your death. What do you wish of me? It has been twenty-five years—and you haunt me still! Will *you* never rest in peace—won't you let *me* rest just a little? What do you wish me to do? What price must I pay—how may I redeem myself? Whatever it is, I shall do it—let me alone! Leave me in peace—*ayyo*, is there no one to save me from this creature? Everyone seeks to remedy my physical illness; is there no one to ease my mind? Go, go away at once—

no, wait—stay—tell me what I must do! Do anything—except stand in silence and torment me. Open your blasted mouth and *say something!*"

The words fell on Vanathi's horrified ears like drops of melted iron. She quivered like a leaf in the wind, from the top of her head to the soles of her feet. She bent, almost despite herself, peering into all corners of the chamber as much as she could.

Someone stood within—just a little further from the Chakravarthy. It seemed to be a woman. Only half of her body was readily visible; the rest was shrouded in the darkness thrown by the pillar's shadows, and smoking *akhil* incense. As far as she could see, though, that woman … ah, didn't she look like the young queen of Pazhuvoor? Was this some sort of a dream? Or had she, Vanathi, suddenly and inexplicably lost her mind? Had she become a victim of *sithabramai*? No, this was no dream—it was all real! There—who was that, hidden behind that pillar? Wasn't that Periya Pazhuvettarayar? Yes, it *was* them, no doubt—but why was the Chakravarthy shrieking such strange words at the very sight of the Pazhuvoor Ilaiya Rani? *I did kill you!*—what on earth did *that* mean?

Suddenly, Vanathi felt a familiar faintness creeping up on her. Her head began to spin—no, the whole palace spun—*chee*! She mustn't fall here—she *mustn't*!

Gritting her teeth, she moved away with dragging footsteps, trying to find her way back—but the corridors seemed to wind forever; her sleeping chamber, it seemed to her exhausted mind, would never come. No, she couldn't walk anymore; she couldn't even stand.

When Kundhavai Piratti returned from the temple later that night, it was to the sight of Vanathi in the corridor, close to her chambers—crumpled in a heap, unconscious.

16

Sundara Chozhar's Delusions

Chakravarthy Sundara Chozhar bade his beloved daughter visit him early the next morning, and commanded his attendants, maids and physician stay away, at a respectable distance. He gazed at Kundhavai as she sat by his side, and caressed her back with a good deal of affection. Ilaiya Piratti's intuition told her at once that her father wished to say something, but couldn't quite gather the courage to do so.

"*Appa*," she began, in a low voice. "You're not angry with me, are you?"

Tears gathered in his eyes. "Why would I be upset with *you*, *Amma*?"

"For having disobeyed your orders and come to Thanjai."

"Yes, well, you shouldn't have. This palace is not quite fit to be the residence of delicately nurtured young ladies. You would have realized that by what happened last night, I think."

"What do you refer to, *Appa*?"

"The girl—the one from Kodumbalur, who swooned—that incident is the one I meant. How is she now?"

"She's fine now, *Appa*. This is something of a habit with her; she used to suffer these fainting fits in Pazhaiyarai too, and always recovered within moments."

"But did you speak to her, my dear? Did she—I suppose she did not mention anything she might have seen or heard in this palace, last night?"

Kundhavai hesitated for a few moments. "Well, yes, she did say something of the sort," she admitted, finally. "She attempted to go up to the upper balconies while we were at the Durgai temple, and heard someone lamenting in a sorrowful voice—and that terrified her."

"I knew it would be so. Do you see it all now, dear child? This palace is haunted—haunted, I tell you. You must not stay here—leave at once!" And Sundara Chozhar's frail body trembled, his bloodshot eyes staring somewhere into the distance.

Kundhavai was quick to note these signs. "But why must *you* stay here, *Appa*? Why must *Amma*? Let's all move to Pazhaiyarai, shall we? I must say, I can't see that this city has done your health any good, thus far."

"Health, my dear?" A cheerless smile bloomed on the Chakravarthy's face. "There is no chance of my recovering at all—and I cherish no hopes about such an eventuality."

"But ... surely such hopelessness is unnecessary? The physician at Pazhaiyarai is certain that he can cure you, *Appa*."

"And you have taken him at his word, sending men to Ilankai to hunt for rare herbs! Some snatches of such news did fall on my ears. I am assured, my daughter, of your boundless affection for me."

"Is that a mistake—for a daughter to care for her father?"

"Not at all, my dear. My heart brims with delight at the good fortune of having borne such an affectionate child. You did not err, either, in sending men for herbs. But the truth is — nothing from Ilankai or the Saavakam islands or even Devalokham, the abode of the Devas themselves, will cure this failing body in this birth!"

"*Ayyayo,*" cried the princess. "Pray don't say such things!"

"You came here, *Amma*, despite all my warnings—and for that, I admit that I am pleased, now. Someday, I had hoped to reveal the secret that corroded my soul and today, I believe I shall have the chance. Listen, my dear: the diseases of the physical body may be cured with herbs and medicines, but how do you remedy the ills of the heart?"

"The Illustrious King who Rules the Three Worlds—what malady could possibly affect *your* heart, Father?"

"Ah, you too use pretty words that spring from the flowery imagination of court-poets! My dear child, I rule not over three worlds; I do not even rule over *one*. My kingdom consists of a small land in a corner of this earth, and I cannot even bear the weight of such a miniscule responsibility, to tell the truth—"

"Pray, why must you, *Appa*? Aren't there those willing and able, I may say, even worthy of sharing your responsibilities? You have two excellent, strapping sons—both of whom are lions on the battlefield; warriors to best all warriors, capable of bearing the greatest burdens—"

"And that, my dear, is what sets my heart racing with terror! Your brothers are the bravest of the brave, it is true, and I showered them with affection, just as I did upon you. But now—I cherish the gravest doubts: I wonder if I would be fulfilling my duty as a father if I were to give them this kingdom. Would you not condemn me, were I to bequeath to them not just a country but a curse as well?"

"What sort of a curse could possibly plague these lands, *Appa*? We count among our ancestors Sibi, who cut out his own flesh for a dove and Manu Needhi Chozhar, who sacrificed his own son for the sake of a cow that lost it calf. Karikal Valavar and Perunar Killi have ruled over these very dominions, while the courageous Vijayalaya Chozhar sat on this very throne, wearing ninety-six war wounds as proud badges of honour. Aditha Chozhar, who had the felicity of raising a hundred and eight glorious temples on the banks of the Kaveri and Paranthakar, who covered the roof of Thillai Chitrambalam with glittering gold, expanded this kingdom; the illustrious Kandaradhithar, who saw the Lord as the embodiment of love, combined piety and grace to rule over this land, a glorious *dharma maharajyam*. To say that this land is cursed—what sort of shadow could possibly fall over it? No, *Appa*, these thoughts are likely the result of some sort of delusion; I must beg you to leave this fort and—"

"You have no idea, my daughter, about what might happen if I do! Do you really believe that I would detest beautiful Pazhaiyarai, and incarcerate myself willingly within Thanjai? My presence, Kundhavai, is the only factor that prevents this ancient kingdom from splintering into pieces. Remember what happened at the theatre last night, my dear—for I was watching everything as well, from the forefront of the moonlit terrace. And I must confess: I even wondered, for a moment, if I must stop the play midway—"

"Pray, why, *Appa*? It was excellent, I thought, and I could hardly contain myself for pride at my ancestors' glorious achievements. Which part wounded your sensibilities?"

"None of it, my dear; I could see no fault in the performance. I was concerned, rather, about the conduct of the audience. Did you not see how they split themselves into the Kodumbalur and Pazhuvettarayar factions and tried to out-shout each other?"

"I did, *Appa*."

"Ah, they dare indulge in such outrageous behavior in my very presence; what wouldn't they do, should I remove myself from this fort! My subjects would splinter the moment I left, and just as Krishna Paramathma's descendents turned on their own and destroyed themselves completely, the people of this *samrajyam* will fall upon each other and ensure that nothing is left of it—"

"You are the sole ruler, the noble emperor of this great land, *Appa*; both the Kodumbalur and Pazhuvoor lords have sworn fealty to the Chozhas; your every command must be carried out by them without a murmur. Should they disobey—why, then, their ruin is the result of their own actions. Why must you concern yourself with their unruly acts?"

"Both these clans have rendered invaluable service to this dynasty for the past two hundred years at least, my daughter. Think: could this *samrajyam* have attained its present heights without their loyalty? And if they were to be destroyed—wouldn't that be an unimaginable loss to these lands?"

"But if it were to be known, *Appa,* that one of these vaunted clans was a group of treacherous rogues, conspiring against you …?"

"What? What is this you say?" Sundara Chozhar threw a keen glance full of undisguised surprise at his daughter. "A conspiracy against me? But who would be guilty of such a plot?"

"Certain men who have sworn eternal fealty to you, *Appa*—men who seek to deceive you even now, with their cunning charade of loyalty. They wish to deprive your sons of their legitimate inheritance, and conspire to make someone else heir—"

"Someone else? Who is the contender to the throne, my dear?" Sundara Chozhar's voice shook with impatience. "Who is this man, whom they intend to bring as competition to your brothers?"

"*Chithappa* Madhuranthakan, Father," Kundhavai's voice was very low. "Here you lie, ravaged by disease, while those wretched creatures spin devious, treacherous webs to supplant you—"

"Aha!" the Chakravarthy sat up straight. "How I wish their efforts might prove successful!"

Kundhavai stared at her father, considerably startled. "But, *Appa* …?" she stuttered. "How could you—you wouldn't turn against your own flesh and blood!"

"Far from it, my dear. I intend, in fact, to do the very best by my sons. They need not inherit this cursed land. Ah, if only Madhuranthakan might agree—"

"And why not? He's practically frothing at the mouth to ascend this throne—he'd do it tomorrow if he could. But *Appa*—surely you aren't about to let such an eventuality come to pass? Mustn't my elder brother be apprised of your intentions—what about his approval ..."

"Indeed, yes, your brother must be asked and not just him; your grandmother, your *periya patti*, must grant approval as well—"

"Which mother would object to her son's ascent to the throne?"

"Why would she not? Surely you have not been in her company all these years, my dear, without understanding her temperament? I took this very throne subject to Sembian Maadevi's most persistent wishes, not to mention crowning Aditha Karikalan as my heir. Kundhavai, my dear—the world knows of her great affection for you. Now, if you could just persuade her, somehow, and beguile her into accepting Madhuranthakan's succession—"

Kundhavai sat as though turned to stone, struck dumb with astonishment.

"Then, my dear, you must leave for Kanchi, meet your brother, and convince him somehow to refuse this kingdom—make him announce his decision of his own volition! We shall crown Madhuranthakan, and then the curse will have no power over us; we shall all live in peace!"

"You keep mentioning some sort of curse, *Appa*," Kundhavai found her voice, finally. "I suppose you couldn't enlighten me?"

"Have you heard tell of the phenomenon of past lives, my daughter? Do you believe in such things? That the memories of your previous birth sometimes come to you in this ... well, my dear?"

"These are grave and important issues, much beyond me, Father. What would I know of them?"

"What of the ten divine incarnations of Mahavishnu, my dear? And have you not heard that the Buddha took many, many births, before his own? What about the countless beautiful tales we have been handed down, about them?"

"I have heard them of course, *Appa.*"

"If the great Gods and learned gurus themselves could have had them—then why not ordinary men?"

"Perhaps."

"I must tell you that I have had strange experiences—visions of my own previous births, my dear. I have told no one about these—they would not believe me, for one thing; neither will they understand them. I am already known to be suffering from various ills; now people would gossip that my mind was afflicted as well, by *sithabramai.* Not content with sending a flow of well-meaning physicians, my devoted attendants will now begin hunting for magicians, those who practice *maandhreegam,* to mend my mind—"

"True enough, *Appa.* There are those who say such things already; that your affliction requires the healing touch of magicians, not physicians …"

"Do they indeed? Well, now you know! But you won't mock me, will you?" pleaded the Chakravarthy. "You won't laugh at what I have to say?"

"Must you even ask, *Appa*? Do I not know what you suffer?" Kundhavai's beautiful eyes brimmed with tears. "Why would I even think such a thing?"

"I know, dear child; I know. That is why I chose to reveal my secrets to you—when I have not trusted anyone else," confided Sundara Chozhar. "Listen to some of my memories from my previous birth, my daughter …"

A beautiful island, surrounded by the sea. Green trees grew with luxurious abandon and where they could not find a foothold, thick bushes overwhelmed the land. A young man lay concealed behind one of them on the seashore, gazing intently at a ship in the distant waters, its sails unfurled to garner the winds. He watched until it vanished beyond the horizon, and then heaved a sigh of relief. "Thank heavens," he murmured. "I'm safe."

He was of royal descent—but his position denied him a throne; to tell the truth, he had no inclination towards one. Three brothers preceded his own father and so, he had never dreamt of ruling his land; neither had he desired it. A huge army had left his lands, crossing the seas to war; the young man had been a part of it, for he had been given a small regiment to command. The army lost; countless died, the young man's regiment among the deceased. He tried to embrace a warrior's death as well and performed a great many valorous feats—but it was not his time to die. Those who had managed to retreat from the battlefield made their way to the harbour, prepared to return home—all except the young man, who did not wish to do so, having lost every single one of his soldiers. The men of his family had distinguished themselves by their courageous feats; he did not wish to be the one to heap humiliation on their untarnished name. He boarded a ship that would leave for his homeland and as it passed a pretty island, took his chance, and slipped into the sea. He swam swiftly, reached the shore and waited until the ship vanished. Then he crept up a tree, made himself comfortable on a low-lying branch, and took in his surroundings. The pristine island's lush beauty captivated him—but it also seemed to be completely devoid of humans. This, however, did not seem to be a disadvantage at the moment—he welcomed the solitude, rather; his spirits rose and he spent the next few hours leaning against the branch, lost in agreeable daydreams about his future.

And then—he heard a shriek. Not just any shriek either, but a human shriek. A woman's voice, to be very exact. He turned—to see a young woman running away, screaming, hunted by a terrifying bear. Even as he watched, it seemed to be gaining on her; the distance between them shortened. There was nothing he could do—no time to even consider options—except for jumping from the branch, snatching up the spear he had left leaning against the tree, and rush to rescue the young woman. The bear had gained even more now and was close—so close that it was about to sink its claws into her neck—when the young man took aim with his spear and launched it. The weapon sank into the animal, which gave a roar that might have resounded in all seven worlds, and turned upon its assailant. The young woman was now free; not so her male counterpart, for the predator now sprang at him. Then began a furious battle between man and beast—and man won, in the end.

The instant combat was done, his eyes swiveled all around, looking for what, he hardly knew, except that—yes, he *did* know what he sought. The young woman.

A coconut tree grew just a little further away, its trunk at a tantalizing slant, providing perfect elevation, and she stood leaning negligently against it. A plethora of emotions flashed in her eyes: surprise, curiosity and happiness, while her face bloomed with the sparkle of youth. That she was a maiden of the forest, largely untouched by civilization, was obvious from her appearance and attire—but there was nothing and no one in the whole world, the young man thought, that might compare to her exquisite loveliness. Her stance, as she leant at a perfect angle against the tree—ah, it was as though a divine artist had come down to earth and painted a charming picture, capturing her beauty perfectly. Perhaps she was a maiden—but even so, she could not be human, he thought brokenly, awed at the perfection of her features. *A celestial being has come down to earth*, he thought, as he approached her—but far from his expectations, she did not vanish. Instead, she completely defied his assumptions, and sprinted away like a startled deer. He followed her for a while but stopped, already exhausted from his battle and unable to match her fleet-foot. Besides, what sort of a behavior was this anyway—chasing after a girl?

She ought to live somewhere on this island, after all, he mused. *I'm bound to come across her again, some time.* He gave up going after her; wandered to the shore, instead, and lay down on the pristine sands, recruiting his strength.

His hopes were not misplaced; the young woman returned very soon—and this time, with an old man in tow. Upon conversation, it became evident that he dwelt on the shores of Ilankai and belonged to the *Karaiyar* caste, making a living as a fisherman. The young man learnt something else of importance as well: that the maiden had been the means of saving him, in the nick of time. Even as the young man had stared at the ship, moving away from the island, a bear had crept up behind him softly, gazing at him as though he were its next meal. Then, it began to inch its way up the tree. The young woman, watching all these events unfold, decided that a distraction was necessary—both to the bear and the young man. Her shrieks were effective: the bear stopped climbing the tree and began to chase her, instead.

There's no need to describe the young man's reaction upon hearing this piece of news, is there? Deep gratitude filled his heart and he made sure to convey it to the maiden—who, however, did not deign to utter a word in reply; it was the old man who did, on her behalf. This state of affairs perplexed the young man considerably until he learnt the truth and when he did, his astonishment vanished: the girl was mute. When he realized that she did not possess the faculty of hearing either, his affection increased by leaps and bounds. As it so happened, circumstances were in the couple's favour; nature itself conspired, it seemed, to nurture their growing affection for each other. The maiden's deficiencies seemed not to bother the young man a whit; her lovely eyes communicated the secrets of her heart; soft truths and sweet words that melted his soul. For, is there any equal to *nayana baashai*, the emotions conveyed through the eyes of a loved one? As if to make up for her hearing, her sense of smell seemed to be extraordinarily powerful; she could divine, just by odour, the wild animal secreted within the vegetation, far away. But what of such petty gifts? When two hearts were joined as one, what did one care for other, lesser faculties? The small island turned into heaven on earth for the young man; days, months and even years slipped by, as though in an ecstatic dream. So drunk on pleasure was he, that he cared not that time flew.

One day, however, his days in paradise seemed to come to an abrupt end. A ship approached the island; several men disembarked into canoes and boats, and came to shore. The young man went to them, keen on knowing their identity, and discovered that they had come for him. A great many untoward incidents had occurred in his country; two of his father's elder brothers had died, while the third had no issue. The young man realized that, far from having no prospects, a massive *samrajyam* now awaited him. His heart churned with confusion; the last thing he wanted was to leave this utopia, and the young woman who had made the island so, by captivating him heart and soul. Then again—he did ache to see his people, those near and dear to him, again. He learnt from the newcomers that grave danger threatened his homeland in all four directions. *Yuddha perigais*, the drums of war thudded in his ears, from somewhere far, far away—and in the end, it was this that played a crucial role in his decision.

"I shall return to you, once I've carried out my duty," he swore to the young woman a thousand times, before leaving. She, having grown up a shy, diffident maiden in a lonely forest, did not even wish to meet these new members of civilization. Instead, she chose to sit upon her old perch—the slanting coconut tree where she had first met him—as he left her shores. He glanced back; to him, her exquisite, large eyes seemed a veritable sea of tears. He hardened his heart, turned resolutely away, settled himself in the boat and off towards the ship.

"To this day, I see that young woman, the *valaignar* maiden, in my mind's eye, Kundhavai. Try as I might, I cannot forget the sight of her, standing mournfully by the tree. And then, something else terrifies me—a picture that shakes me to my very core. It tears into me day and night—it will not let me rest even for a moment—it leaves me trembling and quaking with distress. Shall I tell you about that as well?" asked the Chakravarthy.

"Please do, *Appa*," replied Sundara Chozhar's beloved daughter, in a voice husky with stifled emotion.

ஜ

17

"DO THE DEAD EVER RETURN?"

Thus far, Sundara Chozhar had been speaking as though recounting the experiences of a third person; now, he switched his narrative:

"I am about to tell you something no father would ever share with his daughter, my beloved one—something I have kept locked away within my heart all this time, and never revealed to a single soul save my friend Aniruddhan—and even *he* does not know all. He has no idea, for instance, of the turmoil that rages in my mind. But now—I shall tell *you*. Someone in our family ought to know the truth. Not your mother—but I have thought, for some time, that I could reveal all to you. And today, finally, the time has come. You will not laugh at my fancies, my daughter, but will try and soothe my wounded heart. Why, you would even do your very best to carry out my wishes! It is with that hope that I now speak to you …

"And so it was that I boarded the ship, and set off. When I reached

Kodikkarai, I learnt that Paranthaka Chakravarthy had arrived in Thanjai, and so came here straightaway to seek an audience.

"My grandfather was on his deathbed when I could finally see him. His heart was torn; his spirits depressed. This grand empire that he had built over forty years, piece by piece, was in danger of disintegrating; his firstborn Rajadithyar, in whom he had had every expectation of succeeding him on the throne, was no more, having lost his life in battle. That self-same war had seen my father Arinjayar terribly injured; no one was quite sure about his chances of survival. Kannara Devan's dreaded forces had wrested Thondai Mandalam and were advancing every day; down south, the Pandiyas had seized their chance to revolt. Our forces in Eezham had lost the war as well, and returned home. Tens of thousands of Chozha warriors had lost their lives in countless battles; news of all these encounters had reached my aging, ailing grandfather, and pushed him into a deep abyss of despair. It was at this juncture that we met—and his spirits revived. I had always held a soft spot in his heart, right from my childhood; he had kept me by his side in the palace for many years, unwilling to relinquish me to the outside world. It was with the greatest difficulty that I wrested permission to see combat in Ilankai. I had not been among the men who had returned from the island, and my grandfather's heart was broken, for he had given me up for lost. As it was not known for certain if I was dead, he had sent groups of men in search.

"It was one of these groups that eventually stumbled upon me; when I returned, finally to Thanjai, his grieving heart was rather soothed. Hope had blossomed in him—a *samrajyam* that had begun to fall to ruin in his final days would return to its former glory, somehow, through my efforts; the court astrologers had done their best to nurture that hope. As though to ensure the fulfillment of this prophesy, despite having four courageous warriors for sons, it was I, his only grandson, who was by his side during his last days. He called me to him as he was practically drawing his last breath, and caressed my forehead. Tears poured down his weathered cheeks and he uttered a blessing: "*Appane*, your uncle Kandaradhithar will ascend the throne upon my death; you will inherit it after him. This ancient *samrajyam* will come into its own and regain its magnificence only in your reign." He would repeat these words many times, during those days.

"My only task, nay duty, was to ensure the well-being and prosperity of Chozha Nadu, and I must dedicate my life towards achieving this lofty ideal, he said, and made me swear to honour this pledge.

"My devotion to my grandfather was equal to his love for me; it was no difficulty to promise to uphold his ideals, and carry out his wishes. And yet—my heart was not at peace. That young woman, the *karaiyar* maiden who had saved my life from a bear on that island—what of her? Could a deaf mute, born into a base clan to boot, ever hope to ascend the Chozha throne? For that matter, would she even be able to adapt to life in a palace? What of my countrymen? Wouldn't the citizens of Chozha Nadu make a laughing-stock of me? These thoughts darted through my mind constantly; I was cast into confusion. Other issues served to increase my turmoil: my uncle Kandaradhithar had recently entered into a second marriage; you know, of course, that his fortunate bride was the Mazhavarayar princess. His first wife had had no issue, but where was the guarantee that his second would share the same fate? And if my *periyappa* did beget a son, would *I* inherit the Chozha throne? Of course, I was not the only one to be plagued by such doubts; others besides me had already begun to consider them, and their conversations happened to fall on my ears. But then—I suppose my uncle, the great man that he was, wished to banish such libelous discussions once and forever: when he was made king upon the death of Emperor Paranthakar, *periyappa* Kandaradhithar ensured that I was crowned heir apparent by arranging for a *Yuvaraja Pattabishekam.*

"My dearest daughter, you know the enormous affection our people cherish for your *thambi* Arulmozhi, don't you? Well, they felt the same for me, in those days. Thousands were waiting outside the palace walls, even as the Pattabishekam ceremony took place, within. They wished, you see, to have a glimpse of both the newly crowned king, and his heir apparent, at the same time. I and my *periyappa* obliged them of course, ascended to one of the upper balconies of this palace, and stood by the front balustrade. Below us spread out a veritable sea of faces—all beaming with enthusiasm. A roar went up as everyone caught sight of us. Overwhelmed by their delight, I wondered at my own selfishness: here were tens of thousands of people, voicing approval just because I had been crowned heir—was it really fair of me to spend so much time worrying about a mute girl on a lonely island? What was more important: the happiness of an entire population, or a single girl …?

"Lost in these thoughts, I gazed upon the multitude of pleased citizens below me, scanning each of them—men, women, young ones and old, boys and girls—everyone was there, and all seemed exhilarated upon the occasion.

"But suddenly, I stumbled across a face—a young woman's face overwhelmed with sorrow, eyes brimming with tears, gaze locked onto mine. I had no idea how my eyes managed to find hers amongst the multitude of faces that swam underneath the balcony. But once I saw her, my sight and attention went nowhere else. That face—it grew and grew until it effaced the whole of the crowd gathered below; it blotted out the people standing by my side, the entrance to the palace, the battlements and ramparts of Thanjai fort, even the very sky and earth—everything vanished except for that face, which loomed over me like Devi Parameswari's divine countenance, filled with an unearthly glow. My head spun; legs lost their strength and I, consciousness …

"I learnt later that I fell, and that those around supported me; they assumed that the *Pattabishekam* and its attendant, numerous concerns had been too much and sapped my strength. I had granted audience enough for the day, it was decided, and was brought inside. Once I came to myself, I called my friend Aniruddhan and told him what I had seen. I gave him a description of the young woman, bade him find and bring her to me at any cost. He searched every corner of the city, and returned with the news that he had been unable to find such a maiden anywhere, adding, further, that she had probably been a figment of my imagination. I was furious with him. *What sort of a friend are you, if you won't even do me this favour?* I screamed, and bade men hunt along paths that led from Thanjai fort, towards the sea. Search parties did go out, looking for a trace of her; the men who went to Kodikkarai came back with the news that they had run a mute maiden to earth, in the lighthouse keeper's home. She seemed out of her mind; none of the gestures and ruses they used to communicate worked; she would not return with them to Thanjai. My mind churned when I was brought this news; I knew not what to do. Two days passed as I lurched from one chaotic thought to another. In vain did I try to forget her; I could think of nothing but her, day and night. In the end, I went to Kodikkarai myself in company of Aniruddhan; we sped on our way, driving our horses as swiftly as we could. I grew even more restless as we neared our destination; my confusion increased. If I should find the mute girl—what on earth was I supposed to *do* with her? Take her to Thanjai or Pazhaiyarai and proclaim, *Here is my queen?* My heart and body shrank with shame at the very thought.

"My beloved daughter! In those days, I had acquired a name—completely unnecessary and irrelevant, I might add—for my considerable good looks. I thought nothing of it, but others obviously did, for they talked of it constantly. Despite being named Paranthakan after my grandfather, I was soon awarded the sobriquet of Sundara and so popular did it become that it completely eclipsed my given name. And to think that I—a man who had gained such a reputation—would be bringing a mute girl back to the palace! On the other hand, what else was I to do? It was in a considerably agitated state of mind that I arrived in Kodikkarai—but as it turned out, the good woman had solved all our problems for us. What I learnt there, struck me dumb with horror. The day after the men I had sent left, the girl, it seemed, climbed to the very top of the lighthouse. It was a dark night, with no moon, and the wind had blown itself into a gale. The sea frothed and seethed, rushing into shore and surrounding the lighthouse. The girl stood at the very top, peering down at the choppy waves. No one thought much of this; it seemed to have been a habit with her. And then, a scream—*veeel!*—that seemed to rise over the stormy seas—and the girl had vanished! One or two people glimpsed a woman's body toppling headfirst from the lighthouse into the sea. Boats were brought in and men searched in vain, but nothing could be found. In the end they had to give it up, and it was decided that the sea had taken her ...

"The moment I heard the news, I felt as though a spear had plunged into my chest—such was my pain and sorrow. And yet, after a while, a curious sense of peace enveloped me as well. There was no need, now, to make provision for her. And certainly no need to worry myself to death about her!

"I returned to Thanjai in the same frame of mind, shrouded in a mixture of sorrow and peace. My thoughts now turned fully towards affairs of the state: I went to war, swept into battlefields; married your mother; bore great sons and had the good fortune of having you, my daughter ...

"And yet, my dear ... I could not forget that wretch! Dead she might be, but her form never left my thoughts. Sometimes, a horrible picture unfolded in my mind's eye—one that I never really saw, but was frighteningly real, nevertheless—the picture of a woman tumbling into the sea, from the top of a lighthouse. I saw it both when I was awake, and in my dreams. I awoke screaming during those nightmares, and those beside would rush in with frantic questions, asking if I was alright. Your own mother has wished to know the reason for my distress many times; I have never told her. Sometimes I would say, *Nothing*; at others, I would imagine war-time horrors and recount gory details. Time showered me with his boundless grace and gradually, her memory faded, as did she. At least, so I consoled myself. It seems to me, now, that the dead are far more merciless than the living. My daughter, that *oomaichi*, that mute woman's ghost has never released me—for some time, now, it has begun to haunt me more than ever! Kundhavai, do you believe—do you believe that the dead ever return?"

Sundara Chozhar's eyes darted around, finally settling on, and staring at some point far away. There was nothing in his line of sight, of course. And yet—Kundhavai could not help but notice the tremors that wracked his frail body. A wave of immense pity rose in her heart; her eyes filled. She buried her face in her father's chest and shed tears of love and pity. It seemed to help; the shivers subsided by degrees.

Finally, she looked up. "You've buried this horrible secret within yourself for years, *Appa. How* you've suffered—I'm not surprised that your health failed," her voice was soothing. "But you've shared your heartache with me now, haven't you? I'm sure you will regain your strength in no time."

A spurt of laughter escaped Sundara Chozhar, but why was it tinged with sorrow—and just a smidgen of disbelief? "You do not believe me, Kundhavai," he said, at last. "You do not believe that the dead might return—and yet, last night, that wretched woman's ghost did haunt me—right by that pillar, behind the lamp. I saw her with my own eyes! How can I not believe such a sight—and if I were just jumping at shadows, what about your friend? She did faint at the sight and sound of something terrible, didn't she? Bring her here, Kundhavai," the Chakravarthy's voice shook with haste. "I shall learn the truth myself!"

"Vanathi is just a coward, *Appa*; I've no idea how the valiant Velirs of Kodumbalur could have ever borne such a faint-hearted girl, to be honest. She would shriek and keel over in a faint at the very sight of a pillar looming in the darkness. There's no point in asking her; she's unlikely to have seen or heard anything at all."

"Do you think so, indeed? Never mind her, then; listen to the rest of what I have to say! I did not have faith in the return of dead people either, for a long time; I believed that my weak mind was playing tricks on me. You remember the time we were on a boat on the Kaveri and lost young Arulmozhi Varman, don't you? Just as we were all struck dumb with horror, wondering what on earth to do, a lady rose from the waters, holding aloft the child; she vanished once Arulmozhi reached the safety of our arms. You cannot have forgotten this incident as we have discussed it about a thousand times. All of you were convinced that it was the river Goddess, Kaveri *Amma*n herself, who had saved him—but do you know what I thought? That it was the *oomaichi*—the *valaignar* maiden, who had lifted the child from the waters. You remember that I lost consciousness then too, don't you? You assumed that the danger to the child had overwhelmed my senses, but that was not the truth. After all these years, I must admit—I fainted because it seemed to me that it was the mute girl's spirit that had saved Arulmozhi ...

"Do you remember the day of your brother's *Yuvaraja Pattabishekam*, my daughter? Once the ceremony was done, Aditha Karikalan went to the *anthappuram* to receive the blessings of the royal mothers, didn't he? I was right behind him. And I saw—I saw that wretched *oomaichi's* ghost amongst the ladies, bending its horrifying, ruthless gaze upon him. I lost consciousness once again. Later, when I went over the incident in my mind, certain suspicions reared up in my mind. Why must she stare at Adhithan in such terrifying fashion, I wondered. I suspected that this too, might just be the panicked fancy of my weakened brain. But this time, my dear—this time, when I arrived in Thanjai, all my doubts were at an end. Once, daughter, when she was still alive, I possessed the gift of reading her thoughts just by a look at her face; one glance at her moving lips, and I knew what she wished to say. Now—I have regained that gift, Kundhavai! She has come to me four or five times by now, before midnight, and delivered her warning.

You killed me—but for that crime, I forgive you. Do not sin again! This kingdom belongs by right to one; do not will it away to another! And I understood her message as though she had gained the gift of speech somehow, and spoken the words to me clearly. I knew what I had to do, my daughter—and I look to you, to help me carry it out. This accursed kingdom—this tarnished Chozha throne—need not pass to my sons. Let us bequeath it instead, to Madhuranthakan—"

"*Appa, how can you?*" Kundhavai burst out at this point, unable to bear it any more. "Where's the need to change an arrangement that was agreed upon by the whole kingdom, and has been so for years? And even if *you* should wish for it—would the world truly approve?"

"What does the world's approval matter? My duty is towards *dharma*; to see that justice is done, at all times. My mind was not at peace when I was made heir; neither was I happy at being crowned king. My conscience smote me; it was not right that I, the son of a younger brother should rule, while the elder brother's son remained without a crown. Now, I suffer the result of such a terrible transgression—must my sons undergo the same punishment? Neither Adhithan nor Arulmozhi need rule this land; they need not endure its curse either. Madhuranthakan must be crowned heir while I live. Then, I shall retire to Adhithan's golden palace in Kanchi and spend the rest of my days in peace ..."

"But Periya Piratti must approve of all this, mustn't she, *Appa*?"

"Ah, this is where I require your assistance, my dear. You must convince that lady to come here, somehow—what a strange twist of fate that she, an expert on all matters of justice, must be ignorant regarding this issue? Why must she drive me towards committing such a great sin? What possible grudge could she hold against her own son? Why does she act in a way that is contrary to the very nature of motherhood? There was some justification for her stance, I admit, as long as Madhuranthakan himself was lost in devotion, claiming to spend his life in divine pursuits—but now that he wishes to ascend the throne himself, how unfair to bequeath it to someone else!"

"He may well wish to inherit this land, *Appa*—but what about being worthy of it?"

"Why, what of *that*? The son of Saint Kandaradhithar and one of the most enlightened women of our times, the Mazhavaraiyar princess—how much worthier need one be, pray?"

"Well—well, ignoring the worthiness part of it—what about the approval of the people?"

"If we were to ask our subjects, my dear, they would insist on crowning your young brother king, at once. Would that be just, do you think—and would your brother truly wish it? No, my daughter, this will not serve. Make sure to bring your grandmother somehow, soon—send her a message that I am battling Yama even as we speak—she must come here without a moment's delay if she wishes to see me alive—"

"Unnecessary, *Appa*. Periya Piratti has entertained a wish to renovate the Thanjai Thalikulathaar temple for a while, now. I shall remind her of it, and ask her to visit. In the meantime—I must beg of you to rest, and not overexert yourself."

Kundhavai took leave and left for her quarters, meeting her mother Vaanamaadevi, on the way. "Don't leave my father alone for a moment, *Amma*. The others may perform all the rituals and fasts they please—but you must remain with him."

Vague suspicions that had plagued her for a while were beginning to resolve themselves. Pitch blackness was now beginning to give way, in some places, to light. Her quick mind had already warned that a dangerous web of conspiracy was beginning to wind its treacherous, mysterious tendrils around her father and brothers. What had eluded her, thus far, were the details: what sort of plot was being hatched, and how was it being perpetrated? But she did realize, more clearly than ever, that the Chozha *samrajyam*, not to mention her own brothers' right to it, was being seriously threatened.

And the burden of safeguarding both kingdom and king rested, she believed firmly, on a woman. Kundhavai herself.

18

"WHICH IS THE WORST OF BETRAYALS?"

Enthusiasts of ancient Thamizh History would know that many were the women at the forefront of social activities. Royal ladies were accorded every sign of respect; those born into the Chozha dynasty, as well as those married into it possessed the right to own property. Each had, according to her position in the family, an array of villages, *nansei* and *punsei* agricultural lands and livestock, all assigned to her exclusive use. We ask our kind readers to note, in particular, the various ways these riches were disbursed: many granted resources towards *thiruppani*— sacred works in their names such as lighting temple lamps, stringing garlands for deities, feeding pilgrims and Sivan devotees every day and a great many other charitable acts, which were summarily drawn up and recorded in stone or on copper-plates—*silaasaasanam*, or *cheppu pattayam*—that they may be preserved for posterity.

While it was the norm for female royals to immerse themselves in temple work, Kundhavai Piratti, beloved daughter of Sundara Chozhar, chose to distribute her wealth in quite another fashion. Perhaps it was the precarious state of her poor father's health that weighed on her mind and influenced her decision, but she conceived the notion of setting up infirmaries all over the country. Readers would not have forgotten her successful inauguration of one in the name of Emperor Paranthakar in Pazhaiyarai; Thanjai too, would benefit from such a service, she thought, and had made arrangements to set up a similar infirmary in her father's name. Auspicious Vijayadasami had thus been chosen to throw open the *Adhura Salai*, and to ensure the drawing up of the required inscriptions.

***

The inauguration of the *Sundara Chozhar Adhura Salai* took place with much fanfare within a Garuda *mandapam* directly opposite the Vishnu temple, in the *purambadi* area just outside the fort of Thanjai. Kundhavai had decided on this precise location with reason: Thirumaal, after all, was the guardian of the cosmos while Garudan, his divine mount, was the one who had procured *amudham*, nectar of the Gods. Thanjai's numerous citizens flocked to the ceremony, not to mention Chozha subjects from surrounding villages. Men, women and children had arrived in their finest attire, festooned with whatever jewelry they possessed, to attend the festivities. In addition were to be found Chozha officials, namely the Emperor's *udankuttam* ministers, officers of the *peruntharam* and *sirutharam*; sculptors armed with the duty of chiseling inscriptions onto stone and *viswakarmas*, who would draw up the self-same documents onto copper-plates, and numerous palace menials. The *Velakkara* Regiment arrived in state, with instruments such as *thaarai* and *thappattai* echoing in all eight directions; *Danaar!—Danaar!*—Thanjai's security forces, not to be outdone, descended with a clamour, swords and spears clashing.

The Pazhuvettarayar brothers made a majestic entrance atop their elephant mounts; Prince Madhuranthakar, not quite so fortunate when it came to grand entrances, swayed and weaved all over the place as he tottered up on his white horse, desperate to keep his seat. Princess

Kundhavai, her companions and a few older royal ladies arrived in a dignified parade within a palanquin, while from the opposite direction appeared its ivory-etched counterpart with its palm-tree emblem, bearing the exquisite burden of Ilaiya Rani Nandhini.

The royal women, comprising of Kundhavai Devi, the young queen of Pazhuvoor and various others seated themselves under the blue silk awning erected especially for their use.

Once Periya Pazhuvettarayar made a sign, the proceedings began with a flourish.

Two *odhuvaars*, men in charge of chanting sacred hymns in temples, sang the beautiful Thevaram *pathigam*, "*Mandhiramaavathu Neeru.*" The combination of musical instruments such as *yaazh, mathalam* and their sweet, carefully trained voices, served to cast a spell over the gathered multitude, who listened in complete and utter silence.

Not that this spell seemed to work quite the same magic amongst the royal ladies; two voices rose in low conversation. "Devi," began the young queen of Pazhuvoor, seating herself next to Kundhavai. "You know the tale, I suppose, of this very hymn? Saint Sambandar cured the ailing Pandiya King by singing it, and applying just a hint of sacred ash upon his forehead, didn't he? Why doesn't it possess the same power now, I wonder? Ignoring the hymn itself—what about the *thiruneeru*? Why doesn't it have an effect, any more? No cure seems to work these days without the combined efforts of medicines, herbs, physicians, infirmaries and a host of other things, does it?"

"Truer words were never spoken, Rani," was Kundhavai's forthright reply. "Ah, but those were the days of *dharma*, when righteousness reigned; doubtless, sacred ash was incredibly powerful as well. These days, though, sin has spread its terrible tendrils throughout the world. Why, this very land harbours traitors who conspire against their own king. Pray, when have we ever heard of such doings? Why wouldn't *thiruneeru* lose its magical touch and medicines be needed to cure the mildest ills?" And the princess subjected the Ilaiya Rani to a searching glance.

Nandhini's face, however, changed not a whit. "Indeed? Treacherous bastards who weave conspiracies against our blessed Emperor, you say?" she asked, at her most casual. "And who might they be?"

"Ah, that's just what I don't know. Some point to a certain person; others, to another. This seems to be a matter that requires a good deal of detection and ingenuity; I've made up my mind to stay here a while, to find out what I can," announced Kundhavai. "There's not much you can learn about the world in Pazhaiyarai, is there?"

"An excellent decision," Nandhini's voice was warm with approval. "If you were to ask me, Devi, you would do well to stay here for good— else the *rajyam* will go to the dogs and be ruined! And if you made this city your home, I might be able to lend you whatever assistance I am able. At the moment, I am entertaining a visitor; he might be of immense help as well."

"A visitor?" Kundhavai raised an eyebrow. "Who is he?"

"Kandamaaran, the son of Kadambur Sambuvaraiyar—a young man the height of a coconut tree, and twice its breadth and weight. Have you seen him? He's been ranting about spies and traitors for days, now. You mentioned something about a royal conspiracy, didn't you? What, in your opinion, is even worse than such a terrible betrayal? Do you know?"

"Certainly I do. A young woman who deceives the man she has married, one to whom she is bound by loyalty—can there possibly be a worse betrayal?" And Kundhavai bent her gaze, once more, upon Nandhini—who did not appear fazed in the slightest, at this careful observation. Indeed, a charming smile remained, lighting her exquisite features, much to Kundhavai's disappointment.

"An excellent statement, as usual—but I'm not sure Kandamaaran would agree. The betrayal of friendship is the worst of them all, he would moan—for hasn't the one he considered his friend changed beyond all recognition, stabbing him in the back, quite literally? Not to mention leaving him to die ... and, well, Kandamaaran has been raving about it ever since."

"Who's this man, who dared to subject his own friend to such a dastardly act?"

"A certain Vandhiyathevan, or so I hear. Belongs to the defunct Vaanar clan that used to rule around Vallam, in the Thondai Mandalam. Have *you* ever heard of him?"

Kundhavai's dainty, pearly teeth bit into lush, coral lips. "The name seems—faintly familiar. And … what happened next?"

"What else? His precious friend made good his escape, having stabbed the Kadambur prince in the back. I hear that my brother-in-law has sent men in pursuit of that wretched spy."

"But there's no proof that he *is* one, surely?"

"I'm afraid I wouldn't know; I've merely been repeating Kandamaaran's words. You may speak to him yourself if you wish, and learn the details."

"Indeed, yes; a visit to the Sambuvaraiyar scion does seem to be in order. I've heard that his survival was nothing short of a miracle—has he been in the Pazhuvoor palace ever since he was injured?"

"Yes; they brought him the morning after, and I was saddled with the job of treating his injury as well. His recovery has been slow, to say the least; the wound hasn't healed completely, as yet."

"Not even *your* tender ministrations at his bedside have cured him? Behold me, struck dumb with surprise. Well, Rani, I shall certainly pay him a visit. After all, the Sambuvaraiyar clan wasn't founded yesterday, you know; they've won laurels for their valour from the time of Paranthaka Chakravarthy …"

"My point, exactly, Devi. Besides, we'd have the pleasure of your boundless condescension, stepping into our paltry residence in the guise of visiting *him*, wouldn't we?" came Nandhini's reply, in dulcet tones.

The *pathigams* had faded into silence by now, and it was the turn of the royal documents, or *saasanam*. Emperor Sundara Chozhar's *thirumugam* or communiqué, being first in consequence, was read out:

"As Ilaiya Piratti has seen fit to bestow, in her boundless benevolence, the entire income of the Nallur Mangalam village in favour of the *Thanjai Purambadi Adhura Salai*, and this village was given to our daughter as a *sarva maniyam*, or gift to do with as she pleased, it is decreed, by order of the Emperor, that the *nansei* lands of said village be made tax-free." Once the *thirumandhira olai* official was done, he handed the palm-leaf to the Dhanaadhikaari, Periya Pazhuvettarayar, who received it in both hands with due reverence, pressed it to his eyes and delivered it to the royal clerk, instructing him to enter the transaction in the register.

The next to be read out was Kundhavai's own statement of bequest, her *dhaana silaasaasanam*. The details, meticulously recorded, were clarity itself: that the residents of the above-mentioned village were to be granted the complete enjoyment of the *sarva maniyam* lands; in return, they were to deliver to the *Thanjavur Sundara Chozha Adhura Salai* the following: two hundred measures of rice a year; fifty measures of cows' milk; five measures of goat's milk and a hundred coconuts for the exclusive use of the patients. All these details were chiseled in stone, accompanied by the name of the scribe and, in great detail, those of the officials who had overseen the recording of said gift.

The inscription, once read out, was duly given into the keeping of the heads of Nallur Mangalam village, who accepted the stone with a great deal of deference and placed it atop the elephant, standing patiently nearby.

"Long live Ko Rajakesari Sundara Chozhar, Conqueror of Madurai!" Chants from a thousand throats rose in the air and spread in all eight directions, almost deafening the gathering, while a hundred *parai* instruments delivered a resounding performance, rivaling the voices for sheer exuberance. And then followed chants in a certain pre-ordained fashion:

"Long live Ilaiya Piratti Kundhavai Devi!"

"Long live Warrior among Warriors, Aditha Karikalar, who beheaded Veera Pandiyan!"

"Long live Prince Arulmozhi Varman, Conqueror of Eezham!"

"Long live Madhuranthaka Thevar, scion of *Sivagnana* Kandaradhithar!"

They rose in waves and counter-waves, each higher than the last. And then, finally, came chants in another style. "Long live the Dhanaadhikaari, Guardian of the Granaries, He Who Levies Taxes, Periya Pazhuvettarayar!"

"Long live Chinna Pazhuvettarayar Kalanthaka Kantar, Guardian of the Thanjai Fort!"

By the time these were raised, however, the enthusiasm and vociferousness had died down considerably; it was obvious that they were the efforts of loyal Pazhuvoor soldiers, and that the watching public did not really join in with alacrity.

It was the ambition of Kundhavai to catch a glimpse of the Ilaiya Rani's face during these very moments; regretfully, she could not, despite her best efforts. Had she managed to do so—especially during those raised in praise of Aditha Karikalar—there can be no doubt that even Ilaiya Piratti, possessor of an iron heart, would have quailed in terror.

19

"THEY'VE CAPTURED THE SPY!"

To say that the incidents of the day had roused the worst of Periya Pazhuvettarayar's ire would be an understatement.

Ha! What had this precious inaugural ceremony accomplished except to act as an impromptu means of displaying the people's loyalty towards their precious Chakravarthy and his doltish family?

The people, my blessed foot, he fumed and fretted to himself often. *Idiots! Just lumps of clay, willing to be led around like goats and cows—four thousand people would bleat and follow four—when has anyone ever heard of the masses using their brains, and thinking things out for themselves?* He groaned aloud. *At this rate, the Chakravarthy will send us all to rack and ruin before his reign is out. Endless commands to make this land tax-free or that one free of all obligations! Ha, by the time he gets to heaven, Chozha Nadu won't possess a single village worth a petty coin! No taxes to be collected from anywhere—and yet, money, grains and food are supposed to be sent in an endless train to the battlefield!*

"How am I supposed to accomplish impossibilities?" He raged, sending his own employees scurrying to corners, shaking at his stentorian shouts.

"Pray, *pray* calm yourself, *Anna*," Chinna Pazhuvettarayar came to his aid in the end, preaching patience, of all things. "There is no point in shouting yourself hoarse, thus—we must bide our time and make sure our task is done, and done well!"

These were minor irritants—but when news reached him of Kundhavai's impending arrival at his palace, the elder Pazhuvettarayar's fury knew no bounds.

"What is this I hear about that demon visiting *us*?" he barked, stalking up to his wife. "And what on earth is this nonsense about *you* extending her an invitation—surely you haven't forgotten the abuses she heaped upon me—"

"I overlook nothing—neither a single kind gesture; nor an insult," announced Nandhini, calmly. "Surely you've recognized this particular quirk of my character by now?"

"Why must she come *here*, then?"

"Because she wishes to, I suppose. The Chakravarthy's beloved daughter, isn't she? Bursting at the seams with conceit; of course she wishes to parade her exalted consequence."

"Well, but—why would *you* invite her?"

"I didn't; she asked herself. *I hear that Sambuvaraiyar's son stays at your palace; I wish to see him!* She declared, suddenly, and what could I do? Refuse with a *No!* like a slap in her face? Not that I can't—the time will come, when I shall. Until then, I shall have to bear these indignities with what grace I can."

"I cannot. The thought of even being here, in the palace, at the same time as her visit—no, I cannot even stay in the city! I shall leave, I think; affairs in Mazhapaadi beckon."

"Do, by all means, *Nadha*. I was about to suggest much the same thing, myself. Leave that little poisonous snake to me; I'm an expert at pulling out her fangs and draining her venom. Try not to be surprised, will you, if you should happen to hear some scraps of astonishing news, upon your return ..."

"Indeed? Er—what sort of news?"

"An announcement about Kundhavai Piratti joining in marriage with Kandamaaran, perhaps, or Aditha Karikalan betrothed to Kandamaaran's sister—"

"*Ayyayo*—what is this that you say? What of *our* plans if all this should come to pass?"

"Just the very mention of a deed does not indicate its fulfillment. For that matter, you've been assuring your comrades that Madhuranthakan is the heir to this throne—but that's not the truth, is it? Are all our plans and pains to be wasted on a man who sashays like a woman?" And Nandhini trained her large, exquisite eyes on her lord and master. "Truly?"

Periya Pazhuvettarayar's gaze fell from hers, unable to bear its hypnotic power; his head bowed almost despite himself. "My heart's dearest," his voice was husky, as he took one of her soft hands into his, and raised it to his eyes. "The day of your ascent to this Chozha throne as its Empress is not very far off. Soon, my beloved—soon!"

***

Ever since he heard that Kundhavai was about to visit him, Kandamaaran had been thrown into a flutter of nervousness, flailing in a sea of pleased apprehension. The whole of Chozha Nadu sang the praises of the princess's exquisite beauty, intelligence, and other superior qualities, after all. And to know that she—Ilaiya Piratti—was to pay him a visit—well, wasn't that truly an honour? Ah, he would have willingly submitted to a few more stab wounds in that case! What wouldn't he have given to lie upon this very bed with an injury on his chest, hard wrought in battle? What an incredible honour *that* would have been, to have Kundhavai Devi visit him, and offer her sympathies? Instead, now, he would have to parrot the same story he'd bleated to so many others, about his precious friend's betrayal. A depressing thought.

Amidst all this intruded memories of the conspiracies in which he and others were engaged, against the family of this very lady; his conscience could not but prick him a little.

In truth, Kandamaaran was a principled young man, not much given to devious plots, traitorous thoughts or schemes. Nandhini's unearthly loveliness might have sent his senses reeling, but the very fact that she was another's wife was enough to set a few barriers around his unruly heart. Kundhavai, on the other hand, was a maiden yet — how was he to approach her? What ought to be his behavior? How was he to word his responses—for that matter, how was he to even speak to her politely, knowing that he was engaged in nefarious schemes against her? Or perhaps—perhaps her beauty would bewitch him into weakness, and— no, no, he mustn't, he couldn't afford to let that happen. Why must this precious princess visit him, anyway? There was no reason for her to single him out—let her come to him, then—let her; he'd address a few cutting remarks and she'd take the hint; she wouldn't dare visit him again.

Such were Kandamaaran's lofty intentions—but alas! The moment he set eyes on Kundhavai, they crumbled into nothing. Ah, what a charming young woman! Her enticing beauty, glowing countenance— how modest, and yet how altogether benevolent her gestures—and as for her soothing words as she asked after his health … well, Kandamaaran well and truly lost himself.

His imagination ran riot; he was not unduly given to talking about himself, he gave her to understand, yet made sure to describe his feats of valour as bombastically as possible—although he truly was a humble young man, as anyone knew, not given to embroidering his tales. He didn't wish to bore her with accounts of his indomitable courage, really, but wouldn't she like to see the many impressive war-wounds he'd sustained on his shoulder, chest and elsewhere upon his body?

"I wouldn't have cared even if I'd been murdered, you see, if that bastard Vandhiyathevan had stabbed me in the chest," Kandamaaran lamented. "Now I've been forced to spread around the true story of his betrayal—else, wouldn't I be accused of having shown my back to battle? Why, I'm sure I would even have forgiven him, had he had the temerity to plunge his knife in my shoulder or breast!"

These words, uttered with a wealth of emotional condescension, seemed to ring with sincerity to Kundhavai, who now found herself besieged by doubts. Had she been right to trust Vandhiyathevan? What if she'd been well and truly deceived by that young man? She begged Kandamaaran to describe his encounter with his treacherous friend in detail and he, nothing loath, began on a tale that scaled such heights of imagination that even Nandhini listened, lost in astonishment.

"Listen to this, Devi—that scoundrel took me in properly right from the first, when he stayed the night in Kadambur. Never for a moment did he mention his true purpose in traveling to Thanjavur and here, he managed to weasel himself into the fort by hook or crook, displaying some sort of fake insignia. He crowned his iniquities by even seeking an audience with the Emperor, spouting a spurious tale about carrying an *olai* from Aditha Karikalar. But did he stop there? No, indeed! No, he'd grown so puffed up in his esteem that he had the gall to drag your name into his tangled affairs, lying about carrying a message for you, so was it any surprise that the Guardian of the Fort began to smell a rat? Naturally, he suspected Vandhiyathevan of being a spy and placed him under guard—but Vandhiyathevan managed to stage an escape. You have to hand it to him, Devi—he does manage to get himself out of any manner of tight spots. I must admit, I never for a moment suspected that my friend would be the so-called enemy agent pursued by guards in such earnest. Vandhiyathevan's got a few kinks in his character—he's never been, well, straightforward. I believed that he was just playing the fool, and approached the Fort's Chief of Security myself. I swore that I would capture him somehow, but in return, I had a few stipulations of my own: my friend would have to be pardoned and released; the Chief agreed. I set out in search of Vandhiyathevan at midnight, skirting the fort. I went alone—you see, he was my friend, after all, and the last thing I wanted was to subject him to the indignity of an arrest by soldiers. He'd escaped the guards' clutches within the city—but he would have to approach the fort-walls at some point, wouldn't he? And even had he made it outside, he would still have to conceal himself in the surrounding forest, nearabouts. I reasoned thus and crept along the banks of the Vadavaaru— and then, I caught sight of something by the pale light of the moon: a man scrambling down the steep fortifications. I hastened forward, and once he'd stepped down, confronted him. "What's all this, my friend?" I asked, in all sincerity—and that bastard responded by punching me. What could his measly thump do to a chest that has withstood the mauling of elephants, pray? Still, it galled that he dared to treat me, his friend, this way—and I'd come with the best of intentions, too. I couldn't bear it; I punched him back. We fought furiously for a while. Needless to say, he lost his strength within half a *naazhigai* and slumped to the ground. He begged my pardon, and I, of course, forgave him with all my heart. *Tell me the truth about your presence here*, I reasoned with him. *I swear, I shall help you in any way I can ...*

"*I am exhausted*, he panted. *Please let me sit while I explain.* I took pity on him, and agreed. We began to walk and I led the way—and that was when the bastard showed his true colours: suddenly, he stabbed me in the back! Practically half the knife plunged in, such was his brute force. I began to feel dizzy, and fell. That wretched traitor took his chance and made his escape! By the time I regained consciousness and opened my eyes, I found myself in the home of a mute woman ..."

Nandhini, barely able to contain her amusement at this remarkably embellished tale, laughed to herself; Kundhavai sat still, not quite sure of the veracity of this account.

"You say you ended up in the home of a mute woman," she said, at last. "Who carried you there?"

"That, I'm afraid, is truly a puzzle I can't unravel, at the moment. That female had no idea either—not that she could tell me even if she did. I gathered that she had a son who seemed to have vanished that day—where to, was an unsolved mystery. No one knew anything of his whereabouts; should he return, there might be a chance of learning the truth. Else, we shall have to twiddle our thumbs until the Pazhuvoor men capture my friend—"

"You believe that they will, do you?"

"How could they *not*? He can't possibly tie a couple of wings to his arms and fly away, can he? That's why I tarry here yet—so I may have the chance of seeing him once more. Else, I might have gone home. I still believe, you see, that I might be able to intervene on his behalf and secure a pardon."

"I marvel at your generosity, *Ayya*," complimented Kundhavai. "How incredibly benevolent of you!" *Please, let Vandhiyathevan not be captured*, her heart made a silent, impassioned plea. *I don't care if he's a spy—let him not be caught!*

Hurried footsteps were heard in the palace corridor that very instant. "*Amma!*" shrieked a maid, running into the room. "The spy has been caught—they're bringing him right now!"

Sorrow and dismay reflected almost instantly, on the faces of both Nandhini and Kundhavai. The Pazhuvoor queen managed to school her expression swiftly into one of normalcy.

The Pazhaiyarai princess, however, couldn't.

20

Two Tigresses

The hearts of the three people in the room fluttered in a tumult of emotion, as news filtered in that the spy had been caught—but Kundhavai's agitation was, perhaps, the worst.

"We'll have a peep at the face of this cunning spy, shall we, Devi?" Nandhini proposed.

Kundhavai's reply, when it came, was hesitant. "What do *we* have to do with him?"

Nandhini shrugged. "Oh, very well, then." This, with elaborate nonchalance.

"Perhaps I shall take a look," Kandamaaran offered, staggering to his wobbly feet.

"Pray, don't," Nandhini remonstrated. "You couldn't—you'd fall in a moment!"

"He's right—why *don't* we take a look at this precious friend of his?" Kundhavai seemed to experience a sudden change of heart. "We'd have a good view from this palace's balcony, won't we?"

"Certainly we will," Nandhini rose with alacrity. "If you will accompany me?"

"If it does happen to be my friend, Devi," panted Kandamaaran, "I should like to make arrangements to speak with Uncle—"

"But—how would *we* know?" asked Nandhini.

"In that case, I *must* come with you," And Kandamaaran lurched to his feet, walking unsteadily.

The trio reached the front balustrade of one of the palace's upper balconies just in time to catch sight of seven or eight horses trotting up the road below, carrying spear-bearing warriors. A man walked in their midst, hands secured behind his back, while cavalry soldiers on both sides gripped the ends of the rope tight.

A crowd crawled at the heels of the warriors, gawking at the spectacle.

The man's face, as he staggered in the midst of soldiers, wasn't readily visible to the three people watching atop the palace *maadam*.

Silence descended, a thick, stifling veil, until the sorry cavalcade approached the palace.

Kundhavai's eyes, brimming with a plethora of anticipation and concern, would not budge from the procession.

Nandhini, however, seemed to be dividing her time chiefly between peering down into the street one moment, and glancing up at Kundhavai's face, the next.

It was Kandamaaran who, in the end, broke the heavy wall of brooding silence. "No; that's not Vandhiyathevan."

Kundhavai's face brightened at once.

The strange convoy reached the spot directly below the palace *maadam*, at that instant. The bound man, still staggering between the mounted warriors, raised his head and peered up.

Recognition flashed across the princess's mind at once. *The physician's son!*

"Why, what sort of ridiculous charade is this?" she burst out, stifling the exhilarated relief that threatened to spill out. "What are they doing—binding and dragging this man through the streets? Surely this is the Vaidhyar's son?"

The prisoner opened his mouth as though to say something. The rope that bound him snapped him forward just then, and he was dragged away.

"Is he indeed? But then, what do you expect of my brother-in-law's men?" lamented Nandhini. "They let slip the true criminal, truss up someone else in his place and plague the life out of the rest of us!"

"Ah, I dare anyone to get hold of Vandhiyathevan so quickly; he wouldn't let himself get caught in such a rough-and-ready fashion!" Kandamaaran crowed. "Not for nothing is my friend an Indrajithan, an expert in trickery. He managed to get one over *me*, didn't he—how would he let himself be reeled in by those nincompoops?"

"You still consider him your friend, do you?" asked Nandhini. "After all this?"

"He may have turned traitor, but my affection for him remains unchanged," Kandamaaran declared, stoutly.

"Perhaps these warriors have killed your precious friend," the Ilaiya Rani said, smoothly. "From what I hear, they went in search of *two* spies …" her voice trailed away as she darted a glance at Ilaiya Piratti. *Killed*—the word seemed to operate powerfully, on the princess. It did not take much for Nandhini to understand that the very idea of Vandhiyathevan's death made Kundhavai writhe in agony.

Why, you arrogant little witch, she turned away to hide a smile. *What a wonderful weapon to wreak my revenge upon you. And if I don't make the most of it, I'm not the Ilaiya Rani of Pazhuvoor. Just you wait, my girl—just you wait!*

"Spies, indeed! Of all the ridiculous starts—" Kundhavai tried in vain to smother her anguish under a veil of anger. "For sheer stupidity, I've never seen anything to rival their like—I believe these old men must have lost their little minds! Why must they needs suspect—I sent the physician's son to Kodikkarai on a mission to fetch herbs, and now they're dragging him along the streets, branding him a spy! I'm afraid I shall have to have a word with your brother-in-law—"

"Oh, he's one of yours, is he?" Nandhini enquired. "You mentioned something about suspicions, just now, and I find that I'm subjected to one too: did you send just this one to fetch herbs, or someone else, as his companion?"

"I sent another, in company of the physician's son; I bade one of them travel to Ilankai."

"Ah, I understand everything now; the picture's clear! And it's exactly as I suspected."

"I'm afraid I'm still in the dark. What were your suspicions, and how have they come true?"

"There's no more room for suspicion at all; everything is obvious now. Devi, the man you sent in company of this one—had you already known him? Or was he completely unfamiliar to you?"

Kundhavai could not help but hesitate, a little. "What's all this—new or old?" she offered, finally. "He came to me from Kanchi, bearing an *olai* from my brother."

"That's him, then—that's him!"

"That's who?"

"The spy, I mean. He mentioned that he'd brought an *olai* for the Chakravarthy, here, as well."

"But why suspect him of being one?"

"What would I know of such things? Those are matters for the menfolk. If it comes to that—I can't say the spy behaved in an exemplary manner, himself; he managed to rouse the worst suspicions with his actions, didn't he? Why make a hurried escape from the fort in the dead of the night? Why stab this innocent man, pray, in his back, too?"

"I cannot believe, I'm afraid, that he did. Why drag him all the way to the mute woman's house, to safety, in that case?"

"Why, you might almost have been by his side, the way you describe the events, Devi! I wonder what sort of magic that spy possesses, to be assured of *your* support and sympathy? Why, our guest here insists on calling him his friend, yet. Not that all this matters, any more; a life departed shall never return. If those warriors have killed him—"

Beads of perspiration dotted Kundhavai's fair countenance. Her beautiful eyes turned bloodshot; a lump seemed to have stuck in her throat. *It can't be true*, she murmured to herself, trying to still a heart that beat far too erratically. *Never—it couldn't have happened!* Aloud, she began: "If this spy is quite as wily as your guest claims—"

"Indeed, you are right, Princess," Kandamaaran hastened to offer his opinion. "Vandhiyathevan would never have let himself be captured by these guards."

"Not this time, perhaps," Nandhini shrugged. "But his luck is sure to run out … it's only a matter of time."

Kundhavai bit her lips, striving for self-control. "We're none of us seers, are we, capable of predicting the future?" Then, something seemed to snap. "This is a wonderful state of affairs—the Chakravarthy is ill, abed, and the man I send to fetch herbs for him is being dragged all over the city, and branded a spy! How dared they? What gives them the authority—I shall report to my father at once—"

"Pray, why must the Emperor be put to a great deal of unease and anxiety over this issue, Devi? My brother-in-law is the appropriate person to approach, surely? Perhaps he was unaware of your commission; he might well accede to your requests if he were apprised of it. After all,"

Nandhini smiled. "There's no one in the whole of Chozha Nadu who would deny Ilaiya Piratti her slightest wish, is there?"

It was the young queen of Pazhuvoor who emerged the victor from the day's furious skirmish between the two tigresses. Kundhavai's heart, it was to be feared, sustained a great many wounds, and the princess had to exert her considerable will-power to the fullest in an effort to appear her usual, composed self.

21

THE DUNGEONS

There is no greater conundrum, perhaps, than worldly life itself: who can predict the precise reason for happiness—or sorrow? The sky stays pristine for long and then, suddenly, rumbling clouds charge; thunder crashes in all eight directions; darkness surrounds the earth; lightning flashes threateningly and the rain simply pours.

Sometimes, it seems as though there isn't a whisper of a breeze anywhere in the world. Leaves stay absolutely still—and then, the wind rises to gale force within a matter of moments, uprooting whole trees and sending them crashing to the ground. Lush forests and copses that delighted the senses just moments ago, now present a devastated appearance—like the gardens destroyed by Anumaar, in Ramayanam's Asokavanam.

Kundhavai's life was not unlike such a garden: something very akin to those whirlwinds seemed to be blasting her hitherto orderly existence.

Not a moment's grief had she ever known, until recently. Life, to her, had been one of unalloyed enjoyment, an endless carnival of gaiety and delightful interludes. Her days seemed full of song and dance; pretty dresses and fabulous ornaments; exquisite art and fabled epics, walks in palace gardens and serene evenings upon lavishly decorated boats. Her father, mothers, brothers, ministers, teachers, numerous maids and attendants—everyone in her life doted on her; she was the center of their universe, and they did not scruple to show it. Her only acquaintance with sorrow was from a distance—through sentimental epics, or plays that wrung viewers' hearts.

And so, when it did finally enter her existence, it was with a monumental crash and in everlasting, distressing waves, battering her senses and throwing her into disorder. Her father's health was precarious; the *samrajyam* lay in a perilous state. Her brothers were stationed far away, beyond her call. Her country was about to suffer some sort of catastrophic disaster, according to astrologers and soothsayers who murmured mysterious predictions. Devious conspiracies abounded in secret corners; people seemed fathoms deep in nameless terror.

Kundhavai, the proud descendent of countless generations of iron-hearted warriors, possessed courage enough to weather these and far hardier storms. Her faith in her own intelligence was unwavering; she could destroy any and every peril that threatened, with her sharp wits.

That, at least, had been her belief. Until something happened—something quite inconsequential, or so it had seemed: an unexpected meeting—but one that had shaken her very foundations, quaking her heart, strong as the proverbial diamond, crumbling her iron resolve.

The moment she met Vandhiyathevan—her heart, a bud until then, untouched and unmoved—unfurled into fragrant flower.

But oh, what a misfortune! A bee had found its way into the bloom that same instant, and begun to sink its poisonous fang into the delicate petals, inflicting a sea of pain. *Ammamma*! How agonizing!

Oh, how she writhed at the very idea that the Vaanar warrior might have been imprisoned! As for the cruel insinuation that he might have been killed—her heart nearly broke, then. Ah, the monumental effort she had to make, trying in vain to mask her anguish ...

Many were her near and dear ones; parents, siblings, companions dear to her—and yet, why must she care quite so much about a mere passer-by; someone she hadn't met more than two or three times—and in a formal manner, to boot?

But this was no time to wonder and moan about her wayward heart; analyze her inner turmoil and work down to its root cause. No, she would have to ignore ill omens and bad predictions, thrust away superstition and false reports, gather her spirits and begin her interrogations, accomplish what she had to do ...

She sent a message to Chinna Pazhuvettarayar that she would be visiting him that afternoon, and promptly did so. The women of the palace extended her a warm welcome, showering her with their hospitality; the princess spent a while in their company, discussing various inconsequential matters. Then, she made her way towards the *chithira mandapam*, where awaited Chinna Pazhuvettarayar. He began to escort her around the gallery at once, pointing out the various portraits and describing their merits in great detail. Kundhavai listened with every expression of interest, gazing at the works of art intently.

Finally, they came to the last one, and Kundhavai raised her eyes to his. "There are no words, *Ayya*, to describe the invaluable service rendered by generations of Pazhuvettarayars to the Chozha dynasty."

"That is our good fortune, *Amma*," Kalanthaka Kantar received this compliment with dignity.

"And there's no doubt, either, that nothing can equal such stellar service—save, perhaps, this vast *samrajyam* itself."

"*Thaaye*—what sort of words are these?"

"But surely you could afford to wait until the Chakravarthy's reign is at an end, and he is safe in Kailasam? Must you be in quite such haste to seize the reins of government?"

Chinna Pazhuvettarayar's agonized expression was a clear indication that these words had torn his heart with the swift pain of arrows. Beads of perspiration dotted his forehead; his limbs began to tremble; his very moustache quivered with emotion. "*Amma*," he brushed away the sweat with some agitation. "Pray, why this wrath? Do you seek to send me straight to Yamalokham with your verbal missiles?"

"I do not possess such power, *Ayya*, and well do you know it. Why, the God of Death himself would shudder to enter your presence, wouldn't He? What price a foolish young woman such as myself—"

"*Ammani*, pray drop a little lead into my ears, that I may not listen to such brutal taunts! What have I done to incur this fury? I must beg of you to enlighten me, Devi, as to the reason for this—this terrible grace—"

"Ah, no—who am *I* to speak of your faults? It is rather you, *Ayya*, who must do me a favour and apprize me of mine. Pray, is it a crime, *Ayya*, to send men to gather herbs for my father's health?"

"Not at all, *Ammani*."

"I was the one who sent the Pazhaiyarai Vaidhyar's son to Kodikkarai. You know that too, don't you?"

"I do."

"Today, *Ayya*, I managed to catch a glimpse of that self-same man, bound and dragged by your cavalry, through the streets. Yours was the command to arrest him, wasn't it? And that, despite the knowledge that mine had been the commission?"

"Yes, Piratti—but you may not have known his true identity when you sent him on his mission, perhaps."

"Pazhaiyarai physician's son, a spy? Do you truly expect me to believe that ridiculous tale?"

"But if he were to have confessed to it—what else can we do but believe it, *Thaaye*?"

Kundhavai stared at him, startled. "Confessed? Confessed what, pray? And how?

"That his companion was a spy—and that this other man hadn't begun this journey with the intention of gathering herbs, but to carry a message for someone in Ilankai …"

"That ineffable fool! I suppose he's been spouting a lot of drivel—you do know that I was the one who sent his companion too, don't you?"

"Indeed I do, *Thaaye*. But with all due respect, I am also aware that he has deceived you. That young man, sporting the name of Vandhiyathevan *is* a spy—"

"No, not at all. He's the one who brought me an *olai* from my brother."

"For that matter, he brought one to the Chakravarthy as well, from the crown prince—what of it? Spies must usually make use of some such ruse to accomplish their ends, mustn't they?"

"I suppose you have incontrovertible proof that Vandhiyathevan *is* one, *Ayya*?"

"If he isn't, why must he choose to travel along little known paths, instead of taking the *rajapattai*, like an honest man? Why inquire about the Chakravarthy's fate and future, from the astrologer of Kudandhai?"

"As to enquiring about the Chakravarthy, why, I did much the same, myself. What of it?"

"There is a difference between your query, as the Emperor's beloved daughter, and the tasteless questions of a wayfarer with no connection to the royal family. Only the spy of an enemy could wish for such sensitive information."

"These, of course, are only your suspicions. Any other reason?"

"He could have entered Thanjai fort right royally with my permission; why sneak in with the help of the Pazhuvoor signet ring? Why lie about having received it from Periya Pazhuvettarayar, too?"

"Who else could have given him the signet ring, then?"

"We do not know; that is yet to be discovered."

"What are your men about, if they haven't accomplished that yet?"

"My men, regretfully, are not magicians, *Ammani*. The spy has to be found and arrested before he can be questioned, after all."

"Where's the guarantee that he will reveal the truth, if so?"

"Ah, we have our ways of dragging information out of prisoners, *Thaaye*. There are the dungeons, for instance, and it seems our spy was aware of their existence—why else would he disappear without a trace and escape the fort in the dead of the night? Not to mention stabbing Sambuvaraiyar's son in the back too—"

"Where's the proof that he did?"

"Kandamaaran's own testimony, of course."

"Not good enough; I say that he didn't stab the Kadambur prince in the back!"

"Beg pardon, but did you actually see this for yourself, *Amma*?"

"No—but just one look at his face, and I can tell if a man is innocent, or a hardened criminal."

"That rogue of a spy is fortunate, indeed, for having gained your invaluable support. Alas, that I have been singularly unprivileged in that quarter!"

"You keep referring to him as a spy, *Ayya*."

"If he wasn't, why wear a mask and enter the city of Pazhaiyarai in the company of street-play artists, *Amma*? Why set off towards Kodikkarai port in a disguise? Why secret himself in the forest a whole day, at the very sight of my men? And sail to Ilankai at nightfall—"

"Oh, he managed to escape in a boat, did he? Your men couldn't get their hands on him?" Kundhavai's question was drenched in unholy glee.

"I hate to admit it, but that deceitful mole managed to trick his way out of our nets, and my dolts of men have returned, the physician's son in tow ..."

"Ignoring that wretched spy, *Ayya*—the Vaidhyar's son must be freed at all costs; I sent him on his mission after all, and am certain that he is innocent."

"He may not have been a spy himself, *Ammani*, but there's no doubt that he aided and abetted one. Stuffed my men full of a great many ridiculous tales, that one, and deceived them, enabling the real spy to escape in a boat—"

"Be that as it may, the Vaidhyar's son *must* be released."

"You must absolve me of all responsibility regarding that, *Amma*. Believe me when I say that danger threatens this land from all four directions. Our enemies may rise against us any moment; Veera Pandiyan's precious Abathudhavis have sworn to exact revenge on the Chozha dynasty, not to mention treacherous conspiracies being hatched all over the kingdom—"

"If we were to incarcerate everyone guilty of plotting against the king, *Ayya*, these prisons would run out of room."

"But as long we have some—"

"—you may as well set it aside for the real conspirators. Now, release the Vaidhyar's son at once."

"I am afraid I cannot take it upon myself to do so, *Thaaye*."

"What of the Chakravarthy's own command? Or would you choose to disregard that, as well?"

"There would be no need for one, *Amma*; all the world knows that Ilaiya Piratti's slightest wish is tantamount to a sacred command from the Emperor. Here is the key to the dungeons, Devi—I shall leave it in your care. You may unlock the door and do the deed yourself and while you are at it, kindly do grant freedom to anyone else you feel like honouring with your condescension. You and you alone, will be responsible for the consequences ..."

Kalanthaka Kantar handed over a truly gigantic key, as he made this officious speech.

"Very well, *Ayya*," Kundhavai retorted, while throttling the anger that threatened to overwhelm her. "Loss or gain, on my head be it." She took the key into her possession. "Does that satisfy you?"

"Should this ancient Chozha *samrajyam* find itself at the mercy of unimaginable peril," the Guardian of the Thanjai Fort commented wearily. "I shall count only two women responsible."

"I am one; who's the other?"

"The Ilaiya Rani of Pazhuvoor, of course."

Kundhavai's lips twitched with amusement. "You dare class me with the dictator of the Chozha Empire, Thalapathi? If this ever falls upon Periya Pazhuvettarayar's ears, you'll be banished from this country at once!"

"That is music to *my* ears," retorted Chinna Pazhuvettarayar. "I shall welcome such a fate with enthusiasm!"

ℱℐ

22

SENDHAN AMUDHAN, INCARCERATED

The Chozha *samrajyam*'s Mint, the stronghold churning out gold coins as currency, could be considered a fortress in its own right within the confines of Thanjai; its entrance guarded almost as heavily as the city gates. The sun was sinking beneath the horizon by the time Kundhavai and Vanathi arrived for a visit; goldsmiths had finished work for the day, and were gathered in readiness to depart. Preparations had begun among the sentries to inspect them on their way out—at which precise moment the royal chariot came to a halt outside the edifice, allowing Kundhavai and Vanathi to dismount. The sight of the two elegant princesses stopped both guards and goldsmiths in their tracks; chants rose and deafened those in the vicinity: "Long live Ilaiya Piratti!"

The Mint's Head arrived in an instant and escorted the royal ladies around the premises himself: the enormous fire-pit used to melt gold; the moulds meant for crafting coins and the coins themselves. Those that had been freshly minted that very day lay in a large heap in a corner, their golden tint well-nigh dazzling on-lookers. Each bore the figure of a tiger on one side and that of a ship, on the other.

"Would you look at these, Vanathi? Gold has been pouring into the Chozha *samrajyam* through many avenues—by land and over sea, but thus far, our resilient womenfolk have borne the sole responsibility of carrying the whole; I must say, it was all they could do to fashion it into heavy ornaments and wear them endlessly about their persons," explained Kundhavai. "Lately, though, they've been relieved of that incredible burden, for our *Dhanaadhikaari* Pazhuvettarayar has made arrangements to stamp the gold into these alluring, eye-catching coins."

"But—what use are they, *Akka*?" Vanathi looked puzzled.

"What use—must you display your ignorance so blatantly? Churning out coins such as these will make every commercial transaction a thing of ease; no one will have to weigh the gold, for you may know their worth at just a glance. Subjects will be able to pay their taxes with comfort, while traders won't have to waste their time bartering goods with foreigners; they pay for their products with gold, and receive these very coins as payment. Now you know why our merchants praise Pazhuvettarayar to the skies … and let me tell you something else," Kundhavai Devi lowered her voice to a conspiratorial whisper. "These coins are of immense value to those who plot against the Chakravarthy and his family; they're capable of changing the staunchest subject in the twinkling of an eye, aren't they?"

Her last words seemed to have fallen—faintly, it must be admitted—upon the ears of the official in charge of the Mint. "Indeed, *Thaaye*, some such terrible rumour has reached us as well," he interjected. "Is it any surprise, then, that security has been increased for this stronghold—not to mention the rise in number of those who arrive and exit the dungeons underneath—"

"That there may be a great many arrivals, I can well understand," pondered Kundhavai. "But as for exits—pray, how is that possible?"

"But it is, Devi. Why, someone was brought in this very morning," confided the official. "He was released and escorted away only a *naazhigai* ago."

Kundhavai stared at him, considerably intrigued. *Who could this mysterious prisoner be?*

The princesses wandered around the building, taking leisurely looks at the various centres of operation within and then, approached the rear. The guards opened a small door set in the back wall, and everyone stepped into an ill-lit space, its roof low over their heads. Low growls surrounded them on all four sides, raising the hair on their necks. A little further away stood a menial, holding aloft an oil-torch; its flickering light revealed a multitude of cages around and, once straining eyes grew used to the gloom, the tigers imprisoned within. Some were leopards, others, panthers. A few were lying down but others paced to and fro, their eyes gleaming like burning coals in the feeble light.

"*Adiye*," Kundhavai grabbed hold of Vanathi's hands. "You're not frightened, are you? Don't faint away here, for heaven's sake!"

Her companion chuckled a little. "Why would I be scared of tigers, *Akka*? They're the guardians of our clan, aren't they?"

"The best of guards occasionally range themselves with our foes, my girl. What of the incredible danger that threatens us during those times?"

"I refuse to believe that, *Akka*. Human guardians might conspire against us—but these certainly won't."

"I'm not so sure. These wretched beasts have gobbled up plenty of royal traitors in their time; their blood ought to be coursing through the tigers' veins, after all. Who's to say that it wouldn't have scrambled their brains?"

Vanathi, who had declared her fearlessness just a moment ago, could not help but shiver just a little. "But—what's this that you say, *Akka*? Surely—surely they don't feed men alive to these creatures?"

"They don't. But I've mentioned, haven't I, that the dungeons are situated beneath this very stronghold? Well, there's only one way in and out of that wretched place, and that's through this very *mandapam*. Anyone daring to make an escape would have to enter this room—and then, they'd become the tigers' next, fulfilling meal!"

"Siva Siva—how horrible!"

"I'm afraid that's the way of government, Vanathi; compassion and cruelty go hand in hand. Why, I wouldn't be surprised if they managed to clap me into this very prison, some day. If you'd only heard the way Chinna Pazhuvettarayar spoke to me this afternoon—"

"Well, of all the—! No one in all fourteen worlds of the universe has the power to incarcerate you—and if they did, wouldn't the earth simply open up and swallow the whole of Thanjai? No, what worries me most, *Akka*, is the fate of our physician's son. That poor innocent wouldn't have tried to make an escape, would he?"

"A poor innocent indeed—but who may predict the quicksilver changes of a heart, my dear?"

The tigers' collective growls seemed to reach a higher note.

"They seem to be in quite a fury, don't they?" Kundhavai enquired of a guard.

"Not at all, Devi; merely expressing their delight at having had an opportunity to welcome the Chakravarthy's beloved daughter," came his adroit reply.

"And a wonderful welcome it is."

"Their meal time approaches, besides; they roar at the thought of prey."

"Time for us to leave, then. Where's the entrance to the prison?"

By this time, they had reached a corner of the *mandapam*; the guards moved a few of the tiger-cages positioned at a certain spot. A trap-door was seen to be embedded into the floor; two men bent and opened this promptly. A few steps were visible underneath and everyone went down gingerly, having a care for the deepening gloom. The guards' oil-torches shed a flickering light, made hazier by the lingering smoke; their passage had to be in a careful single file, a precarious walk along a narrow passage that seemed to meander.

If the growls of tigers above-stairs had been terrifying, the moans, groans and sorrowful cries of human prisoners below were enough to make anyone's heart shudder with a mixture of pity and terror.

And yet, amidst all this hopelessness—wonder of wonders!—a golden voice rose in song:

"Ponnaar meniyane!
Pulitholai araikkasaithu
Minnaar senjadai mel
Milirkondrai aninthavane!"

None of the so-called cells in the dungeon had been laid out in an orderly fashion; some thrust forward and others, pushed back. The guard paused in front of each and held his torch aloft; some contained only one prisoner, while a group of men were squashed into others. A few had been bound, with sturdy chains, to large iron rings buried in the walls, while other cells saw the prisoners allowed relatively more freedom. Kundhavai peered into each one and the moment she ascertained the identity of the occupant, the cavalcade moved on.

"What a torturous fate," Vanathi lamented, once, as they passed room after dingy room. "Why must all these people be shut up in these horrible dungeons? Isn't there such a thing as a court or a trial?"

"Such things certainly are part of the process for ordinary crimes," Kundhavai explained. "But these cases are different: those who conspire against king and country, foreign spies and the men who have aided them are the ones thrown here. They might be released, perhaps, if pertinent information has been extracted—but this doesn't work all the time, nor with everyone. They might not have anything to reveal ... and the fate of those, I must admit, is wretched indeed."

They had been walking steadily all this time; the hymn *Ponnaar Meniyane* was beginning to sound closer by the moment. A cell was soon approached and in the light of the torch held aloft could be seen a youngster barely out of boyhood. Someone already known to us: Sendhan Amudhan, of course.

His youthful face and the sheer innocence in his bright eyes, shorn of worldly guile, captivated the princesses, who peered at him with considerable interest.

"Were you the one singing, just now?" Kundhavai enquired.

"Yes, *Thaaye.*"

"You seem to be in excellent spirits."

"There's no need for me to be otherwise, *Amma*. God, in his munificence, is everywhere—even this prison."

"Upon my word—these seem to be the words of no less than a great saint! Pray, who are you? And what were you, in the world outside?"

"I'm neither a great saint nor a lesser one, *Amma*. I performed the task of delivering flower garlands to the lord, a great many *poomalais*. Here, though, I've had the good fortune of dedicating a garland of songs—a *paamalai!*"

"Not just a saint, I see, but a poet as well. Is it only this song that you know—or are there others?"

"I'm aware of a few more, but I've been singing this one ever since I arrived."

"Have you? Why?"

"I was brought here through the *Thanga Saalai*, *Amma*, and my eye was caught by newly minted, dazzling gold coins. Naturally, my heart bethought itself of *Ponnar Meniyan*—Siva Peruman himself, He Who Glows like Gold—"

"You are singularly fortunate: many would feel a multitude of desires at the very sight; you, however, are reminded of the lord's divine features … but tell me, do you have no relations? What about your family, my boy?"

"Only my mother, who lives by the lotus pond, just outside the Thanjai fort."

"Her name?"

"Vani Ammai."

"I shall visit that good woman and tell her of your enthusiastic residence, here."

"I'm afraid that would serve no purpose, *Amma*. My mother cannot hear; neither can she speak."

"Wait—is your name Sendhan Amudhan?" Kundhavai's voice was filled with astonishment.

"Indeed, Devi ... but I can't conceive of how you know—"

"What crime has led to your incarceration?"

"I had no clue as to my misdemeanor until yesterday, *Ammani*—but today, I've had some inkling of it."

"Have you, now?"

"I believe I've been accused of aiding and abetting a spy—and that's the reason for my imprisonment. Or so I've learnt."

"Why, which spy benefited from your assistance?"

"I happened to meet a stranger at the entrance to Thanjai fort, one evening. He asked me room for the night, upon which I took him home. It never occurred to me, though, that he might have been a spy—"

"What name did he give you?"

"Vallavarayan Vandhiyathevan, He informed me, besides, that he belonged to the ancient Vaanar clan ..."

Kundhavai and Vanathi traded glances; their meaningful looks seemed a mirror to their hearts, engaged in silent but sapient communication.

The Kodumbalur princess turned her gaze towards Sendhan Amudhan. "Tell us everything, *Appa*."

The young man obliged, nothing loath. Everything came pouring out, from meeting Vandhiyathevan at the fortress gates to being caught by Pazhuvoor men on the banks of the river.

"To think of you going to all that trouble for the sake of someone you barely knew—why did you?" asked Vanathi.

"Some people evoke a strange response in us, *Thaaye*—we like them on sight; to give our lives for their cause seems perfectly reasonable. As for the whys and wherefores—what can I say, except that there seems to be no earthly basis for such a feeling? Some people, on the other hand, make us want to club them over the head until they're dead! Today, they shut up a man in my cell for a while—and I'd be hard put to describe my anger at him. Thankfully, I wasn't made to suffer his company for long; the Pazhuvoor Ilaiya Rani's men released him—"

"Did they, now?" Kundhavai's pearly teeth bit into her coral lips. Her brows drew together in a scowl; fury made her breathing erratic. "And— who was it, taken away with such unseemly haste? Do you know?"

"Why ever not? The Pazhaiyarai Vaidhyar's son, or so I heard."

"And what were the horrors to which he subjected you—that made you want to clobber him, as you so emphatically put it?"

"My uncle's daughter—my cousin Poonguzhali—resides in Kodikkarai, and this man had the audacity to speak of her in such terms that—suffice it to say that I could not bear the slurs he cast on her; they made me furious. And yet, he did impart a piece of good news—and that proved enough to ensure his safety at my hands."

"Extraordinarily heartwarming news it must have been, too. What was it?"

"He seemingly accompanied Vandhiyathevan to Kodikkarai, and it was this scoundrel who managed to betray my friend, trying to get him into the clutches of the Pazhuvoor men. Not that he managed it—"

"He didn't?" The voices of Vanathi and Kundhavai blended in astonished delight. "In other words, the spy escaped, did he?" Wasn't this why they'd gone to all the trouble of descending into the dungeons—to discover this information?

"Indeed, *Ammani*. My friend escaped; Poonguzhali ferried him to Ilankai in the dead of the night. Those in pursuit—including this wretched rogue—were doomed to disappointment!"

The princesses stared at each other, eyes brimming with the exhilaration that threatened to overwhelm them.

"Your happiness at this spy's escape does seem to be a little excessive, *Appane*," Kundhavai gazed at Sendhan Amudhan. "It seems to me that you deserve to stay in prison!"

"If that were so, *Thaaye*, then the two of you ought to be thrown into the adjacent cell," quipped the young man.

The ladies gurgled in amusement; the sound of their merry peals of laughter seemed to echo off the dungeon's gloomy walls, almost as alien to the damp and darkness as Sendhan Amudhan's divine hymns.

"You're certainly someone to be reckoned with," Kundhavai said, finally. "A bad, wicked boy; at this rate, you'll turn everyone into rogues with your sweet voice and heavenly songs. I see that I have no choice but to postpone my immediate duties and petition the Fort's Guardian for your release."

"Pray, *pray* do not do so, *Thaaye*—there's a man in the cell next to mine, who's been pestering me a hundred times each day, to teach him a song. *If you do, I shall impart to you the secret location of the ancient Pandiyan crown and necklace, in Ilankai!* He swears, and I must beg of you to leave me here," declared Sendhan Amudhan. "That I may learn his precious secret!"

"That you may rot here—or until you go as insane as your dungeon-mate, I suppose? What of your beloved mother, Vani Ammai, then?"

Kundhavai Piratti left soon after, along with her entourage.

Within the space of half a *naazhigai*, a few soldiers arrived at Sendhan Amudhan's cell, released him from prison and escorted him to the gates of Thanjai—towards freedom.

༄

23

NANDHINI'S NIRUPAM

That evening saw Nandhini seated on her elegant *hamsa thulika* couch in the *latha mandapam*, writing a *nirupam*, an epistle.

Her slender body quivered as a fragile vine in the breeze sometimes, as she penned the words. Huge, heaving sighs escaped her. The day was almost done; a not unpleasant chill pervaded the area—and yet, despite a devoted maid fanning her mistress with peacock feathers, Nandhini's forehead, smooth and gleaming as marble, was dotted with beads of perspiration.

Her missive was as follows:

"Great Prince! Having gathered every scrap of courage, I yet write this with enormous hesitation and dare I say it—fear. Of late, news of every kind about the state of the kingdom has fallen on my ears. You, I regret to say, would seem not have given these the slightest notice; neither have you deigned to visit Thanjai, despite repeated requests from your poor, bedridden father. Sometimes, my tortured imagination wonders if I am the reason for

your absence. Should I but meet you once, all my doubts would be at an end. Would your gracious highness condescend to grant me this wish? If the prospect of visiting Thanjai displeases you, an alternate meeting-place could be arranged with all convenience at the Kadambur palace. I am, after all, in the position of your grandmother now; pray, what objection can there be, to our meeting and conversing with each other? The bearer of this missive, the valiant son of Sambuvaraiyar, is worthy of our trust; you may send any reply you choose, through him."

A tormented soul wedded to misfortune,

Abhagyavathi Nandhini.

In truth, the Pazhuvoor Ilaiya Rani had expended a great deal of thought over this effusion, hesitating over practically every word. Once done, she raised her head to glance at the maid, still fanning her. "Find the young prince of Kadambur and bring him here."

The maid duly carried out the command and once Kandamaaran arrived, retired to a respectable distance.

Sambuvaraiyar's son could barely meet Nandhini's eyes; he chose, instead, to glance at the garden beyond the *mandapam*, almost shuffling his feet.

"Pray be seated, *Ayya*." The faint quiver in Nandhini's voice brought his gaze to hers in a moment; he found himself scrutinizing her face keenly.

"I'm not surprised that eyes that have gazed upon Kundhavai Devi's fair countenance can barely stomach mine," Nandhini smiled a little.

The words fairly broke Kandamaaran's heart, while her quizzical smile turned him almost faint. "Not a thousand Kundhavais could match a single Nandhini Devi," he managed to stutter.

"Doubtless, you would soar to Devalokham itself and seize Indra's throne if she merely lifted a finger—but you won't even oblige my request to seat yourself. Is that it?"

Kandamaaran sat down instantly. "Should you so wish it, Devi," he declared, grandiloquently, "I shall ascend to the very Brammalokham and chop one of Brahma's heads for your edification!"

This very gratifying announcement did not quite seem to have the desired effect. Nandhini shivered, and looked away. "Brahma does, after all, have four heads, even after Siva Peruman's execution," she said, in a low voice. "Your deed would still leave him with enough to survive."

"Speak of anything, Devi, but Kundhavai; I must beg you not to sing her praises," Kandamaaran spat. "My blood fairly boils when I remember the way she empathized with Vandhiyathevan, that traitor to friendship—"

"Still, credit must be given where it's due—to you, I mean. Your fantastic tales scaled such heights that I was astounded," Nandhini's lush lips widened into a smile. "As for that splendid account of the furious combat between yourself and your friend—*well!* What a fertile imagination!"

Kandamaaran had the grace to blush crimson. "I had to find a way to explain our meeting, hadn't I?" he offered, at last. "That was the only one I could think of—and besides, it's true, isn't it, that he *did* stab me in the back?"

"Wouldn't it be of benefit, *Ayya*, if you were to recall everything that happened that night once more?" asked Nandhini.

"Do *you* doubt me as well, Devi?"

"Not at all—but it seems to me that a few aspects may have slipped your mind. Some day, Vandhiyathevan will be imprisoned and brought here to trial; your testimony must be strong enough to send him to prison, mustn't it?"

"I find that I'm not very keen on that, Devi. I should still wish to forgive him if he's arrested."

"Allow me to express my approval of your generosity, *Ayya*—still, I must beg of you to indulge my wishes and go over the events of that night exactly as they happened, so we can come to some conclusion between ourselves. Now—on your journey through the vault, you came across me and Periya Pazhuvettarayar. You remember that, I hope?"

"Certainly. I don't think I shall ever forget *that* meeting as long as there's life in this body."

"And do you remember what you said, on that occasion?"

"Not really. I do remember feeling stunned in your presence, but the exact words escape my memory—"

"Mine, however, remains intact. *Ayya, many are the tales I have heard about your daughter's bewitching beauty,* you said. *But now, I see that none of those accounts have done her justice ...*"

"*Ayyayo*—did I really—good God, I had no idea—I didn't really say that, did I? Was that why his face turned such a shade of red? He doesn't quite like me much, even now—"

Nandhini laughed gently. "That doesn't quite matter. *You* cherish some regard for him, don't you? That, I assure you, will do well enough."

"If I may confess the truth, Devi ... *I* don't quite like him either," Kandamaaran admitted in a rush. "There's no point in concealing that from you, I think."

"No matter. *I* like him, you see, and that will answer excellently." A sigh, filled with gratitude, escaped her. "Ah, how fortunate I am! I wonder what penances I performed in births past, to have wedded such a one as him?"

These words only served to confuse Kandamaaran a good deal; he stood silent, not quite knowing what to say.

"Be that as it may," Nandhini continued. "What did you do, once you'd left us?"

"The guard led the way, holding aloft the torch; I followed, my mind overwhelmed by your presence. We opened the secret entrance that led outside the fort. I stepped forward—when someone stabbed me in the back. That's all I remember. Vandhiyathevan must have known somehow that I would exit the fort at the precise point, and lain in wait for me outside."

"No, *Ayya*—I must tell you now, that your assumption is extremely erroneous."

"But Devi—what's this? Surely you haven't taken his part as well?"

"Why, pray? What am I to gain by doing so—for that matter, what does *he*? I do know, however, that here's how it must have happened."

"Tell me, then, Devi—do, please!"

"Vandhiyathevan wasn't waiting outside ..."

"No? Who else, then?"

"No one. I did say that Vandhiyathevan wasn't lying in wait *outside*, didn't I? He was waiting, *Ayya*, within the treasure vault!"

"What? But—how could that possibly be, Devi?"

"He did disappear completely, that evening, without a trace. Now, how could he have accomplished that? Think, now: somehow, he managed to stumble into the vault and learn all its secrets. Later, he followed you; once the door was opened, he struck you in the back and made his escape. Perhaps his conscience smote him later; he carried you to that mute woman's home, and fled ..."

"Indeed ... yes, of course! This is how it must have happened—Devi, I do believe you've hit upon the truth. Why did this never occur to me—for that matter, to others? If anyone should ask me to name the most intelligent person in the whole of Chozha Nadu, Devi, I would give yours, undoubtedly. There are those who are beautiful, and those quick of wit—but very rarely do beauty and brains blend in Brahma's creation; very few are blessed with both. You, Devi are one of those gifted beings!" Kandamaaran announced, voice bubbling with a mixture of respect and awe.

"Do these words come from your heart, *Ayya*—or are they just bland praises offered by men to women of their acquaintance; just *mukasthuthi*?"

"My words are as pure as my intentions, Devi; I speak nothing but the truth as I know it."

"In that case—will you trust me completely, *Ayya*? And do me a favour?"

"I shall do whatever is in my power to accomplish."

"You must journey to Kanchi for me."

"To Kasi even, should it so please you."

"Such a vast distance is unnecessary. I shall entrust you with an epistle, to be delivered to Prince Aditha Karikalar. Your mission shall also include extending him an invitation to the Kadambur Palace, as a guest—"

"But Devi, what's this that you say? Pray, you can't be unaware of the plans—the schemes set in motion regarding royal affairs by your husband, my father, and several other Chozha lords and chieftains—"

"Certainly not—in fact, I have in my possession a few other facts as well: did you know, *Ayya*, that your family, mine and several others, commanding the greatest respect, stand at the threshold of grave peril this very moment? And do you know the person responsible for such a state of affairs?"

"Pray, tell me, Devi."

"That conceited wretch who visited us this very afternoon."

"*Ayyayo*! Surely you can't—you can't mean Ilaiya Piratti?"

"Indeed I do. That poisonous snake—for only a snake can foresee the treacherous intentions of another; it takes a Nandhini to plumb the depths of Kundhavai's wicked schemes—sent your precious friend Vandhiyathevan to Ilankai. Not to gather herbs; that's the greatest lie ever to sully anyone's ears! That little witch couldn't care less about her father's health. No, as far as she's concerned, neither Madhuranthaka Thevar nor Aditha Karikalar must ascend the throne after him; it's her beloved younger brother Arulmozhi Varman who ought to rule this land—for she can play him like a puppet, and rule this empire in his stead! And then, Kundhavai will forever hold forth as the Empress of the Chozha *samrajyam*—and would you like to guess at the Emperor? Why, your friend Vandhiyathevan, of course!"

"Ah, is that so, indeed? This terrible fate must never be allowed to come to pass—it must be stopped—my father and the Pazhuvettarayar brothers, they must be informed at once —"

"That would serve no purpose, *Ayya*; they wouldn't lend the slightest credence to these theories. No, her devious schemes ought to be countered by tactics that would render her machinations powerless. And those can be evolved—with your help, if you would but offer it."

"I await your commands, Devi!"

"This *olai* must be delivered with the greatest of care, to Aditha Karikalar in Kanchi. Will you accept this commission?" And Nandhini handed over the palm-leaf, along with the accompanying cylinder.

Kandamaaran, consumed by a combination of lust and barely contained longing, ignored them and snatched at her hands. "Say the word, Devi," he stammered, huskily. "And I shall do anything—*anything* …"

Something reached their ears that very instant—a sort of frantic flapping.

Pazhuvettarayar was hastening down the passage that led from the palace to the *latha mandapam*. The maid, caught unawares at his unexpected arrival, shrank back, startled. A large, triangular bird-rest dangled from the ceiling, acting as a perch to a large parrot. Caught mid-stride and barely aware of what he was doing, Pazhuvettarayar snatched at the hapless creature; the fury that had taken over his mind spread to his hands, tightening around the bird which flapped its wings, trying ineffectually, to escape.

Creech! shrieked the parrot, unable to bear Pazhuvettarayar's cruel grip.

24

AS WAX IN FLAME

The bird's terrified screech, coupled with the maid's startled cry, almost made Nandhini and Kandamaaran jump out of their skins. Periya Pazhuvettarayar here! The Kadambur Prince's face blanched with sheer, unadulterated terror. And to think he'd just revealed his dislike of the *Dhanaadhikaari* to Nandhini!

He wondered if the old man could've possible overheard him. A moment later, something even more dreadful occurred to him: what if the *kizhavan* saw them conversing and—and assumed the worst? After all, everyone knew the peculiarities of men who married at a ripe old age—perhaps *that* was why he was hurtling towards them in such a flaming fury. *What's he going to do once he does get here, I wonder? Well, whatever happens, I shall just have to grin and bear it.*

All these and more thoughts crashed through Kandamaaran's mind within a matter of moments, wave upon frantic wave. And yet, that day provided him with an opportunity to witness something truly beyond the pale; something that he hadn't even imagined he might see in his wildest dreams—that went against every one of his imagined eventualities.

Nandhini's beautiful eyes widened; her luminous face brightened even more as Periya Pazhuvettarayar approached them swiftly. "*Nadha*, I was worried you might stay away too long," she purred, her dark eyes training themselves upon his face. "But you've come—ah, how pleased I am!"

Her sweet voice fell upon his ears; his eyes fell upon her exquisite face—and Periya Pazhuvettarayar's fury vanished as if it had never been. Before Kandamaaran's startled eyes, the old warrior melted as wax in a flame. "Well, yes, my task was done," with a ridiculous smile on his face. "And so, I—well, I returned home." Then, his gaze fell on the Kadambur prince. "What is this boy doing here at this hour? Plaguing you with asinine love poems, I suppose?" He tittered, pleased with his own attempt at humour.

Kandamaaran's face burned with embarrassment; Nandhini, however, seemed to enjoy her husband's witticism thoroughly. "I'm afraid he knows little about love and still less about lovesick poems," she laughed even louder than Periya Pazhuvettarayar, if possible. "All he does know is to fight and suffer wounds for his trouble. He's healed now, thankfully—in fact, he was speaking to me, just now, about leaving for home."

"Ah, boys these days! Words fail me when I try to praise their valour. Indeed, I received four and sixty war wounds from twenty-four battles in my day, but never once did I find the slightest need to seek my bed. This brave young man, now—it has taken him days to even rise from his! But then, it would not be fair to compare our respective wounds: mine were all borne on my chest, shoulder, face and head—but his was on his back, was it not?" Pazhuvettarayar's scornful laugh echoed around the *mandapam*. "It is only fair that he should take months to heal ..."

"*Ayya!*" Kandamaaran's fury was a sight to see; his voice throbbed with barely retrained anger. "You stand to me in the position of my father—which is the only reason for my forbearance—"

"Is it?" Pazhuvettarayar's hand flew to the sword at his waist. "Else what would you have done, boy? You little—"

"*Nadha*," Nandhini chose this moment to intervene. "Surely you must know that this young man's injuries are not just upon his body, but deep in his heart, as well? He has been wounded gravely, you must know, by the terrible betrayal of a man he considered his friend—such a dastardly act of stabbing him in the back, too! His physical wound may have healed, but the one sustained by his soft heart—that is grievous, indeed. Surely it's our bounden duty, my lord, to not exacerbate his pain—to prod a festering lesion with a sharp stick, so to speak? You do remember what transpired that night—the night this estimable young man was stabbed—don't you, my lord?"

Her exquisite eyes, glowing with fervour, must have held some obscure message—for Periya Pazhuvettarayar's demeanor underwent a lightning change.

"Oh—ah, yes. Of course, you are right; this youngster is innocent. His father—a very dear friend of mine—naturally, it would not do to take offence at his meaningless prattle. Be that as it may, Nandhini—my purpose in visiting you was to impart a vital piece of information; this boy may know as well, I suppose. The authorities have arrested someone suspected to be a spy, in Ilankai's Maathottam. An *olai* meant for Prince Arulmozhi Varman was found on his person; from his description, I suspect him to be Kandamaaran's precious friend. A slippery eel, that rogue," commented Pazhuvettarayar. "He managed to give our own men the slip, didn't he?"

Neither man noticed the swift change of expression upon Nandhini's countenance.

"*Ada*, he's escaped, has he?" Kandamaaran exclaimed, voice dripping with dismay. "To Ilankai, you say?"

"Frankly, *Nadha*, I can't say I'm surprised," Nandhini chimed in. "If I've said it once I've said it a hundred times that your brother is supremely unfit to bear the guardianship of this fort. What of his pathetic men, then?"

"I must confess, I did not lend credence to that fact before, but now—I begin to think you may be right, after all. Here is another choice bit of information, too: apparently, a Pazhuvoor signet-ring has been recovered from this mysterious spy in Maathottam; as to how he came by it, he refused to reveal, even upon interrogation—"

A slight, small sigh escaped Nandhini. "How very strange, to be sure. Pray, how on earth did *he* end up with a palm-tree insignia? Does your beloved brother volunteer any explanation that might shed some light on this very peculiar state of affairs?"

"Him!" Periya Pazhuvettarayar harrumphed his displeasure. "You would be hard put to contain your laughter, if you listened to his ridiculous explanations! That wretched signet-ring, Kalanthakan says, could not have been given by anyone but—you!" And he exploded into hearty peals of thunderous laughter that seemed about to bring the roof of the *mandapam* upon their collective heads, while leaves on the trees outside trembled and quivered with apprehension.

"My brother-in-law, the jester," Nandhini joined in her husband's laughter. "There's no one to equal his wits in all fourteen worlds of this universe!"

"Listen to a few more of your brother-in-law's hilarious conclusions— why, I cannot contain my amusement at his choice tales, culled from his vastly colourful imagination. That trickster, that Indrajithan ran into you while you were journeying towards Thanjai in your palanquin, Kalanthakan deduces; he met you once more within this very palace, that magician. And therefore, he concludes in vastly logical fashion, that *you* must have been the one to give him the ring! And if yours had not been the hand that delivered it directly, it must have reached him through the *mandhiravadi* who visits you in secret often!" Pazhuvettarayar fairly shook with mirth, all his very impressive teeth gleaming in the light. "Ah, my sides ache at the wonderful tales he spins, trying in vain to smother his own stupidity—!"

"My mistake, to assume the existence of my brother-in-law's wits; there's as much sense in his head as plants on a pestle! And yet ..." Nandhini's expression changed in an instant. "I cannot but wonder, *Nadha*, at your silence at his outrageous claims—" Where, just a few moments ago had danced a smile, now rose flames of fury; fine eyes fairly glowed with sparks of sheer wrath.

That warrior among warriors, lion in the battlefield, the general who had faced the most fearsome opponents; withstood spears and swords, often bearing them upon his bare body without a flinch—faltered at the slightest signs of Nandhini's displeasure. Periya Pazhuvettarayar's defenses crumbled; his features and his very demeanour seemed to experience a strange weakness. "Of course not—surely you do not think I would simply listen to his accusations without a murmur—why, I tore into the hapless idiot and left him practically sobbing—had you seen him, Nandhini, you might have pitied him yourself—"

Kandamaaran, mute witness to these admittedly intimate arguments, squirmed in considerable embarrassment. Something very like fear snaked around his heart at the very thought of Nandhini, while markedly different feelings arose at Pazhuvettarayar's plight: pity and loathing. Nevertheless, he had no business in a quagmire of this couple's making, and wished to leave as soon as he could. "*Ayya*," he cleared his throat with some discomfort.

"My brother-in-law's iniquities seem to have made us forget our guest," Nandhini interceded smoothly. "He may leave for home just as he wishes, mightn't he, my lord?"

"Why, certainly, certainly. I daresay his father might be worried out of his mind, considering his lengthy absence."

"I am, in addition, entrusting him with an *olai*. I have your permission to do so, I hope?"

"A palm-leaf? To whom?"

"The prince in Kanchi."

"Him? To receive …" Periya Pazhuvettarayar's eyes flitted from Nandhini to Kandamaaran, clouding with suspicion. "An *olai* from you? Why?"

"If Ilaiya Piratti can send a palm-leaf to her precious younger brother through our guest's friend, why mustn't the Pazhuvoor Ilaiya Rani send one to the elder? And charge this young man with its delivery, besides?"

"The *olai* in the possession of this boy's friend—that was written by Ilaiya Piratti, you say?" Pazhuvettarayar's surprise was evident. "How did you manage to discover this?"

"Pray, why else would I need the services of a magician? For that was how I gleaned this bit of information, you know—with his magic spells. You've seen my brother-in-law's ridiculous men and their supreme inability to perform even the smallest tasks: those who managed to find out about the signet-ring in his possession couldn't tell you that the *olai* he held was in fact, entrusted to him by Kundhavai, could they?"

"To tell the truth, they were not the ones who brought me this piece of news; I managed to wring it from Anbil Aniruddha Brahmaraayar, just returned from Rameswaram …"

"And did *that* Brahmin at least inform you of Kundhavai's commission?"

"No."

"Pray recall my words of warning to you, *Nadha*. Have I not always maintained that everyone in this *samrajyam* plots to deceive you? You believe me now, I hope? The *mandhiravadi*'s claims alone weren't enough to satisfy me; I made sure to have the physician's son, imprisoned in Kodikkarai, brought to me as well, and subjected him to an interrogation. He confirmed what I'd heard—that it was indeed Ilaiya Piratti who had sent her *thambi* an *olai* …"

Periya Pazhuvettarayar felt all at sea, to the truth; blindfolded and let loose in a dark forest, into the bargain. He cast a glance of dislike at Kandamaaran, standing nearby; was it really necessary to carry on a conversation of this nature in that wretched boy's presence?

"Our story can wait, however," Nandhini changed tack suddenly, aware of the shift in her husband's mood and reading his thoughts to a nicety. "There's no need for our guest to tarry any longer." She turned to Kandamaaran. "This *olai* has to be delivered into the hands of the prince at Kanchi, *Ayya*. Should he honour it with a reply, kindly receive and relay it to me with the greatest care. And you won't forget to issue him an invitation to Kadambur, will you?"

"What of my father, Devi?" Kandamaaran asked, with some hesitation. "I may tell him that this commission carries the Pazhuvoor lord's approval, mayn't I?"

"Do, by all means," assured Nandhini. "The Pazhuvoor lord's sentiments match mine at all times. Don't they, *Nadha*?"

"Yes—yes, of course," stammered Pazhuvettarayar, nodding obediently. None of this made any sense to him; his senses reeled—and yet, he could not seem to gainsay Nandhini the slightest, either.

Once Kandamaaran had made his thankful way out of the chambers, Nandhini turned to her husband. Her exquisite eyes locked themselves upon his, enveloping him in her magnetic gaze. "Your faith in me appears to have suffered a blow, *Nadha*," her voice, touched with something of the lilting tones of a parrot, caressed him. "My brother-in-law's devious words would seem to have had their effect ..."

"Never, Nandhini—not in the slightest!" The old man announced. "The spear in my hands or the sword at my waist may betray me, perhaps—but you, never. My heart may not believe in the paradise of warriors, but your words shall never evoke anything but trust!"

"If that were indeed the truth, why subject me to the indignity of searching questions in that boy's presence?" Nandhini's eyes brimmed with tears that began to course down her cheeks. "The humiliation of it—!"

Her sobs shook Pazhuvettarayar to the depths of his soul. "My heart—my dearest!" He hastened to wipe her tears, stricken beyond belief. "Pray, do not punish me thus …!" Nevertheless, it took him a while and all his considerable effort, before consolation had any effect. "And yet, my heart," he ventured later, hesitantly. "Some of your activities do not, I admit, make the slightest sense to me. Do I not have the right to know the whys and wherefores of all that you do, beloved one?"

"Yours is the right to ask what you will, just as mine is to answer—that, my lord, is not the bone of contention here. All I ask, *Ayya*, is that you don't interrogate me in front of strangers," explained Nandhini. "Now—you may demand of me what you please."

"Why must you send an *olai* to Aditha Karikalan? Why the need to extend an invitation to Kadambur palace?" Pazhuvettarayar demanded. "Surely you know that he is the first obstacle to our grand plans—our prime foe, in fact?"

"A mistaken assumption, my lord—our greatest enemy is that female snake from Pazhaiyarai; not the crown prince. Pray, why do you think I took such pains to draw her to our palace? The same reason for my inviting Aditha Karikalan to Kadambur, of course. I must beg of you to recall what I've mentioned often; haven't I always said that Ilaiya Piratti has evolved some sort of devious scheme? Well, I've managed to rout it out: she means to do away with every single contender to the throne, and ensure that her beloved younger brother Arulmozhi Varman inherits Thanjavur. That's the reason for her frantic *olai* to Ilankai, not to mention her presence in the capital at this moment. Her plots may be defeated only with far more powerful counter-plots; on no account must that conniving witch be allowed to get away with her conspiracy. *Now* you know the reason for my palm-leaf to Kanchi, I hope?" Nandhini directed a look at Periya Pazhuvettarayar that stole through his defenses, cleaved his very heart and befuddled his senses thoroughly.

"Yes—yes, of course," stammered the valiant old man. "I see it all, my dear!" Nothing was more obvious than the fact that he understood not a word.

"This ancient Chozha *samrajyam* stands tall today, spreading in all four directions, *Nadha*, resting upon your laurels and those of your great ancestors. I promise you, my lord, that this unfortunate creature shall not rest a moment, night or day, until I see you ascend the golden throne of Thanjavur for at least a day!" Nandhini proclaimed, her voice throbbing with emotion. "Until then—should my actions ever rouse the slightest particle of doubt, kindly end my life with a single blow of your trusty sword!"

"My heart's dearest," burst out Periya Pazhuvettarayar. "Pray, *pray* do not torment me with these cruel words!"

25

MAGNIFICENT MAATHOTTAM

It has been aeons since we last saw our friend Vandhiyathevan; we have tarried in Thanjai far too long. Only a few days, to be very exact, but it seems a very long time, indeed.

Within this short period, however, Vallavarayan had managed to travel along the Ilankai coastline and reach the city of Maathottam, situated on the banks of the Paalaavi River, beyond the seas of Rameswaram. A vastly pleasing sight it presented too, surrounded by lush greenery and pleasant orchards, cool and soothing to the eye, just as it doubtless had been during the times of Thirugnana Sambandar and Sundaramurthy Nayanar. Mangoes and jackfruit; coconuts and *kamugu*; plantains and sugarcanes grew in profusion along the shores; monkeys swung gleefully from branches; bees hummed, their song a soothing buzz; parrots spoke in shrill tones, their lilting words caressing the ears.

The sea sent waves battering against the fort-walls of the city, crashing and thundering around the manmade barrier.

All sorts of vessels thronged the port of Maathottam, from large ships to miniscule crafts, nestling cheek by jowl; produce freshly transported from them to the shore lay heaped in huge mounds, like small mountains.

These and more presented a tableau that seemed to be much the same as in the times of Naayanmars—barring a few differences. The crowds of devotees usually surging towards the Kedheeswara Temple seemed to have thinned considerably; soldiers dotted areas that once teemed with devout *bhakthars*, singing the praises of God, lost in divine bliss. Warriors marched here and there, armed to the teeth with swords, shields, spears and daggers.

The last hundred years had seen the city transform, slowly, into a *yuddha kendhram*, a war centre. Armies that landed in Eezham from Thamizhagam usually did so here; those that left the island chose this city as well, for departure. Maathottam had changed hands several times, patronized at periods by the kings of Ilankai, and the Pandiya kings at others. Ever since the reign of Emperor Paranthakar, though, it had come under the control of the Chozhas.

It was at the entrance of such a war-obsessed city's fortress that Vandhiyathevan found himself, one day. He announced his wish to enter Maathottam, and to seek an audience with the Chozha commander. Upon the sentries' categorical refusal to admit him, he decided that he would make use of the same tactic that had once come to his aid in Kadambur: he rushed at the guards, almost milling them down, trying to get through the gates with main force. Such behaviour could not be borne of course; he was arrested in an instant and brought to the fort's chief of security. Vandhiyathevan vouchsafed the information that he bore an *olai* meant for Arulmozhi Varman, the details of which he could reveal to no one but the Chozha commander himself. He was searched summarily, upon which an *olai* addressed to Ponniyin Selvan was discovered upon his person—along with the Pazhuvoor signet-ring.

The commander of the Chozha forces stationed in Ilankai at that time happened to be Kodumbalur Periya Velaar, Boodhi Vikrama Kesari, who was closeted with Aniruddha Brahmaraayar when news of the arrest was delivered. There was little he could do at that moment, preparing as he was, to embark on a journey to Rameswaram in the minister's company; his men were instructed to keep the young man under guard, that he might be interrogated upon Periya Velaar's return.

Vandhiyathevan was escorted to a ruined mansion, thrown into a room and locked in. Sentries took their place at his door.

This turn of events did not dismay our hero unduly, to tell the truth. The long journey had exhausted him; his arrest was, he exulted, a blessing in disguise. Surely he could snatch a day or two of well-deserved rest, relieved of traveling at breakneck speed?

His expectations were fulfilled on the first day—but the second day afforded no such respite.

The adjacent room began to resound with mysterious sounds and shrieks. Someone began to berate another; his blistering reproaches and bombastic, high-flying speeches were worthy of a better audience. "Here—*chee*! *Chee*—! Get away! Don't come near me—take a step and I'll kill you!—careful, your life isn't your own—I shall send you to Yamalokham—one kick and you're dead!"

The yells and threats went on a good while; the identity of the recipient of his wrathful speeches as yet unclear. All that could be heard was one voice; none was raised in reply. Could it be a deranged soldier, perhaps? In that case, Vandhiyathevan may as well bid goodbye to all hopes of a peaceful night; these roars would put paid to even the briefest snatches of rest—hah, how unfortunate!

"You won't listen to reason, will you?—You won't?—Very well, then, beware—you won't like what I'm about to do!"

The next instant, something landed in Vandhiyathevan's room with a thump; the young man jumped up, startled out of his wits. He peered at the new arrival, a little shaken—and laughter bubbled up almost despite himself. His unexpected guest, who had been precipitated into the room in such an uncouth fashion, turned out to be none other than—a cat.

"Ha, you've even learnt to laugh at me, have you? Go ahead, then!"

came the voice from the other room. "But don't you *dare* come in here—do you hear?"

A lunatic, no doubt: why else would he argue with a measly cat? Or even assume that it would be capable of laughter? And yet—for all his amused puzzlement, something niggled in the back of Vandhiyathevan's mind. That voice—it seemed very familiar, as though he had known and heard it often—but where? And whose was it? He cudgeled his mind for an answer but drew a blank.

He gave it up after a while: what did it matter, after all? Who cared about the occupant of the next room? He lay down once more and tried to gather the wisps of sleep, flitting away. In vain, for he could not reclaim his slumber, but soon enough, another problem arose: something soft brushed against his soles. He opened his eyes—to the cat. Good God, how was he to even close his eyes with this dratted feline rubbing against his feet? He aimed a kick at it and the cat sheered away. Vandhiyathevan tried to sleep once more, only to feel something brush against his arm. He opened his eyes—to find the wretched animal snuggling to him, a lovesick expression on its scraggy face.

He pushed it away again; it shrank back; he closed his eyes. This time it crept around to his head and made itself comfortable, swishing its bushy tail across his forehead.

Vandhiyathevan was a consummate warrior, having faced swords and spears with indomitable courage but a cat, twitching its tail against him was more than he could bear. He rose, picked up the animal by the scruff of its puny neck and walked to the wall that divided his room from the next. The top part had crumbled away a little; he threw the cat through the opening with all his strength.

And then, a commotion the likes of which he hadn't heard so far broke out in the next room. Human shouts blended with feline shrieks and screeches to produce sheer cacophony. "Go—get lost!" screamed the voice again; the cat's pitiful yowls were heard for a while, fading away gradually. And then—silence.

Sleep stole over Vandhiyathevan once more—a half-sleep, it must be admitted, but one that seemed to come with its own perquisites: a wonderful dream where Ilaiya Piratti sat down by his side, and caressed his forehead. Ah, what a difference between that cat's scrubby tail and the princess's gentle, petal-soft fingers!

He awoke suddenly, awareness flooding in, and lamenting the loss of the marvelous dream.

Someone was tapping on the wall from the other side. That lunatic, no doubt.

"Who's there? Who threw the cat in here?"

Vandhiyathevan stayed silent. But wait—what was this scratching sound, like cat trying to—no, this was no feline attack; someone was trying to clamber over the wall on the other side.

He made no attempt to rise but lay still, listening to the variety of sounds; his hand, however, hovered over the hilt of his dagger, prepared to use it at the slightest excuse.

First to appear at the crumbled opening atop the wall were two hands. And then, a turban. A face followed, reaching the top and peering over the wall.

Ah—but this was Azhwarkkadiyaan, wasn't it? He looked a little different, owing, of course, to his head-cloth, but there was no doubt that it *was* the stout, squat Vaishnavite.

How did he get here, anyway? And what's he doing here? Perhaps he knew about my presence—but the question is: will he help? Or prove a hindrance?

"Well met, great devotee of Vishnu," announced Vandhiyathevan, sitting up. "The most magnificent Saivite *sthalam* of Kedheeswaram bids you welcome!"

"Is it you indeed, *Thambi*? I wondered if it might be—who else can sit in here, still as a statue, like an *amukkuppillaiyar*, scarce a sound escaping him?"

And Azhwarkkadiyaan jumped into the room, large as life and twice as natural.

26

A Bloodthirsty Dagger

The Veera Vaishnavite's presence in that room, not to mention his purpose, worried Vandhiyathevan considerably, but not by a flicker of eyes did he betray his unease.

"How wonderful this is, to be sure," he began, instead. "My thoughts wandered to you just moments ago—and here you are, jumping over walls into this room! That old saying about deities smashing through roofs to shower devotees with riches certainly is true."

"You were meditating upon my exalted person just now, were you, *Appane*? Why, pray? Why dwell upon this pitiful human being, when you could have paid your respects to the divine Lord Rama, which would at least have aided in your spiritual journey—"

"What a coincidence! You deserve a mouthful of sugar, as they say, for I *was* reminded of Ramabiraan at first—I could see the Rameswaram temple *gopuram* on the other side of the sea. After all, wasn't that the site of the lord's worship of Siva Peruman, washing away the terrible sin of Ravanan's murder—"

"Stay, *Thambi*, wait a—"

"I cannot, *Swami*, upon my word, I cannot; my legs ache with having stood and waited and stayed and the last thing I want to do is wait even more. Pray, take pity on me and seat yourself. Now, where was I? Ah, yes: my thoughts flew to Ramabiraan and by natural association, towards his most devout follower, Anumaar and whom should I think of, then? You, of course. And here you are, hard upon the heels of my wayward thoughts! Did you jump over just this wall—or emulate the monkey God and leap over the whole sea?"

"You do Anumaar grave injustice, *Thambi*, by daring to speak of us in the same breath. For He—ah, that great being arrived in Ilankai, vanquishing Akshaya Kumaran and a great many other demons while I, well, I couldn't even get a *cat* to obey me. Just look—my legs are black and blue, courtesy that wretched feline!" And Azhwarkkadiyaan displayed limbs that were indeed, considerably scratched.

"*Adada*, my condolences. On the other hand—why brangle with a cat, of all creatures?"

"Mine was not the fault—it was all that spitfire's, bad-mannered wretch!"

"How's that, *Swami*?"

"I came here in search of you; I gave the guards the slip, clambered over the courtyard wall, jumped in—and where should this cat swish its tail but right where I should happen to land? All my foot did was to brush against it ever so slightly but that blasted creature flew at my legs and scratched them bloody with its sharp little claws. Take this from me, *Thambi*, a valuable lesson: you can brawl all you want with a tiger, but never accost a cat—"

"I've managed to learn the secret now, I think."

"You have? Which one?"

"That pitiful creature came in here, caressed my forehead with its tail, snuggled up to me and behaved, altogether, with the utmost affection. At no time did it ever scratch me—but it provided *you* with this preferential treatment! Why was that, do you think? Because, my dear Nambi, it happened to be a Veera Saivite cat, harbouring a deadly hatred for Vaishnavites—!"

"Ah—oh! Now, why didn't this explanation ever occur to me? If only I'd had the slightest suspicion—I'd have engaged in holy battle and thrashed it—"

"The good Gods be praised, then, that you don't have your precious staff with you now—for I don't mind telling you that I've been experiencing something strange, myself; I feel the blood of Veera Saivites coursing, red-hot, through my veins; my dagger, secure in its scabbard, screams for a taste for Veera Vaishnavite blood! I've managed to stifle its cries, though, in kind consideration of the great assistance you've rendered ..."

"I'm afraid I don't recall any such aid, *Appane*."

"You did speak to me about your sister, the Pazhuvoor Ilaiya Rani, didn't you?"

"I did."

"And didn't you show her to me even as her palanquin passed us, on the way to Kadambur?"

"Indeed, yes—what of it?"

"Patience, Nambi. I glimpsed that very same equipage on my way to Thanjai; the bearers almost ran into my horse on purpose. I went over at once to demand an explanation—"

"And the occupant?"

"Who else but the young queen of Pazhuvoor, Nandhini Devi?"

"Fortune truly does favour you; I tried my very hardest to seek an audience with her but couldn't—and yet, you did so with the utmost of ease!"

"Isn't that the way of luck, always?"

"Fair enough. What next?"

"I mentioned your name and that I was the bearer of a most important message—"

"I've seen plenty in my time, my boy, but never anyone such as you, able to trot out a humongous parcel of lies without a hint of shame—"

"My ancestors had a great predilection for bards, Nambi; they were experts in penning verse, themselves."

"What does that have to do with anything?"

"The blood of generations of poets courses through my veins; my imagination runs riot at times. Ignoramuses such as you, though, dare to label my effusions as lies—"

"Oh, *go on*. What else?"

"Nandhini Devi, however, has excellent taste; she appreciated my creative genius and handed over the Pazhuvoor signet-ring, not to mention an invitation to the palace—"

"Did you make use of it?"

"*Wouldn't* I? I did so at once and the Ilaiya Rani, considerably impressed by my own account of my incredible bravery, offered a commission."

"And that would be …?"

"The Pandiya dynasty's crown and Indra's valuable necklace are hidden somewhere in this island's hill country, courtesy Ilankai's royals. *Find them somehow and bring them to me*, she commanded. Never in my wildest dreams did I ever imagine that that might prove an almost impossible task …"

"There are tales that the treasure stashed in Periya Pazhuvettarayar's vault amounts to more than a thousand donkey-loads; all those gold ornaments aren't enough to satisfy her, I suppose. Well—what did she promise you, in return?"

"Chinna Pazhuvettarayar's exalted position would be seized from him and given to me."

"In that case—*Thambi*, my boy, you'd allow me unlimited access into the fort wouldn't you?"

"Well, of all the—! How on earth can I ever become Thanjai's Chief of Security if I'm stuck in this prison?" Vandhiyathevan's voice dripped with a perfect blend of sorrow and dismay.

"Well, why are you?" Azhwarkkadiyaan demanded. "Stuck here, I mean. Do you even *know* the reason for your imprisonment?"

"I brought the Pazhuvoor queen's signet-ring with me, hoping that it might possess the same power it had in Thanjai and, well—I realized my mistake soon enough."

"As well you might! Kodumbalur Periya Velaar is the Senathipathi here, isn't he? Really, *Thambi*—don't you know of the eternal hostility between the Pazhuvoor and Kodumbalur clans?"

"My incarceration was the result of my ignorance, I shall admit. I've no idea what to do ..."

"Well, you needn't worry—"

"No?"

"—for I'm here to facilitate your release."

"Oh."

"If you'll remember, I asked you once for aid and you refused. Still, *Thambi*, I'm here now, to help you out. Come with me, and we shall make our escape at once."

"You'd better leave right away, Nambi."

"Why, *Appane*?"

"My dagger has begun to weep in earnest. *Blood*, it shrieks, *Oh, for a drop of a Vaishnavite's blood!*"

"Your wailing dagger is welcome to some, if that's what will silence it. After all, I've enough without having to worry about the loss of a few drops. Come on, now."

"I regret that I must refuse."

"Your reason?"

"My eyes are practically closing of their own accord with exhaustion. It's been days since I slept the night through, and I've decided to take advantage of what room I have, at the moment. Why else do you think I even flung that wretched cat away?"

"Why, what's this, *Thambi*? So this is how you carry out Kundhavai Piratti's commission, is it? What about all your wonderful promises to her—that you wouldn't rest a moment; that you'd travel day and night until you manage to deliver this *olai* into the hands of Ponniyin Selvan himself?" And Azhwarkkadiyaan slipped a palm-leaf out of his waistband, handing it out to the young man.

Vandhiyathevan received it with alacrity, relieved almost despite himself about the Vaishnavite's intentions. He'd suspected Azhwarkkadiyaan of trying to wheedle secrets out of him; that didn't seem to be the case, though.

"How did you come by this?" he asked.

"By means of Kodumbalur Boodhi Vikrama Kesari, who, incidentally, also returned this signet-ring," Nambi handed over the Pazhuvoor insignia. "He's granted you release, by the way: you're free to continue your journey when you please."

"My thanks to you, Nambi."

"Save these expressions of gratitude; some day, you may find a way to repay my services in full."

"You wouldn't happen to know the prince's location, would you, *Ayya*?"

"No one is privy to that sort of information; all I know is that he's traveled from the hill country to Anuradhapuram. As to *where* exactly he is—that's something we'll have to find out." Azhwarkkadiyaan cleared his throat. "The Senathipathi has bid me act as your guide on the journey. I should like to accompany you—if I may."

A small seed of suspicion sprouted once again, in Vandhiyathevan's mind. "I should like to seek an audience with the Senathipathi before I leave," he ventured, finally. "May I, *Swami?*"

"By all means; in fact, you certainly ought to," Azhwarkkadiyaan answered promptly. "It wouldn't be appropriate to leave without delivering a report on Vanathi Devi, would it?"

Vandhiyathevan stared at the Veera Vaishnavite, wondering if Azhwarkkadiyaan did, indeed, possess magic tricks at his finger tips.

27

THROUGH THE JUNGLE

Kodumbalur Periya Velaar Boodhi Vikrama Kesari occupied the post of the Commander of Chozha forces; a man advanced in years and with the distinction of having trained in one of the harshest schools known to mankind: the battlefield. Many were the conflicts the veteran had engaged in and emerged from—not to mention dispatching enemies to a warrior's heaven. In addition to all these excellent qualifications, his was an ancient clan; one that claimed kinship and intimate friendship with the Chozhas.

It had only been a few years since his brother Siriya Velaar embraced death and his armies likewise a wholesale defeat, on the battlegrounds of Ilankai. It was not to be wondered at, then, that the present Senathipathi strove tooth and nail to wipe the stain of ignoble defeat, re-establish the valour of the Kodumbalur clan and by extension, that of his own brother. Thus his presence in war-torn Eezham, coordinating Chozha forces despite his considerable age.

A while ago, we saw the enormous difficulties in waging war smoothly due to the Pazhuvettarayars' interference, didn't we? What had once just been rivalry between two clans had now mushroomed into something very like bitter hatred, courtesy these tactics. By rights, the discovery of the Pazhuvoor signet-ring upon his person ought to have landed Vandhiyathevan in hot water—had not the Velaar touched upon this very topic with Aniruddha Brahmaraayar. This proved to be a stroke of luck: the Chozha *Mudhanmandhiri*, who had learnt the truth about the young man from Azhwarkkadiyaan, now urged his disciple to approach the Velaar himself and explain Vandhiyathevan and his presence in Ilankai.

Whatever his prejudice, Senathipathi Boodhi Vikrama Kesari, looking the valiant Vaanar warrior up and down, must have formed a favourable opinion. "Were you treated right, *Thambi*?" he enquired, his voice warm with friendliness. "You were lodged and fed well, I hope?"

"Indeed I was, Senathipathi," Vandhiyathevan replied promptly. "Nothing was denied me: I had five or six guards at my door, ready and willing to do my every bidding; I had a great deal of space at my disposal; I even had a cat sent for my night's meal—except that this Veera Vaishnavite had to jump in at that moment and ruin my appetite. And what must happen, *Ayya*, but for that wretched cat to turn out to be a staunch Saivite! It flew at this Thirumaal devotee, scratched him with its claws and made its escape—"

"Hah, this young man can certainly tell a tale," chuckled the commander. "Is this all true, Thirumalai?"

"He claims that his ancestors were poets and their blood courses through his veins, making his imagination run riot—or some such thing. Aside from that, he's right; a hissing feline did do me grievous injury," Azhwarkkadiyaan admitted.

Kodumbalur Periya Velaar practically split his sides, laughing at the bloody scratches liberally adorning the Vaishnavite's body. "To think that a cat was the cause of these marvelous war-wounds!" he crowed, rocking with mirth. "A good thing, then, that you have this warrior for protection on your journey through the jungle—"

"I don't need one, Senathipathi; my trusty staff is more than enough. It was a mistake, I admit, to have met this young man without it—"

"In that case, *you* may as well be his; make sure that he is fed well, before you start. Food is rather scarce these days in Ilankai, *Thambi*; Mahindan's marvelous forces have broken the banks of lakes and ponds hereabouts and farming has practically come to a standstill. Not that there are men available even if resources there be, in plenty. When the locals are starving, how would it be possible to feed our armies? It isn't as though the necessary grains and rice are sent from our homeland, either …"

"I'm not exactly ignorant of these circumstances, Senathipathi; I witnessed the women of Pazhaiyarai's valorous Padai Veedu settlements petitioning Ilaiya Piratti about the same issues: *We hear that our men are starving, in Ilankai—*"

"Oh, did they? Very well; what was her reply, pray?"

"*You have no cause for worry*, the princess assured them. *As long as Periya Velaar is the Senathipathi in Ilankai, there shall be no question of our warriors starving—*"

"Ah, did she, now? A good many dynasties in the world boast of great women among their ranks, but I tell you: there is none who can match our Ilaiya Piratti—"

"Beg pardon, Senathipathi, but there *is* another with equal claim to that honour—"

"Is there, *Thambi*?"

"Certainly. Vanathi Devi, the Kodumbalur princess, of course."

"Ah! You, my boy, are positively wicked, I assure you! Your silver tongue would seem to render me speechless. And so, *Thambi*—you managed to see the light of my life, Kodumbalur's hope in Pazhaiyarai, did you?"

"Indeed I did, *Ayya*. I'd have been hard put not to—for, how may one not be privileged to meet someone who never leaves Ilaiya Piratti's side? Both the princesses honoured me with their presence on their elephant, bidding farewell as I left the city. The princesses Vanathi and Kundhavai are as inseparable as the light and its glow; the flower and its fragrance; the body and its shadow—"

"*Adede*, this youngster's wit surpasses all my expectations! Thirumalai, make sure you escort him to our treasury; provide him with as many clothes and ornaments as he wishes—"

"They may remain where they are, *Ayya*; I shall make sure to take them when I return."

"And, well, I suppose—has Ilaiya Piratti sent me no message about my daughter, Vanathi?"

"I'm sure you'll understand, Senathipathi, that I don't wish to lie."

"Certainly, certainly; there is never any need to do so, to anyone."

"In the matter of this staunch Vaishnavite, however, I must beg for an exception; my head shall explode if I have to tell him the truth—"

"Do not, pray do not, my boy. Well ... no message from the princess, I suppose?"

"None for you, Senathipathi, but ..."

"But—what?"

"There are for the, ah, concerned individual. She's charged me with a few messages regarding Vanathi Devi, to be delivered to the prince in person—"

"Upon my word—never have I seen a young man so astute!" The Senathipathi caught Vandhiyathevan to his chest and embraced him heartily. "Well, enough time has been wasted," he said, finally. "You may take your leave."

"Must this Vaishnavite torment me with his presence on my journey, *Ayya*? If I could travel alone ..."

"What is your objection to him?"

"Oh, mine isn't the objection; it's the dagger at my waist, you see: it's as staunchly Saivite as he's a Vaishnavite, and has been screaming for his blood for days. Should it ever escape my strict guard, well—I'm afraid I might not be responsible for the consequences."

"Leave that bloodthirsty blade here, then, and take another. You cannot find the prince on your own; no one knows where he is, and you will need Thirumalai to guide you. Besides, he carries an important *olai* for his highness as well. You would do well to travel together—but make sure that you do not enter into petty squabbles and ruin your mission."

And then, Periya Velaar signed Vandhiyathevan to come closer. "He will not be a hindrance to you, *Thambi*," he whispered into the young man's ear. "But take care, in any case. Find out his message to the prince, and make sure to tell me."

Vandhiyathevan had suspected Azhwarkkadiyaan of being his spy; now, it seemed that the opposite was true. The situation pleased him a good deal.

***

Warrior and Vaishnavite set out that very night with an escort that consisted of two guards.

The first two days of travel took them in the eastern direction. In the beginning, they passed through villages and towns; a certain number of people were around. As they went on, however, human habitation thinned out, giving way, gradually, to forest. They encountered smaller, squatter trees and left them for massive, towering ones that seemed to touch the very skies. Now, they were unmistakably in the jungle, the vast *aranyam*. Sometimes, they stumbled across lakes with banks broken at places, dried out, the water long gone. Farms stood desolate and untended while elsewhere, in a vast clearing, appeared an unexpected body of water. The banks of the Paalaavi River had been destroyed as well and the water, instead of flowing down the bed had scattered here and there, stagnating in random holes and depressions.

They tramped through the forest, taking in these sights. Vandhiyathevan listened as Azhwarkkadiyaan spoke to him at length about the long-drawn out conflict, the ravaged territories and the widespread destruction it had caused in these parts. War was an imaginably devastating force, he declared often; not unnaturally, this led to a great deal of argument between them.

Two days later, their direction changed; they were now traveling south. The jungle grew denser with each step; the plains gave way, gradually, to a landscape dotted with boulders and small hillocks. Huge mountain ranges rose in the distance, their peaks piercing the sky. The forest seemed more perilous by the moment. Strange, terrifying sounds emerged from within its depths, mingling with the melodious notes of birds.

Talk rose, now, about the appalling attacks by wild beasts along the path. Jackals, leopards, bears and elephants, Azhwarkkadiyaan informed, lived in these jungles.

"Jackals are dangerous when they hunt in packs, aren't they?" asked Vandhiyathevan, his mind flashing to the memory of his nightmare in the Kadambur palace.

"I daresay, but a single jackal's howl is ten times worse than a whole pack's," revealed Azhwarkkadiyaan.

"How can that be, *Swami*?"

"Leopards and jackals combine forces to hunt, in these parts. The leopard would conceal itself in certain nooks while the jackal would prowl here and there, smelling out its prey. It would set up a single howl at the sight of men, deer or other such mellow creatures; the leopard would leap out at once, pounce and make a kill. A jackal that acts thus, as a spy for the leopard, is called an Ori—"

A loud rumble, not unlike the roar of the oceans, reached them at this point, interrupting their conversation. "We've come pretty far from the sea, haven't we?" Vandhiyathevan ventured. "What's that roar?"

"There's a pond or lake hereabouts, I suppose," Azhwarkkadiyaan replied. "Probably a herd of elephants come for a drink."

"*Ayyayo*! What if we're caught in the middle—"

"There's no need to fear them at all; a herd poses no threat. All we have to do is stand aside, and they'll leave without even a glance at us."

By this time, one of their escorts had clambered up a tree and was peering in all four directions.

"*Ayya! Ayya!*" he shrieked. "A lone elephant—a mad one! It's crashing through the trees and trampling everything in its path!"

"*Ayyo*—how dreadful! What do we do now?" Azhwarkkadiyaan stared around, petrified. "How do we escape?"

"You wouldn't flinch at a dozen elephants, but you're trembling at just one?" Vandhiyathevan looked puzzled.

"One crazed mammoth possesses the strength of a thousand sane ones, *Appane*; nothing and no one can withstand its sheer, brutal power—"

"Three of us have spears, while you possess a trusty staff—"

"Not a thousand spears can have the slightest effect upon an insane elephant—there! I see a steep hillock—we might manage to escape by the skin of our teeth if we climb onto it—**run**!"

Azhwarkkadiyaan suited action to words and set off at top speed; the rest followed at his heels. Once they had covered a certain distance, though, a fresh difficulty beset them: they almost stumbled into a steep, sheer ravine. It barred their way, cutting across the path that led to the hillock. They came to a standstill at its very edge while the lone elephant thundered behind them, closing in with every moment. Its murderous rage had doubtless been fanned by the sight of the humans; it was a wonder that the whole universe had not splintered into a thousand fragments as it raised its trunk and trumpeted a mighty, ear-splitting roar that crashed through the forest.

The men clapped their hands over their ears, almost deafened; they threw caution to the winds and scattered in all four directions.

The elephant stomped closer. Closer—and closer ... it seemed to have trained its sights upon Azhwarkkadiyaan, and made its way in his direction. Should the Vaishnavite take two steps backwards, he would topple headfirst into the deep ravine. There was no way to escape along the side either; the foliage was much too dense—not that he could run, in any case.

Vandhiyathevan did lift his spear into his hands—but it seemed, to his horrified eyes, that not even Indra's famed celestial weapon, *Vajrayudham*, could slow down the ferocious animal. He lost his nerve; his hand dropped, weak and useless.

Danger threatened with every passing moment—but Azhwarkkadiyaan's actions, at that juncture, almost made Vandhiyathevan collapse into laughter.

"Stop! Stop where you are, you stupid beast!" Nambi raged at the crazed elephant. "Don't take a step more—or I'll kill you and make sure you rot under mounds of earth!" He shook his staff almost in its face. "Careful!"

28

THE KING'S ROAD

lone, crazed elephant would not pay the slightest heed to Azhwarkkadiyaan's frantically waving staff or his high-pitched screeches of retribution, would it? It raised its trunk once again, emitted an outraged screech and trampled forward, leaving crushed bushes and creepers in its frenzied wake.

There was no doubt: Azhwarkkadiyaan was about to meet his end at the hands—or rather feet—of an elephant.

The two valiant warriors who had been their escorts stood where they were, yelling out "Hoy—hoy!"—ineffectually, of course.

As for Vandhiyathevan, he picked up the spear that had fallen to the ground, with the creditable intention of trying to attack, or distract the lunatic animal.

This was the moment Nambi chose to fling his staff at the elephant.

The next instant, he vanished.

His turban flew off his head, coming to a mournful rest on a tree-branch.

Before anyone could wonder about the Vaishnavite's fate, something else happened—something that distracted everyone instantly, from Nambi.

The elephant, intent on its prey, edged towards the ravine—and then, suddenly, fell on its knees, leaning forward.

A loud, terrifying trumpeting sound echoed through the dense forest, shattering the silence.

The next instant, the elephant slipped and fell into the terrifyingly deep chasm—as though a mountain had skidded off the earth. Huge rocks and boulders crashed through the undergrowth as it rolled down the side, and a cloud of dust rose into the air, thick and stifling.

It took Vandhiyathevan more than a few moments to gauge the situation and re-construct what had happened.

Azhwarkkadiyaan had waved his staff so hard that he lost his balance, Vandhiyathevan guessed, and with the ravine immediately behind him, fell in, headlong. The elephant, following him, had placed two feet almost into the chasm—but could not regain stability, once it felt itself slipping. Its enormous weight, not unlike that of a small mountain, had turned enemy, sending it crashing to the depths of the gorge!

A crazed elephant, and a human who resembled one, had met the same fate, and now shared the same grave.

Vandhiyathevan's skin prickled at the very thought; his body shivered.

His heart felt heavy with sorrow. The last few days had seen all his doubts about the Vaishnavite vanish; indeed, he had begun to cherish something very like affection, for Nambi.

A man such as that—must *this* be his fate?

No more would Vandhiyathevan receive his invaluable assistance or his guidance in traversing this dangerous path: no, he would have to accomplish this humongous task all by himself.

He tiptoed to the edge of the ravine where he had seen both man and beast vanish, and peered cautiously into its depths. All he could see, at first, was a cloud of thick dust, barring his view. By degrees, the earth settled, revealing glimpses of crushed bushes and pulped foliage along the side, the result of the pachyderm's rapid journey to the bottom.

"Well? You're not just going to stand there like a stock, are you? What's this, a play for your entertainment?" The voice made Vandhiyathevan nearly jump out of his skin. "Give me a hand, why don't you?"

It was all the young man could do, to not topple off the edge and follow the elephant, in his astonishment. He peered down in the direction of the voice.

And there was Azhwarkkadiyaan—hanging on for dear life, from a thick root that happened to poke out beside a steep rock, almost by the elephant's path.

It was as though a cloud had lifted. Vandhiyathevan's depression vanished in an instant; needless to say, his witticisms returned in full-force. "Ah, most revered Vaishnavite, you've managed to grant Gajendran salvation," he crowed. "But stayed behind in Thirisangu's heaven, have you?" He clapped his hands, summoning the guards. Then, he unwound his waistcloth, handed one end to them with instructions to hold on tight, and let the other down into the chasm. Azhwarkkadiyaan let go of the root and gripped the cloth tight, whereupon the three men above gasped and heaved, finally dragging the heavy-set Vaishnavite onto the forest floor.

For a while, it was all Azhwarkkadiyaan could do to simply lie on the ground, almost lifeless, except for the deep, heaving breaths that shook his body. The rest stood around him, pouring out consolation and relief, by turns.

And then, the Vaishnavite sat up with a speed that was astonishing. "We must resume our journey at once," he prodded them. "We ought to reach the *rajapattai* before nightfall. Where's my head-cloth? And my staff—where's it gone?"

"There's no need for this haste," Vandhiyathevan assured him. "You may rest awhile, yet; we can travel a little later."

A jackal howled at that precise moment.

Another added its melodious note, the next instant.

A hundred, two hundred more joined in a chorus, joyous notes mingling.

Somewhere beyond them, bushes began to rustle suspiciously, the rippling movement stretching down towards the chasm. There was no need to explain that leopards were now tracking their way towards the ravine, slinking stealthily amongst the foliage.

Vultures and other birds of prey began to circle in the air, high above the gorge.

"An elephant's death is no ordinary matter; every carnivore in the vicinity, not to mention ravenous birds will converge upon this area within a few minutes, eager to feast upon mighty Gajendra's remains. Unless you cherish a deep desire for us all to become side-dishes to the main course, I suggest we make a move towards the *rajapattai*," explained Azhwarkkadiyaan. "Well?"

This time, Vandhiyathevan raised not a word in objection. The four quickened their steps along the forest path as much as they could.

When the sun sank in the west, they had achieved their objective.

The king's road presented a very cheery picture indeed, as people thronged the thoroughfare; chariots and carts rumbled along, intent on their destination. Elephants walked majestically, carrying travelers who seemed completely unfazed by their mount; Vandhiyathevan gaped at the sight. *Was it truly an animal such as this that had been the cause of such mind-numbing terror in that forest?* He could barely speak for astonishment.

"So, where does this road lead?" He asked, when he had gotten over his surprise, somewhat. "Where have we come from? Where are we going?"

"We've joined the *rajapattai* that connects Anuradhapuram and Simmagiri," Azhwarkkadiyaan informed him. "Thampallai is still half a *kaadham* away; we shall be there by nightfall, I daresay."

"Surely we could've traveled by the *rajapattai* all the way? Why the treacherous journey through the forest?"

"The king's road would've meant a hundred check-points, minute inspections and interrogations; we'd have been stopped completely at Anuradhapuram, with no hope of further travel. News has reached me that the person we seek is somewhere in the vicinity of Simmagiri, which is why I chose a shortcut. There's still no guarantee that we shall find him," Azhwarkkadiyaan sounded doubtful, all of a sudden. "I can only hope that he hasn't veered off in another direction …"

Houses, villages, market-streets, carpentry-workshops and iron-smithies crowded on both sides of the *rajapattai*. Most of those who lived and worked in these parts seemed to be Singalavars. Despite warriors from Thamizhagam crisscrossing their paths often along the king's road, those who lived on either side went about their business without the least sign of fear or nervousness.

"Who controls these sections, now?" asked Vandhiyathevan.

"Chozhas have captured up to Thampallai; beyond, the Simmagiri Mountain and fort still lie in Mahindan's hands."

"And the people?"

"Mostly Singalavars. You see, Ponniyin Selvar changed the very face of war, here: the conflict is narrowed to the Chozha forces and Mahindan's men—and that, only upon the battlefield. For the rest—the people may go about their daily lives without the slightest fear of disruption. As for the Buddhist monks, they're in the seventh heaven of delight. And not for nothing either: our prince has issued orders to rebuild all the ruined *viharams* in Anuradhapuram. Did you ever hear anything like it? Why wouldn't the monks be nearly off their heads with joy? When I meet the prince, I'm going to tell him that I don't like what he's doing—not a scrap!"

"Certainly you must; who does the prince think he is, anyway, doing things that don't meet your approval?" demanded Vandhiyathevan. "He's not some exalted being with a horn on his head, is he?"

"Not that, perhaps, but *Thambi*—there's something about him, some strange power; even people who speak ill of him fall under his thrall when they meet him, and find themselves succumbing to his personality. No one dares say a word against him. I know of only one person who can— who possesses a power stronger than his; the ability to influence him ..."

"Indeed, yes; who may doubt the wonderful Veera Vaishnavite's utter control over the prince? Didn't he dispatch a completely crazed elephant with merely the power of his divine staff?

"You misunderstand me, *Thambi*. To pit my poor little self against Arulmozhi Varmar ... why, that would be nothing less than sacrilege! I could dispatch lunatic elephants with my staff; grapple with tigers, bears and lions even, with my bare hands, but when I am in the presence of Ponniyin Selvar ... I can scarce believe it myself, but my courage fails me. My heart skips a beat and begins to melt; my throat closes up, and I can barely speak a single word—"

"Who were you speaking of, then, as having the power to influence *him*?"

"The whole world is privy to it but you've no idea at all, I suppose? Who else but Ilaiya Piratti? Princess Kundhavai's slightest wish is his command; the equivalent of the very Vedhas."

"Indeed? Pazhaiyarai's Ilaiya Piratti, eh? I did wonder if it was your sister, the Pazhuvoor Ilaiya Rani Nandhini Devi ..."

"Nandhini possesses her fair share of influence—but hers is of a different nature altogether."

"Is it?"

"Say, a man is about to fall headfirst into hell; now, Kundhavai Devi would stop him, and ensure that he was saved from a gory end by escorting him to heaven. That's a kind of power, certainly. Nandhini, on the other hand—ah, do you know *her* capabilities? Her influence is a shade stronger, I must admit: she'd convince the man that hell was in fact, heaven, and make him jump in of his own volition, delirious with happiness!"

A thrill of emotion coursed through Vandhiyathevan as he realized that the Vaishnavite was perfectly right: how well had Azhwarkkadiyaan estimated Nandhini's character and the fantastic, spell-binding web of intoxication she could weave, over unsuspecting mortals! Could it be true that she *was* his sister?

He said nothing more, lost in these thoughts; they walked on, wrapped in silence.

The sound of horse-hooves broke their reverie; they seemed to come from the opposite direction. Within moments, four stallions thundered up the road, raising a storm of dust and passed our pedestrian travelers at the speed of lightning. But those few short moments were enough for Vandhiyathevan to recognize at least one of them—ah, wasn't this Parthibendra Varman? An intimate of Prince Aditha Karikalar at Kanchi, wasn't he? *And one who doesn't like me much, either. What's his business here and where's he off to, now? For that matter, when did he even arrive in Ilankai—and why?*

The horsemen had gone past when a strong, authoritative voice cracked over them like a whip. "Stop!"

The stallions obeyed at once; the whole cavalcade turned. One, who seemed to be the leader among them, trotted forward, while the rest followed. He was, as Vandhiyathevan had guessed from his fleeting glance, Parthibendra Pallavan, whose acquaintance we made in Maamallapuram.

Now, he subjected Vandhiyathevan to a hard stare. "Well, upon my word—" he shot out. "What on earth are *you* doing here? What of all those fantastic tales about you vanishing from Thanjavur like a puff of smoke? I thought you'd have been hanged and quartered by the Pazhuvettarayars by now for sure—"

"I'm afraid disposing me wouldn't be quite that easy—for the

Pazhuvettarayars, or anyone else," came Vandhiyathevan's smooth answer. "I'm a scion of the ancient Vaanar clan, aren't I?"

"Indeed. You've no equal when it comes to sliding out of any difficult situation; saving yourself by the skin of your teeth—"

"When it is necessary to do so, *Ayya*, certainly; I make use of any and every ruse I can come up with—and I shan't hesitate to give my life too, if that would answer. And, I'd much rather do so, battling the noble descendent of the Pallavas ..." Vandhiyathevan drew his sword out of his scabbard. "... than at the hands of the petty Pazhuvettarayars!"

"*Chee*—are you suggesting that I fight you? And in these lands, so far from home? Not at all, *Thambi*. I'm on an important mission and have no time to tarry. What of the prince's mission?"

"Done, *Ayya*. I've delivered the *olai* meant for the Chakravarthy, as well as the one for Ilaiya Piratti."

"Have you, now? What's your business here, then?"

"I've cherished a desire to sightsee Ilankai for a long while, now: I decided to take the chance to do so, in company of this Vaishnavite—"

"Ha, this man seems familiar too, for some reason—"

"Doubtless, Maharaja, for I visited the crown prince, once, to enquire about my sister's whereabouts," answered Nambi. "You were by his side at that time if I remember right ..."

"Your sister? Who's she, pray?"

"The present young queen of Pazhuvoor; Nandhini Devi."

"That sleek, poisonous cobra! Why, when I think of the devastation in the country as a result of her evil machinations—you, as her brother, ought to be skewered on a spike ..."

"I've sworn to impale myself upon a *kazhumaram* one day, Maharaja; I shall send you a message on the appointed date, and you shall carry out the sacred deed with your own blessed hands—"

"Unlikely; your impalement would require a hundred hefty men—I certainly shan't be able to manage it. Be that as it may, have you heard anything of the prince's whereabouts?" Parthibendran demanded. "Do you know if he's reached Anuradhapuram?"

"I'm afraid we peasants aren't likely to be privy to such sensitive information, Maharaja. Our journey was along the forest path—why, we had quite an adventure, with a crazed elephant stomping after us, and you should have seen—"

"Oh, *enough* of your ridiculous tales. You know," Parthibendran wheeled around his stallion. "I wouldn't be surprised if I did manage, some day, to carry out your wishes and impale you upon that sharp spike …"

Azhwarkkadiyaan's attention had been divided, all this while, between a conversation with Parthibendran, and a keen scrutiny of the Pallava prince's entourage.

The horses galloped away, and the Vaishnavite turned towards Vandhiyathevan. "Did you take a good look at the other three men, *Thambi*?" His voice brimmed with eagerness. "Did any of them seem familiar to you?"

"Never seen them," was the young man's prompt answer.

"I suppose not; no, you'd have had no reason. I have, however— two of them at midnight, within the ruins of the Thiruppurambiyam memorial—good grief, the terrible oath they swore!" Azhwarkkadiyaan trembled at the very memory.

"Really? And what was this horrifying vow?"

"To destroy every trace of the Chozha dynasty, down to the last soul, with no hope of revival …"

"Ayyayo!"

"I can't, for the life of me, understand how they came to be here before us—those clever, cunning rogues," Azhwarkkadiyaan shook his head. "And now they've managed to latch themselves to this Pallava ruffian too …" He lapsed into silence.

Something he'd learnt in Kodikkarai now rose in Vandhiyathevan's memory: a piece of news—about two men arriving just a day before him, and hurrying towards Ilankai almost right away—ah! Hadn't it been Poonguzhali's elder brother who had ferried them, too?

Could those two be part of the trio accompanying the Pallava prince? If so—what was the connection between them?

The four had been walking steadily all his while—and the holy city of Thampallai was fast approaching, with every step.

ೞ

Hidden Meanings and Explanations

Singalavars

Sinhalese

Thirisangu

At the end of his lifetime, this prince wished to ascend to heaven in his own mortal body, but was denied the privilege on the grounds that it was against the laws of nature. Sage Vishwamithrar then created a brand-new heaven for him much to the dismay of Indra and the Devas, who later persuaded him to change his mind. The sage did, which left Thirisangu literally in a limbo, hanging midway between the true heaven and earth, in a half-finished celestial abode. It's said that Thirisangu dwells there for all of eternity, upside down. Thus, he became a byword for someone who's caught between his desire, and his destination.

29

THE MAHOUT

Two thousand years ago—and a thousand years before the time of this saga—ruled a Sinhala king by name Valahambahu, whose time on the throne saw Thamizh forces invade Ilankai. Valahambahu made his escape from the capital, biding his time in a mountain cave in Thampallai. Later, he gathered his forces, launched a counter-attack and re-captured Anuradhapuram. Brimming with gratitude for the cave that offered him sanctuary, he enlarged and sculpted it into a temple; within, he established a great many Buddha statues, large and small as a gesture of appreciation.

It would seem that the sculptors responsible for a hundred odd statues of Lord Buddha were not content with exhibiting their talents thus; they added a few Hindu statuettes for good measure. Visitors to Thampallai may still see these wonderful works of art in the cave shrine.

To Vandhiyathevan, it seemed as though he had entered a brand new world, when he stepped within the sacred confines of the holy city. The scent of fresh flowers sent his senses whirling, for lotus buds and *shenbagam* blossoms lay in huge, fragrant heaps at street-corners. Devotees bought these by the dozens, laying them tenderly in pretty *olai* baskets, before taking them to the temple. Crowds of men and women thronged those streets; Buddhist monks, clad in characteristic saffron robes dotted the area as well. Occasionally, great chants of "*Sadhu! Sadhu!*" rose among the crowd.

Vandhiyathevan wandered in a daze, astonished beyond all bounds at these wondrous sights. "It was my impression that we were entering a war *kendhram,*" he turned to Azhwarkkadiyaan. "But we seem to have stepped right into a Buddhist *kshethram,* haven't we?"

"Not surprising at all, considering that it's been one for a thousand years," commented the Vaishnavite. "And renowned, as well."

"But—you did say that it was under the control of the Chozhas, didn't you?"

"I reiterate; yes, it is."

"I don't see Chozha warriors anywhere."

"They'd likely be found at the Padai Veedu settlements outside the city. Those are the Prince's orders."

"Which prince would that be?"

"The one we're searching for, of course."

"Now that you remind me, I wish to ask you about him, myself. We've just seen off Parthibendra Pallavan, who's poked into every corner of this place and gone without even a glimpse of the prince—what's the point of *us* looking for him here?"

"That fool Pallavan might think the prince isn't here, but there's no reason for me to take his word. I mean to find out what I can, myself. After all, the demon Iraniyan announced that there was no such God as Hari, but did devout Prahaladan actually believe it?"

"Ah, you put me in mind of something that must be addressed at once: you entered the lists against every Saivite you ran into, back home—now here are dozens of Buddhist monks, and yet you walk by my side without the slightest sense of outrage! Why, valiant Vaishnavite? You haven't been cowed by their large numbers, have you?"

"What's this fear you speak of, *Thambi*? What does it look like?"

"Black as a demon and large as an elephant. Don't tell me you've never seen it."

"No." Azhwarkkadiyaan seemed to lose interest in the conversation, approaching two men by the roadside, who seemed to be Thamizh. He entered into dialogue with them for a while and then returned.

"Well? What sort of questions did you put to them, Vaishnavite? No doubt you wished to know who was the greater, Siva Peruman or Vishnu. But you'd have been doomed to disappointment—everyone here is bound to declare that Buddha Bhagavan is the greatest," Vandhiyathevan grinned. "You *have* noticed the simply enormous dimensions of the statues here, haven't you?"

"I'll have you know that I bundled away all my Veera Vaishnavite sentiments in Rameswaram, *Thambi*; I'm here on strictly official business."

"What did you ask those men, then? The prince's whereabouts?"

"Quite to the contrary, I wished to know the reason for the festivities in the city, today."

"What was their answer?"

"Two Chinese travelers are about to visit; the Buddhist Viharam has arranged for a welcoming ceremony, which explains the festivities."

"And where are they coming from—these Chinese travelers?"

"They arrived yesterday and left for Simmagiri, apparently. They've begun their return journey and will be here soon, I hear."

"Where's Simmagiri?"

"A *kaadham* from here, and still under Singala control. You can have a view right from this site, if it's daylight. There's an almost impregnable fortress on top and a cave with beautiful art-work, glistening as though painted only yesterday; likely the travelers made the journey to see them. They must have had a job of it too, climbing that mountain and getting down ... look over there!"

A large, well-decorated elephant was making its slow, ponderous way, in the direction of Azhwarkkadiyaan's finger. Two men sat in its *ambaari*, their appearance and attire proclaiming their Chinese nationality; a mahout sat majestically upon the animal's neck as well, holding an *ankusam*, a goad. A multitude thronged around the mount at once, raising shouts and chants.

"Well, *Thambi*?"

"Indeed, Nambi, I've never *seen* an elephant this size—*Amma*! Should we begin to look for a chasm, do you think?"

"Unnecessary; all we need to do is stand by the side of the street."

They suited action to words; the elephant tramped past them, the crowd following in its wake.

Vandhiyathevan's attention was centred completely upon the travelers upon the *ambaari*. Ah, what *bhakthi* was theirs that prompted them to cross entire seas; travel through alien lands and unknown countries, in search of holy places connected with the Buddha! It was only fair that they be welcomed with such fanfare and pomp—and yet, wasn't it nothing short of miraculous that their journey should be made possible here, even in these times of terrible war? Must be Arulmozhi Varmar's arrangement, all of this; no one else could have come up with such a benevolent gesture. But where *was* the prince? Would they ever be able to find him? What if all this trouble he'd taken, traveling in the company of this Vaishnavite, was for nothing?

"Were you watching, *Thambi*?"

"Certainly I was."

"And what did you see?"

"The Chinese have really flat faces, you know? As for their peculiar clothes—"

"That wasn't what I meant."

"No?"

"The mahout. You didn't notice him at all?"

"Er—no. Should I have?"

"Good grief, *Thambi*—you didn't see the way his eyes fairly glowed when they fell upon us?"

"They did? What'd he put in them—oil torches?"

"Well, upon my word—! I'm not sure if I should gape at your stupidity, or Ilaiya Piratti's folly in entrusting such a sensitive mission to a careless oaf … never mind that, now. Come, let's go on."

The duo followed the travelers and the surrounding crowd, at a little distance.

The elephant swayed to a stop in front of the Buddhist Viharam; the mahout whispered something into its large, flapping ears, and it obediently knelt on the ground. The Chinese disembarked and were promptly extended a warm welcome by the band of Buddhist monks gathered at the Viharam's entrance. Conches blew; *alatchi* bells pealed merrily; flowers showered upon the honoured guests from the monastery's upper balconies, accompanied by the sacred chant of "*Buddham Saranam Gachaami!*" The newcomers vanished inside, followed by most of the gaping crowd.

The mahout, who had clambered off the elephant's neck even before his passengers had climbed down, now bade the animal rise, walked with it and upon letting his gaze settle on four men who stood a little further away, gave the mount into the care of one of them. He pointed out Azhwarkkadiyaan to another, and said something. Then, he walked away with the other two, turned a street-corner and vanished from sight.

The one who had had Nambi pointed out to him now approached our duo. "*Ayya*," he began, in a low voice. "Would you be willing to come with me?"

"That's what we've been waiting for," Azhwarkkadiyaan replied.

"An insignia of some kind?"

Azhwarkkadiyaan produced the Kodumbalur signet-ring, given into his possession by the Senathipathi.

"Very well. If you will follow me?" They duly did.

A lonely, twisted little forest path appeared, once they had left the city behind. A little along this way and they reached a ruined *mandapam*, some distance from the roadside. Their instructions were to wait there for a while, informed their guide. As for the man himself, he scrambled up a tree and began to scrutinize the path they had just taken, intently.

"All these hide-and-seek games," Vandhiyathevan complained. "What's all the mystery about? I don't understand any of this."

"Patience. All will be revealed, soon."

Two horses were tethered behind the *mandapam*; this bothered Vandhiyathevan a little. *Why only two?*

And that mahout—what could possibly be the mystery surrounding him? Vandhiyathevan had sent him a fleeting glance, before transferring his attention to the Chinese travelers. He tried in vain to retrieve a memory of the *paagan*, to no avail; nothing surfaced.

"Who was the mahout, Nambi? Tell me, why don't you?"

"Take a guess at his identity, why don't *you*?"

"Was he—was it Ponniyin Selvar?"

"From the way his eyes gleamed for just a moment when they rested on us—it would seem to be so."

"What if others should recognize him the way you did?"

"I shouldn't think anyone would—who on earth would expect the prince to jaunter off playing mahout to two Chinese travelers, pray? Besides, no one here has seen him in person."

"You mentioned that those travelers returned from Simmagiri, didn't you?"

"I did."

"Didn't you also say that the place was still under Singalavar control?"

"I won't deny it."

"Then—is the prince returning from a sojourn amongst enemies?"

"Why stop with just Simmagiri, pray? He's been to other places as well, such as Mahiyangaanam and Samanthakoodam in the company of the Chinese—places still under our foes, I might add."

"But—why would he subject himself to this sort of mortal peril?"

"The intense desire to gaze upon the many wondrous works of art at these *kshethrams*, of course!"

"Well, of all the—! What sort of a prince is he, and what desires are these? And this is the childish youngster that the Kudandhai astrologer swore would one day become the *Eka Chakradhipathi*, the sole emperor at whose feet other, lesser kings would count it fortunate to lay their heads!"

"Did the Kudandhai Jothidar indeed predict such a future, *Thambi*?"

"Don't tell me you believe all that too."

"I don't believe in predictions, *Thambi*; I've no need to depend on astrology, either."

"You haven't? Why?"

"*Because I know ...*"

Abruptly, the clip-clop of horse-hooves reached their ears; the sound approached them with every moment. The scout atop the tree scrambled down and brought forward the two steeds. He climbed onto one and bade Azhwarkkadiyaan mount the other. "A cavalcade is about to pass this way soon; we're supposed to join them," he informed Nambi.

"What about me?" Vandhiyathevan demanded.

"My orders are to bring only this individual."

"Upon whose command, pray?"

"I'm not authorized to reveal his identity."

"I must see the prince at once; I'm the bearer of most important news."

"I'm afraid I know nothing of such things, *Ayya*."

"Patience, *Thambi*," counseled Azhwarkkadiyaan. "I shall petition the prince on your behalf for permission to escort you and seek an audience."

"You of all people must know the importance of my message, Nambi—and how speedily it must reach its recipient."

"Give me the *olai* then, and I shall deliver it to him."

"Don't even think about it."

"You've no choice, then, but to cultivate patience. I can see no way out."

"No?"

"Not even the slightest."

Vandhiyathevan's heart churned and seethed; Azhwarkkadiyaan was being summoned to the prince's presence—of that, there was no doubt. And here the Senathipathi had bidden him learn the Vaishnavite's message to the prince—how was Vandhiyathevan to do that, pray?

The cavalcade of horses thundered towards them, passed them by, and vanished down the road at the speed of lightning. The two men, mounted in readiness by the *mandapam*, snapped the reins, preparatory to depart.

What occurred next was completely unexpected.

Vandhiyathevan grabbed hold of the man on the horse, gathered all his strength and shoved him off. The man went sprawling with a shriek, and Vallavarayan seized the chance to mount the stallion. A swift kick to the side and the steed practically flew down the path, followed by Azhwarkkadiyaan on his mount. The felled warrior rose in an instant, drew his dagger from his waist and flung it with a flurry of raucous threats. Vandhiyathevan had the forethought to flatten himself against the horse's back; the warrior's dagger flew past and buried itself harmlessly, into a tree.

The horses galloped along the path. Both took care not to approach too close, nor stay too far behind the three that led the way.

"Well done, *Thambi*," Azhwarkkadiyaan's words of praise reached the young man—but Vandhiyathevan, wracked by worry about the consequences of his actions, vouchsafed no reply. Why, oh why had he crossed entire seas, traversed forests in alien lands and appropriated someone else's horse on a mission such as this—all for the sake of a young woman's request?

The stallions sped on their way along the path, almost equal to the speed of the wind, and the mind.

30

FAST AND FURIOUS BATTLE

To Vandhiyathevan, holding onto the horse's mane for dear life, it seemed as though they were on a journey that might never end. Ha, had this wily Vaishnavite shown his true colours at last? Was he a traitor, leading him straight into the jaws of *sathru*, the enemy?

The jungle rose around him on both sides, dark and gloomy, almost sickening in its vastness. As for the dangers that lurked within—who knew what peril lay concealed amidst the towering trees, rustling, shadowy bushes and tricky paths? Leopards, bears, elephants, poisonous creatures, all these had already made the forest their home—and to them could be added dangerous human foes; who knew? Hadn't he heard that Thampallai was the last Chozha outpost in the south, after all? Where was this man taking him, then?

The moon's faint illumination helped, thankfully, to see his way. Pearly beams danced atop trees that rose majestically into the night sky; their restless, darting rays dappled the forest path, throwing into relief the shadowy forms of the three horses just ahead. Sight might be denied at times, but the thunder of hooves upon the ground assaulted the ears every moment.

And then, other sounds began to intrude—sounds that one might not expect in the middle of a dense jungle: human voices raised in delight; voices lifted in song and dance with unbridled enthusiasm—ah! Chinks of light through trees in the distance—the light of oil-torches and the unmistakable, bright glow of oven-fires, placed underneath huge cauldrons the size of kilns. A camp of some sort, obviously—but who were these soldiers, so caught up in cheer and joy that they cared not about being in the very middle of a forest? Chozha warriors? Or—the foe?

Vandhiyathevan had little more than a few moments to muse on such weighty issues; before he had gotten very far in attempting to deduce the identity of the camp members, one of the horses just a little ahead of him snapped to a stop—and wheeled around, swiftly.

Its approach escaped Vallavarayan's notice until it was almost nose to nose with his own. The rider leaned forward, curled his fingers into a fist and punched him hard, in the face. Even as Vandhiyathevan, stunned beyond all recognition at the knock, floundered, his senses fuzzy and disordered, the unknown grabbed his knee and pushed hard.

Thud! Vallavarayan fell to the ground in an ungainly heap; his horse, plainly horrified at such strange happenings, reared up and galloped to a safe distance.

By this time, the man who had unseated him in such ignominious fashion jumped down and approached our fallen warrior, who was struggling to get back on his feet. He bent and in one swift motion, pulled the dagger from the waist of a still fazed Vandhiyathevan, and flicked it away.

The Vaanar warrior regained his senses in an instant—not to mention his considerable fury which reached outrageous proportions at this dastardly act. He jumped up at once, muscles straining; curled his fingers into fists as strong as *Vajrayudham*, drew back his arm, and punched his opponent full in the face. His enemy, naturally, was loath to take this example of brute force calmly, and jumped promptly into the fray.

Battle broke out, fast and furious.

They grappled with each other, not unlike the demons Gadothgajan and Idumban; pounced on each other and rolled on the ground, locked in each other's arms like a certain other famed pair of yore: Siva Peruman, disguised as a hunter, and the Mahabharata warrior Archunan. They fell apart and then closed in with the ease of trained wrestlers, and it was as though two *dhikkajams*, the celestial elephants that guarded all directions had suddenly decided to cast all caution to the winds and begin brawling.

Azhwarkkadiyaan and the men who had galloped ahead stood at a distance, and in the dancing moonlight that dappled the ground amidst restless, rustling tree branches, frankly gaped at the spectacle unfolding in front of their astonished, unblinking eyes.

Soon, the sound of footfalls reached them; a few warriors pushed aside the closely woven tree-branches and stalked forward, holding aloft oil-torches. The sight that met them stopped them in their tracks and they stood still, eyes wide. Within moments, a considerable crowd had gathered around the combatants.

In the end, Vandhiyathevan it was, finally pushed onto the ground. The warrior who had bested him in combat promptly sat heavily on his chest, and yanked at the waistcloth around his waist, slipping out the *olai* adroitly. None of Vandhiyathevan's desperate efforts to prevent him had the slightest effect.

The moment he had his hands on the coveted palm-leaf, the man practically leapt off the fallen Vaanar warrior and walked swiftly towards the light shed by the torches held by the watching men. A quick sign from him, and two men ran across to Vandhiyathevan; they pinned him to the ground so securely that he could hardly move a muscle.

"You wretched Vaishnavite!" he screamed, consumed by fury and a desperate helplessness that made him gnash his teeth. "How dare you— how could you betray your friend? Get that *olai* from him—**get it**!"

"I'm afraid that's a task much beyond my abilities, *Appane*," was Azhwarkkadiyaan's tranquil answer.

"*Chee*—you coward! I've never seen the likes of you—ah, that I trusted you, vile Vaishnavite, to guard me on this journey—!" Vandhiyathevan fairly shrieked his aggravation.

Azhwarkkadiyaan climbed down from his horse in leisurely fashion, and made his way towards the young man on the ground. "You little idiot," he whispered into his ear. "Your precious *olai* has reached its intended recipient. Why do you screech so?"

The men holding aloft the torches now peered intently into the face of the man reading the palm-leaf. Recognition flitted through them at once—and a huge shout arose.

"Long live Ponniyin Selvar!
"Long life to the Destroyer of our Foes!"
"Long live our Ilango, our prince!'

Chants such as "Long live the Chozha scion!" rose in accompaniment as well, threading through the trees and filling the entire jungle. As if in echo, birds in the trees, disturbed from their sleep by the rousing shouts, chirped and twittered, rustling feathers and flapping wings: *Sadasada— padapada*!

By now, men other than those already gathered pulled aside tree branches and creepers, and thundered towards the clearing, attracted by the noise. The warrior darted a glance around him, taking note of the swelling crowd. "You'd better return to the *paasarai*, all of you, and make arrangements for the feast. I shall join you within a few moments."

The quiet words had instant effect; they melted away, clearing the area as though one man.

As for Vandhiyathevan, he still lay on the ground where he had fallen, the bearer of considerably painful bruises and injuries from the fight—but such was his stunned astonishment that he scarce felt their fiery throb.

Aha—so this is Prince Arulmozhi Varmar! Ah, the strength in his hands; how swift were his blows, how hardy! People do say, don't they, that even if you had to be knocked out, better that you suffered it at the hands of your betters? And what better fate can befall me than to sustain blows at the hands of such a toughened warrior as this? Why, here's a prince with the handsome features and majesty of Archunan—the wonderful endurance and strength of Bheemasenan; who can wonder, then, that the whole country sings his praises so volubly?

And now, the time has come, finally, to introduce our readers to the young prince who gave this epic tale its name; a warrior without equal, who carved an indelible name for himself in Thamizh history; who earned such fame for his House that it took its place, forever and ever, among the great pantheon of India's ruling dynasties; the emperor who would one day assume the grand title of Raja Raja, and be renowned as one of the greatest rulers of the world—but who was known, at the time of this tale, as simply Arulmozhi Varmar. We must beg a royal pardon for having brought him to the notice of our readers so late—and it is only natural that they feel some resentment. But what can be done, pray? Our hero Vandhiyathevan has met him for the first time only now; how may the rest of us have done so, before?

Arulmozhi Thevar walked up to Vandhiyathevan; that young man looked up startled, wondering if he were to be treated to a taste, once more, of that warrior's hardy knuckles.

Then, his eyes fell upon the prince's pleasant countenance, brightened by his smile, and his suspicions fell away.

"*Varuga, varuga!* Well met, dear friend; I bid you grand welcome to the fair isle of Ilankai. You braved a long journey indeed, across land and sea, to meet with your Chozha comrades, didn't you? Were you satisfied with the valorous welcome I extended upon your arrival?" The prince's smile grew wider. "Or do you wish, perhaps, to enjoy something much more—shall we say—energetic?"

Vandhiyathevan leapt up at this, and folded his palms. "Your gracious sister's *olai* has reached you safe, great prince; I am delighted to assure you that my duty is at an end. I have no further need of this life and no need, either, to make any attempt to safeguard it. By all means, let's do battle, study a few more chapters of *Yuddha Kaandam* and test our mettle, should it so please you!" He announced with alacrity.

"Ah, well may you declare so; why shouldn't you, indeed? Your life and safety are now my concern and mine only—else how may I even look Ilaiya Piratti in the face? This palm-leaf seems to bear the writing of my beloved sister, my friend," the prince continued. "Did she entrust it to you herself?"

"Indeed, your highness; I had the great good fortune of receiving it from her own illustrious hands. Ever since then, I have striven to reach you without a moment's pause, traveling over land and sea, night and day," Vandhiyathevan paused for a breath.

"I quite see that; you couldn't have managed to get here within such a short space of time, else. I'm at a loss to see how I can repay such dedicated service." The prince stepped up to Vandhiyathevan and wrapped him in a warm embrace.

Every single bruise seemed to vanish as if by magic; the injuries were as though they had never been. Pain and exhaustion fell away in an instant. Vandhiyathevan felt as though he had left earth somewhere far behind.

The heavens embraced him; he was in paradise.

ॐ

Hidden Meanings and Explanations

"People do say, don't they, that even if you had to be knocked out, better that you suffered it at the hands of your betters?"

Such are Vandhiyathevan's sentiments when he's recovering from Arulmozhi Varmar's blows; the phrase Kalki uses is "*Kuttup pattaalum modhirak kaiyaal kuttup pada vendum ...*" which literally means that if you're going to get a knock on the head, it might as well be by a bejeweled hand, ornamented with rings.

31

THE ELELA SINGAN KOOTHU

A dried out pond in the middle of the jungle served as a clearing big enough to accommodate roughly a thousand Chozha soldiers who had set up *thaavadi*, a camp. Huge stone ovens dotted the area as well, bearing enormous vats and cauldrons with a variety of rice, *koottanchoru*, for their delectation. Any number of side-dishes bubbled away nearby; their collective aroma made everyone's mouths water. Meantime, as difficult as it was to wait until the cooking was done, the men had elected to spend their time in song and dance; their enthusiasm knew no bounds when they saw that their beloved prince had arrived to bear them company. The commander in charge of the border-force found it extremely difficult to quell their exuberance and instill some sort of discipline but he managed, in the end, to make them all sit in a half-moon formation, and maintain silence.

A huge tree had been cut down and a little of its trunk left poking above the earth; the prince took his seat upon this makeshift throne.

No more did he look a simple mahout. Now, his attire proclaimed his high office: a gleaming, golden crown upon his brow; delicately wrought *vaagu valayam* ornaments at his shoulders; pearl necklaces draped on his chest and a beautiful silk *peethambaram* at his waist—he appeared the prince he was, with the border-force's commander, Vandhiyathevan and Azhwarkkadiyaan seated around him.

It was time for the Elela Singan Koothu to begin—a historical play meant for the edification of the prince.

Just as the Chozha forces had captured a good deal of Ilankai at this time, so had they, a thousand years ago; their leader then had been one Elela Singan. Ilankai's ruler had retreated from battle and hidden himself in the hills in a bid to escape him; his son was named Dushtakamanu and a notorious warrior he was, too, cherishing great dreams of recovering Ilankai from Elela Singan some day. One night, when he'd been very young, the prince had lain in bed, his arms and legs folded close to his body. *Pray, child, why do you lie thus, at great inconvenience?* Asked his mother. *Why do you not stretch your limbs and sleep at peace?* Dushtakamanu's answer had been swift. *Thamizh warriors bludgeon me on one side, while the sea crushes me on another; what am I to do but hold myself close and snatch rest in grave discomfort?* Great deeds were naturally expected of such a child, and Dushtakamanu did not disappoint: he gathered an army when he came of age, and went to war with Elela Singan. His men scattered in all four directions, unable to bear the onslaught—but Dushtakamanu's wits did not desert him. He came up with a ruse, approached Elela Singan with great daring, and communicated it to him. "My pitiful army has gone to pieces, unable to battle your massive forces; I'm the only one left. You, Sire, possess the distinction of being born in a noble dynasty; therefore, I put forward a proposition. Let us fight each other, you and I; to the victor shall belong the kingdom of Ilankai. As for the other—he shall attain the illustrious heaven meant for heroes!"

The young warrior's indomitable courage impressed Elela Singan a good deal; he accepted the challenge with alacrity and instructed his men to not interrupt the proceedings on any account.

Battle began, fierce and furious; Dushtakamanu's soldiers, who heard the news, gave up retreating and wandered back, one by one. Soon, a large crowd had gathered around the battling duo.

And it went on and on, for hours. Dushtakamanu fought with the furious desperation of one battling to claim his birthright; Elela Singan, who had begun to sympathize with this spirited youngster almost despite himself, held back a little, and did not use all his considerable force and acumen. In the end, he embraced a warrior's death; upon Dushtakamanu's coronation, the young man erected a memorial in his honour, and lavished praise upon the valour and compassion of the fallen king.

Arulmozhi Varmar's men threw themselves into this rare piece of historical drama and brought both Chozha and Ilankai kings to life, singing and dancing with abandon. Indeed, the actor who donned the role of Elela Singan played dead in the end so convincingly, that those around him wondered for a moment if life had indeed left his body. The prince and the rest of the spectators enjoyed the performances to the hilt, often raising their voices, shouting "Aha!" in praise, as and when the occasion demanded.

The ilango directed his attention towards Azhwarkkadiyaan once, in the midst of the play. "Thirumalai? The battle between Dushtakamanu and Elela Singan has been drawn with the most beautiful colours in the Thampallai cave temple—they're as fresh as though done yesterday. Have you seen them?"

"Not yet, *Ayya*," replied Azhwarkkadiyaan. "We glimpsed you even as we entered the city, you see; there was no time to visit the shrine."

"You must, Thirumalai. Ah, their beauty and lustre is not to be missed. Our Thamizh Nadu boasts a great many works of art, but Ilankai's possessions are a vast deal more spectacular."

"The paintings here aren't about to sprout legs and wander off, your highness; they can be viewed at any time. You, on the other hand— seeking a royal audience is no easy task; we managed it only by the skin of our teeth as it is. Parthibendra Pallavar, who arrived here just a little ahead of us had already turned back, not having had the felicity of meeting you; we ran into him just as he was leaving," Azhwarkkadiyaan explained.

"Indeed; the commander informed me as well, that my beloved brother's friend was in search of me. You couldn't hazard a guess as to the purpose of his visit, could you?"

"Certainly I can; Crown Prince Aditha Karikalar has sent him to escort you to Kanchi."

"*Ada*, you're privy to that information, are you? Then you'd seem to know the contents of the *olai* your precious friend brought me after so many trials and turmoil, wouldn't you?"

"Your sister has bid you to Pazhaiyarai at once. You see, your highness, I concealed myself inside an arbour and watched as she gave this *olai* in secret, to the Vaanar warrior ..."

Vandhiyathevan, seated behind Azhwarkkadiyaan, pinched the Vaishnavite hard.

"Ah, these wretched jungles," Nambi slapped his back. "Bees and insects that sting even at night ...!"

"*Che*, how dare you?" The prince snapped, considerably incensed. "You'd dare play off your tricks on my beloved sister, would you?"

"I'm sure I cannot regret what I did, your highness; it was why I managed to bring this man to you, braving a great deal of danger, after all. As Buddha Bhagavan is my witness, no one knows what I had to go through to get him here in one piece; with his remarkable propensity to pick fights at the slightest provocation, he'd certainly never have made it, had he come through Anuradhapuram and I'd have had his death on my hands. That's why I dragged him through the forest—and even there, he tried to go head to head with a mad elephant! I dealt it a fatal blow with my trusty staff and brought him to you, safe and sound!"

"Oh? Was that the reason for your visit, then? To ensure his safe arrival?"

"Not at all, *Ayya*; I've brought my fair share of messages."

"What are they?" asked the prince. "Quick, man!"

"Chief Minister Aniruddhar thinks it best that you stay right here in Ilankai, for a while."

"Good grief. Three elders, and three messages, all at variance with each other." The prince shook his head. "What am I supposed to do, now?"

"Your highness," Vandhiyathevan intervened, at this moment. "Forgive me—but it's your sister's message that must take precedence over others; hers are the instructions you must follow."

"Must I, indeed? Why?"

"It's what your heart says—deep within, you yearn to respect your sister's wishes. And if it shouldn't please you to do so, *I* ought to," Vandhiyathevan quipped. "Ilaiya Piratti's orders are to bring you to her as soon as I can, you see."

Prince Arulmozhi Varmar turned his attention fully to Vandhiyathevan; his keen gaze swept up and down the Vaanar warrior. "Ah," he murmured to himself. "It was for a brave friend such as you that I've been waiting, all these years ..."

ஃஓ

32

KILLI VALAVAN'S ELEPHANT

By the time the *koothu* came to an end, it was time for the night-meal as well—preparations had concluded moments ago. Bundles of lotus-leaves were brought up and spread in front of the soldiers; *pongal* and a side-dish, a *kariyamudhu* was served as well, piping hot.

As the famished men fell to, the prince began to circulate amongst them. He asked after their health, their food and whatever else he might have been concerned about. Those who had been signaled out for this honour found themselves buffeted by waves of sheer happiness; their neighbours congratulated them upon this stroke of excellent fortune.

Chozhas' Ilango, the young prince, had already been the object of considerable affection—now, with recent events, his popularity touched new heights amongst his men. They were aware, all of them, of his not inconsiderable efforts to procure rice and grain from their homeland; the prince also made the effort to go amongst his men and enquire after their welfare and family, man-to-man, boosting their morale, so to speak, and it was this gesture, more than anything perhaps, that endeared him to his soldiers.

It was not very surprising, therefore, that they tried to stop the prince when he passed among them, gathered courage and posed some sort of question in a bid to hold him in conversation. Most of these seemed to be centred on one concern: *When were they going to launch an offensive against Pulasthya City?* The prince's answers were all different. *What was the point of attacking Pulasthya Nagaram when Mahindan had retreated to Rohanam,* he said, to some. *Patience,* he advocated to others; *the rains were still heavy and it was advisable to wait until the monsoons were done.* A few men were vociferous in their protest of lazing away days in sleep and meals when there was work to be done, while others petitioned him for a visit such as this at least once a month. "That will help us be patient," they declared.

Mealtime enquiries at an end, the prince made his way towards his own *padai veedu,* set at a discreet distance from the camp, making sure to take Azhwarkkadiyaan and Vandhiyathevan with him.

"You saw it all, didn't you? You saw how enthusiastic those soldiers were? Ah, if only I'd had Thanjai's unstinting co-operation, the whole of this island would have been ours by now," the prince shook his head. "A wonderful opportunity has been lost—there's no question of waging war here during the rainy season; our warriors will have to sit twiddling their thumbs for the next three or four months at the very least."

"Your anxiety over local affairs is astonishing, your highness," commented Azhwarkkadiyaan. "The Chozha Empire is practically imploding, across the sea—the splendid realm established by Vijayalaya Chozhar, nurtured and strengthened by brave warriors such as Paranthakar and Sundara Chozhar is in grave danger of disintegrating due to civil unrest and untold perils!"

"Indeed, yes; you've brought me important messages, both of you, while here I am, wasting precious moments over my petty concerns ... well, now: you may tell me everything. I should like to hear from the beginning, starting—" the prince pointed towards Vandhiyathevan. "—with him."

Vandhiyathevan duly obeyed, embarking on the story with his departure from Kanchi, describing everything he'd seen and heard upon his journey. Casual mentions were made of the various spirited stratagems he'd employed to escape from truly precarious situations—although, of course, really, he was loath to draw attention to himself and wouldn't have brought up the subject if the prince hadn't, no, not at all—and finished with the following peroration: "Your beloved father is as good as imprisoned, *Ayya*; those who flaunt their relationship with your family, the very lords and chieftains who've sworn fealty to your dynasty have evolved terrifying conspiracies. Ilaiya Piratti is rightly concerned, and subject to a great deal of worry. You must leave here at once, and come with me to Pazhaiyarai; there's not a second to be wasted."

This was the sign for Azhwarkkadiyaan to take up his tale and he told it well, acknowledging the truth of Vandhiyathevan's own adventures and touching, in addition, upon the alarming plot hatched by assassins in the Thiruppurambiyam memorial. Matters being so, Chief Minister Aniruddhar felt, he emphasized once more, that the prince would do well to stay where he was, instead of entering the country when it was in such turmoil.

"It isn't just a question of remaining here; the *Mudhanmandhiri* wishes you not to undertake further expansion of our territories. He urges you to gather your forces at a point in Northern Ilankai; the conspirators are sure to reveal themselves sooner or later and an army in Eezham is bound to be of great assistance in case of such an eventuality," Azhwarkkadiyaan explained. "Further, the Chief Minister wishes me to inform you of this: the armies quartered at present in Pandiya Nadu—the *Kaikkolar*, *Vanniyar* and *Vellalar* Regiments—are all willing to lay themselves down, body, heart and soul, in the prince's service!"

"Good grief, Thirumalai—what does your precious master think of himself? An Anbil Chanakya, along the lines of the one from

Pataliputhram?" demanded the prince, visibly incensed. "What am I supposed to do—fight my own family and relations?"

"Those aren't his intentions, *Ayya*, and he'd certainly be the last to instruct thus. What he does wish you to understand however, is that those who scheme against the Chakravarthy—who have begun to plot against the empire as a whole—must be punished when the time is right," argued Thirumalai. "Surely yours must be the hand that helps achieve this aim?"

"And pray, what gives me the right to sanction such a punishment? If there indeed be any truth in the rumours of conspiracies, it is for my father, to take appropriate action; how may I act without his express command, in a way that might contravene his authority?"

"Your highness," Vandhiyathevan intervened at this point. "Your father, I regret to say, is no longer his own master; the Pazhuvettarayars keep him under such close guard that he may as well be a prisoner, shackled by their men in his own palace. Your elder brother has sworn a pledge, it seems, to never set foot in Thanjai. With no protectors in the vicinity, shouldn't it be your duty to ensure the safety of the empire? Your responsibility should spur you onto leaving for Pazhaiyarai at once shouldn't it?"

"Now *that* doesn't make a lick of sense; what's the point of the prince going to Pazhaiyarai, pray?" argued Azhwarkkadiyaan.

Said prince spent a few moments, lost in thought. "Lust for land, ah, that's a wicked snare," he murmured, finally. "The sins that have been committed in this world, all for the sake of a kingdom, the urge to rule … you know that I visited the Simmagiri fort today, don't you? You're aware of its history, I hope?"

"I'm not," Vandhiyathevan admitted.

"I shall tell you. Hark! Around five hundred years ago, this island was ruled by a king called Thaathusenan. He had two sons: one was named Kasyapan, the other, Mahallan. Thaathusenan's commander and Kasyapan entered into a plot; the latter threw his own father into prison, and ascended the throne. Mahallan fled across the seas and into Thamizh

Nadu. Sometime later, a wall was built around Thaathusenan's prison; he was killed. Kasyapan, who had been quite nonchalant about his actions until then, began to be terrified that his brother might return and avenge his father's death. He came to this very Simmagiri and decided that he would hide himself here, as his foes might find it impossible to scale its sheer heights and storm the fort. Eighteen years were spent thus, in terrified concealment. Mahallan did arrive one fine day, the Pandiya army, with whom he'd managed to strike an agreement, in tow, and approached the fort of Simmagiri. Kasyapan saw what was happening, and suddenly, lost what wits he'd had. He, who'd kept himself safe all these years by hiding away, now threw the doors open walked out in a fit of brazen idiocy, fought his brother and lost his life! And yet, that rogue—that scoundrel who'd killed his own father—commissioned a series of wonderful paintings in his fort. I viewed them today when I accompanied the Chinese travelers. *Adada*, words fail me when I try to describe their incredible beauty; would you believe it if I told you that those works of art were drawn several hundred years ago, and yet, they remain as fresh and lustrous, bursting with vibrant colours as though done only yesterday ..."

"Permission to pose a question, *Ayya*?" Azhwarkkadiyaan murmured.

"Must you ask? Certainly."

"The fort of Simmagiri lies in the hands of foes, still, doesn't it?"

"It does, and I've no intention of making preparations for its capture. Nothing will accrue of that enterprise but wanton bloodshed."

"That's the least of my concerns *Ayya*—but I did wish to ask you this: was it well done of you to have entered the fort of an enemy, thus? Was that not a tad reckless? Where was the need to disguise yourself as a mahout to Chinese travelers of all things, pray? I didn't dare believe my own eyes when I saw you at the elephant's very neck; I could be certain of your identity only when I glimpsed your brows draw together. Is it wise, I ask you, to subject yourself to this sort of peril?"

"My life is hardly worth that much, is it, Thirumalai? When I think of the number of Chozha men who've sacrificed their lives in the name of duty on this very island ..."

"In the battlefield, yes, and they embraced a warrior's death—but you, on the other hand, have been subjecting your person to needless risks—"

"I wouldn't quite call it that, Thirumalai. I had two reasons for wishing to enter Simmagiri: one was to gaze upon the beautiful paintings within the fort, and I managed to realize that ambition—"

"And the other, your highness?"

"I received news the instant Parthibendra Pallavar set foot in Thirikona Malai, but didn't wish to see him that day because ..."

"Because...?"

" —I knew that the Chief Minister had arrived in Maathottam for his part; I was in expectation of news from him as well. And if I should receive messages from two elders at the same time, I shall have had to abide by the first—"

"Well said, your highness," Vandhiyathevan exulted. "I win, don't I?"

"Beg pardon, but this man used a silly a trick, a ruse to take you in—"

"He didn't; I fell for his tricks all by myself. I saw him trip the man meant to escort you here, leap upon his horse and gallop away; I believed that he needed to be taught a lesson—"

"You certainly did; ha, each one of your hefty lessons might have weighed a ton! My back and chest throb even now when I think of it; is it fair to treat an envoy thus, I ask you? Be that as it may, if you'd just agree, now, to come to Pazhaiyarai—"

"I'm reminded of an old verse—Thirumalai, an ancestor of mine, Perunkilli Valavan by name, possessed a wonderful elephant. It's said that one of its legs could stand in Kanchi; another in Thanjai; a third would be firm upon Eezham while the fourth would stomp down in Uraiyur.

"Kachi orukaal mithiyaa oru kaalaal
Thathuneerth thanthanjai thaanmithiyaap—pitraiyum
Eezham oru kaal mithiyaa varume nam
Kozhiyar kokkillik kaliru!"

Witness the imaginative genius, if you please, of the poet! This very island has thousands of elephants tramping up and down hills and valleys, but what's the use? If I but had just one elephant, like the one that's the subject of this verse, I too could be in Kanchi, Pazhaiyarai, Madurai and Ilankai all at the same time, couldn't I?"

Vandhiyathevan and Azhwarkkadiyaan practically split their sides with laughter, at this peculiar fancy.

"Well, you certainly don't possess such a magical mount," Nambi said, finally. "What's to be done, now?"

"It's been decided that Pazhaiyarai is our destination, hasn't it?" Vandhiyathevan demanded. "What else needs to be debated?"

"Cease your squabbling for a while, you two. We're leaving for Anuradhapuram tomorrow, where I shall have to meet Parthibendra Pallavar," announced the prince. "Whatever decision I make will have to wait until I learn what he has to say."

33

THE STATUE'S MESSAGE

By the time the sun rose the next morning, Arulmozhi Varmar, Azhwarkkadiyaan and Vandhiyathevan were well on their way towards Anuradhapuram, traveling along the forest path for a while before stepping onto the *rajapattai*. That the prince hadn't opted for an escort of a few well-chosen guards was a source of enormous astonishment—and yet, to Vandhiyathevan, it didn't seem as though he had ever attempted a journey as uplifting as this one. To ride upon the glorious king's road, shielded on both sides by majestic trees at that early hour, was a fabulous experience in itself and adding to it was the pride bubbling within—he'd carried out the Pazhaiyarai princess's commission with flying colours, hadn't he? Not to mention having fulfilled one of his life's greatest ambitions: to meet the most beloved son of Chozha Nadu; the one whose valour, good sense and amiable character were being praised sky-high by every citizen of the country—and what a meeting *that* had been, to be sure! All the fantastic tales of the prince's quirks were true, it seemed; hadn't he whipped his horse about in a flash and practically barged into Vandhiyathevan, sending his senses reeling? This, then, must be the secret of Arulmozhi Varmar reaping victory after victory upon every battlefield; the source of his power over every battalion; his unorthodox martial strategies probably took his enemies by surprise, rendering them powerless ... but surely his prowess in war was not the only reason for his widespread acclaim? Witness his behaviour with his men—the genuine camaraderie, and concern for their wellbeing? It wasn't a surprise that they conceived for him a slavish affection. And not just the warriors either; one look at the people of this conquered land, and it was obvious that they practically worshipped him as well. Could anyone guess, from the well-maintained roads and towns, that this was a war-ravaged country? Ah, how carefree were these people as they walked along the streets! How joyous these villagers, living on either side of the road looked, as they went about their business? Not the slightest hint of terror or sorrow marred their clear faces. Why—the happy laugher of children and the gentler, softer tones of relieved women surprised him more than anything: what sort of a strange prince was Ponniyin Selvar? A man who refused to confiscate food from the very mouths of the vanquished and insisted on importing grains and pulses by the shipload, from his homeland?

Memories of the Pazhuvettarayars' simmering resentment, and their numerous complaints to Sundara Chozhar about this strange state of affairs surfaced in Vandhiyathevan's mind. Almost despite himself, comparisons between Aditha Karikalar's ruthless, rough-and-ready methods and Arulmozhi Varmar's benevolent approach thrust themselves forcibly into his cogitations. That he was forced to entertain such derogatory thoughts about a man who had been his master until recently, was extremely distasteful—and yet, such comparisons were inevitable every time he happened to catch sight of a pleasant, open countenance on both sides of the *rajapattai* towards Anuradhapuram. *Ammamma!* Dare he even imagine such a sight in the lands conquered by Aditha Karikalar? Wouldn't the terrain be ripped apart by the shrieks and howls of tormented souls?

All these and more inspired Vandhiyathevan with such a desire to engage the prince in discussion upon every subject he could think of—and those were numerous — that he could barely control the words tripping over his tongue, but alas! The opportunities to indulge in such intimate conversations while riding across the countryside on a swift horse were next to none. And yet—one occasion did offer itself; Vandhiyathevan was quick to seize it.

They were almost upon the city, when a huge statue of Buddha Bhagavan by the roadside caught his attention. Not by much, though; he'd seen simply too many such dotting Ilankai to be impressed. Ponniyin Selvar, on the other hand, seemed to think differently; the sight of him suddenly reining in his horse and coming to a halt forced Vandhiyathevan to do the same. Azhwarkkadiyaan, who had been trotting a little ahead of them, wheeled his steed around and headed towards them.

For a while, Ponniyin Selvar stared at the large, majestic statue without blinking an eye. "*Adada*, what a beautiful work, to be sure," he murmured.

"I'm afraid I don't quite see the charm of these humongous statues— they're *everywhere* in this country!" lamented Vandhiyathevan. "Frankly, what's the point?"

"Your speech mirrors your thoughts exactly, doesn't it?" The prince threw an amused glance at the Vaanar warrior. "A pleasing trait."

"One that Vallavaraiyar has begun to emulate only today, your highness," quipped Thirumalai.

"My companions decide my character, Vaishnavite," Vandhiyathevan rallied. "Ever since I set eyes upon you in Veera Narayanapuram, my powers of imagination have touched new heights—but once I saw the prince, honesty became my policy."

Said prince, however, was not paying attention to this war of words and appeared, instead, to be lost in contemplation of the divine Buddha. "There are only two forms in the whole world, I believe, that encompass sculptural perfection," he commented, at last. "The Buddha, and Natarajar, the King of Dance."

"But Natarajar is never fashioned along such huge proportions in our land, is He?"

"Some of the ancient kings of Ilankai were truly great men," began Ponniyin Selvar. "Their territories may have been small, but their hearts were large and their devotion, even greater. This—fashioning enormous statues of Buddha Bhagavan—was their way of exhibiting the feeling that overflowed their souls, and they erected enormous *stupams* too, in honour of the religion that ruled them. When I gaze upon these magnificent specimens, gigantic sculptures, elaborate viharams, and then turn my eyes towards the tiny temples of my own land ..." he paused, and sighed. "My heart shrinks with humiliation."

The prince dismounted upon these words and walked up to the statue; he gazed intently at the divine feet, the *padma paadham* for a few moments, taking in the lotus buds that were placed as simple decoration. Then, he placed his hands upon the Buddha's feet, touched them to his eyes in prayer, and mounted his stallion as before.

As the tiny cavalcade proceeded slowly, Vandhiyathevan darted a glance pregnant with meaning at the Vaishnavite. "Upon my word, it almost looks like his highness might convert to Buddhism at this rate!"

His low words reached Arulmozhi Varmar, who turned a comprehensive glance upon his companions. "My devotion to the great Buddha is attendant upon certain reasons—for His *padma paadham* delivered a very important message."

"Did they? But not a word reached our ears ..."

"With reason; the communication was conducted through the medium of silence."

"And what might this message be? May we know?"

"Buddha's lotus feet requested me to arrive in the vicinity of the pond near the Fountain of Lions in Anuradhapuram," confided Ponniyin Selvar. "... at the twelfth *naazhigai*, tonight."

⁊ꙅ

34

ANURADHAPURAM

The sun was vanishing over the horizon by the time they set foot in Anuradhapuram. Vandhiyathevan, catching sight of one of Ilankai's most venerated and ancient cities, gaped at it speechless, lost in amazement.

Much had he heard from those who had visited it; a certain picture had emerged in his mind based on their overwhelmed descriptions. But now that he had seen it for himself—ah! The splendid city's resplendence beggared description, and went beyond all bounds of his puny imagination. *Ammamma*, what a massive fortress—walls of such a length!—it didn't seem possible to guess just how far they went on both sides, before finally circling around the city! And as for the spires that towered above them; the *gopurams*, lofty *mandapams* and *stupams* that competed with one another in height—how numerous, and how far apart these edifices! How was it possible for such a proliferation of grand mansions, palaces and towers to exist within these walls? Why, what were the grand cities of Kanchi, Pazhaiyarai and even Thanjai, before such magnificence? Perhaps one or two—such as Pataliputhram in Ashokar's times; Ujjaini during the rule of Vikramaditya and Kaverippattinam, under the great Karikal Valavan—ah, these cities, perhaps, might equal Anuradhapuram in splendour; certainly none from present day could even be considered a rival ...

The closer their approach to the entrance; the larger the crowd surging towards the fort-walls. Tamils and Singalavars; men, women and children; *bikshus* and householders all thronged towards the city as though in eager anticipation of a chariot festival, perhaps; the arrival of our travelers caught the attention of some of them, who began to point them out, and whisper among themselves. Ponniyin Selvar, upon whom none of these signs were lost, gestured to his companions, veered off the *rajapattai* and onto a smaller, little-used short-cut. They trotted on for a brief space, before coming to a stop at the base of a small hillock surrounded by leafy trees. "Our horses have traveled for hours, today," he looked at the other two. "We'd better rest here awhile and enter the city after dark."

The trio dismounted and made themselves comfortable on a large, convenient boulder.

"Such a crowd, pouring into the city!" Vandhiyathevan exclaimed. "There wouldn't be a festival of some sort today, would there?"

"The biggest of them all, in fact," replied the prince. "Considering how many there are, that's certainly something."

"I was worrying about this huge war that everyone swore was decimating Eezha Nadu ..." Vandhiyathevan shook his head. " ... only to come here and find everyone off their heads, celebrating a grand *thiruvizha*."

"You mentioned the Sri Jayanthi festivities in Pazhaiyarai, didn't you?"

"True, but in a city that happens to be in Chozha Nadu ..."

"And Anuradhapuram is in Eezha Nadu. What of it? It's Sundara Chozha Chakravarthy who rules those lands after all, and his benevolent sceptre that extends its authority over this island too ..."

"But—aren't there enemies lurking here, still?"

"Probably—again, what of it? Must their nefarious activities be allowed to affect ordinary citizens? War may rage in the battlefields, but towns and cities must be able to rejoice in their festivals ... Thirumalai, what do you say?"

"Foes may lurk here but so do traitors over there, and while our foes at least gather forces out in the open, there's no saying what stealthy depths conspirators may descend to, which is why this servant feels that your highness would do well to prolong your stay on this island, conducting festivals or ferocious battles, as the case may be," Azhwarkkadiyaan paused for breath, having delivered this lengthy peroration.

"Your statement would actually be quite amusing, if it weren't so ridiculous," Vandhiyathevan denounced him roundly. "If plotters and schemers were so dangerous, wouldn't it make more sense for the prince to be amongst them? Isn't that the very essence of fearlessness; the hallmark of a true warrior?"

"Oh, please—as if walking straight into a trap without the slightest attempt to safeguard oneself, ignoring every ounce of commonsense or advice, is the trait of every hardened warrior," Azhwarkkadiyaan scoffed. "Why don't *you* suit action to words then, lion-heart that you are? Instead of turning tail and running over here—"

"Cease your squabbles, you two," Arulmozhi Varmar poured oil over troubled waters. "We don't want a war right here, do we?"

Darkness fell, and was the sign for the three travelers to slip into the city. No one was detained at the gates that day, it seemed; fortress sentries simply stood in place, watching anyone walk through without batting an eyelid and our three heroes managed to enter the fort without hassle, mingling with the crowds.

Inside, Anuradhapuram appeared to be bursting at the seams as an endless stream of people wove along the streets in dizzying fashion, while chants of *"Saadhu! Saadhu!"* rose deafeningly. Here and there, Vandhiyathevan spotted mansions and viharams that were crumbling, while still other monasteries were being renovated; the latter, at any rate, must have upon the prince's orders, he decided. As to what might have prompted this liberal gesture ... that was genuinely puzzling. Why must the prince expend such extraordinary effort towards winning over the people of a conquered land? Battle and destruction were, after all, nothing new, here: Singala rulers had been warring with Thamizhagam for a thousand years, and instead of torching and razing the capital of their sworn enemy, reducing this city to ashes, here was the ilango, permitting tumbled-down buildings to be renovated, and festivals to be conducted! Astonishing indeed—but there was something else going here, he was sure. Something mysterious, as yet unexplained.

And then, a theory swam into Vandhiyathevan's curious mind, beginning to take gradual shape. Yes, that must be it, surely: this prince had no say in Chozha politics; there was no place for him in Thanjavur, after all—Aditha Karikalar was the Crown Prince with the right, hopefully, to ascend the throne someday, and contending for that same, supreme position was Madhuranthaka Thevar, which meant that Arulmozhi Varmar was probably engaging in these measures to carve a kingdom for himself on this little island—and who knew? His ambitions might well have some foundation; now what was it that the Kudandhai astrologer had predicted? Something about, yes ... *The Dhruva star never vacillates; it shines steadily, always holding its position. That, Thambi, describes Emperor Sundara Chozhar's youngest son, Prince Arulmozhi Varmar. Nothing can shake his courage and determination; he is as valiant as he is compassionate and trustworthy. Those who believe in him shall never find their trust betrayed* ... And this was the warrior with whom he now found himself; the man to whom his arduous journey had led. Vandhiyathevan felt as though his heart might burst with contentment.

They were now at the entrance of an old mansion that looked like it might drop onto their heads at any moment, and dismounted. This area was a little apart from prominent streets and was, consequently, devoid of people. The prince clapped thrice; the next instant, a door on one side of the mansion slid open as though by magic. No one seemed to be there, however, and he walked forward in the darkness. Curiosity got the better of Vandhiyathevan, who turned and peered out to know the fate of their horses—not that he got very far in his quest.

"Our steeds know their way," informed the prince and gave the Vaanar warrior no more time to dawdle; he gripped his hand tight and practically dragged Vandhiyathevan along with him. For a while, their path was in darkness but before long, chinks of light appeared in the distance; soon it grew bright, and Vallavarayan realized that they had arrived at the interior of an ancient palace.

"We'll have to be a little careful here, I'm afraid," the prince murmured. "This is Chakravarthy Mahasenar's *anthappuram*, after all; he might make a sudden appearance and throw us out at a moment's notice."

"Mahasenar who?" asked Vandhiyathevan, staring all around him.

"The Emperor who ruled the kingdom of Ilankai, over six hundred years ago. He did a great deal of good for the people, and is supposed to still haunt this city; they hang cloths in trees, believing him to shiver in the cold! No one has lived here either; this palace has been empty ever since his death."

Servants waited, eager to serve the prince and his companions; once the trio bathed and dined, they ascended to the palace's balcony from where could be had a glimpse of the whole city, spread out beneath in a beautiful vista. As comprehensive as their own view was, they chose a spot from where those below could not enjoy the same felicity, and seated themselves.

"Didn't you mention, *Ayya*, that the Buddha statue wished you to be somewhere at the twelfth *naazhigai*?" Vandhiyathevan queried.

"There's time, yet—look above, the moon has only just risen," the prince explained. "Once he's ascended to that point right above the *thaagabaa*, will be the time for us to set off."

A *stupam* rose like a large hillock against the sky, where he pointed. As these edifices were erected above a speck of Buddha Bhagavan's sacred remains, they were referred to as *Thaathu-garbam*—which gradually underwent linguistic changes to become *thaagabaa*. Vandhiyathevan stared at it, amazed. "Why did they erect such massive monuments?"

"In the beginning, to exhibit the greatness of Buddha Bhagavan to the general public. Later, as a means of displaying the kings' own magnificence," the prince tone was dry. "And they did excel—each *stupam* was bigger than the previous one!"

A little later, something almost akin to the thundering roar of oceans fell upon their ears; Vandhiyathevan peered down, in the direction of the uproar. A huge crowd, an army of people came surging up the street in the distance, wave after endless wave, and amidst them seemed to float large, dark shapes the size of whales—elephants, in their hundreds. A thousand torches flickered and gleamed amongst them like the refection of twinkling stars upon the sea, while the people themselves numbered in lakhs.

"Good heavens," Vandhiyathevan gaped at the moving, heaving mass below. "This almost looks like an invasion—"

"Not at all," the prince intervened. "Just the biggest celebration of this island—the *Peraherath* festival."

The closer the peoples' approach, the greater Vandhiyathevan's astonishment; his eyes fairly popped out of his head, for he had seen nothing like it in his life, ever.

First came thirty elephants in an orderly fashion; all decorated with elaborate, rich golden plates covering their forehead and trunk. The one in the middle seemed the most ornately bedecked of them all, swaggering majestically. Upon its back reposed a golden casket, encrusted richly with the nine precious gems; a golden umbrella shielding the whole. *Bikshus* sat atop the elephants surrounding the one in the centre; they waved whisks liberally embellished with silver. Others walked amidst the mounts, holding aloft torches, *kuthuvilakkus* and other lamps, elaborately fashioned. The golden plates and ornaments upon the majestic pachyderms, the silver handles on the monks' whisks flashed and glittered in the light of the lamps, captivating everyone.

A massive crowd followed the elephants, and amidst them were approximately hundred people, all in strange attire and ornaments, dancing. A good many carried the *udukkai* as well, beating to a rhythm, while still others played more instruments. *Appappa!* What a wonderful dance, too—the Devaralan and Devaratti's performance in the Kadambur palace was nothing—*nothing* at all, compared to this magnificence! Some of the dancers leapt into the air, spun twice or thrice and descended to earth gracefully; mid-air, the rolls of cloth and *kunjams*, little spheres embellished with ornaments tied around their waists, whirled out in eye-catching arcs like flower-adorned umbrellas. The sight of a hundred or so dancers, swinging up in the air and spinning thus, their ornaments along with them—ah, you needed two thousand eyes, not just two, to appreciate the splendour of the spectacle. And a couple of hundred thousand ears as well, to perceive the beauty of the instrumental play that accompanied the dancers for the *udukkai, thunthubi, mathalam,* conches, *parai* and others bellowed together at their highest pitch; it was a wonder no one's ear had been deafened yet.

Once the dancers and the surrounding crowd had moved past the trio, thirty more elephants came into view, decorated as richly as the preceding mounts; the one in the centre carried a well-adorned casket with a golden umbrella on top; the *bikshus* around waved their whisks gently. Dancers followed these elephants as well—but this time, they were costumed to resemble Rathi, Manmadhan, and the Three-Eyed God Himself—and the people around them danced and leapt in devotion mingled with ecstasy.

"Well, of all the—!" Vandhiyathevan exclaimed. "How on earth did Siva Peruman arrive here?"

"Brought over by the Ilankai king Gajabahu," was the prince's reply. "It may have been meant to be just a brief visit—but stubborn deity that he is, Sivan stayed here for good."

"*Oi*, Nambi—you see who's the greater God, now? Do you understand—" Before Vandhiyathevan could continue, several more elephants arrived, complete with adornments as the previous groups; this time, the people who followed them were interspersed with dancers dressed in feathers, beak-like noses meant to imitate Garudazhwar, Thirumaal's sacred mount, leaping high, spinning, twirling, dancing and shaking their beaks in most enthusiastic fashion.

"Well, *Appane?*" Azhwarkkadiyaan pounced. "It looks like Lord Vishnu has made an appearance as well, upon his divine mount!"

Another elephant convoy appeared, accompanied this time by dancers armed to the teeth and dressed in full battle regalia, prancing about with their swords, spears and javelins. *Danaar! Danaar!* Their sharp weapons flashed and clashed according to the beats that thrummed around them, and the mesmerizing rhythm of their dance.

The elephants that swaggered up last of all were followed by dancers holding aloft a *silambu* in each hand, swirling and twirling to the beats, the anklets jingling and jangling with every step. The dancers themselves varied their movements at each turn, bursting into frenzied dervishes at one moment; turning into gentle, soothing angels the next, showing off the lilting softness of their movements.

Vandhiyathevan stood staring at these extraordinary scenes; along with the strange melodies, sounds and beats, poured into his ears the legend behind the wonderful festival—as narrated by the prince himself.

As much as there was a history of strife, there had been times when the kings of Thamizhagam and Ilankai had extended the courtesy of friendship to each other as well; Gajabahu of the emerald isles ringed by the sea, and Cheran Senguttuvan had been two such. The former had been present when the latter conducted festivals in honour of the famed *pathini* Kannaki, the woman revered for her devotion to her husband; Gajabahu had stayed behind to enjoy more such celebrations. Later, when Cheran Senguttuvan repaid that honour with a royal visit to Ilankai, it was Gajabahu's turn to commemorate the occasion with festivals, and he did so with aplomb: Siva Peruman, Thirumaal, Karthikeyar and Kannaki all figured in the massive festivities. Once he discovered his peoples' keen enjoyment, the decision was made to conduct it annually, conferring a signal honour upon Buddha Bhagavan by placing Him at the head of the procession while the other deities followed. Custom prevailed, took root and gradually became entrenched into Ilankai's cultural psyche, and the festival continues to be celebrated until this day in a grand fashion—the most famous *thiruvizha* of the island.

"But I don't see the deities anywhere," Vandhiyathevan objected.

"You did glimpse the golden casket upon each elephant that walked amidst several others?"

"Have they locked up the *deivams* within those little boxes?" Vandhiyathevan wondered. "What're they afraid of? That they might make their escape to Thamizhagam?"

"Good God, no," Ponniyin Selvar chuckled. "The first casket contains the sacred tooth of Buddha Bhagavan Himself, carefully guarded by the people; the greatest treasure of the Buddhists of this island. The sacred relict has been preserved for centuries and is paraded in a procession upon an elephant, during these special occasions."

"What about the other caskets?"

"They couldn't find the teeth of Siva Peruman, Vishnu, Murugan and Kannaki, I'm afraid," the prince smiled. "The others contain ornaments that usually adorn those deities in their temple and are paraded in place of human relics."

Vandhiyathevan sank into deep thought, for a few moments. "Good lord, if Periya Pazhuvettarayar had come to war here, instead of you ...?"

The last of the procession turned a street-corner at that moment and was soon lost to sight; the mingled commotion of people, elephants and instruments began to die down.

"We've only a *naazhigai* until our meeting," announced the prince, slipping down from the platform. "Time to leave." The trio descended to the street and took the direction opposite the procession. As almost the entire population of the city had followed the Peraherath parade, scarce anyone accosted them, and they soon reached a lake of enormous dimensions. Water lapped at the shore gently while moonbeams played upon the surface, turning the waves into sheets of sheer, eye-catching silver.

The men stepped down to the lake's banks and walked on; the sweet scent of *shenbagam* flowers bade them welcome while various other blooms, stark white in the moonlight, hung heavily upon bushes. Here and there, small hillocks and man-made ponds met their vision as well; upon one of these was a spout fashioned like the face of a lion, with water gushing out of its mouth to make a pretty waterfall. They walked up to the banks of this pond and waited.

Vandhiyathevan glanced around him. The image of the Buddha statue by the road, outside Anuradhapuram swam into his mind.

The lotus buds at the Buddha's feet! The prince must have counted them, and arrived at the twelfth naazhigai. And they'd been buds—not fully unfurled flowers—which denoted night—and now that Vandhiyathevan cudgeled his memory, he did seem to remember, faintly, the presence of a small vessel, a *gindi*, shaped like the face of a lion. *It probably indicated this very pond—it must have!*

This is all well and good, but who is the perpetrator of this mysterious message, arranging for this assignation? Even more important, what about the perils of a meeting such as this? To top it all off, the prince has prevented us from arming ourselves—why? Perhaps—is there going to be some sort of a romantic interlude? Is that the whole point?

Romance—ah! Vandhiyathevan's heart churned; his mind flew the next instant, over sea and towards Pazhaiyarai; the images of Ilaiya Piratti and Vanathi Devi floated before his mind's eye. He wondered if he could pick the prince's brain and discover something—anything.

"Ha—this place seems to resemble the elaborate gardens of an ancient palace," he opened his gambit.

"You're not far off; it *was* one. A thousand years ago, Dushtakamanu's palace used to be situated nearby—look over there! Parts of his residence still exist."

Vandhiyathevan threw a cursory glance at the dilapidated buildings and mansions at a little distance. "That might have been an *anthappuram*, and the princesses would have come here to play about in the water—a *jalakreedai* in this very *thadaagam*, perhaps!"

"Did you know—something really strange did happen in this *nandavanam*, as a matter of fact. A thousand years ago, King Dushtakamanu's son Saali was taking a leisurely walk, one day. He caught sight of a girl filling her pitcher from this very *thadaagam*, and watering the flower-bushes in the garden. He fell in love with her at once, learning only later that she belonged to the Chandaala caste, and was called Asokamala. Despite her lowly status, he stayed stubborn in his determination to marry her. *If you persist in your infatuation, you will be denied the throne,* declared his father. *Who cares? It's Asokamala I want,* announced prince Saalivahanan. Can you even imagine another prince in the whole world, making such a daring assertion?"

The picture of Poonguzhali, paddling her boat in the choppy seas of Kodikkarai suddenly flashed into Vandhiyathevan's quick mind. Hah—was it on account of her that the prince had chosen to relate this tale? Was he thinking of her now, this very moment?

Even as he wondered how best to bring up the subject of Samudhra Kumari, something rather magical occurred.

The Fountain of Lions was designed in such a way that the interior wall curved inwards, allowing for a stone seat that could accommodate two. Suddenly, the feeble light of a lamp appeared to one side of this tiny alcove.

The hand of a man holding aloft the lamp, appeared, followed by the wise countenance of a Buddhist monk.

Vandhiyathevan stared at this fantastic *indrajaalam*, mouth agape, eyes wide as saucers. Such was his eagerness to know what might happen next that he even stopped breathing, for a few moments.

ॐ

35

THE THRONE OF ILANKAI

The *bikshu* stared around him by the light of the lamp in his hands. No sooner did he seem to set eyes upon the prince and his friends, than the feeble light and lamp vanished. Moments later saw the monk step down the stairs adjoining the *thadaagam*. He approached the ilango—and in the pearly, gentle light of the moon, looked unto his blessed countenance.

"Welcome, welcome, Devapriya, most beloved of the *Gods*! The *Vaithulya Bikshu Sangam* awaits thy gracious presence this very moment; the Maha Thero Guru has arrived in person, showering us with his divine grace. Indeed, words fail me; my heart overflows with gratitude at thy prompt and punctual arrival!"

"This humble servant is flawed in innumerable ways, Your Holiness—but I do possess a few virtues; keeping my word is one of them," answered the son of Ponni. "I may go so far as to promise that this is an oath I have never broken thus far."

"I had learnt that the city was bereft of thy presence, even as late as dusk. That, I must confess, worried me a good deal."

"Had I come earlier, I might not have been able to keep my word and so, I arrived at the appointed moment."

"Indeed, yes! Dark and ominous clouds gather upon the horizon in a vain bid to blot out the glorious sun and destroy its luminous presence— this, we do know. And yet, the blessed winds of Lord Buddha's grace and compassion shall disperse all into nothing. Be that as it may—who are these people? They are well-known to thee, I hope? And worthy of thy trust?" enquired the monk. "Are they capable of keeping their word as well?"

"I trust these men, Your Holiness, as I would my own two hands. Should you so decree, however, I am willing to leave them here and come alone," offered the prince.

"Ah, no—I am unwilling to shoulder such an enormous responsibility," refused the monk. "It is true that our destination is as safe as can be—and yet, the path is long; who shall divine the dangers that lurk behind each pillar, as the saying goes? These men may accompany thee, by all means."

Vandhiyathevan, who had been listening to this entire exchange with bated breath, felt his heart heave with the tumult of emotion. That the prince reposed such confidence in him—even to the extent of risking his presence on a perilous, confidential mission such as this—thrilled him beyond measure.

An extremely important event was to happen tonight; that was certain, his heart whispered, almost thrumming with excited anticipation. The question was—what?

***

The three men followed the monk, who went ahead, guiding them up the *thadaagam* steps and to the back, into a chamber carved out of stone. He went to a wall and did something in the dark—upon which a pathway appeared. A light blinked, within. The *bikshu* hefted a torch; as soon as the three newcomers crowded in, the entrance disappeared. The sound of water falling from the *singamuga thadaagam* reached them faintly from beyond the walls; else, they would have found it difficult to believe that they had been standing on the banks of that very pond just moments ago.

The group continued their journey along a narrow, underground passage that wound round and round confusingly, and seemed to have no end in sight. The sound of their footsteps echoed off the walls in terrifying fashion. There were moments when Vandhiyathevan was shaken by the horrifying suspicion that the prince had wandered, all unwittingly, into a trap.

The path widened in a while, ending in a *mandapam*—and what a *mandapam* it proved to be! Only a fraction of the space was visible in the monk's feeble torch-light—but even this was enough to proclaim the fact that the columns were of solid marble. Statues of Buddha Bhagavan dotted the floor in all four directions. Buddhas who stood; sat in meditation; lay down; blessed eager devotees or were themselves lost in prayer … ah, how many, indeed!

They crossed the marble *mandapam*, this time, into another narrow passage. And then, another hall which seemed to possess pillars embellished with bronze plates, glowing with the subdued fire of rubies in the torch-light. The roof was covered in bronze plate as well, filled with beautifully wrought art. Buddha statues dotted the floor.

Past, in the same fashion, a *mandapam* supported by columns of a strange, rare yellow wood of some kind; another with pillars embellished with delicately carved ivory, and a *mandapam* with columns wrought with gold and precious stones. Despite their frantic pace, Vandhiyathevan still found time to touch and marvel at random pillars. What surprised him enormously was that not only was the prince *not* subject to the same temptation—he didn't even seem to notice them.

*Mandapam*s of metal all having been crossed, they arrived, finally, at a simple one of hewn stone. This vast space presented a truly astonishing sight: while the previous halls had been devoid of anything but the statues of the Buddha, this one contained signs of life—a great many monks. Their calm faces shone with a surreal glow and in their august midst was seated the Maha Thero Guru. In front of him stood a magnificent golden throne, set with the legendary nine precious gems. Beside, on a low table, rested a bejeweled crown, sword, and sceptre. Torches blazed in all four corners of the *mandapam*; the throne and crown well nigh dazzled in their bright glow.

The monks rose with one accord, as soon as the prince and his escorts entered the space. "Long live the Buddha," chants arose, collectively. "Love live *Dharmam!*" came another. "*Sangam Vaazhga!*" echoed a third.

The prince approached the Maha Thero Guru, and folded his hands respectfully.

The Master, the one who led the *bikshu*s present towards enlightenment in this world, pointed to a simple, unadorned seat next to him, and signed that Arulmozhi Varmar be seated.

"Maha Guru," the prince put forth, in respectful tones. "I must request that you, my senior in age, accomplishments and *dharma*, take your seat, first."

Once the Adhyatchaga Maha Guru had done so, the prince followed.

"Our Maha Bodhi Sangam is cast into transports of delight at thy arrival, great prince, Beloved of the Gods. Thy presence here could not have been an easy accomplishment, as thou hast encountered a great many obstacles in a bid to accede to all our stipulations. There can be no doubt, thus, that thou art most worthy of Buddha Bhagavan's immense grace!" As the Master stopped his speech in the Pali language, the monk who had acted as their escort translated it into Thamizh. The rest of the monks chanted "*Saadhu! Saadhu!*" as a way of expressing their appreciation.

"We are greatly indebted to Bharathavarsha, the illustrious land that bequeathed to us the way of the Buddha," the Maha Thero continued. "And yet, it saddens us to say that various royals of the Chozha, Pandiya, Malayalam and Kalinga kingdoms have taken every opportunity of assaulting this island, heaping the curses of the Gods upon their hapless heads by the ignominious looting of various Buddhist viharams and monasteries. But why hold only thy kings responsible? Our own rulers have scarcely been honourable, descending to grave crimes, planting discord within the Sangam; flattening the monasteries of monks who dared to disagree with their edicts, and offering them up Agni. Once, Buddhist viharams had the satisfaction of occupying at least half of this vast, sacred city, boasting dimensions two *kaadhams* in length and a *kaadham* in breadth; today, almost all are in ruins. No royal family has given orders thus far to repair, and restore them to their original, ancient splendour. No, that stroke of good fortune—the immense honour of issuing the command to restore our monasteries, has been bestowed on none other than Prince Arulmozhi Varmar himself. Most beloved of the Gods, words cannot do justice to the Buddhist Maha Sangam's delight, at thy commendable act ..."

The prince bowed, accepting this benediction with every semblance of respect.

"In addition, this ancient, blessed city was deprived of the Peraherath festival as well, for a long time. The Pandiya dynasty captured this land a hundred years ago, and the Ilankai royal family of those times was forced to flee to Pulasthya Nagaram. The festival which was stopped abruptly has not been revived until thy edict this year, that it may be conducted as it was, in ancient times. Aside from thy gracious permission, thy benevolence in sanctioning the requisite financial assistance has pleased the members of this Sangam immensely, as well ..."

"Maha Guru," the prince bowed again. "If there is aught that this servant can do to please your noble selves, lay the command, and it shall be done."

"Indeed, yes, Prince," the Adhyatchagar smiled. "The Buddhist Sangam has every expectation of thy service, in the future. A few more words need to be said, before that issue can be touched upon. Thou hast knowledge, of course, of the various incarnations of the Buddha before He made his last, most illustrious appearance. The Great One took form as the noble Sibi Chakravarthy with the sole purpose of showing kindness to every life-form and announcing to the world, the merit of such virtuous actions. He cut up his own flesh and weighed it on scales, with the express intent of saving the life of a little dove. Thou and thy people the Chozhas call thyselves the descendents of Emperor Sibi. This, it is said, is the reason for one of thy dynasty's famed titles, *Sembian*. Thus far, however, the Buddhist Sangam had placed no faith in such claims; this was, they believed, just another fable circulated by crafty priests of the Chozha ruling clan. Now, however—having seen thy gracious acts of benevolence—we conclude with much satisfaction that the Chozha's claim of descent from the illustrious Sibi is undoubtedly just. Thy great clan has had its sight clouded to the Buddha's infinite compassion by the veil of illusion until now, and remained in ignorance; on this day, however, that divine grace has fit to reveal itself before thy self, and reside in thy form. Indeed, it would not be an exaggeration to say that we have received a celestial sign of this momentous event. There …!'"

As the Adhyatchaga Thero turned behind, several monks carried forward a seat, upon which lay another *bikshu*. His entire body shook without pause; his hands trembled; head shivered; teeth clinked and clanked as they clashed; lips quivered—even the brows, framing his bloodshot eyes, throbbed incessantly.

"Three and thirty crores of Gods have come upon this *bikshu*," announced the Maha Thero. "Listen to the words They bestow upon thee so graciously—and heed them well!"

Strange words in a language that seemed alien, spilled with frightening speed out of the quivering lips of the monk, who shook as though possessed by some powerful entity. Once his outpouring stopped, the Adhyatchaga Guru took over: "The most bountiful Gods, the *muppaththu mukkodi* Devas have chosen thee, fortunate one, to offer their boundless blessings. In an age long gone, Devanampriya Asokar, Most Beloved of the Gods, ruled over this vast Bharatha land and spread the divine word of the Buddha throughout the world. Now, the Devas have chosen thee for a most generous benediction: thou too, shall follow in his footsteps and rule the world, the Emperor of a magnificent *samrajyam*. They wish that thou shall carry the word of the Buddha to all corners of the world, just as Emperor Asokar once did. They command thee to begin this great task from the sacred city of Anuradhapuram just as thy spiritual forbear once did, from the splendid seat of his capital, Pataliputhram. What is thy answer, Prince, to this, the Gods' divine command?"

"The Devas are immensely powerful beings, Maha Guru," answered the prince. "They shall do as they please—but I, ignorant servant that I am, do not quite understand what their great work entails. What is it, exactly, that I am to accomplish?"

"*That* is within my own capacity to explain." The Adhyatchagar made a sign, and the possessed *bikshu* was instantly removed from their presence. Once the group vanished, the Guru bent his gaze upon the prince. "I draw thy attention to the throne in front of us, highness. Observe the golden crown and the sceptre. Every ruler belonging to the royal family of Ilankai was acknowledged as a king by the Buddhist Sangam only after having sat upon this throne, wearing this crown and holding this sceptre. This is the seat that once held Chakravarthy Dushtakamanu, Emperor Thissa, Beloved of the Gods, and Mahasenar! This crown adorned their illustrious heads; this sceptre rested in each of their hands. Now, this throne—one that has given birth to kings for aeons—that has provided us Emperor after Emperor for a thousand years and more, awaits thee. To sit upon this embodiment of magnificence, wear this crown and hold this sceptre is an honour beyond any mortal, royal or otherwise. This honour is now thy own. Wilt thou accept?"

Vandhiyathevan, listening to this masterful peroration avidly, now felt a thrill course through his veins. His arms and legs throbbed with eagerness and anticipation: couldn't he—oh, couldn't he just bundle up the prince and place him on this marvelous throne?

Said prince, however, sat quite still; there wasn't even a flicker of expression on his youthful countenance.

"But how can this be, Adhyatchaga?" he asked now, his voice low and tranquil. "King Mahindan, who sat upon this throne and took up the mantle of Ilankai, is still alive, isn't he? Even if the place of his refuge at present is unknown ..." his voice trailed away.

"The ruling dynasty of this island must change, Prince, and it will. Centuries ago, King Vijayarajan arrived from the vast lands of Vanga, enriched by the Ganga, and established a proud lineage: from this line has sprung king after great king, guarding these lands, ensuring peace and justice. Unfortunately, their time came to an end; their successors perpetrated unimaginable cruelty, misused their power; destroyed the very fabric of civilization and earned the immense displeasure of the Gods. Those born into this dynasty committed terrifying acts that tainted their souls: fathers killed sons; sons hacked their fathers; brother assassinated brother; daughters did away with mothers, and daughters-in-law felt no compunction about murdering mothers-in-law. The Gods decree that such criminals no longer deserve the privilege of spreading the word of the great Buddha. Mahindan, who last ascended this throne, lost the right to kingship, not to mention the fact that he has no heirs. It can be seen, therefore, that the royal line of Ilankai *must* change—and if such change is imminent, this Buddhist Sangam has the right to determine the first of the new line of kings. Our choice has now fallen on thee. Should thou accept, thy coronation shall take place at once, this very night ..."

Silence fell within that *mandapam* for a few moments—the deep, impenetrable stillness that reigns within the core of the earth and in the depths of oceans. Vandhiyathevan felt his nerves thrum with exhilaration and anxiety; his excitement rose to an almost unbearable pitch.

This was the moment Ponniyin Selvar chose to rise with immense dignity, and fold his hands with respect towards the Buddhist *bikshus*. Vandhiyathevan shivered, almost at the end of his tether. There—this was it—the moment was at hand! The prince would seat himself on his throne—and Vandhiyathevan would seize the crown and place it on his head himself!

"I prostrate myself at your feet, great saints," said the prince. "I find myself bereft of words at your immense generosity; the affection and benevolence that must have prompted this Sangam's offer of the ancient

Ilankai throne. I regret to say, however—that this charge is beyond my power to accept. I'm Chozha born and bred; the lands and rivers of that country fed me; slaked my thirst. My arrival here was at my father's command. I am powerless to make any decision regarding these matters without knowing his opinion ..."

"Surely," the *bikshu* intercepted, at this point. "Dost thou not know that Sundara Chozhar now lives a life without liberty, almost as though he were a prisoner himself?"

"I'm not unaware of his paralysis, or that he's tied to his sickbed, unable to move of his own accord. Be that as it may, I am bound to obey his lawful representatives—those who possess the power of ruling the country in his name. Should I accept this throne, I would be guilty of conspiring against them ..."

"If this be thy objection, it should be no great feat to send a group of envoys to Thanjavur, on the Sangam's behalf. Thy beloved father's patronage towards Buddhism is well-known; the Chozha Emperor would not reject our petition ..."

"The citizens of this island might, however. Who indeed, has the right to give away their kingdom without their approval?"

"The very citizens thou mention would consider thy ascension to their throne an immense honour; a stroke of great fortune."

"Everyone may consider it so, and congratulate themselves, as you say—but there is one person whose approval I value above all else in this world; one person, whose opinion I consider binding—my sister. My mother may have given birth to me; Ponni, the benevolent river Goddess may have saved my life ... however, it is to my sister that I owe my awareness of the outside world; she it was, who lit the light of knowledge in my ignorant mind. But there is a voice I must respect and bow to, even more than hers—the voice that whispers deep inside my heart. Great monks, my conscience refuses to let me accept the rare gift that you have chosen to bestow upon this ignorant boy. Forgive me, Your Holiness ..."

Silence fell in the *mandapam* again. Vandhiyathevan alone could hear the sound of blood thrumming unpleasantly in his very veins.

"Great prince," began the Adhyatchagar, after a few moments. "Thy answer surprises me not at all. Something of this sort, in fact, was expected. This refusal only serves to prove thy supreme worth; thou art more deserving of the honour of ascending the throne of Ilankai than any of thy contenders. Those of us here, who possess knowledge of *dharma*, are sure of it. However, to exert undue pressure—no, that cannot be thought of. Time shall be offered, to reflect upon our offer carefully; one year from now, we shall send forth a message and then wilt thou have the opportunity to give us thy considered, final answer. There is, however, one thing that thou would do well to remember: many are the monasteries that have been ruined beyond repair, caught in the midst of war, in this ancient city. All, except this, the Maha Bodhi Viharam. We have sustained no hurt, so far—chiefly because it has been constructed underground. Those leaders of the Sangam gathered are the only ones who know the way to this monastery. It is impossible to come here, without one of us to act as guides. The Kings of Ilankai visit exactly once in their lifetime—to be crowned by the Buddhist Sangam; such is the secrecy that shrouds this sacred route. Thy friends and thee must swear to us an oath: no breath must reach the outside world of thy visit here, or the subject of our discussion. Should anyone breach this pledge, thou shall lay thyselves open to the most terrible curse of the Gods!"

"There is no need for such drastic measures, Adhyatchaga; I made my friends aware of the need for secrecy when I asked them to accompany me," assured Ponniyin Selvar. "And I shall never break my oath."

***

Half a *naazhigai* later saw Prince Arulmozhi Varmar, Azhwarkkadiyaan and Vandhiyathevan walking in the moonlight along the streets of Anuradhapuram. The latter, who had managed to keep his lips sewn shut within the monastery, now let loose with all the power of a broken dam.

"I'm not denying that Chozha Nadu possesses every sort of natural wealth and beauty—but it's not a patch on this beautiful country, let me tell you. They offer the throne of their precious emerald isle on a golden platter, and what do *you* do? Kick it away like a heap of pebbles!" Vandhiyathevan was ranting now, drawing on a reservoir of pent-up irritation and disappointment. "What absolute—*nonsense*! Oh, and what can one say of those wonderful *bikshus* who actually pitched upon you as a candidate to rule their precious kingdom! There I was, a pillar amongst all those columns—they could've just handed their crown to *me*, couldn't they?"

In vain did the prince try to soothe ruffled feathers. "Didn't I tell you about Dushtakamanu's son Saali, who gave up his right to this throne— all for the sake of his beloved Asokamala? Didn't a single word of that heart-warming tale enter your brain?"

"Oh, it did, it did. What I want to know is—which pretty maiden have *you* set your heart on?" demanded Vandhiyathevan. "Who's the girl that stands between you and your throne?"

"Not one, my friend, but two marvelous young ladies. I've fallen in love with Truth and Justice, you see—and it was on their account that I refused Ilankai."

"When I look at you, I see a youth your highness, but when I listen to your speech—wonder of wonders, you sound exactly like a doddering old man in the twilight of his life."

"As to that—which of us here knows the oldest of us all, and the exact moment our lives are about to end?"

They were walking by the side of the street, alongside an old mansion.

The sound of clapping hands reached them from the opposite side. Someone stood there—a black, indistinguishable figure.

"Come with me," said the prince, walking with some urgency to reach it. The others followed.

They were merely halfway across the street—when a huge commotion arose behind them. The group turned. The front balcony of the mansion they had been walking under, was crumbling to the ground! Had they not crossed the street just moments ago, it would have collapsed on their heads. Within the space of a moment, three lives had been saved—and such lives, too!

Which of us here knows the oldest of us all and the exact moment our lives are about to end?—ah, how true were Ponniyin Selvar's words?

Vandhiyathevan stood rooted to the middle of the street, ruminating on this even as the others walked away. He came to his senses, hurried to catch up with them—and caught sight of the figure now fully visible in the gleaming moonlight. And then he stood stock-still again, unable to believe his eyes.

Because—how could this be? No, no, this was utterly ridiculous—it wasn't possible ...

How could the Ilaiya Rani of Pazhuvoor whom he'd last seen in Thanjai, appear in Anuradhapuram? And what was she doing here at midnight?

The figure vanished the next instant, leaving only two men, behind.

36

THE TRUE MEASURE OF WORTH?

Vandhiyathevan hastened towards where the prince and "Nandhini" stood—but even before he reached them, suspicion began to rear its head: *Was* she, in fact, Nandhini? Nothing of the elaborate silks or glittering ornaments she'd worn before were now upon her person; she was dressed in the simple attire of ascetics. Her face certainly seemed to resemble the charming countenance of the Pazhuvoor Ilaiya Rani ... but there was a subtle difference as well. Now what could that be?

The moment he arrived, the mysterious lady glided away, disappearing into the dark shadows of the homes lining the street. Vandhiyathevan hurried forward with the intention of following her—but the prince halted him in his tracks by the simple expedient of grabbing his hands.

"Who was that woman, *Ayya*?" The words tripped on Vallavarayan's tongue. "I thought I recognized her ..."

"The guardian deity of the Chozha clan, no doubt," offered Azhwarkkadiyaan promptly, as he joined them. "Look over there," he pointed. "We'd have been paying our respects at the divine feet of Buddha in person, if we hadn't moved away in the nick of time!"

They turned their attention to where Thirumalai pointed—and saw that the mansion's upper half had crumbled down to the road, the rubble resembling a small hill that looked like it could swallow an elephant whole. What, then, of three puny humans?

"It would seem that our patron deity arrived at exactly the right time and clapped to get our attention," mused Ponniyin Selvar.

"Your highness, *who* did you say she was?" Vandhiyathevan asked, with considerable surprise.

"Whom did she seem like, to you?" asked the prince in return. "And why did you try to follow her?"

"That Vaishnavite might have called her the Chozha's guardian deity—but I beg to differ," Vandhiyathevan suggested, slowly. "To me, she seemed, rather, like an avenging fury out for Chozha blood ..."

"What does that even ... *who* do you think she is?"

"It's just my brain playing tricks on me, I expect—but she seemed to be Nandhini Devi, the young woman Pazhuvettarayar's lately married," admitted Vandhiyathevan. "That thought didn't occur to you too, by any chance?"

"I didn't really observe her closely, but you were probably hallucinating," said Azhwarkkadiyaan promptly. "How could the young queen of Pazhuvoor possibly be here?"

"I'm afraid it's not just his brain playing tricks; his eyes must have as well, because," intercepted the prince. "This has happened to me too. I've sometimes wondered about that mysterious resemblance, myself. Come, both of you; we may talk as we walk."

Rather than pass underneath the shadows cast by houses, the trio chose to stride in the middle of the street, bathed by pearly moonlight.

"Your highness," began Azhwarkkadiyaan, after they'd been walking a while. "She clapped her hands and gave you a message, didn't she? What was it?"

"Two foes have arrived, out for my blood—and that these *sathrus* are awaiting the right moment to assassinate me."

"Why, that witch!" Vandhiyathevan burst out. "Was she referring to us by any chance?"

"She wasn't that specific, to tell the truth," Ponniyin Selvar laughed a little. "It wouldn't matter even if she had; my lady has mentioned before that I've an incredibly strong grip on life—and this isn't the first time she's dragged me away from danger."

"Well, I happen to know their identity, *Ayya*; they're the two men in company of Parthibendra Pallavar, currently in search of you," Thirumalai revealed. "I managed to catch a glimpse of two shadowy figures in the ruined mansion that almost buried us whole—that must have been them."

"*Oi*, Vaishnavite—why on earth didn't you mention this before?" Vandhiyathevan demanded. "Go on, the two of you; I shall make a thorough search of that ruined place and—"

He turned to go back but was stopped by the prince, who clutched his hands again. "There's no need for that, now; I doubt if they can be found there, anyway—all that will be taken care of, later. But you—you must stay by my side until I command otherwise, do you understand?" The prince's gaze settled squarely on Vandhiyathevan's face. "Because I trust *you*, my fearless warrior. Who knows what other horrible dangers lurk within the shadows, nooks and crannies of this ruined, dilapidated city? And wasn't it your presence, *Veera Sikamani*, that made me disdain the protection of my personal security detail? Consider my plight: if *you* desert me in the middle of the street, what will I do?"

The soft words of entreaty sent Vandhiyathevan into an ecstasy of drugged delight. "*Ayya*," he stuttered, voice husky with emotion. "Never shall I leave your side—not even for a moment!"

"And I shall never leave *you*," Azhwarkkadiyaan promised. "You're the prince's guard; I'm yours."

They reached the interior of Emperor Mahasena's ruined palace within the next few minutes. Comfortable beds had been made up for them on the old-fashioned bedsteads in a spacious room that had once belonged to the royal, and the trio lay down at once. The moon sailed in the velvety sky, sending its cool, pale rays to eavesdrop upon them through the chinks in the window on one of the walls.

"Hundreds of years ago, Ilankai's emperors, kings and their queens would have taken their ease in this very chamber, residents of this palace. And moonbeams would have crept up to the windows even then, just as they do now," commented Arulmozhi Varmar. "Vandhiyathevare, they'd be horribly disappointed to see us ordinary mortals in the place of their royals, wouldn't they?"

"You have my permission to comment any which way you please about your poor self and this pathetic Vaishnavite, *Ayya*, but pray don't class *me* with the masses," Vallavarayan said elegantly.

"Oh, of course—you must forgive me; it simply slipped my mind. I'm in the exalted presence of the scion of Vallam royalty, aren't I?"

"Indeed you are, *Ayya*—and if you happened to hear a poet's song upon one of my ancestors, this Vaishnavite here might spontaneously combust in jealousy and go up in smoke."

"I'll elect to see him off, in that eventuality. Thirumalai is an advocate of chaste Thamizh in any case, and wouldn't hesitate to give his life for that cause—like the famed King Nandhivarma Pallavar," the prince grinned. "Go right ahead; I'd like to listen."

Vallavarayan hesitated. Then, he threw caution to the winds and began:

"En kavikai en sivikai
En kavasam, en thuvasam

En kariyee(thu) en pariyee(thu)

Enbare—man kavana

Maavendhan Vaanan

Varisai parisu petra

Paaventharai, venthar

Paarthu!"

"Thirumalai," asked Ponniyin Selvar, once he'd heard the verse through. "You possess some expertise in Thamizh, don't you? Care to elucidate?"

"I can only assume that you wish to test me, *Ayya*—but I shall oblige anyway. Here's the scene: dozens of petty kings and chieftains wait humbly at the entrance of Maavendhar Vaanar's elaborate, ornate palace, hoping vainly for a glimpse of his royal highness. Not that they're successful; they've been superseded by the much more respected Paavendhars, the kings of songs, as it were, and the Vaanar Emperor is lost in appreciation of their verses. As a mark of his admiration, he decides to honour them with gifts worthy of a royal: flower-decked state umbrellas; flag-staffs studded generously with precious gems; elephants and horses. The kings standing in line glare at these offerings showered upon poets and promptly—er— go up in smoke. "*Adada*, this is my umbrella!" groans one; "Isn't this my palanquin?" laments another, while others moan about their elephants and horses being borne away—and by poets! For, the Vaanar Emperor is giving away all the expensive gifts the petty kings had placed reverently at the feet of their liege-lord. And that, your highness, is the meaning of this verse—assuming that I'm right, of course?"

"Could you be otherwise? *Adada*, what a beautiful song, to be sure—and so wonderfully creative too! What a pity that we've no idea about the poet's identity. Truth be told, oh scion of the Vaanar clan, no one cares if your ancestors ruled a huge kingdom or a small one; that they managed to garner a poem such as this in their praise—ah, what more does a dynasty require, Vandhiyathevare? Who better to occupy these royal quarters than you, descended from a lineage as illustrious as theirs? Why, you deserve to lie not in Mahasenar's couch, but the famed Dushtakamanu's decorated bed itself! You're certainly worthy of all these honours and more, aren't you?"

"Indeed *Ayya*, yes! I've often thought so—and I couldn't be happier that you, at least, see me for what I am. Alas, though—who cares about a man's true worth these days? Certainly not those silly *bikshus*, for instance, or they'd have handed me the throne of Ilankai, wouldn't they? But what do *they* do? Try and stuff the crown on your head—and you didn't even want it! Oh, you've no idea how furious I was at that moment. I would've grabbed that stupid thing and placed it on my own head—but I was worried that this petty Vaishnavite might compete with me, and gave up the notion at the last moment," Vandhiyathevan finished, with a very saintly expression on his face.

Arulmozhi Varmar fairly roared with laughter at this remarkable speech; Vallavarayan's heart thrilled at his merry peals of mirth. He decided to press his advantage and assumed a mortified expression. "It's all very well to laugh at my expense," he grumbled. "But there's nothing in it for *me*. When do I get my due, eh?"

"My venerable prince, descended from the glorious Vaanar dynasty—I mentioned two maidens by the name of *Sathyam* and *Dharmam*, didn't I? It never occurred to you, I suppose, that they were reason enough for my having refused the throne?"

"Now that you mention them, I declare, I've quite made up my mind. You see, I'd rather had my eye on those two lovely ladies for a while now … but I've decided that I'm never going to associate with them, or even allow myself to be distracted by their considerable charms!"

"*Adada*, have you, now? And what, pray, is the reason for this terrible decision? Have some pity, do. Why this deep and dark hatred for them?"

"Nothing quite so dramatic. You mentioned that you'd fallen in love with them, didn't you? And given up the kingship of Ilankai for their sakes? Well, I'm a gentleman and I follow the code of noble conduct set down for scions such as me: never let it be said that I coveted another's women!"

"*Oh*," Ponniyin Selvar dissolved into peals of laughter again. "Oh, I've never met anyone as amusing as you!"

"Laugh all you want, *Ayya*, but my stomach fairly burns, I tell you," Vandhiyathevan muttered, morosely. "You've every right to refuse throne, crown and sceptre, I suppose, but couldn't you have just pointed to me and said, *Here's a worthy candidate right by my side; give them to him?*"

Arulmozhi Varmar collapsed helplessly, chuckling with merriment. "Vandhiyathevare," he said, once he'd finally recovered somewhat, although his voice still wobbled. "You ought to know by now that accepting a throne isn't quite as easy as it looks—especially if it's being offered by Buddhist monks. It's simply *not* done. The consequences of such an impulsive decision would be unimaginable, because it wouldn't be right. Religious leaders, my friend, should concern themselves with such issues alone, and not overstep their boundaries. Poking their exalted noses into politics and statecraft bodes ill not just for royal affairs, but religion as well. And that's not all: the *bikshus* who offered me Ilankai today don't represent all the Buddhists of this island; they're just the leaders of one faction. There are two others just like this one, and had I accepted the throne from tonight's Sangam, I'd have been forced to rule under them and knuckle under their authority," he explained. "The other two Sangams would have turned our instant enemies."

"The noble scion of illustrious Vallam kings understands the situation here, I presume?" Azhwarkkadiyaan needled.

"Perfectly," Vandhiyathevan snorted. "I thought idiots like the ones who bashed each other over the superiority of Sivan and Thirumaal existed only there—apparently, there are plenty here as well."

"Pray, don't start bashing each other up now, you two," warned the prince. "The night speeds upon its way—hark! The Peraherath festivities must have come to an end; people are returning. It's time we caught some sleep."

"Well, I can't. But if I knew something more about the lady who clapped her hands and saved us being buried alive … perhaps."

"I don't know who she is either," admitted the prince. "But I've no objection to sharing what I've learnt about her so far. If you're interested, come a little closer, and I shall begin my tale."

ॐ

37

KAVERI AMMAN

The prince began his tale as Vandhiyathevan and Azhwarkkadiyaan hurried to the foot of his bed, and settled comfortably on the floor.

"Once, when I was a child, I was sailing along the Kaveri with my parents. My older brother and sister were in the boat too, talking amongst themselves but I—I was intent on peering over the boat into the river, watching the current make little eddies in the surface, and pretty Kadamba flowers getting caught in the swirls. I remember how sad I felt when I saw one of the blooms sucked in by the water and fluttering desperately. Sometimes, I leaned over the boat and tried to fish them out. And once, when I was engaged in picking a particularly helpless flower—I slipped and fell in! Since I'd toppled into the water headfirst, I floundered and thrashed, barely able to breath.

"That dull *thud* when my head hit the sandy river bed—how well I remember it. Neither can I forget the tumbling waters practically hurling me down-river, and the vague shouts and cries of people from somewhere far away. I began to suffocate, thinking that I was done for: the river would fling me straight into the ocean and there, it would end. When I thought of my parents, my brother and sister and how terrible they would feel when they realized that I was gone … well, I couldn't bear it. And then, I sensed someone grab me with their hands and hold me close. The next instant, whoever it was brought me up and I was out. Water dripped everywhere, from my head, eyes, nose and mouth, but I could still see the hands that had pulled me to safety. And then, I saw the face that belonged to those hands. Only for a few moments—but it was etched indelibly, in my heart. She seemed vaguely familiar, but I couldn't recognize her.

"Those hands handed me to someone else and the next thing I knew, I was in the boat. My mother, father, sister and brother crowded around; their sorrow, sympathy, love and boundless affection consumed me completely. Once there'd been time to calm down, people began to remember that I'd been saved by someone, and to inquire about their identity. They asked me as well. I looked around, but couldn't spot that divine face anywhere. I blinked, unable to answer them and in the end, everyone decided that it must have Kaveri Amman, the river Goddess herself who'd dragged me from the brink of death. A special ritual of thanksgiving and elaborate *poojais* would be conducted each year on the anniversary of my re-birth, so to speak.

"I, however, wasn't convinced, or relieved about these arrangements; what had once been a simple wish to see my saviour evolved, gradually, into a sort of obsession. I neither knew nor cared if she was a human just like the rest of us or the divine Kaveri herself, walking the earth—I wanted to see that face; that beautiful face that now resided, untarnished, in my memory. My ambition drove me to the river often and I would look here and there, hoping against hope that that angel, the Goddess would simply rise up from the waters and grant me another vision. That she was, likely, a human being was a conviction that grew from strength to strength as days went by. This gave way to another pre-occupation of mine: staring at every single older woman, whenever I had the chance to visit festivals in various places. As time passed and my own perceptions sharpened, I realized that staring at older women wasn't, perhaps, the best of manners. Years flew and I'd almost given up any hope of glimpsing her divine countenance again.

"Roughly a year ago, I set foot here as the *Maathanda Naayakan* of the Southern Armed Forces. Senathipathi Boodhi Vikrama Kesari had already captured parts of this island; Anuradhapuram had, however, changed hands several times and was, at that time, in Mahindan's grasp. Our armies had laid siege to the city; I'd decided to take advantage of the impasse and tour various sections of Ilankai. The Senathipathi saw me off with a thousand of his hand-picked warriors. I decided to make good the opportunity and traveled into forests, up and down hills, vales and followed the rivers within Chozha-occupied dominions, learning every bit of the territory by heart. You might know by now that there are several islands off Ilankai shores; I visited these, as well. Exploring various sites this way, we set up camp in the middle of the forest, a few *kaadhams* north of this city. As it so happened, we'd decided to stay in the vicinity of the *Yaanai Iravu Thurai*, where the seas north and south of Ilankai approach very closely and practically join, through a narrow strait. Sometimes, it's said that herds of wild elephants make a crossing to the north at this point and hence, the name. And something rather mysterious occurred, during our stay there.

"Each night, an unearthly voice would rise in wailing lament, close to our camp. None of us could quite make out if the howls belonged to man, bird, or beast. All we could sense was a heart-rending, wordless sorrow that seemed to sear our soul and make the hair stand on end. The sentries stationed at the boundaries of the camp were the first to hear it; they ignored it at first. And then, others began to hear the wails too, at other sections of the camp. Some came to me about it; I didn't pay much attention to their tales of terror. *If you're going to tremble at ghost stories, this is no place for you,* I warned them. *Go home and nestle into your mother's lap!* Not surprisingly, they were stung by the reproof and decided to rout out the source of these strange cries each night: were they human, or otherwise? The next time they heard the lament, they rushed over there. The owner of the voice took to their heels the moment they approached; to them, it seemed to be a woman. They couldn't catch her, though. Not that the wailing stopped; we could still hear it now and then, around the camp.

"I ignored it as best as I could at first—but the same couldn't be said of my soldiers who, it seemed, could find nothing else to talk about. Some of them grew really terrified at these unearthly sounds and finally, I decided that I'd have to do something about it—find out what, or who was underneath it all. One night, I and my men decided to follow the direction of that wordless wail. We went after it and caught sight of a woman erupt from within a scraggy bush. She stared at us, dumbstruck for just a moment—and then began to run. A voice whispered within my mind that a whole horde in pursuit would have no chance of capturing her; I ordered the others to stay where they were, and went alone. The figure turned once, saw just me after her and hesitated. Then she waited, as though to let me catch up.

"Now, I don't mind admitting that I'd become, well, terrified, myself. I hesitated too, for a moment. Then, I gathered my courage, stilled my beating heart, and crept up to her. The moon's pale rays fell full upon her face. A slight smile played upon that divinely beautiful countenance. In an instant, I recognized her: Kaveri Amman—that Goddess who'd saved me from a watery grave all those years ago ...!

"I simply stared at her for a few moments, stupefied. Then, I managed to work my way out of my trance. *Amma*, I asked gently. *Who are you? When did you come here? Why? Oh, how long I've been searching for you! And if you'd wished to see me, you had but to come to me—why wail and howl around this encampment?* I almost screamed at her. *Why this sorrowful lament?*

"My lady didn't utter a word; for all my entreaties, I might as well have been addressing a wall. A few moments later, tears began to roll down her cheeks; the sight broke my heart. It seemed to me that she wished to say something, but the words simply wouldn't come. Some sort of unearthly, inhuman sound came from her throat. And then—I understood. She was mute.

"Ah, the despair and sorrow I felt then! I stood rooted to the spot, unaware of what to do. Abruptly, she caught me in a hug and kissed the top of my head. I could feel her tears fall upon me. The next instant, she'd gone. She ran, and never looked back.

"I didn't follow her. My soldiers surrounded me when I returned to camp and rained questions on me. *She's neither ghost nor ghoul,* I told them bracingly. *Just an ordinary woman who seems to have endured immense heartbreak and become deranged, likely, as a result.* I issued them strict instructions to leave her alone if she ever returned, and not to harass her in any way.

"All through the next day, I was plagued by a notion: would it be better for everyone concerned if we just packed our provisions and dismantled camp? I couldn't come to a decision, though. Deep down, in my heart of hearts, resided the hope, I suppose, that she might appear again. The day slipped away, lost in these thoughts; night was upon us. My expectations were not in vain; we heard her lament once more, just outside the camp. I prevented my soldiers from following me and set off alone, in the direction of the wails.

"My lady awaited me just as she'd done last night, a smile lighting up her face. She stared at me for a while, obviously wishing to tell me something. I, however, didn't possess the art of comprehending her message.

"She took my hand then, and bade me come with her. This may sound strange—but I felt not the slightest compunction in following where she led. The way she held aside thorny branches on our forest path so they wouldn't scratch me in the slightest, melted my heart. Some distance away, we came upon a hut. A tiny earthen lamp flickered, within. In its feeble light, I saw an old man lying on the floor. His body shook and shivered as though with unbearable cold; sometimes, he almost seemed to leap up a little, so severe was the shaking. His teeth were gritted; eyes were bloodshot, almost sparking with heat; his lips were muttering and murmuring something; words which no one could understand ...

"You remember, don't you—that monk we saw tonight, in the Maha Bodhi viharam underground, who shook and shivered? They said that thousands of Devas, celestial beings had possessed him? Well, I was reminded instantly of the old man I'd seen in the hut. I began to wonder if the Gods had indeed come upon the *bikshu*, or if the poor monk had simply been seized by the terrible ague, the shivering fever that's so prevalent around these parts. I didn't bring up the subject though— and why should I have, indeed? Why expand upon my suspicions and destroy the faith of those pious, devout monks? You know, sometimes, I wonder if I hadn't made a mistake, granting permission to the residents to celebrate the Peraherath festival this year—half of this glorious, sacred city has already been destroyed; what would happen if the fever sank its poisonous tendrils into the people? The rest of the population would have to take to its heels as well …"

Arulmozhi Varmar's voice trailed away, as he lost himself in thought.

"*Ayya*," Vandhiyathevan prompted, after a while. "This wretched city may ruin itself by all means—but what happened inside that hut?"

"Nothing much, really. My lady clearly felt that I mustn't stay there long; she grabbed my hand and almost dragged me outside. Then she delivered her message, using a sign language unique to her; I understood at once. *Do not tarry in these parts; else, you will be susceptible to this terrible fever. Break camp and leave at once.* She managed to communicate all this using gestures, and made sure I understood. I realized then, that it was her boundless love and concern for me that made her go to such lengths. I decided that the Gods themselves had ensured my safety, and decided to follow her orders to the letter: I gave orders to break camp that very night, and leave at once.

"The joy my soldiers felt was indescribable. They heaved a sigh of relief—for they wouldn't have to listen to that horrible, moaning lament again …"

இ

38

(He)art Speaks!

The prince stopped, mid-sentence. "That sound—did you hear something, by any chance?"

His listeners, intent on the story, shook their heads collectively and disclaimed all knowledge of any sound whatsoever.

"Wait," said Azhwarkkadiyaan abruptly. "Isn't this place a little … warmer than before?"

"I seem to smell smoke too," volunteered Vandhiyathevan.

"*Ayya*, this area isn't dangerous, is it?" Azhwarkkadiyaan asked, worried.

"Should there be the slightest hint of peril, rest assured that Kaveri Amman will come to our rescue," the prince promised. "Now, to continue—"

"We broke camp and left at once—but it appeared that the dread fever had managed to strike: at least ten of my soldiers fell victim to this ague. *Ammamma*! I've never seen the likes of such a terrible malaise; that wretched disease can turn the bravest warrior into a quivering mass of terror. Men who've seen a hundred battles and think nothing of bloody injuries all over their body become nervous wrecks within three days of infection, and blubber about "wanting to return home." I reflected that it had been the Chozha guardian deity Durga Parameswari Herself who'd taken human form as a mute woman, and arrived to warn us. Not that she left us to stumble along later—I sensed her loving hand guiding us past wild beasts eyeing us for prey; pythons crawling on our path; shadowy enemies—and so much more. She disappeared as swiftly as she made her presence felt. A few days were all it took for me to understand her expressive face and animated gestures, and communicate in the same fashion. My heart, in fact, could read hers perfectly; so attuned to her was I, that I acquired the gift of sensing my lady's presence in the vicinity. In fact, even now ..." the prince's voice trailed away. "Get into your beds, both of you; act like you're fast asleep even if you don't feel drowsy— *quick*!"

The two scrambled into their beds at once and even, to their credit, tried to screw their eyes shut—but the avid curiosity that consumed them refused to let them close.

Even as they stared through the slits of their eyelids, a figure approached the moonlit window—the same one they'd seen opposite the crumbling mansion on an Anuradhapuram street.

Came the faintest hiss; Arulmozhi Varmar obeyed the summons and went to the window. The figure outside made some sign; the prince pointed to his companions on the beds and had the satisfaction of receiving some sort of answer to that too, in sign language.

Arulmozhi Varmar issued instructions to his friends to follow him at once, and left the mansion. The trio walked in the footsteps of the older woman a long time, it seemed, along a dark path shrouded by tall, gloomy trees. Abruptly, a stunning sight met them in the pearly rays of the moon:

huge, dark elephants clustered thickly in the distance, guarding a massive *stupam*. Vandhiyathevan's breath stuttered in his throat—but the lady simply walked towards the giants, completely unfazed.

"What wonderful stone-work, to be sure," an astonished Azhwarkkadiyaan muttered in his ears. "That proportion and finish— don't they look absolutely real?"

It was only after this comment that Vandhiyathevan realized the truth—and though the bewilderment abated somewhat, surprise did not vanish completely.

Each of these massive stone pachyderms standing cheek by jowl possessed two lung tusks as they almost nestled into each other, fashioned as if to bear a mountainous *stupam*. One, among the hundreds that loomed against the sky, had a broken tusk. Their guide approached this elephant and moved the boulder that rested at its enormous foot. A stairway was revealed underneath; she went down and the others followed. Once they'd descended and walked along a narrow passage, they came into a *mandapam*. Two large *agal* lamps burned, within.

The lady tweaked the wick of one and picked it up. She made a sign that only the prince may follow her. The others fidgeted a little, for the dangers of a solitary excursion with this woman worried them not a little, but once they gleaned the lady's intentions—she was raising her lamp now and showing several paintings on the *mandapam* walls—their concern subsided, somewhat.

***

To the prince, observing the art keenly, the pictures seemed to portray several scenes of a story in an orderly fashion. The paintings were done and displayed according to the prevailing fashion of the times—much like the tales of Lord Buddha's glorious incarnations in viharams—but these had nothing to do with the Great One's life; they were centered upon a woman. And her countenance bore a startling resemblance to the lady who stood by Ponniyin Selvar now. It wasn't too difficult to understand that these paintings were meant to portray the life of his mute guardian.

The first of these panels showed a young woman standing by the shore of an isolated island, the sea lapping at the beach, and her father rowing out to fish in his canoe, returning to land with his catch. The next showed the girl walking along a forest path. A young man sat upon a branch; he looked like a prince. A bear was clawing its way up his tree but the prince seemed unaware of this danger, staring elsewhere. The young woman screeched a warning and ran; the bear gave up its quarry and pursued her. The prince jumped down and threw his spear at the beast. They fell upon each other, and a fierce battle ensued. The young woman leant against a convenient coconut tree and watched the combat avidly, eyes gleaming. In the end, victory was the prince's; the bear fell to the ground, dead. The young prince approached the girl and tried to express his gratitude.

Tears rolled down her beautiful face and she stayed silent, offering no answer. Then she flitted away and returned with her father. The fisherman explained that his daughter was mute—a revelation that depressed the prince. The sorrow changed to delight soon enough as he began, and soon developed, his acquaintance with her. The flowers of the forest bloomed in his hands to be fashioned into exquisite garlands; they decorated her lustrous hair, or wreathed her neck. Those lonely woods saw them strolling through dense jungle, hands entwined, lost in themselves.

Paradise didn't seem eternal however; a large vessel appeared in proximity to the island. Several soldiers descended to shore, found the prince and paid him their respects. They begged him to return with them to the ship; the prince consoled the young woman with many soft words and took his leave. Soon, the ship that bore him disappeared over the horizon. The young woman lost herself in grief after his departure; her days were spent in mournful tears. Her father, who had sensed the direction his daughter's life was taking, and who couldn't bear her distress, took her in his boat across the sea. He came ashore in the vicinity of a lighthouse, where both were welcomed by a family. Soon, they travelled upon a simple bullock-cart to a large city, surrounded by high fort-walls. There, in the balcony of a beautiful palace stood the prince, wearing a gleaming crown. Several people surrounded him, attired in rich silks and elaborate jewelry.

The young woman stared at the sight, dismayed and sorrowed beyond imagination. Her heart gave away; she ran away, on and on, until she reached the seashore. She climbed atop the lighthouse—and jumped.

The waves in whose arms she'd spent a lifetime, carried her now; a boatman cruising in his vessel spotted her bobbing in the waters and dragged her to safety. Her demented look convinced him that a ghost possessed her and in his kindness, he left her in a local temple, where the priest blew a handful of *vibuthi* in her face and thrashed her with a clump of Neem leaves, according to ritual practice.

The temple was roused to frantic activity and visitors one day, for a great queen had arrived to pay obeisance to the deity. The priest informed the royal of the demented woman from the *valaignar* caste. The queen was with child, and learnt that the refugee was pregnant as well. She took the young woman with her and in due time, the latter gave birth to twins, in the royal gardens. The queen paid a visit and asked to raise one of the children as her own—only to be refused. Soon, however, the mute woman began to have second thoughts: wouldn't it be much better for both babies to be raised in affluent surroundings?

Her heart was made up; she fled the palace in the dead of night without anyone the wiser. For years she roamed the forest, a lonely spirit with a heartache that couldn't be assuaged—an ache that could be soothed, sometimes, by the sight of her beloved children. Rare enough were the opportunities offered her—and sometimes, the pain would be excruciating; the desire to see her children from afar at least, unbearable, and she would secret herself by the trees clustering the riverside. These were the moments she lived for, when the king, his queens and children glided along the river on elaborate royal barges. She would feast upon the sight for a while, and then slip away between the trees. At one time, though, a child fell into the water; no one noticed. She plunged into the river, brought him up and delivered him into safe hands. She submerged herself in the water almost at once, reached the opposite shore, and melted into the forest.

***

Every single one of these incidents had been etched most realistically on the walls of the *mandapam*s with a red *kaavi* stick. Prince Arulmozhi Varmar took them all in, heart brimming with intense eagerness and astonishment. At the final panel, he turned to her. *I was the child rescued from the river; you were my saviour,* he mimed. The lady embraced him lovingly, and kissed his forehead.

She then escorted him to another section of the *mandapam*, and showed him more paintings. These were not scenes from her life, but warnings about the various perils and dangers that threatened the prince and she took some pains to reveal them, through drawings and elaborate gestures.

The prince's companions saw it all, standing at a strategic corner. Vandhiyathevan couldn't help but compare the lady's face with Nandhini's own; strange thoughts flitted through his mind, and uneasy suspicions. This, however, was hardly the right time to expound on them and he preserved a discreet silence.

They exited the *mandapam* guarded by stone elephants; the lady, still serving as their escort, now began to ascend the *stupam*, towards the summit while the rest marveled at her phenomenal stamina. Vandhiyathevan himself was exhausted by now but marshaled his fading resources, and climbed without a word.

Halfway up, they paused and looked out—to see a section of the old city engulfed in flames.

"Ah!" An exclamation was surprised out of the prince. "Mahasena Chakravarthy's ancient palace is burning ..."

"Was that where we were bedded down …?"

"Indeed, yes!"

"And if we'd spent the night there in sleep—"

"We'd have been offered up to satiate Agni Bhagavan's hunger, of course."

"How can you be so sure that that *was* our camp? It *is* quite far out …"

"I'm sure—for the paintings within the *mandapam* were kind enough to inform me."

"But we heard nothing …"

"Unsurprising. Art is its own language, you know; a unique mode of communication. Very few people can converse in it comfortably."

"Dare we ask if this—ah, art—conveyed some other information to you?"

"You may, and it did. Secrets regarding my family, for instance. Furthermore, it also warned me to leave Ilankai as soon as possible —"

"Hah! Long live art and all of its marvelous languages!" Vandhiyathevan exulted. "*Oi* Vaishnavite, it looks like I've won. *Now* what do you say?"

"The paintings didn't stop with that, did they, Your Highness? Correct me if I'm wrong, but didn't they warn you of the following too? As long as you're in Ilankai, it would be best to avoid sleeping under roofs; walking beneath houses and tarrying under trees …" Azhwarkkadiyaan drawled. "I'm right, aren't I?"

"You are," smiled the prince. "As to how you knew …"

"You might claim expertise in the language of art, your highness, but this servant has some little acquaintance with facial expressions. I spent quite a while watching your guardian deity's animated countenance as her ladyship communicated with you."

"Not bad at all. Now, there's only a *jaamam* left of the night; I suggest we continue to the top of the *stupam* and snatch some sleep while we can," announced the prince. "We can resume our journey at dawn."

***

The sun's sharp rays stung Vandhiyathevan to wakefulness, the next day. As though the very real occurrences of the previous day hadn't been enough, a whole host of conspirators, arsonists, mute women, deaf men, bears clawing up trees, ghosts, ghouls, ranting Buddhist monks and gleaming crowns paraded through his nightmares at random, making even sleep an unnerving experience. With morning came the bright sun, though, banishing terrible dreams and awful spectres; his confusion and panic vanished.

The prince and Azhwarkkadiyaan had already arisen and prepared themselves for travel, by the time Vandhiyathevan banished the mists of sleep from his brain. He dressed himself as well and the trio descended the *stupam* without delay. Taking care to keep to the middle of the street, they wended their way to the Mahameha Vanam which contained, within its hallowed precincts, the sacred and much venerated Bodhi tree, a thousand and five hundred years old.

Devotees—both Buddhist monks and others—surged towards this tree, circumambulating and showering the trunk with fragrant flowers. Prince Arulmozhi Varmar paid his respects as well.

"Kingdoms that hold the world in thrall and their rulers may be swallowed by the march of time but this Bodhi *virutcham* stands even now— proof that *dharmam* still, and will always, endure," he said to the other two, scrutinizing his surroundings as he did so. Three horses were tethered in a corner, ready for travel, and three men stood by, holding the reins.

Their faces brightened once the prince approached, and they folded their hands with much respect. Arulmozhi Varmar enquired something of them, and then turned to Vandhiyathevan. "It was indeed Mahasenar's palace that burnt down last night—where we were supposed to have rested. These men were anxious, lest we might have lost our lives in the conflagration. Now that they've seen us safe and sound, their delight and relief know no bounds."

"A thousand and five hundred year old tree might still stand—but it's been aeons since justice died a slow and painful death," Vandhiyathevan quipped.

"Don't you dare say that," Azhwarkkadiyaan butted in. "How could *dharmam* have died as long as I'm hale and hearty?"

The trio climbed onto their horses, and left Anuradhapuram through the North Gate. They attracted no attention as crowds of people still thronged the city streets, leaving through all four gates, now that the festival was at an end.

The small town of Mahindhalai was situated approximately a *kaadham* north-east of Anuradhapuram. "This is where Mahindar, Emperor Ashokar's son first spread the word of the Buddha. Ah, how great was his good fortune?" mused the prince. "Fate didn't force him to march across lands with his armies nor slink around the city in a desperate bid to escape murderers and assassins!"

"So much for his good fortune, then," commented Vandhiyathevan.

The prince was surprised into a rich chuckle. "Never, ever leave my side," he informed the young man. "The most terrible catastrophe would turn into pleasurable amusement, in your company."

"And the most enjoyable pastime into intolerable bore," quipped Azhwarkkadiyaan.

A huge, swirling dust storm rose ahead of them on the road, at this very moment. The loud *thud-thud-thud* of several horses could be heard, galloping forward at breakneck speed. A small cavalry regiment was visible within the next few moments; the lances in the soldiers' hands glittered in the morning sun.

"*Ayya,*" murmured Vandhiyathevan, instantly on the alert. "Unsheathe your sword at once!"

39

"HERE'S BATTLE!"

The prince unsheathed his sword the moment Vandhiyathevan's whisper reached his ears—and the Vaanar warrior pulled out his own weapon almost simultaneously. Onlookers might have been forgiven for thinking that they ought to have been handled by giants—for these were no ordinary blades but monstrous weapons, the famed broadswords wielded by legendary warriors. They had been handed over only that morning by the trio that had met the prince's party, by the Bodhi tree in Anuradhapuram.

The prince jumped down from his horse. "Get—down—this—instant, you impudent idiot! I've had enough of your prattle!"

And then, he turned to face Vandhiyathevan.

"Your fate shall be decided here and now, my fine young buck," said the prince evenly. "Everything else can wait."

Vandhiyathevan stared at his idol, speechless. Was this all real? Or just a cruel prank played by his over-active, exhausted imagination? And yet—the prince was on the ground, which meant he couldn't stay on his horse in high and mighty fashion. He got down slowly, still trying to make sense of it all.

"Well, *Ayya*? What on earth are you waiting for—a royal welcome? Ha, I wouldn't be surprised if you did. After all, you mocked me last night, didn't you? You sang songs about how my ancestors waited at the front door of yours, yearning for a glimpse of your precious forefather—and then to crown it all, they even lamented the poets carting away their umbrellas, palanquins and flags! And I, listening to this farrago of nonsense—how do you think *I* felt? That's when I decided that I'd teach you a lesson you'd never forget," the prince gripped his broadsword with both slender hands, and began to whip it around like a discus, coming closer to Vandhiyathevan with each moment. "Not a step further, until then!"

Ah yes, we did mention that these weren't ordinary blades, didn't we? Indeed, no man could hoist one with a single hand; so massive was its weight that both hands were needed to merely lift it.

To see the prince heft up that huge sword effortlessly and swing it around, it seemed unbelievable that he'd been raised in a royal palace with every comfort known to man, and had lived a luxurious life since the moment of his birth. At one moment, he seemed, suddenly, the embodiment of those ancient warriors of lore—Bheeman, Archunan, Aravaan and even Abhimanyu—who'd met and matched a dozen warriors at a time; at another, his formidable bearing reminded everyone forcibly that here stood a prince descended from the line of illustrious Chozha emperors such as Vijayalayar, decorated with ninety-six scars, and Rajadithya Thevar who'd met honourable death on his elephant.

Never at any time loath to combat, Vandhiyathevan began to swing his sword around as well. He used both hands and at first, his movements were unsure: his mind chaotic with thoughts chasing one another; hesitation and doubt churned his heart. With each moment, though, the reluctance retreated; his heart and hands steadied; his thirst for swordplay, always ready to be indulged, now took centre-stage. His eyes and mind forgot that the man in front was the prince of Chozha Nadu, his highness Arumozhi Varmar who deserved his complete and unquestioning loyalty—now, it was just The Foe. His brain stopped wondering about the reason for this unlooked for fight, and concentrated solely on the sword swinging in the Foe's hands. All he thought about was its glittering movement; its probable path: how could he escape its murderous edge—and even more important: how on earth could he wrest it from his enemy's grasp and deliver a killing blow?

The swords began to clash, first slowly, in the *chavukka* rhythm, and then gained reasonable speed in the *mathyama* rhythm and then the blows came faster and faster, approaching the highest, the *thuritha* rhythm. "*Danaar! Danaar!*" They smote each other, the sound of metal ringing through the air almost tearing the ear-drums of their watchers.

As far-sighted as he was, not even Azhwarkkadiyaan could guess the motive behind the prince's actions. That there *was* a reason for this uncalled-for fight, he understood. It could be, for example, a ruse to know more about the approaching cavalcade; force them to halt, discover their identity and then decide on a course of action—all of which required time. Having thought out so far, Azhwarkkadiyaan promptly decided to add his mite: he dragged the horses of the combatants and ranged them across, held their reins and stood by, effectively blocking the road.

The cavalry regiment approached with every moment. Azhwarkkadiyaan saw the tiger flag fluttering in their midst; a great load rolled off his heart. Clearly, the newcomers were on their side—but *who* were they?

The answer to this question was supplied in the next few minutes by the *kattiyakkaararkal* who accompanied the cavalcade for this very purpose, and made an announcement in stentorian voices:

"Make way for the Senathipathi who destroyed Mahindan's feeble armies in the Eezham War and forced him to flee the battlefield— Kodumbalur Periya Velaar, who claimed Veera Pandiyan's head in the battle on the banks of Vaigai—Boodhi Vikrama Kesari Maharaja—make way!" roared a voice like a clap of thunder. "*Paraak! Paraak!*"

"Make way for the scion of the Pallava dynasty—Warrior among warriors, who claimed Veera Pandian's head—the Parakrama Boopathi, lion amongst men who defeated the Vengi forces in the Vada Pennai Battle—Parthibendra Pallavar—*Paraak! Paraak!*" came another sonorous voice.

Approximately thirty armed men astride horses arrived in their wake, with Parthibendran and the Senathipathi mounted most majestically on white stallions in their midst.

An immense elephant, complete with *ambaari*, followed them.

At some distance came an infantry regiment, rather blurred, it must be admitted, by a massive cloud of dust.

Members of the cavalry at the head of the column, however, seemed rather displeased at this most unexpected roadblock and several voices rose, loud with annoyance.

"Who's there?"—"Move, at once!"—"Make way, do you hear?"

And then, little by little, the irritated voices subsided, giving way to agitated murmurs—then, conversations in hushed tones—and then, finally, to loud bursts of stunned appreciation: "Aha—oho!"

Soldiers jumped down from their horses, surrounded the combatants and began to watch avidly.

Boodhi Vikrama Kesari and Parthibendran descended from their horses as well, pushed past the jostling warriors and made their way to the frontline.

"Good God, do you *see* that?" Parthibendran stuttered, roused to wrath at this extraordinary sight. "Remember what I said about that wretched Vallam brat? Of all the impudent, rag-mannered devils—*look* at him! Daring to cross swords with the prince himself—" his hands began to draw out his own. "I'll be damned if I let this atrocity go on—"

"Come, come now," interrupted Boodhi Vikrama Kesari, his iron hand gripping that of the Pallava prince. "What wonderful sword-play, to be sure—and it's been ages since I saw such excellent foot-work ..."

By this time, the three hundred odd infantrymen had joined them as well; they formed a wide circle around the combatants, intent on the proceedings.

And now, a young woman descended from the *ambaari* on top of the elephant. She sidled between the watching soldiers, negotiated her way through the crowd, and managed to station herself on the frontline.

Ah, the thrill of exhilaration that lit up her face, at that moment! Impossible to describe, that. Her beautiful eyes darted here and there, following the flashing swords. When the fighters sprang forward and back in the thick of battle, her slender waist echoed their movements sinuously. Within moments, her fingers reached towards her lustrous hair, plucked a pretty *neelothpalam* flower and began to twirl it this way and that. The stalk danced every which way, following the direction of the swords— and by now, we needn't trouble ourselves to introduce this young lady to our readers: surely they couldn't have forgotten Poonguzhali?

For a while, battle progressed with the prince directly in her line of sight. By degrees though, the warriors moved, step by step and completed a half circle and eventually, it was Vandhiyathevan who faced the young woman.

Now, Vallavarayan hadn't devoted all his attention to battle; his eyes had swirled around the audience, darting lightning glances here and there, taking in the swelling numbers. They alighted on Poonguzhali at this precise moment.

Astonishment made his concentration falter for just an instant— but that was enough for the prince. His broadsword descended upon Vandhiyathevan's blade with the brutal ferocity of Devendran's famed *Vajrayudham*. The Vaanar warrior staggered; his sword slipped from grasp and clattered to the ground.

The audience erupted into a cacophony of shouts and applause that rivaled the ocean's tumultuous roar, at that moment. And yet—a young woman's enthusiastic trill of laughter broke through it all, refusing to be drowned out.

Vandhiyathevan bent with some effort, trying to pick up the fallen blade again—but he reckoned without the prince.

His highness Arulmozhi Varmar sprang forward, and crushed him in a comprehensive hug.

"You didn't fall to my sword; you matched me blow for every blow—but alas that the lances in a woman's eyes should have beaten you!" He grinned. "Nothing to be ashamed of; it happens to the best of us."

Vandhiyathevan would have tried to explain himself in the face of this lighthearted sally—but by this time, Senathipathi Boodhi Vikrama Kesari and Parthibendran had arrived at their side.

"Mine was the hand that signed off this boy on a commission to you, your highness," the Senathipathi shot out his words. "Has he overstepped his bounds? I must confess—we reeled at what we saw, moments ago."

"Indeed, yes, Commander—I couldn't stand him at all. Nag, nag, and nag for hours on end, asking, *Where's war? Where?* In the end, I couldn't stand it—and I simply had to show him: *Here's battle!*" quipped the prince.

The audience roared in approval once more, at this answer.

The Senathipathi approached Vandhiyathevan and patted his shoulder in a comradely fashion. "Ah, it's been many days since I saw such excellent sword-play, *Appane*—and you're certainly well-suited to be the prince's companion, let me tell you! Sometimes, his shoulders fairly heave with the need for martial pursuits—after all, a descendent of Paranthaka Chozhar who won the title *Kunjara Mallan* for himself, isn't he?" chuckled the commander. "Those who cannot engage in combat with him when he pleases will find their days as his comrade numbered!"

The prince had made his way to Parthibendra Pallavar by this time. "News came that you've been in search of me, *Ayya*, and I made haste to meet you," he said, politely. "Is my brother well, in Kanchi? What news of my grandfather?"

"Your elder brother and your grandfather have made me the bearer of an extremely important message, and I've already been forced to spend four or five days in an effort to locate you—which means that there isn't a moment to waste," was Parthibendran's terse reply. "And so—"

"So I gather, or you wouldn't have arrived here hotfoot, *Ayya*," intercepted the prince. "Which is why I must beg your indulgence in revealing their messages at once."

"Not in the middle of the road, we cannot—and certainly not with such an immense audience," pointed out Senathipathi Periya Velaar, who had arrived at their side by this time. "Look—that ruined *mandapam* over there might aid us in our task. That's one thing we can be thankful about in Ilankai, I suppose—there is no dearth of structures collapsing to rubble."

The whole gathering, accordingly, trooped over to the crumbling edifice, some distance across the road.

40

MANDHIRALOSANAI

Vandhiyathevan snatched a moment with Azhwarkkadiyaan on their way to the *mandapam*. "I can't gauge his highness at all," he murmured plaintively. "These unexpected fights—why, the other day he wrestled me to the ground while today, he practically forced a sword-fight on me. The least he could've done is given some notice," he groaned. "This friendship is proving to be fraught with danger ..."

The prince, who seemed to possess the ears of a lynx, sidled through the moving throng to join them. "Indeed, yes, *Ayya*—my friendship is likely to prove dangerous to anyone. You might've guessed that yesterday, I should think," he added, candidly. "If you've set your heart on a life of ease, you'll need to stay at least ten *kaadhams* from me."

"That isn't precisely what I meant, your highness. I'm willing to lay down my body, heart and soul in your service when danger threatens, but if you *will* insist on thrusting these quarrels—"

"I'm surprised you haven't tumbled to the truth of his strategy, *Thambi*," the Vaishnavite interjected. "We were about to be accosted by an unknown, armed cavalcade—what better ruse to know their identity, and buy some time to plan accordingly? After all, not many can resist the lure of a sword-fight, can they?"

"Thirumalai is right, of course," acknowledged the prince. "But there's another reason. The truth is—anyone who becomes my friend magically transforms into an instant target for the loathing and hatred of many. It's my custom to inflict quarrels on the one whose friendship I crave; only those who don't mind these squabbles can stay with me for any length of time."

"Well, in *that* case—! Never mind waiting for *you* to start; mine shall be the honour of quarreling with you, henceforth. By the way, I, your sister's envoy, forgot to deliver another, very important message and I should like to do it soon—at once, in fact." Vandhiyathevan hurried on. "Of course, if you've any objection and wish to take up your sword again, then by all means—"

"I don't," chuckled the prince. "Let me know this precious message."

"A certain young woman was part of the audience during our sword-fight. She held a *kumudham* flower too—you even mentioned that I'd fallen for the lances in her eyes ... do you know who she is?"

"No. Frankly, I didn't notice her all that well; I'm not in the habit of gawking at women."

"The message I'm about to deliver is from her, to tell the truth—and it simply slipped my mind. Well, why wouldn't it? Ever since our meeting, I've only had time to grapple with you in the streets and try to escape crumbling houses! Hence the lapse and somehow, I never could find the right moment to tell you. But today, I happened to catch sight of her and remembered that I'd never passed on her message. That was when I faltered and you took the opportunity to beat down my sword, and—"

"Leave all that be; now who's that girl, and why on earth must she send me messages?"

"She's Poonguzhali, *Ayya!*"

"A beautiful name, but completely unfamiliar to me, I'm afraid."

"Do you at least recall *Samudhra Kumari?*"

"Samudhra Kumari ... Samudhra Kumari," the prince mulled over the words. "Doesn't ring a bell, I'm sorry to say—in fact, I don't even remember seeing her."

"Do try to cudgel your brain into dredging up the slightest memory— if you don't, she's certain to break her heart. Picture this: there you were in Kodikkarai, awaiting the boat that would carry you to your ship. This young woman paddled ashore at that very moment in her boat, all by her lonesome self. You watched her, astonished. She approached your camp, eager to know your identity, and you turned to the lighthouse keeper. *Who is this young lady,* you asked, and he replied that she was his daughter, his Kumari. *Oh,* you exclaimed at once. *Is she, now? Forgive me, for I believed her to be Samudhra Kumari herself!* The girl hasn't forgotten a word of that brief conversation—and frankly, it was with her help that I managed to cross the sea and set foot in Ilankai ..."

"Now that you mention it, I seem to retain a very hazy recollection of some such incident—but what on earth is the daughter of Kodikkarai's oceans doing in the vicinity of Anuradhapuram, of all places? In the company of this regiment too ... or is she here on your account?"

"Not at all; I can't even imagine her journeying all this way just for my sake. That simply doesn't make sense. If she's here on anyone's account, it has to be yours—but I'm afraid I couldn't guess the reason."

Vandhiyathevan's eyes searched the crowd as he spoke, finally alighting on Poonguzhali, walking demurely by the Senathipathi's side, head bowed. For all her meekness, he rather suspected that her attention was focused completely on the prince; all her senses were attuned to him and she kept flicking lightning looks in his direction out of the corner of her eyes. Instinct might have warned her, perhaps, that she was the subject of their discussion—else there was no reason for her sudden, newfound submissiveness, at complete variance with her usual, confident demeanour. *Ammamma*! Could mere words do justice to her sparkling eyes—so restive, darting here, there, everywhere without a pause?

The ruined *mandapam*, lacking a ceiling but compensated by beautifully sculpted pillars, was soon at hand. The disadvantages of a missing roof could be ignored somewhat due to the leafy branches of the surrounding trees that provided welcome shade. The tumbling structure was even supplied with a sort of raised platform in the centre, which provided a convenient seat for the prince, the Senathipathi, and Parthibendran.

Vandhiyathevan and Azhwarkkadiyaan stood a little apart.

Poonguzhali chose a pillar behind which she stood half concealed—but with a vantage point which allowed her to observe the prince and Vallavarayan closely.

Warriors of the cavalcade ranged themselves in two rows around the *mandapam*, forming themselves into something approaching a tight, impenetrable *viyugam*. Horses and elephants formed a neat line, beyond.

"What message from my elder brother and my grandfather?" asked the prince of Parthibendran. "I'm eager to know everything."

"The Chozha Empire is besieged by immense peril, your highness—doubtless, you too, are aware of this fact …"

"I couldn't help but know this, *Ayya*; the Chakravarthy is ill and abed …"

"That, I'm afraid, is hardly the only danger that threatens; the *samrajyam* as a whole is in dire straits. Those in a position to wield considerable authority have turned conspirators, spinning webs of deceit calculated to snare the Emperor, the crown prince and your own exalted self. They've decided, all on their own, that your elder brother shall be divested of his right as heir and further, to place idiotically pious Madhuranthakan—that sly, hypocritical cat with his clacking *rudhraksham* necklaces!—upon the Chozha throne. The Pazhuvettarayar brothers; the Sambuvaraiyars; Irattai Kudai Rajaliyaar and Mazhapaadi Mazhavaraiyar are some of the deceitful rogues who've ranged themselves on his side. We needn't fear that their pitiful efforts might come to fruition however; the Northern and Southern Chozha forces still acknowledge our suzerainty, not to mention the illustrious Thirukkoyilur Miladudaiyar and Kodumbalur Periya Velaar. Their unflinching loyalty and considerable resources, combined with our armed forces shall trample these fragile webs of deceit within moments. And yet—it would be foolishness to waste too much time in planning strategy; that would turn out to be an advantage to our enemies. No; our conspirators' treachery ought to be nipped in the bud.

"And that's why, your highness, you see me, the bearer of imperative summons from your elder brother and your grandfather. They wish you to come to Kanchi without a moment's delay. Your grandfather thinks, further, that you brothers oughtn't to be separated at this point, offering easy targets for your foes. I shall take further leave to reveal your brother's deepest desire: it's never been his wish to barricade himself within a royal palace and rule from a capital; he's practically straining at the leash to marshal a well-armed navy, travel to far-flung countries, and have the tiger flag fluttering atop their palaces. Ever since those wretched Pazhuvettarayars scuttled his northern campaign by flinging every single obstacle they could lay their hands on, his restlessness has grown by leaps and bounds. His aggression and lust for war are now ten times what they were. Once you arrive in Kanchi, a massive force shall descend on Thanjai, destroy the betrayers, those treacherous leeches and when you've been crowned Emperor—"

"Good God, *no.*" The prince, who'd been listening to this speech with the greatest respect and a flattering degree of attention, clapped his palms over his ears. "Don't—*pray* don't speak such terrible words. I and the Chozha throne have nothing to do with each other, after all."

"Naturally, the subject shall not be mentioned if it displeases you. Discussion about the succession is, of course, your brother's prerogative as it's yours; an issue that may well be resolved between yourselves as siblings—indeed, it must be. And yet, destroying our foes is a subject that requires complete accord between your noble selves. Make preparations for a journey to Kanchi at once; we shall join hands to destroy the Pazhuvettarayars, the Sambuvaraiyars and all their cohorts in one fell stroke. It ought to be easy to dispatch that hypocritical Siva devotee to his much-vaunted heavenly abode as well, and then ... well, you and your brother may settle everything as you see fit," finished Parthibendran with a flourish.

"And is all to be decided by just us, *Ayya*?" came the prince's gentle question. "What about my father, the Chakravarthy? Must we not know his opinions about these startling developments? My brother might have received tidings from him—a personal message of sorts, regarding these issues. Perhaps you're aware of any such communication?"

"I see that there's nothing to be done but make a clean breast of things, your highness. There's no more point in prevarication, or subterfuge: to put it plainly—there's simply no way of knowing your respected father's opinion. The Chakravarthy can no longer call his soul his own and is a prisoner of the Pazhuvettarayars. None may seek a royal audience, convey or receive messages without their express approval. How, then, may one learn his opinion about anything? Your brother made every effort to bring him to Kanchi—to the extent of building an ornate golden palace—and petitioned him to perform the *grihapravesam* to honour his new home. Not that he received even an acknowledgement ..."

"There's nothing new about the fact that my father is ill and unable to leave his bed ..."

"*Must* your honoured father—the most Illustrious Emperor of the Three Worlds—journey to Kanchi on foot, your highness? Aren't there elephants and horses aplenty; vehicles and carts enough to transport entire armies, within our dominions? Pearl-studded palanquins and golden chariots to carry the entire royal family? Wouldn't a hundred thousand chieftains and lords within these very borders fall all over themselves to shoulder your gracious sire where he wills? But that, my prince, is not the reason for his inability to travel; one may trace the root of all these evils to the Pazhuvettarayars. They've incarcerated his royal person; the Thanjai palace is now but a lavish prison. Come, your highness—come with us …" Parthibendran made a last, impassioned plea. " …if you wish to save your beloved father's life!"

These emotional words, it was obvious, had had their effect on the prince. That his heart was now in turmoil was apparent; for the first time since the conversation began, his radiant face fell; his countenance faded and worry settled itself between his shapely brows.

Having spent some time lost in thought, he finally raised his head and looked straight at Boodhi Vikrama Kesari. "Might I know your thoughts, Senathipathi? Chief Minister Aniruddha Brahmaraayar was here a few days ago—as you know, a most trusted and valued confidant of my father—and he counseled me to stay in Ilankai for a while. You, as I remember, agreed. In answer to my query of why I should twiddle my thumbs here in the absence of war, you put forward several theories and convinced me. You see the Vaishnavite over there? He's arrived with the same message from the Chief Minister. As for Ilaiya Piratti," the prince paused. "Words can't do justice to my respect for her; my journey to Ilankai was, in fact, at her bidding. She has now communicated with me as well through this Vaanar warrior—and to tell the truth, there's not much of a difference between hers, and Parthibendrar's messages. She, on the other hand, wishes me to come to Pazhaiyarai—while my brother wants me in Kanchi at once. Your view, Senathipathi?"

"Until this morning, your highness, my considered opinion was that you ought to remain in Ilankai; in fact, I spent most of last night debating the issue furiously with Parthibendrar. I may add, in passing, that his most impassioned arguments failed to convince me, but what this girl—the one that's standing right there—told me, this very morning, changed my mind instantly," admitted the Commander. "I now believe it imperative for you to leave for Kanchi at once!"

The prince's attention now turned to Poonguzhali, who'd been gazing at him through the corner of her eyes, half concealed by the pillar. "I've heard tales of Mahabharatham's Abhimanyu being massacred by several foes at once," he said to himself. "But I seem to be in danger of being hacked to pieces by mere messages ..." Aloud, he asked, "Well, what *is* this news of hers that has thrown everything and everyone into disarray?"

"As to that," said the Velaar. "She can tell you, herself."

Poonguzhali took halting steps, emerging slowly from behind the pillar, and finally stood in front of the prince. Her gaze darted in all four directions—towards the Senathipathi; Parthibendran; Vandhiyathevan and Azhwarkkadiyaan a little farther ... but for some reason, her strangely uncooperative eyes simply refused to alight on the prince.

"Go on, girl," prompted the Senathipathi. "Quick, now!"

Poonguzhali parted her lips in a vain bid to speak—but her throat, in most perverse fashion, refused to work.

"Oh, no," murmured the prince. "Has the whole world turned mute, now?"

That was it. Poonguzhali raised her large, expressive eyes and gazed at him once—for the tiniest fraction of a second. But even that seemed too much: those eyes began to well up with tears and trickle down her cheeks.

The next instant she flitted away, vanishing into the dense thicket of trees a little beyond.

The assembled group frankly gaped at this bizarre spectacle.

Vandhiyathevan, the first to gather his wits, took a quick step forward. "This isn't the first time she's done something like this, *Ayya*," he explained. "She ran away from me once; I followed and caught up with her. Allow me to do the same, now."

"Do, by all means, but before that," said the prince. "Perhaps the Senathipathi might tell me the gist of her message?"

"That may be accomplished easily; two words will suffice," offered said Senathipathi at once. "War ships. The Pazhuvettarayars have sent two of these massive vessels, filled to the brim with soldiers; they are anchored even now in a canal of the Thondaiman River, cunningly concealed. And they are here ..." the Commander paused. "To take you prisoner."

41

"LOOK OVER THERE!"

A faint, rueful smile lit up the prince's face at Senathipathi Boodhi Vikrama Kesari's dramatic announcement. "It would seem that my heart's turmoil is at an end at last," he murmured almost to himself.

"Senathipathi!" Parthibendran chose to—rather predictably—explode in spectacular wrath, and rose at once. "*What* did you just say? This—is this the truth? Ah, why didn't I know before? *Now* I see why you practically dragged that lunatic girl all the way here—but I ask you again: is it really true that the Pazhuvettarayars have sent war ships to imprison his highness?"

"If one is willing to believe what this girl swears she heard and saw with her own ears and eyes—then, yes, it is."

"Thirukkovilur Miladudaiyar's predictions have come true, then. Ah, truly, that wily old man was the only one to see through those scheming Pazhuvettarayars—but Senathipathi, why do you sit still, having known this—this terrible news for so long? How *could* you? How could they—!

337

Sending men to arrest the great-grandson of the illustrious Paranthaka Chozhar—the most beloved son of Emperor Sundara Chozhar—the prince dearly loved by every Chozha citizen, the very apple of their eyes—the cherished younger brother of crown prince Aditha Karikalar—ah, has it come to this, indeed? What more are we waiting for? Let's start at once and march all the way to those treacherous ships, raze them to the ground and give them a most indecent burial on this very island. And then, we shall carry out everything as planned ... why hesitate?" Parthibendran spluttered and practically spewed fury at a great rate. "*Do* get up, all of you!"

"Some suspicion about your reaction did cross my mind, Parthibendra," the Senathipathi gazed up at him. "Which explains my silence until now, about the girl's message. Haste will not help us here; we ought to think about what we know and plan accordingly ..."

"Think? And plan? What on earth are we supposed to *think* about, pray? Your highness," he turned to Arulmozhi Varmar at once. "Do tell us what elaborate plans we're supposed to make. Whatever concerns you may have had before, surely they've all crumbled to dust now? The Pazhuvettarayars deserve to be annihilated, don't they?"

"It would be best to learn the Senathipathi's sentiments first," was the prince's noncommittal reply. "Why don't we? *Ayya*," he turned towards the commander without the slightest sign of outrage or anxiety. "What is it that you say we must think about?"

"The men who are here to imprison—forgive me; my tongue simply refuses to even say the wretched words—your gracious highness, well ..." the Senathipathi hesitated. "What if they are here upon the Chakravarthy's express command?"

"Oh, *here's* a wonderful jest!" Parthibendran went into a cackle of sarcastic laughter. "And is the Chakravarthy in any position to issue commands of his own? The Pazhuvettarayars have divested him of all authority and practically shackled him to his bed, haven't they?"

"The Pallava Commander is completely right," Vandhiyathevan butted in, at this point. "I saw the pathetic state of affairs with my own eyes and it's true—the Pazhuvoor lords do treat him little better than a prisoner. No one can seek an audience with him or even speak a few words without their express approval. Ah, the treatment they meted out just because I dared to utter a word … *appa*, my hands still ache from Chinna Pazhuvettarayar's iron grip!" And Vandhiyathevan massaged his wrists in remembered pain and loathing.

"Well done, Vallavaraya—say it like it is, boy! You know, I didn't quite do you justice," exulted Parthibendran. "Let the prince and the Senathipathi know the truth about Thanjai!"

"He's made known everything that needed to be known, so I shall spare him the repetition," said the prince, and then turned to Vandhiyathevan. "You offered to bring back our runaway, *Ayya*, but I see you here, still. I'd like to learn this precious message firsthand, so escort her to us please. She seems slightly wanting, from what I can see—tread lightly, won't you?"

"Certainly I will, your highness—I'm on my way as we speak. But please know this: never, not for a single moment shall I entertain the idea of the Pazhuvettarayars laying a finger on you, let alone arresting you," Vandhiyathevan declared as he stalked away. "Not as long as there's life in this body!"

"You haven't revealed your opinion yet, Senathipathi," said the prince, continuing the conversation.

"I will, now: Attempt no meeting with the men sent by the Pazhuvoor brothers. Rather, depart for Kanchi at once in Parthibendrar's ship. I, for my part, shall journey to Thanjai, seek a personal audience with the Chakravarthy and learn the true state of affairs …"

"As well stick your head into the lion's gaping maw," Parthibendran snorted. "You'll never make it out of that place alive—rather, a straight passage to Thanjai's famed dungeons would be your fate. You wouldn't even, I wager, be able to see the Emperor—"

"How *dare* you? Who in Chozha Nadu possesses the temerity to even attempt such a thing? No one is man enough to stop me from seeking an audience with the Chakravarthy either—and another thing: Chief Minister Aniruddha Brahmaraayar is there, as well—"

"Yes, he's present—and a fat lot of good *that* is. Not even he can manage to wrangle a meeting with the Emperor and—why, there stands his own trusted disciple. Why not ask his opinion?"

"Ah, yes," the Senathipathi turned towards Azhwarkkadiyaan. "This Vaishnavite's presence completely slipped my mind. Why this profound silence, Thirumalai? You have not turned mute, have you—like the prince mentioned just now?"

"God has given us ears two, Senathipathi, but only one mouth; therefore, *Use your ears twice as much as your mouth; listen more and talk less*, has always been one of my Guru's cherished maxims," Azhwarkkadiyaan stated in dulcet tones. "In particular must I follow this priceless rule, he's decreed, when bearing witness to discussions involving royal affairs of extreme delicacy and—er—discretion."

"And a wonderful disciple you've proven to be, thus far. But do favour us with your opinion, now that we're asking you ourselves."

"Favour you with my opinion on what, exactly, Senathipathi?"

"The issue that has us all in a raging discussion at the moment. What course of action do you think the prince must take, at this juncture? Stay in Ilankai? Or leave for Kanchi?"

"Permission to reveal my honest opinion? I will, if his highness will allow it."

Arulmozhi Varmar, lost in reverie until that moment, now raised his head to stare at the Vaishnavite. "By all means, Thirumalai. There's no reason for you to hesitate," he encouraged. "Let me know what you think."

"Find the most guarded prison in Ilankai—in a highly secret location—and place the prince there, under additional and highly efficient security, of course."

There was perfect silence for a moment. And then, "What sort of ridiculous nonsense is this?" demanded the Senathipathi.

"You could've hardly picked a worse time for your tomfoolery," spat Parthibendran.

"I'm neither indulging in a practical joke, nor am I spouting nonsensical drivel," Azhwarkkadiyaan said, quite calmly. "You asked me for my honest opinion and I gave it. Last night, the prince was almost buried alive under a crumbling mansion as he walked along the streets of Anuradhapuram. Later, we were resting in an old home, and left it briefly on some pretext. The house went up in flames within the hour. You may confirm the truth of these incidents with his highness, if you please!"

One look at the prince's expressive face, however, and the two listening men knew that everything that Azhwarkkadiyaan related had, indeed, happened.

"On whose account did these dangerous events occur, pray? Ask him, *Ayya*—for who on earth would burn down mansions to assassinate either me or Vandhiyathevan?"

"There's no doubt about it—someone's trying to murder his highness, of course," Parthibendran jumped up at once. "This makes it imperative that the prince accompany me to Kanchi—"

"Not on your life!" Azhwarkkadiyaan remarked crisply. "If that's the alternative, we may as well ship him off to the Pazhuvettarayars—"

"*What* did you say, you—you impudent rogue Vaishnavite ...!" Parthibendran unsheathed his sword with a hiss.

"Thirumalai ...!" The Senathipathi exclaimed, scandalized, while simultaneously pushing Parthibendran back into his seat. "How could you say such a thing? You ought to know that the Pallava scion's loyalty to the Chozhas is unquestionable; that his integrity is such that—"

"Indeed, Senathipathi, I'm well aware that Parthibendrar's fidelity is beyond reproach and that he cherishes the very greatest regard for them—but is that enough, pray?"

"I can vouch for the fact that Parthibendrar would give his life for those who claim friendship, Thirumalai," offered the commander.

"That may well be true—but I should like to ask him just one question; pray request him, Senathipathi, to honour me with an answer. When we were in the vicinity of Thampallai, the evening of the day before, we saw him in the company of two men. Who were they? Ask him where they are, now."

"I ..." For the first time in the discussion, Parthibendran looked rather disconcerted. "I came across them in Thirikonamalai," he said, with visible hesitation. "They swore they knew the prince's location and that they would take me to him—but vanished without a trace in Anuradhapuram. Why do you ask, Vaishnavite? You wouldn't happen to know anything about them, would you?"

"I know them as two among a vicious group of conspirators who've sworn to destroy the Chozha dynasty without a trace. What's more—I suspect that they were the ones behind the attack on his highness in Anuradhapuram ... ah!" Azhwarkkadiyaan exclaimed suddenly. "Look over there!"

He pointed to a place, a little distance from the *mandapam*. Amidst the dense shrubbery and thickly clustering trees stood a handsome young man and a pretty lass; it could be seen that these were Vandhiyathevan and Poonguzhali. The Vaanar warrior, who'd been speaking seriously, suddenly whirled and flung away a dagger. It sailed through the air and landed in a thorny bush.

A pained *screech!* rose from within.

ℒ

42

POONGUZHALI'S DAGGER

Vandhiyathevan, pursuing Poonguzhali post her dramatic exit from the ruined *mandapam*, came upon her graceful form leaning against a tree. Closer still, he could see that she was sobbing a little.

"Poonguzhali," he murmured, making his voice as pliant and comforting as possible.

She jumped at his approach and whirled around. "*You*," she muttered, and turned away again.

"Yes," Vandhiyathevan admitted. "You're furious with me, aren't you?"

"I'm not."

"Why're you snapping off my nose, then?"

"I *hate* men."

"The prince as well?"

Poonguzhali whipped around to stare at him, her eyes blazing fire. "Him, especially!"

"What's he done to deserve your loathing?"

"He never even looked at my face—doesn't remember me at all."

"But he does—why, when I mentioned your name, he exclaimed, *Wouldn't I know Samudhra Kumari?*"

"Liar."

"You can ask him yourself, if you wish."

"If—if he did remember me, why didn't he say a single word?"

"He did; you were the one who took off like a startled hare."

"Not *that* kind of talk. The things people say when they meet someone they know and ask after them, to … you're lying! He didn't spare me a glance."

"There's a reason for that, Poonguzhali."

"There is?"

"These are terrible times for his highness."

"Who says so?"

"Every single astrologer; the Kudandhai Jothidar told me so, personally."

"What exactly did he say?"

"That the prince would be forced to endure a great many perils in quick succession; what's more, his companions will have to suffer them too. *He* knows this as well, which is why he tries to pick quarrels with his friends and drive them away. He'd rather that his problems ended with him, and affected no one else."

"Why're you with him, then?"

"You saw what happened a little while ago, didn't you? He subjected me to the same tactic—halted in the middle of the road and practically forced a sword-fight on me! The only reason we stopped was because of your party's timely arrival."

"Wouldn't you leave him no matter how much he tried to drive you away?"

"Certainly not. I'd stay by his side and endure everything he does."

"You really like him, don't you?"

"Very, very much."

"Why?"

"I can't put my finger on it. Somehow, I liked him the moment I set eyes on him."

"Me too!" Poonguzhali blurted—and then bit her lips, her lovely face crimson with embarrassment at having admitted such a fact.

"I know. That's why I came here to escort you back. Now, come."

"*No.*"

"Don't make me drag you by force, my girl."

"Don't make me use my dagger," Poonguzhali slipped her hand to her waist and pulled out a wicked weapon.

"Why do you threaten to kill me, you little wretch? This is your way of paying me back for having reminded the prince about you, I suppose."

"You never mentioned a single word—stop lying!"

"As you please. Now get back to that *mandapam*, tell the prince what you know about the two warships come to imprison him, and then get lost."

"I've told the Senathipathi every single thing I know."

"Nevertheless, the prince would like to hear everything from you."

"Can't. I shall turn speechless in his presence."

"Well, you're in luck: the prince cherishes a soft spot for mute women."

"*Chee!*" Poonguzhali spat, raising her dagger. "How dare you make me the butt of your silly jokes?"

"You're not going to come with me, then?"

"No!"

"Please yourself," Vandhiyathevan shrugged, turned away, and took two steps. Abruptly, in one swift move, he turned, plucked the dagger from her hand and flung it with a flourish.

The blade twirled through the air for a very long time and finally landed in a dense bush—from which came a pained shriek.

It was impossible to judge whether the sound had been made by man or beast. Poonguzhali, who had glared at Vandhiyathevan with unspeakable fury at his deed, now stared at the bush, stunned. They glanced at each other, considerably astonished, and made their way slowly towards the bush near which the dagger had seemingly fallen.

Droplets of fresh blood shone on the leaves and earth—but there was neither animal nor human; not to mention Poonguzhali's dagger. Both had vanished.

"You see the truth of my words now, my girl? Danger surrounds the prince on all sides; no one can guess where or how it may strike. I threw your knife on the spur of the moment—but it's obvious that someone was concealed within those bushes. Now, think: why would someone do that, except to wait for the right moment to assassinate him? Remember the two men you mentioned in Kodikkarai—the ones your brother ferried to Ilankai? You were suspicious of their motives, weren't you?" Vandhiyathevan rattled on without a pause. "You'd better keep these things in mind: is it really fair to talk about liking the prince and then leaving him in the lurch?" He finished finally, rather breathless.

"But—what if he orders me to leave?" Poonguzhali hazarded.

"We simply mustn't. No matter what."

Poonguzhali mulled over this for a moment. "Shouldn't we find out who was hiding in that bush?" she asked, finally.

"Impossible to accomplish that—especially in a jungle as dense as this one. Waste time too much and we might drive the prince into a real fury. Everyone would just leave us here, so stop dawdling and come with me now!"

"All right, then," Poonguzhali acquiesced, and the two of them made their way towards the rest of the congregation in the *mandapam*.

***

They were surrounded by men and questions from all sides, once they reached their destination. "Why did you fling that dagger?"—"What was that shriek?"

"Probably a jackal or leopard, crouching in the foliage," Vandhiyathevan was dismissive. "I suspected its presence and threw the knife. We went closer and investigated, but found nothing."

"Ah, who cares?" The Senathipathi shook his head. "Just question the girl."

Poonguzhali had been staring at the prince ever since her return—and now, finally, he raised his eyes to gaze at her.

Chee, be still, my beating heart! What's this lump that chokes my throat? Why do my eyes well up with tears? You silly, weak little girl—what's happened to your famed courage? You've never flinched at roaring seas and dreadful hurricanes; why does your heart fail you, now? You could match a dangerous leopard's cold stare for stare—why does your sight dim in his presence? Poonguzhali, for the sake of everything you care about, don't falter and earn the name of a lunatic once more! Raise your head; look up at the prince; answer his questions in a firm, clear voice. Don't betray yourself! What can he do to you, after all? The world calls him Benevolent, Dhayaalu—one whose compassion is renowned. What could he do to you, a harmless, pitiful girl ...?

The prince smiled very slightly.

"Samudhra Kumari," his voice seemed to reach Poonguzhali as though from the very depths of the ocean. "Do you remember me?"

43

"I'm a criminal!"

Do you remember me, Samudhra Kumari?"

Remember you, Ponniyin Selva? What a question to ask, my prince, after thousands of years lost in each other, our souls intertwined, our hearts mingled forever! Dare you ask if I remember—or perhaps it's you who has forgotten? Forgotten the many years spent in my boat—ah, when we rowed into the heart of the ocean, bobbing gently upon white-tipped waves, aware of nothing but our own exhilaration? And then, suddenly, black clouds rolled around us, blotting out the sun and we stood up in our rocking craft, clutching each other's hands; you've forgotten the aeons we spent, just the two of us, haven't you? Forgotten the raging storm that battered the seas; the screaming gales, churning waves which raised our little craft right to the very heavens one moment; flinging us right down to Pathalam the next, and the endless days we spent, drawing strength from each other and riding out the cyclone? And then, one day, we flew alongside the birds in the sky—have you forgotten that too? You gathered a handful of sparkling stars and set them in my hair; diamonds in my dark tresses. You even caught up the poorna chandran and held it up to my face: **There, gaze at your lovely golden countenance upon this silver plate,** *you said—and you've forgotten!*

Once, you dived down to the very depths of the ocean while I waited, heart hammering in my chest; soon, you re-appeared, hands overflowing with lustrous, glowing pearls and corals, and strung them around my neck in a necklace! You might have forgotten these momentous events, but how could I? How could I forget, your highness, those luxurious afternoons we lay upon lush, grassy forest floors, drinking each other in, while the tree branches above us bent with the weight of fragrant flowers, making a scented arbour as they leant towards the surface of lakes gleaming with blue waters? How could I forget the hundreds of nightingales singing sweet songs with their mates, while a thousand bees buzzed in accompaniment and a hundred thousand butterflies fluttered their delicate, silken wings that shone like jewels, dancing in ecstatic abandonment? They're etched in my heart, my prince, no matter how many lives I live and you look up and ask me if I remember you—how could you? Of course I remember you, Ayya; I remember you very well indeed ...

Thus did Poonguzhali's naïve heart lament; stuttering with the need to pour out eloquent thoughts—but her coral lips betrayed her. "Yes," was all they would murmur.

"Ah, you speak at last, Daughter of the Oceans! I've seen so many heart-wrenchingly beautiful Goddesses and fairy-beings chiseled on the pillars of countless mansions and palaces in this island—for a moment, I wondered if you were one of them; a figure of stone. Thankfully, you spoke just now and broke that illusion. Do me a favour and continue; my heart yearns for the sound of your melodious voice. Now, you seem to have given the Senathipathi news; two large warships lie concealed in the Thondaiman River, and that they are full of soldiers. This is true, isn't it, Samudhra Kumari?" asked the prince. "You did see those vessels, did you?"

"Yes indeed, *Ayya*—with my own eyes," she said.

"I can hear a little more of your voice, now; my ears are gladdened.

Very well, to proceed—you paddled into a small canal once you'd caught sight of the ships; you intended to lie concealed within the dense forest until they left. This was when a few soldiers disembarked and came ashore, near where you were secreted, in fact. You didn't really wish to listen to their talk, but they were so close that you couldn't help but overhear. This is what you related to the Senathipathi, isn't it?"

"I told him exactly what I'd heard and seen."

"Naturally. Your first instinct, when you understood the essence of their speech, was to communicate a warning to the commander. You left the moment the soldiers had gone apart and made your way to the Senathipathi as fast as you could. By the way, how did you manage that, Samudhra Kumari?"

"Half the way in my boat and the rest, I walked through the forest."

"And your intended destination, *Amma*?"

"Maathottam at first, as I'd understood that the Senathipathi could be found there—but on my way, I heard that he was in Mahindhalai. Oh, the trouble I went to, just to manage an audience with him …"And Poonguzhali turned to glare in the Boodhi Vikrama Kesari's direction, her eyes glinting with the power and fury of summer lightning. "I've lost count of the number of people who barred my path!"

"Meeting a military commander is no easy task; if you only knew the trouble my friend over here went through, to accomplish the same thing—well, you'd be astonished. Be that as it may, the very fact that you were stubborn enough to ignore the obstacles, meet him and deliver your news says a great deal. But would you mind repeating your message to me, Poonguzhali? What were those soldiers talking about, when you were listening from within the foliage?"

"My tongue falters at the very thought, your highness."

"Do, anyway, for my sake."

"They—they said that they'd come to take you prisoner."

"Upon whose command were they bent upon this mission? Was that mentioned?"

"I didn't believe it—I thought it very likely the Pazhuvettarayars' wicked plot."

"You may divulge your suspicions later; do keep to the subject and tell me exactly what they said, Samudhra Kumari."

"That it was the Chakravarthy's command."

"Excellent. And the reason for such an order—did they mention that too, by any chance?"

"Yes. That you—that you conspired with the Buddhist monks of this island and tried to crown yourself king—oh, I wanted to *murder* those wretched excuses for men with my own hands when I heard this—"

"What a thing to say, my girl. You ought to know, surely, that the Chakravarthy's envoys ought not to be, er, mauled. Very well; is there anything else of importance that you remember from their conversation?"

"That the Senathipathi mustn't know of this on any account, for he'd try to help you escape. They'd have to find a way to seek you in person, deliver the Chakravarthy's command and escort you themselves ..."

"Which was why you decided to move heaven and earth to find the commander at once, I suppose. You've done me an unimaginable service, Samudhra Kumari; now pray stand aside, for I must discuss certain matters of great importance with these men. But don't run away like last time—or make me send Vandhiyathevar to retrieve you!"

The Daughter of the Oceans obligingly moved, and concealed herself behind a pillar; this time, she chose a spot which would let her have an unobstructed view of his face.

Two bees had tumbled headfirst into a pot of honey; they floundered to the rim, and then began to glory in the exquisite taste of nectar. Poonguzhali's eyes found themselves in just such a convenient, blissful position, from where they could delight and drown themselves in the sweetness of the prince's chiseled, handsome features. Her heart, however, was a different matter; it fluttered within her, unwilling to remain silent. Her soul had tasted a little of heaven and was brimming with such ecstasy that it wished to break free and fill the very universe.

***

"You're the chief of a clan that has bound itself to ours for generations, *Ayya*," the prince now addressed himself to Senathipathi Boodhi Vikrama Kesari. "One of my father's closest friends and I, certainly, never considered you any different from him. You, on your part, never treated me any less than your own son—for which reason I must make to you a petition," the prince opened his gambit. "Pray, don't stop me from carrying out my duty." Before the stunned Commander could think of a rejoinder, he whipped around to meet Parthibendran squarely in the eye. "By the same token, *Ayya*, I must make you this request: you're my esteemed elder brother's dear friend. My brother's counsel is no less in my opinion than God's own, and I treat yours the same way. I beg of you now: please don't stand in the way of doing what I believe to be my duty."

Parthibendran and the Senathipathi glanced at each other, their eyes conveying their fear and concern simultaneously.

"I am afraid I do not understand the import of these words, your highness," began the Commander. "I am one of those who have spent a majority of their lives on the battlefield; men such as I have never been experts in the art of dissembling. You speak of carrying out your duty—pray, tell us exactly what this may be, and how you propose to accomplish it."

"My duty, as I see it now, is to submit to my father's command. He's sent two warships with soldiers to imprison me; why must I importune them needlessly? There's no need for them to wander all over this isle for me; I propose to give myself up. This, in my opinion, is what I ought to do …"

"Never!" Parthibendran barked at once. "I shan't even *think* of allowing this as long as there's life in this body. Be warned that I shall do everything in my power to stop you!"

"Pray calm yourself for a moment," the commander counseled Parthibendran, and then turned towards the prince. "You explained your duty in some detail, *Ayya*; now pray, allow me to describe mine. I am the last man representing the illustrious Kodumbalur Velir clan; the others embraced death in service to the Chozha *samrajyam*; almost all of them, in one battlefield or the other. Who knows—some day, this might be my fate as well. I must, therefore, beg of you to listen to my words with as much patience as you can muster. Last year, the Chakravarthy named you the *Maathanda Naayakar* of the Southern Chozha armed forces—you, my prince, who had spent a lifetime in the luxury of royal palaces until then. He sought a personal audience with me: *The prince's departure feels as though my very soul is being wrenched from my body. And yet, to keep him chained to this palace just to satisfy my whims would be unhealthy; he must leave the confines of this city and prove himself a warrior, just as his brother did before him. But should some danger threaten him—ah, my life shall depart that very instant! Yours shall be the responsibility of keeping him from harm ...*

"Does it make any sense that the Emperor, your honoured father who placed such an onerous charge on me last year would simply turn around and issue commands to imprison you? And what indeed, has been your crime that merits such punishment? To accuse you of plotting and scheming to grab Ilankai—how absurd! A fabricated piece of outrageous nonsense; who would even believe it?"

The prince, who had been listening politely enough to the Kodumbalur Periya Velar's impassioned speech until now, judged it the right moment to intervene. "I can't comment on who might or might not believe it—but I certainly can."

"What on earth do you mean, your highness?"

"That it's true: I did conspire to seize the throne of Ilankai."

"But what's this that you say, *Ayya*?" Vandhiyathevan demanded now, taking a step forward. "Until some time ago, you were droning on about *Sathyam* and *Dharmam*—and now here you are, uttering such enormous lies that ... Senathipathi, pray don't heed a single word he says. Last night, the Buddhist Maha Sabha did offer him the throne, crown and sceptre of Ilankai; his highness refused to accept. I and this Vaishnavite right here were witness to this," he finished, breathlessly.

"Allow me to put forth a question, Vandhiyathevare." A slight, teasing smile appeared on Ponniyin Selvar's face. "Do men who plot and scheme usually do so in the presence of witnesses? Did it ever occur to you that I might've refused the throne of Ilankai precisely because of your presence?"

Vandhiyathevan subsided, dazed at this apparent possibility.

"In case you're still plagued by suspicion, my Vaanar warrior, kindly clarify with your Vaishnavite companion," the prince elaborated, still with the rather mysterious smile on his face. "Ask him about Chief Minister Aniruddha Brammaraayar's message. *The Buddhist monks of Anuradhapuram will likely offer you the throne of Ilankai; refuse, in the presence of witnesses*—this was his instruction; you may confirm the truth of it with Thirumalai."

The assembled gathering was stunned into silence.

"Kindly listen to me, *Ayya*," the prince turned to the Senathipathi once more. "I did, once, cherish the great ambition of ruling this pretty island — and I blame my sister for lighting in me that fire; the fire that eventually grew to a blazing inferno. *Your palms possess the signs of the Conch and Discus, Thambi*, she would say. *You are destined to rule an empire—but this isn't the place for you. Depart for Ilankai at once, and seize its throne for yourself!* The words might vary but her sentiments never did, and she made sure to fan my desire into flames at every opportunity... and therefore, I *am* a criminal. The Chakravarthy wasn't far off the mark when he branded me one, and ordered my arrest ..."

"Now just a moment, your highness. If these were your sentiments regarding Ilankai—then this island ought to consider itself truly fortunate. Neither you nor your honoured elder sister, Ilaiya Piratti is to be held responsible; rather, it is the Emperor himself who must shoulder the blame—if blame indeed there be, which I do not accept for one moment. He has spoken to me more than once of his desire to see you grace the Ilankai throne and it was he, in fact, who brought up the subject first with Kundhavai Devi; your sister is guilty of no crime but that of conveying your father's wishes to you—which clears you of any culpability whatsoever ..."

"By the same token, *Ayya*, surely there can be no objection to go to my father? I could tell him everything that happened, and these two shall corroborate my account. As to what comes next, well. It shall be my duty to abide by his wishes, whatever they may be ..."

"We're wasting our time with these pointless speeches, Senathipathi," Parthibendran's voice sparked with barely controlled fury. "I've said this before: there's no point in beating about the bush. It's time and more that we lay the truth—and the complete truth—before the prince. Now, which of us should perform this office, do you think?"

"Leave it to me and pray, do cultivate a little patience," counseled the Senathipathi. Next, he did a rather peculiar thing: he looked about him furtively, and then turned to the prince. "I tried with all my power to keep this, well, frankly unsavoury episode from sullying your ears, your highness, but my efforts seem to have been in vain. I see now that I shall have to broach this extremely distasteful subject to you: you know, undoubtedly, that Periya Pazhuvettarayar has, at this late date, married a woman by name Nandhini. This female, your highness, is nothing but a witch armed with the most hideous and dangerous black magic. It is no secret that she has ensnared Periya Pazhuvettarayar using a variety of spells and has him groveling at her feet. He, for his part, has no compunction in carrying out every fell command she delivers. Imagine the fate of that courageous old man, born into an ancient and valorous clan, now the bearer of this blemish ..."

"None of this is exactly news to me, Senathipathi," the prince objected. "Surely all of Chozha Nadu has been talking of this for months?"

"But that is not all: thus far, it was only Pazhuvettarayar who lay intoxicated but now ... forgive me, your highness—but it now appears that she has begun casting her devious spells upon the Chakravarthy himself. Can it be wondered at, that he has sent warships to arrest you?"

"Careful now, Commander," the prince's low voice held a hint of menace. "Not a word against my father's honour. Whatever his commands and the circumstances surrounding them, I consider them God's own ..."

"And we do not refute this, your highness—yet, the fear that it isn't just the Chakravarthy's honour but his very life that is in danger, does terrify us. Why, I myself did not know the truth about Nandhini until yesterday, when Parthibendrar made known the whole—and now, it is essential that you are in possession of these facts as well ...

"That last, final battle in the vicinity of Madurai three years ago ... well, Parthibendrar, your brother Aditha Karikalar and I were in council almost every moment, planning each detail of the campaign. The Pandiya forces were annihilated; Veera Pandiyan fled the field and tried to hide away, just as he had done once before. We were determined that it must not happen—and this time, we had sworn not to enter Thanjavur without his head as a trophy. We decided that such an onerous task could not be entrusted to another, and to accomplish it ourselves. We followed the foe and discovered that he had holed up in a hut near a small temple. Your brother bade us guard the entrance and went in; when he walked out, he held Veera Pandiyan's severed head in his hands. We returned, ecstatic that our task was now complete. But we were ignorant, *Ayya*, of the small, incredible drama that had unfolded within the hut in those few moments. The young woman sheltering Veera Pandiyan begged your brother to spare her lover. Your brother kicked her away and chopped off the enemy's head.

"That woman—the one who dared to plead for the life of Chozha Nadu's most dangerous foe—was none other than Nandhini, your highness! And she, indeed, is the one who married the seventy-year-old Pazhuvettarayar and now lords it over everyone as the Pazhuvoor Ilaiya Rani. One may now guess her purpose, her all-consuming ambition in making her home here, can we not? For, what else can it be but to gain a bloody revenge for Veera Pandiyan's execution? To tear out the Chozha clan by its very roots? No one in her presence has ever failed to be caught in the snare of her considerable beauty; Vandhiyathevan, here, can attest to this. As for the terrible group of conspirators who have sworn complete annihilation of the Chozhas—ah, the many tales our Vaishnavite can tell! Who else but Nandhini could have kept them rolling in the wealth they require to fund these treacherous plots?

"And now, it seems that our illustrious Chakravarthy himself has fallen victim to that wily witch's dangerous lures; rumours of his wishes to place Madhuranthakan upon the throne have reached our ears. Therefore, your highness, it is my considered opinion that this is hardly the right time for a visit to Thanjai …"

"I'm stunned at what I've heard so far, Senathipathi—but this has only served to re-affirm my decision: if this be the mire my father has sunk in—if these are the terrible perils that surround him—then my place is by his side. What does the throne of Ilankai matter, or even this petty life? No, there's no reason to hesitate, and let no one dare to stop me, either," finished the prince, most majestically. And then, his eyes swiveled, eventually resting upon Poonguzhali, who had been standing by the pillar, watching him unblinkingly.

"Come here a moment, Samudhra Kumari."

She took a few slow steps forward.

"You've done me a great service by bringing your message, my girl— but now, I require a little more of your assistance," began the prince. "You'll oblige me, won't you?"

What is all this? Surely a fantastic dream? I came here, hoping to help him in any feeble way I could and here he is, asking for my assistance—this petty little boat-girl! I came hoping for a boon from God *but here is my deity, holding out His hands, begging* **me** *for alms!* These thoughts flitted though her mind even as her lips uttered the words, "Your slightest wish shall be my command, your highness."

"You informed me of the two warships that lay concealed at the mouth of the Thondaiman River, sent for arresting me, didn't you? I wish to reach them at once," the prince paused. "Will you be my guide?"

"Refuse, girl," growled a voice from somewhere, and it took Poonguzhali a moment to recognize that it belonged to the Senathipathi.

It was only then that that besotted young woman, lost in some exotic fairy dream so far, realized the appalling complications of her position: had she paddled over tumbling rivers, stumbled over hill and dale to warn the prince about the horrible peril that awaited him—only to be asked to deliver him right into its gaping jaws?

Now, she understood the full import of that growled out *Refuse, girl!* from the Senathipathi, for, a thousand, thousand voices echoed the same command: the trees rustled; the pillars of the *mandapam* groaned and rumbled; the birds on the branches shrieked and twittered: *Refuse!*

But stay ... what was this feeble, gentle voice in her heart? *Wait, Poonguzhali,* murmured this voice. *Think—for here's your chance! Do as the prince asks, and you could be in his company for two whole days. You shall be by his side; you could gaze at him as long as you wish without his knowledge. The breeze that touches him will caress you too; his melodious voice will fall on your ears as often as even you could wish. At last, at last, you pitiful girl— you will get a chance to fulfill the tiniest part of your hopeless, futile fantasy. As for what might happen next—frankly, who cares? Accept, Poonguzhali ...*

"You hesitate, Daughter of the Oceans. Won't you help me?" The prince's voice held just the slightest hint of cajolery. "Will I have to find my way to these ships all by myself?"

This, as far as Poonguzhali was concerned, clinched the issue. "I shall be your guide, your highness," she offered.

The loud, pointed rasp with which Senathipathi Boodhi Vikrama Kesari cleared his throat, then, was something akin to the earth's loud rumble from its very depths, just preceding a monumental earthquake.

"Far be it from me to stand in your chosen path, your highness," he announced portentously, taking a step forward. "You ought, however, to accede to a request of mine: until you reach these ships, your safety is of paramount importance and therefore, my responsibility. Your friends described, at some length, the attempts made on your life. These assassins have not yet been caught; we do not even know their identities. Forgive me for speaking plainly—but I have my doubts even regarding this girl, here; she may well have done her part in assisting these murderers. Perhaps her tall stories of two warships awaiting you are just that— stories borne of a creative fancy. Why not, indeed? A while ago, your friend grabbed her dagger and threw it into the foliage, where it clearly hit something—or someone. Whose pained lament was it, then? This girl may act your guide, by all means—but she must travel upon our elephant. I shall, moreover, accompany you until I see these precious ships in the Thondaiman River with my own eyes. This, your highness, is my sworn duty, and nothing can swerve me from it!"

"By all means, Commander." There was a pronounced twinkle in the prince's eyes as he listened to this impassioned speech. "Far be it from me to keep you from carrying out your sworn duty!"

44

A Rampaging Elephant

Senathipathi Boodhi Vikrama Kesari nudged Parthibendran a little aside and held a short, private conversation. Then, he issued several separate commands to his soldiers.

"It seems that my purpose in coming here has been completely defeated; I'm forced to return empty-handed, *Ayya*," Parthibendran admitted, as he took leave of the prince. "Karikalar will be furious with me, but you're stubborn in your decision. All I can be sure of is that none of this is my fault, and everyone here is witness to that."

"Must you leave at once?" ventured Arulmozhi Varmar. "Surely you could accompany the Senathipathi as far as the Thondaiman River ..."

"And be a party to this—this travesty? No, thank you, your highness; I'd rather be spared that dubious honour, to tell you the truth. My ship still lies anchored in Thirikonamalai. I shall have to embark soon and be on my way to Kanchi," explained Parthibendran. "Karikalar must be apprised of all that has happened here." He turned to Vallavarayan. "Well, boy? What of your decision? Aren't you going to accompany me?"

Vandhiyathevan looked a little startled at this direct approach. "Er, no," he said, finally. "I'd like to stay with his highness."

"Suit yourself," Parthibendran shrugged. "You're going to regret this, is all I can say." He left soon and as per the Senathipathi's command, a few soldiers accompanied him.

"I'm not sure I understand what that Pallavan was getting at," Vandhiyathevan turned to Azhwarkkadiyaan, puzzled. "Why would I regret not going with him? You wouldn't happen to know anything about this, would you?"

"Didn't you see those two war-horses murmuring together? The Senathipathi has cooked up some sort of scheme with him, and I've no doubt we'll be treated to the fruits of their wonderfully devious strategy—such as it is," Azhwarkkadiyaan surmised. "If you want to know what I think—this Kodumbalur curmudgeon is at the root of all our problems now."

"He is?" Vandhiyathevan looked at him, wide-eyed. "What's he got to do with all this?"

"Everything, *Thambi*. You can't be unaware that one among the bevy of royal princesses currently residing at the Pazhaiyarai palace belongs to his ancient, peerless clan."

"You're talking about Vanathi Devi, of course."

"Naturally. The Senathipathi has evolved some sort of complicated ruse by which that young woman is bound in marriage with the prince, who will then be conveniently placed upon the Ilankai throne. That seems to be his ambition at the moment—for his was the hand that prodded the Buddhist *bikshus* into setting up that elaborate ceremony, offering the prince this island. You'd think someone who actually muddled through all this would at least make the effort to keep his stratagem a secret—but not our marvelous, magnificent Senathipathi. No, rumours of his clumsy efforts reached Thanjai of course, which prompted Chief Minister Aniruddhar to visit Ilankai, not to mention sending me to the prince. Whatever happens, Vandhiyatheva, we ought to make sure that we stay alive—for you and I, young man, might have to stand witness in Thanjai to the prince's refusal to accept the throne of Ilankai!"

By this time, the Senathipathi's affairs, whatever they were, seemed to have been resolved and all his soldiers barring four, departed for their separate destinations.

The prince's party was the last to leave: he swung up on his well-bred stallion in company of the Senathipathi, Vandhiyathevan, Azhwarkkadiyaan, and set off north. Poonguzhali, for her part, clambered upon the elephant that stomped behind them as though it owned the very earth. The only other atop, was the mahout.

They travelled upon the *rajapattai* for a while but it soon became apparent that this was not going to be easy: word had spread, somehow, about the prince's impending arrival. Ilankai's northern provinces were heavily populated with Thamizh folk in those times, and the road was choked with people eager to catch a glimpse of their hero. "Long live Prince Arulmozhi Varmar!" rose chants from raucous groups here and there. "Long live Senathipathi Kodumbalur Periya Velaar!" echoed more shouts further along the road. Some even circled the resplendent horses, following the small cavalcade in large, determined factions that grew so unmanageable that the stallions could barely wade through.

***

Upon the prince's strenuous objections and various spirited discussions with the Senathipathi, the decision was made to shift from the king's road to smaller, lesser populated forest routes. This might have proven a wise decision, for it meant that the general populace was gradually, gently pried away and left behind—but forest tracks abounded in vegetation and animals, which provided their own set of problems. A small, idyllic lotus pond barred their path after a while—and on the opposite banks stood a large gathering. At the precise moment the prince's party was sighted, the *kombu* and *perigai* blared out, while the beats of *thaarai* and *thappattai* reverberated around the forest.

"Just a moment, your highness; I shall find out who these people are," promised the Senathipathi, and promptly cantered forward. He returned within a very few moments. "The people hereabouts have learnt, somehow, of the prince's journey through these parts," he announced. "They are here to give the welcome that is his due."

The people edged forward and at the first sign, surrounded the prince. They stared at him avidly, feasting upon his splendid profile; they raised chants and showered him with benedictions but even among those, "Long live Arulmozhi Varmar, King of Ilankai!" seemed the loudest and certainly the most frequent.

A smile appeared on the prince's lips. His eyes lit up, and his chiseled features brightened. He called one of the men in the crowd, who seemed to be their leader, up close. "Why have these people spontaneously crowned me the monarch of Ilankai?"

"This island has suffered without a charismatic leader for years, your gracious highness," announced the man, with every sign of obsequious civility. "It is our earnest wish, therefore, that Ponniyin Selvar assume control and ascend the throne— this is, in fact, the most heartfelt desire of every single resident of this land. Thamizh, Singalavar, Saivites, Buddhists, ascetics and householders all have but one wish and one name on their lips: yours," he finished.

The welcoming party had made arrangements for a lavish feast, and it would have been the height of ill-manners to leave without partaking of it. When, accordingly, the prince's party left after the requisite speeches and elaborate farewells, time had flown.

***

Vandhiyathevan and Azhwarkkadiyaan found time to snatch a private conversation in the midst of these splendid celebrations.

"You see what I meant, *Thambi*? About all this being the Senathipathi's plot?" Azhwarkkadiyaan burst out. "He's sent a party in advance and whipped up people into planning celebrations—"

"The Senathipathi's hand *is* rather obvious—but what I don't understand is, why?" Vandhiyathevan demanded. "Does he nurse vain ambitions that the prince might be so moved by the local population and their petitions that he'd instantly change his mind and accept the very throne he refused just yesterday?"

"That could be one of the results he expects, certainly," Azhwarkkadiyaan acknowledged. "But there's another, more straightforward motive: stalling our journey."

"I've no idea how that would help the Senathipathi in any way."

"I don't either, but I've no doubt that all will become apparent by and by. Look at the prince's face, *Thambi*," Azhwarkkadiyaan nudged Vandhiyathevan. "Is that the expression of someone enjoying himself?"

It certainly didn't seem to be so, when Vandhiyathevan glanced at the ilango. Arulmozhi Varmar, whose luminous face usually glowed with good-humour even when his lips uttered angry words, now looked furious. His brows were drawn together in irritation, and his intelligent eyes showed their abstraction. He was lost in thought.

***

Poonguzhali, for her part, was lounging on the opposite banks of the lotus pond, lost in her own reverie—for this journey hadn't really turned out to be as delightful as she had expected.

For one thing, she had fully anticipated a great deal of privacy in the prince's company when she could have struck up conversation with him, and which might have provided her the opportunity of revealing—at least just a fraction—the emotional tumult that raged in her heart. She was doomed to disappointment, for the window of opportunity didn't even open a smidgeon; Ponniyin Selvar was perpetually surrounded by a band of men.

No, all she'd gain from this God-forsaken journey would be the blame of having delivered him straight into the hands of his enemies ... and frankly, why must she? It wasn't too late even now; she could simply slip away from these very banks and run ... at the very least, she'd have escaped the Senathipathi's fury.

Che, what can that old man's anger do—how can anyone's fury harm me, for that matter? No, that's not what I'm worried about ... but why should my desires be razed? Burnt to ash? How long will I have to endure this fire that races through my veins, that threatens to consume me? Ah, why am I still alive? Why couldn't a bolt of thunder simply crash down this very instant and blast me to smithereens? No, there's no point in wishing for such things. I've done so a thousand times but they never do happen. This life of mine will not end by itself—not unless I do something—not until I take matters into my own hands ...

Wait—what's this that's happening? I'm not dreaming, am I? No, certainly not - but how is it that the dagger, the very one that the prince's friend snatched from my hand and threw by the ruined mandapam, end up by my side? Who could have flung it here? Certainly not someone who wishes him well. Had they aimed it at me, perhaps? Oh, how unfortunate that it didn't pierce me but fell by the side! But this might be all for the better, in a way—once I've done what I promised, once I've given him up to those hateful foes, I shall plunge this dagger in my heart, and give up my life in his presence—no, cheechee! Why must I subject him to such pain? Far better to end my life when he's gone—I shall climb into my boat, sail to the middle of the sea and do the deed ... ah, you've returned to me, my precious dagger—and I'm incredibly grateful for those who performed such a service.

Or perhaps ... perhaps this dagger had been meant for the prince—hadn't the Senathipathi mentioned that innumerable dangers threatened his highness? Now, why couldn't a wonderful opportunity present itself, one where I intercept a knife meant for the prince, where it pierces my heart instead of his? Why couldn't fate allow me a chance to give up my life on his account? And if it did, the blood would soak my skin as the life slowly left my body and in those last moments ...

A strange, not unpleasing vision unfolded in her mind's eye: a dagger had pierced her breast and blood gushed from her wound. The prince came running up. *Ah, Poonguzhali,* he mourned. *Why must you die for my sake?* The words thrilled her so much that blood fairly spurted from her heart. The prince sprang forward and gathered her onto his lap, whereupon her blood liberally coated his clothes and limbs. Poonguzhali's laughter rang out. *Your highness,* she breathed with difficulty. *Now do you see what's in my heart?*

Foolish, foolish girl, the prince shrieked. *I've known your heart for ages—must you die for this?*

Such was the exhilaration that coursed through Poonguzhali that she began to chuckle to herself.

"You lunatic!"

The words startled her out of her splendid reverie; she jumped and saw Vandhiyathevan looming ahead.

"The prince is furious as it is about the endless delays and here you are, lounging about like an idiot," he ranted at her. "Come on!"

Still chortling, Poonguzhali slowly untangled herself, ran towards the elephant and clambered up. Then she clasped her dagger to her heart and began to whisper sweet-nothings to it.

***

A most unexpected incident occurred, a little after they had resumed their journey. An arrow whirred past the travellers from the dense forest to their right. There was no doubt that it was meant for the prince and would have found its target—had he not acted on instinct within a split second and yanked his reins even faster, whipping around his stallion. As it was, the arrow flew so close that he felt a sharp gust as it whistled past him and burrowed into the turban of Azhwarkkadiyaan, who happened to be right by his side. Such was its speed that it carried off the Vaishnavite's turban; Azhwarkkadiyaan turned around, clutching his head in considerable surprise and alarm.

The Senathipathi stopped dead at this, startled; the whole party looked stunned.

Poonguzhali, for her part, could not help but mourn the fickle arrow that had missed her entirely, thus robbing her of splendid martyrdom.

"Your highness," said the Senathipathi, once he had managed to regain his composure somewhat. "You see, now, the reasons for all my safety measures. Imagine our plight if I had simply sent you alone ..." He turned and commanded his warriors to enter the forest and search for the perpetrator. They plunged in accordingly but returned after a while, reporting that they had found no one.

The Senathipathi began to make elaborate plans now, for the rest of the journey. "We must place his highness in the midst, and form ourselves into a protective cordon around him," he began a traditional battle formation.

"If I may intrude, Commander," intercepted the prince. " ... with a request?"

"Perish the thought, your highness," the Senathipathi returned, looking shocked. "Speak not of requests, but command me as you wish."

"It's my earnest desire to reach home alive, that I may lay my case in front of the Emperor, and prove my innocence ..."

"Your honoured father will be the last to suspect, or accuse you of any crime."

" ... not to mention the subjects of Chozha Nadu as well. There shall be no further need to keep this soul in my body once I've carried out my mission—but I certainly don't wish to become a corpse before I achieve my purpose."

"If there should be the slightest breath of danger threatening you, *Ayya*, this Kodumbalur dagger shall plunge into my heart that very instant!"

"Very honourable I suppose, but it would serve no purpose; your death would be Chozha Nadu's incredible loss."

"Could there be a greater, more heart-wrenching loss to this country than yours, Sire? And if this servant were to be the cause, could I, could this *kodumbaavi* even bear to live another moment?"

"In that case, it becomes even more important that I stay alive."

"There is nothing quite so important in this world, I should say."

"Now there—I've an idea."

"By all means, *Ayya.*"

"As long as I'm astride a horse, perils such as the arrow just now, might occur again. You ought to consider that possibility, at any rate ..."

"I do not understand: do you suggest that we walk? Or else—"

"You do know that I communicate excellently well with elephants—and that they respond in kind, don't you?"

"Certainly; I am aware, in fact, that you disguised yourself as a mahout and toured a great part of this island."

"In which case, you ought to have no objection to my adopting that disguise once more. The present mahout shall ride upon my horse, instead."

The Senathipathi seemed a little thrown by this surprising request and looked around, desperately hoping for some sort of objection. None came, however, and he turned to the prince reluctantly. "What if the mahout, er, doesn't know how to ride a horse, your highness?"

"He may return by foot."

"And that wild girl—she seems to shy away a little too much from people—if she should argue that she will not share the *ambaari* with you—"

"Then she may jump down and walk by the side."

"As you please, your highness."

The prince sprang from his horse at once and strode towards the elephant. Poonguzhali gazed from the top, her dark, limpid eyes round and wide in complete astonishment. He ordered the mahout down with a few swift words, clambered up, and settled upon the elephant's neck in his place.

The journey, delayed for a while, now resumed.

As for Poonguzhali ... that young woman now touched the very heights of excited exhilaration. She didn't seem to be riding upon an ordinary elephant; no, she leapt up from its boring back and scaled the skies in an instant. She flitted about the heavens; she peeked into celestial abodes; her spirit, glorying in this unlooked-for adventure, sampled a rare taste of the unearthly bliss that never could be understood or realized by mere mortals.

But stay ... what was this that fell on her ears—the exquisitely lovely song of the Devas? Such rich notes; such divine music—no ... no music, no matter how heavenly, could be this melodious; this was the prince speaking, wasn't it?

"Samudhra Kumari," came the sweetest voice she had ever heard. "You're not disgusted at having to ride with me, are you?"

"The gift of having done penances in at least seven previous lives, *Prabhu*."

"Tell me: would you be very frightened if this elephant were to—ah, suddenly run mad?"

"Not even the very heavens crashing down would alarm me Sire, as long as you're by my side."

"Where have you tied up your boat, Poonguzhali?"

"Very close to *Yaanai Iravu Thurai, Ayya*."

"The bank on our side, or the opposite?"

"The opposite, as I couldn't find a suitably isolated spot anywhere else."

"And how did you cross the *Thurai*?"

"The tide had gone out when I entered, *Ayya*, so I simply walked through, mostly. At some points, I swam across."

"Now, if this elephant were to enter the sea ... would you be very afraid?"

"Not even if you pushed me into the sea," she chuckled. "I'm the Daughter of the Oceans, aren't I? Weren't you the one to name me so, after all?"

"We shall ride to where you've secreted your boat, and then make the rest of the journey in it—but you'll have to be the one to row us both, I'm afraid. That's well within your power, isn't it?"

"These hands have paddled boats since I was ten, *Ayya*; not, I'm proud to say, the flower-soft, useless limbs of royal women. Didn't your friend Vandhiyathevar tell you about how I rowed us both to Ilankai?"

"He did—but you'll have to accomplish the same thing today much faster. I must reach the ships anchored at the mouth of the Thondaiman River as soon as I possibly can."

"But—why do you force me to be a party to this heinous deed, Sire? I scrambled over forests and hills as fast as I could to save you from imprisonment, but you've now made me guide you to the very same fate I sought to help you escape. Must you inflict such torture on this poor soul?"

"You know that my father, the Chakravarthy, is ill, don't you, Poonguzhali?"

"Yes, *Ayya*—also that the people have begun to talk about the comet blazing its way in the sky."

"My father's life could end at any moment, couldn't it?"

Poonguzhali stayed silent.

"And if such an event should occur, do you think it right that he should depart this world, wondering and suspecting that I conspired against him to seize the throne?"

"But he wouldn't. This is nothing but those devious Pazhuvettarayars' plot—"

"And even to them do I wish to prove my innocence ..."

"Why, *Ayya*?"

"Because, Poonguzhali—ruling a land is the last thing I wish to do."

"What else, then?"

"Climb into a boat and sail the endless seas forever! Ah, the tales I've heard about vast islands that dot oceans just like this one! I've always wanted to visit them all. To see these new countries; know their people and communicate with them ..."

"Surprise, surprise."

"What is?"

"That your desires happen to mirror mine so exactly. And when you do set off on these journeys—you'll take me, won't you?"

"Aid me in carrying out my current pressing duties, first. And you will, won't you?"

"Your wish is my command."

"Now, see the ropes descending from both sides of the *peedam* you're sitting on? Take those and bind yourself securely."

"Why, your highness?"

"This elephant is about to go on a rampage. Careful, Poonguzhali!"

The prince leaned forward, almost over the pachyderm's broad forehead, caressed it fondly, and began to whisper into its ears.

Abruptly, the animal's speed increased.

He murmured something more ...

... and the walk turned to a run.

The elephant raised its trunk, uttered a loud, ear-splitting roar, and began to storm along the path. The forest suffered as it might during a vicious hurricane: *sadasada—padapada*! Branches and even whole trees crashed to the ground; the earth vibrated with the force of its monstrous tread. All eight corners of the world seemed to shiver and quake even as birds, shaken out of their nests on hitherto safe trees, flapped their wings in fear, screeching and twittering in alarm. Animals, supposedly safe within the jungle, shrieked and stampeded in confused patterns, weaving in and out of the forest.

"*Ayyayo!*" shrieked Senathipathi Boodhi Vikrama Kesari. "The elephant has run mad!"

Despite the prince's considerable warnings, Poonguzhali could not help but feel a twinge of panic; her expressive face reflected her fear.

She was caught with no hope of escape into a vicious, humongous whirlpool in the ocean, being swirled round and round helplessly; the prince swung around with her too and so did their mount, the furious elephant.

She screwed her eyes shut, heart in her mouth.

The elephant raged on, crashing through the undergrowth like a dark thundercloud surging with a gale.

Eventually, it reached *Yaanai Iravu Thurai*.

It was here that the seas of Ilankai's east and west met and mingled and it was here, in the narrowest part of the strait that connected the northern and central parts of the island, did the elephant descend— with a mighty splash, like a mountain hurled into the ocean by Lord Hanuman himself.

ॐ

On Hidden Meanings and Explanations

" ...whose luminous face usually glowed with good-humour even when his lips uttered angry words, now looked furious..."

During Vandhiyathevan and Azhwarkkadiyaan's tete-a-tete, Kalki describes the furious expression that cloaks Prince Arulmozhi Varmar's face thus: *Avar mugathil ellum kollum vedithana*—which, literally translates into, *Sesame and kollu seeds bubbled and burst in his face*. To a modern English reader this might seem absolutely nuts, until they understand the context: the prince was so furious that one might have garnished *ellu* and *kollu* in the heat that suffused his countenance—it would have been equal to that of boiling oil.

45

The Prison Ship

Yaanai Iravu Thurai passed in the blink of an eye. In its hurried wake flitted back the trees of the forest; the birds of the jungle ... ponds, lakes, habitations, temples, *mandapams*—everything, everything seemed to simply leap back in a flash and vanish into oblivion. An intrepid herd of deer tried to keep pace with the runaway elephant for a while, but was defeated and soon retired from the lists. The massive pachyderm, however, simply kept storming forward, forward, endlessly, trampling through the foliage and soon, Poonguzhali lost track of the distance, or even hours. It did, she noticed, still seem to be within the confines of Eezha Nadu, much to her considerable surprise. By this time, it ought to have made a complete circuit of the entire island at least thrice—or so it seemed to the stunned girl.

Wait—this enormous pachyderm isn't just stalking through Ilankai; it's tramping through the very earth from the southern end to the north. I—I'm flying round and round Bhoolokham on its back and so is the prince!

It was true that tendrils of terror wrapped around Poonguzhali for the first few moments the elephant began to rampage through the forest; the experience was new to her, and there was the added panic of not knowing what exactly was about to happen. The prince, however, turned around twice or thrice to smile at her—and she felt her trepidation and reluctance evaporate. Soon, the last of her terror disappeared and exhilaration of a kind she'd never experienced before, a thrill of ecstasy, enveloped her.

She swayed atop the majestic *mathagajam*—but only for a while; within moments, somehow, she'd left behind the dull, tedious earth and found herself in heaven. Now, she was seated in state upon Devendran's incredibly regal Iravatham, his famed white elephant, and was taken in a majestic procession through sky lanes. The eternal *karpaga* trees showered divine flowers upon her, while celestial beings such as *gandharvas* followed her train strumming their legendary instruments and sprinkling exquisitely musical notes in the air. Beautifully dressed and ornamented *apsara* women danced around her, while the heavenly avenue fairly dazzled with row upon row of brilliant lamps on both sides! And thus did many aeons pass.

Why, now Iravatham seemed to be slowing down and somehow, it seemed to have descended to the earth—in Eezha Nadu to tell the truth, for the mahout was leaning over and patting its broad, smooth forehead, whispering sweet-nothings into its—*cheche*, this was no ordinary mahout; it was the very Lord of the Gods himself, Devendran—wait, no, this was the prince, wasn't it?

The elephant came to a juddering halt by the side of a pretty pool ringed with dense trees, and stood still.

Poonguzhali, now in full possession of her senses, peered at the opposite banks, considerably worried: had a welcoming party of villagers appeared here as well, ready to shatter the silence and—dare it be said—her happiness? But no; there was nothing. She looked behind to see if the cavalry was at their heels, but there wasn't even the slightest scuffle of a hoof.

She turned to stare at the serene pond. Every single fragrant *alli* and *sengazhuneer* flower upon the surface simply unearthed itself, flew up and surrounded her; stems, vines and all. They crept up her shoulders, nuzzling and caressing her blooming cheeks, delighting in her embrace. And then, those wicked flowers went a step further: their vines wound themselves around her slender figure, almost crushing her in their soft grasp, suffocating her with their sweet, over-powering scent.

With a mighty wriggle, Poonguzhali cast off their smothering kindness; the vines and flowers fell apart. The next instant, it seemed as if she'd tumbled and fallen headfirst to the ground, for the elephant bent its forelegs first; then its hind legs, and finally sank to the forest floor.

The prince hopped off the mount's neck. "Well, Poonguzhali?" He grinned up at her. "Don't want to get down yet, do you?"

Poonguzhali came to her senses, even as her body quivered. "It's no easy task coming down to earth from heaven, is it, *Ayya*?" she mumbled, as she descended with reluctance.

The elephant rose again and lumbered off to one of the trees by the poolside, breaking off a luscious branch and stuffing it into its gaping maw.

Arulmozhi Varmar, for his part, strolled to the bank and sat down. He looked up at Poonguzhali, shy and hesitant, and bade her take a seat by him.

***

The still waters reflected Poonguzhali's flushed face which, already crimson with her recent exertions and her heart's tumult, now seemed to rival the beautiful *sengazhuneer* flowers in its exquisite, fresh colour.

"I really do like you, Daughter of the Oceans," said the prince slowly, gazing at her vivid image in the gently rippling waters.

The white and red lilies whose ardour seemed to have subsided somewhat, now rose up all over again and smothered Poonguzhali with petal-soft kisses!

"Do you know why?" he continued.

Sky, earth, pool and flowers whirled and twirled in a mind-numbingly glorious dance, before her dazed eyes.

"Everyone I know wants me to be a puppet manipulated by their strings," the prince explained. "You're the only one happy to carry out *my* wishes. Rest assured that I shall never forget, Samudhra Kumari."

Miraculously, Poonguzhali's figure transformed into a musical *yaazh*; her nerves, into its slender strings. Golden hands touched the delicate instrument and strummed the strings; exquisitely lovely notes dipped in honey, wafted through the air.

"The Senathipathi and Parthibendrar used every weapon in their arsenal to stop my journey; you saw how the commander tried to throw every obstacle he could think in my way, even sending word to villagers in advance and preparing welcome-parties. As for Parthibendrar, he's flown hotfoot to Thirikonamalai—planning, no doubt, to get to his ship and reach the mouth of the Thondaiman River before us. Ah, they think I'm unaware of their plots and schemes," mused the prince. "But I've managed to outwit them all with your aid ..."

And then, suddenly, Poonguzhali felt as though Yama's envoys had made it their personal mission to drag her down to hell and crush her alive in a press—for she realized the enormity of what she had just done. "They did nothing but try to help you escape your foes, *Ayya*—but I ... miserable wretch that I am," she began to sob. "All I've done is deliver you into prison!"

"*Adede*, I've been entertaining the highest opinion of you so far, Poonguzhali—but you're just the same as *them*."

"And they were right. I wouldn't have done what I did of my own accord; your pretty speeches turned my head and made me ... but I've come to my senses, now. I'm leaving." Poonguzhali jumped up.

The prince stretched out his hand and clasped hers gently, in a bid to stop her.

The celestial maidens of the heavens did not seem to have much to do at that moment, it seemed, except to blend the wonderfully fragrant essence of sandalwood with lustrous moonbeams, and sprinkle a few scented drops on Poonguzhali.

Her legs lost their strength; she quivered and sank down almost bonelessly, unable to do anything else. Then, she covered her face with her hands and began to sob.

"I wished to tell you something important, Samudhra Kumari, but if all you're going to do is weep, there's nothing to be done but continue our journey."

She brushed away her tears at once, and looked at him expectantly.

"There's a good girl. Now, you were right when you said they wanted to help me escape imprisonment—but do you know their motive?"

"They adore you of course, and would do anything to protect your sacred person. *I'm* the demon who—"

"Patience, my girl. Of course they adore me—and do you know why? Some astrologers and palmistry experts seem to have had nothing to do but make dazzling predictions: apparently, some day, I shall become an emperor. And so they wish to dump me on a throne, all of them, and stick a crown on my head, those rapacious schemers ..."

"And why mustn't they, *Ayya*? Forgive me but I fail to see why it shouldn't be so, for you deserve to rule not just this but all the three worlds as the supreme emperor—"

"Ah, you echo their sentiments too, my girl. Listen to me—and listen carefully, Poonguzhali: there's no greater prison in this world than a royal palace; no more dangerous sacrificial altar than a throne and no punishment more terrible than wearing a crown all your life. The others wouldn't have understood this—but you, I believed, would be an exception."

Poonguzhali's exquisite eyes fluttered like a delicate, beautiful butterfly's wings; she gazed at the prince out of limpid, wide eyes.

"The truth now, Poonguzhali: if someone forced you to stay chained to a throne all your life, would you submit?" The prince demanded.

She considered this seriously for a moment. "No," she said finally, her tone ringing with decision.

"Well, then. Why do you wish *me* to undergo such a stringent punishment?"

"But—you're a royal."

"What of it? Thankfully God, in His infinite mercy, spared me the harrowing burden of kingship: there's my older brother, heir and crown prince, not to mention the son of my uncle, who has an eye to the throne himself—"

"Ah!" Poonguzhali exclaimed. "That's come to your ears, has it?"

"Well, really—you didn't imagine that I'd remain in blank ignorance of such a development, did you? The Thanjavur throne is certainly in no danger of disintegrating without an occupant. Not to mention that the last thing I want is to wear a crown and govern a land ..."

Poonguzhali gaped at him. "What *is* it that you wish for, then?"

"Now *that's* the question I've been waiting for. And I shall tell you: what I should love, beyond anything, is to trample through endless forests and jungles on a majestic elephant, like a gale-force *sandamarutham*—just like we did, now. I should like to sail the vast seas on ships; to climb the tallest mountains ... do you know, I've heard tales of islands and huge land-masses just like Ilankai and our own Bharatha *kandam* beyond these oceans; I'd like nothing better than to visit them all and gaze upon their marvels ..."

Poonguzhali listened to this effusion open-mouthed, as though she would devour each word. "*Ayya*," she cut in, when her eagerness threatened to consume her. "Will you take me with you on all these journeys?"

"I hope in vain, Poonguzhali. These are just my paltry wishes," sighed the prince. "As to whether there's any chance of them coming true—who can say?"

These words served to drag her to the real world, as it were. "If that's the case, *Ayya*—why do you wish to go to Thanjavur now?"

"I began to answer that question when you changed the subject and we wandered all over the place talking of other things. Now ..." the prince paused. "There's a woman on this island, Samudhra Kumari, who doesn't possess the ability to speak, and who roams here and there, like one deranged. Do you know her?"

Poonguzhali sat up, astonished. "I do, your highness. But—why do you ask?"

"That, you shall know later. Answer this: how, and what do you know of her?"

"I lost my own mother in infancy, *Ayya* and knew something of a mother's love only at her kind, affectionate hands. She's my *guru*; my God. What else do you wish to know about her?"

"Does she have a home—some place that is her permanent abode? Her *vaasasthalam*? Or does she spend her life thus, wandering like the restless wind?"

"There's an island called Boodha Theevu with a small, rock cave, as you approach Ilankai from the direction of Kodikkarai; this is her habitual dwelling-place. In fact, that's where I saw you first ..."

"What're you talking about?"

"The truth. My lady has drawn a few excellent paintings inside the cave—and I saw your likeness in a few of them. In fact, that was why I was stunned when I saw you in Kodikkarai."

"I see it all, now. Wonder of wonders ... things that never made much sense to me, now seem clear. Do you know of the bond that exists between me and this lady, Samudhra Kumari?"

"Some such thing I suspected, your highness," Poonguzhali admitted. "But I'm unaware of the nature of your relationship."

"She's my step-mother; the lady who, by rights, ought to be seated on the throne of Thanjavur."

"By all the Gods! Truly?"

"And yet—who may guide the hands of fate? No one can do anything; that's the truth. For some time, now, I've known that my father harboured some secret, a grievous sorrow that ate at him—and finally, I realized the truth. He has been labouring under the misapprehension that my step-mother is dead—and worse, at his own hands. And it has now fallen upon me to divulge the truth—that she's very much alive. That should soothe his wounded heart, and perhaps go some way towards assuaging his horrible affliction. You know, of course, that he is very ill. This life of ours is a transient one; no one can predict what might happen at any moment. There's a comet glowering in the sky now of all things, setting up a whole flurry of rumours and conjectures, none of which are doing my father any good. This makes it all the more imperative for me to tell him my discovery—and this, Samudhra Kumari, is why I have to go to Thanjai as soon as I possibly can. Now do you see how valuable your aid has been?"

Poonguzhali, who had been listening avidly to his speech, now heaved a great sigh. "Dear God," she murmured. "Why must you thrust so much joy and sorrow into one paltry lifetime?" Then, she turned to the prince. "That this witless servant has been of some little service to you is the result of a thousand penances in previous lives, your highness. But—forgive my asking—why was *my* help necessary? Surely the Senathipathi and the others, if told this truth, might have been able to assist you better?"

"The answer is that I didn't. Wish to tell them the truth, I mean. To men whose only ambition is to set me on the Thanjai throne somehow, details such as these would hardly count. Besides, this is a part of my father's personal life and the last thing I want is to lay the facts bare for their edification. Not that they'd have understood it, even if I had.

But stay, Daughter of the Oceans. There's something else I need from you—which was why I halted the elephant here, anyway. The great men who prophesied my rise to kingship—the astrologers, I mean—also foretold a great many perils and dangers that would threaten my life. Should something of that nature hinder my journey ... should I find myself unable to meet my father, *you* must. Seek an audience with him somehow, and make sure that he knows that my step-mother's alive. And if he should so wish it, make arrangements for him to meet her. You must be the one to take her to him. Will you do this for me, Poonguzhali?"

"Nothing shall stop you, your highness; as for those petty perils— why, they'll take to their heels in your presence. You'll reach Thanjavur just as you wish—"

"Promise me, anyway—in case something does happen."

"Certainly, your highness."

"You know that I couldn't have entrusted such an important secret to just anyone, don't you?"

"Fair enough. You've assigned me my task and now, I suppose, my usefulness is at an end," Poonguzhali voice was laced with the tears that started in her eyes. "Permission to take my leave, your highness?"

"What's all this nonsense about desertion when we haven't even reached the mouth of the Thondaiman River yet? Or sighted the Chozha vessels come for me ... pray be patient; curb your anger and climb onto the elephant once more. Bear with my presence just a little—you're free to go where you please once we've caught sight of the ships bearing tiger flags."

Without a word, Poonguzhali rose and began to walk slowly towards the elephant; so did the prince. The massive animal bent in obedience to his whispers; they clambered upon its back and though it did not rampage through the forest as before, the pace was swift.

"I mentioned some of the things I liked doing best, Samudhra Kumari," the prince began to roll the ball of conversation. "Shouldn't it be your turn, now?"

"Yama's mount, the buffalo, is my favourite animal, and climbing to the top of boulders in the dead of the night to watch flickering *kollivai* ghouls is such a treasured pastime that I usually lose track of time ..."

"You're a strange girl. You know that, don't you?"

"Call me a lunatic, rather, like your friend did; it wouldn't bother me. As for the other things I like ... well, sailing in my little boat endlessly, especially if there's a storm about—oh, I'm deliriously happy when gale-force winds attack my craft, taking it right up to the skies one moment; crashing it down to *pathalam* the next ...! There's nothing I love best. In fact, our elephant's rampage through the forest reminded me of my adventures in the sea, and I've never been more ecstatic!"

"If Muruga Peruman had mounted a quest to win your smile, my girl, he'd have lost the battle even before he began," chuckled the prince. "None of the tactics he used, to win Valli—setting a wild elephant to scare her out of her wits—would have worked on you at all!"

***

"Oh!" screeched Poonguzhali, as they approached the mouth of the Thondaiman River. "What's this?"

"What?" demanded the prince eagerly. "What is it?"

"The ships with the tiger flags aren't where I saw them," she moaned. "You're bound to think the worst of me—and to think that the Senathipathi's doubts are about to seen as the truth—oh, everyone's going to suspect me of having brought you out here on a pretense—"

"I certainly won't be one among their number," the prince said, firmly. "There's no reason for you to lie so atrociously and drag me all the way here; no motive—"

"Isn't there, your highness? It could be—it could be love, couldn't it? A foolish girl could have fallen for the charms of one praised as Manmadhan for his beauty and Archunan for his valour—and indulged in a fantasy, couldn't she?"

"Such a far-fetched suspicion might occur to the Senathipathi if he were here—but you and I, my girl, are far too sensible to entertain even the idea of such an idiotic fable."

"Forgive me, *Ayya*—but would those be your sentiments about a certain female of the warrior clan, dwelling in the Pazhaiyarai royal palace? A princess called Vanathi Devi?"

"Indeed, yes—I haven't forgotten her, nor the many schemes the Senathipathi and my sister are weaving to somehow bind us both; perhaps that hapless girl cherishes some desire of ascending the Chozha throne herself. Be that as it may, I'm not responsible for the ambitions of others," the prince snapped. "Now, Poonguzhali—where were the ships when you last saw them?"

"There, at that end," she pointed. "How could I forget?"

"Well, that mightn't be a problem. The ships could have drifted a little away," the prince reassured her. "No harm in walking down to the shore and making sure."

"Good riddance to bad rubbish, if they're gone," Poonguzhali shrugged. "Why on earth must we hunt for them?"

"Those may be *your* sentiments, but no one would be more disappointed than I, if that were true," the prince said briskly.

***

Three hundred years ago, Manavanman, the prince of Ilankai, had sought refuge in Kanchipuram; Maamalla Chakravarthy, then the Pallava emperor, had sworn to restore his lands and sent a large army, accordingly. Those hordes had landed on the island at this spot; the so-called Thondaiman River had been only a small pond at that time. The army had immediately deepened and widened it for the accommodation of the large numbers obliged to make camp and in due course of time, the pond had turned into the Thondaiman River. The many curves it sported at its mouth, coupled with the dense trees nestling along its banks, made it convenient for large ships to lie concealed from the prying eyes of those on sea.

It was in one of these lagoons, where the river widened enough for ships to lie anchored that Poonguzhali had caught sight of those sent to imprison the prince. But they were not there now—in other words, the sails and standards that might have given away the vessels were absent. But what they saw when they approached the site, seemed even more unbelievable.

A ship seemed to have moved away from deep water and sunk in the muddy quagmire just adjacent. Its sails and flags hung in a tattered mess; there was no sign of men anywhere. Poonguzhali immediately recognized it as one of the two she had seen, two days ago.

She sank into astonishment at the realization that a ship sent to imprison the prince now lay imprisoned, in a marshy bog!

46

Tumultuous Hearts

The prince murmured something into the elephant's ears, upon which it sank to the ground. They clambered down its back hurriedly, and made their swift way to the ship lying wrecked upon the shallow banks.

It was a pitiful sight: the sails were ripped apart and the mast hung forlornly, obviously battered. The prince, acting upon the suspicion that there might still be survivors inside or lurking thereabouts, clapped his hands. Poonguzhali curved her palms around her mouth and called out. Their efforts were to no avail. There was only one thing to be done, now: see the lay of the land for themselves. Accordingly, they waded into the water, reached the ship and climbed aboard, holding precariously onto the balustrade.

The lower decks, they soon saw, were a disaster: the planks fractured, letting in a great deal of water and swampy mud—which immediately put paid to an admittedly far-fetched notion that the ship might still be sea-worthy. For one thing, it would be well-nigh impossible to even drag it to water and as for pushing it to shore, that would require the strength of not just one elephant but several, not to mention a horde of men. Carpenters would have to slave over it for months to return it to its original, pristine condition.

The prince maneuvered himself across the deck and reached down to pick up the tiger flag, lying mangled between the collapsed sails and masts. That it distressed him, was obvious. "Poonguzhali," he turned to the girl. "Was this one of the ships you saw?"

"So it seems," she answered. "The other must have been completely wrecked and drowned, I suppose." Her voice rose with something very like glee.

"You seem very enthusiastic," commented the prince.

"Why wouldn't I be?" she demanded. "The ships that were supposed to imprison you have been smashed to bits and have likely disappeared into the depths of the ocean, haven't they?"

"You're wrong to be so delighted, my girl. Something terrible has happened—it's worse that I've no idea *what*—and the sight of this mangled tiger flag is extremely dispiriting. What was the fate of the soldiers and sailors aboard? That confuses me even more—and now you say that the other ship has likely sunk. Do you really think so?"

"That's what I suspect—and I don't mind admitting that that would be an excellent thing."

"It would certainly be nothing of the sort—and I hope you're wrong. The other ship might have seen the fate of this one and moved prudently to safer, deeper waters. I don't understand why this one should have come so close to shore, either. Chozha sailors are descended from families that have fairly lived upon the ocean for thousands of years; it's uncharacteristic of them to have committed such a ridiculous mistake. Whatever their motive, some of this ship's crew, at least, must have survived and either climbed aboard the other ship, or managed to hole themselves somewhere, hereabouts. Come—let's see what we can find."

"Go where, you highness? Find what, or whom?" Poonguzhali asked. "Dusk is deepening, and night surrounds even as we speak."

"Where did you leave your boat, Samudhra Kumari?"

"But—it would be right in the middle of the river now, wouldn't it? We've managed to come here so quickly because of the elephant and that, only because *you* were the mahout. If we'd travelled by boat, it would have taken midnight."

"In that case, we may as well search the riverbanks before night-fall. The trees are dense, here; they might well prevent us from seeing the other ship anchored out in the sea, couldn't they?"

***

They left the elephant grazing placidly and began to walk along the banks. The shore was reached very soon and beyond lay the serene, calm sea. Not the slightest sign of choppiness could be seen; not a wave marred the stillness of the glistening surface, like an alluring emerald plane. Far, far beyond, the green of the sea and deepening blue of the sky blended into the horizon.

There was no sign of a ship anchored far off, or even a boat. Nothing but a few stray birds, fluttering from water to land!

Having stood there for a while, staring around at the place, the prince came to a decision. "Let's return to the wrecked ship."

They began to walk back the way they had come.

"I shall never forget your aid, Poonguzhali," began the prince, finally. "But it's time we parted ways here."

She stayed silent.

"You understand me, don't you? I'm determined to stay on the ruined ship. The Senathipathi and the rest of my party will find their way here in the end; I shall consult with them, and determine my next course of action. You, on the other hand, have nothing further to do—find your boat and get going. Remember what I said about my father ..."

Poonguzhali hesitated a little. She leaned against a convenient tree, nearby. Its low-lying branches hung invitingly; she reached a hand and caught one of them.

"Well, Samudhra Kumari? What is it?"

"Nothing at all, your highness. I shall take my leave of you here and now. Farewell."

"Offended, Poonguzhali?"

"Offended ... what right does a petty girl have, to be annoyed or upset at you? I haven't grown quite so puffed up in my own conceit, I think."

"Why have you stopped, then?"

"Not offended, *Ayya*—just tired. It's been two days since I last slept. I think I'll rest for a while hereabouts and then go in search of my boat."

That was the day after Pournami; the moon rose slowly in the eastern sea, and a few dull rays fell upon Poonguzhali's face.

The prince paused, and scrutinized the pale, wan countenance. He took in the haggard features that betrayed bone-tired weariness; eyes that showed a worn-out spirit and strove to close all by themselves.

It was only natural, he mused, for the lotus to fold in upon itself at moon-rise ... but the beautiful blossom that was Poonguzhali's face wasn't just furled—it was crumpled, worn and dulled with fatigue.

"If it's been two days since you slept, my girl," he asked. "How many days has it been since you ate?"

"The same, *Ayya*. You see—pangs of hunger didn't dare attack as long as you were with me."

"Ah, heedless idiot that I am ... I never even thought to ask if you'd broken fast when the rest of us gobbled down the choicest foods at this afternoon's feast. Come, Poonguzhali—let's make our way to that wrecked ship. I remember seeing spilled grains on the deck; we could gather them, cook a little something for the night and then, you may leave ..."

"I shall likely lie down and go to sleep wherever I am, once I've eaten, *Ayya*—I'm drowsing as I speak."

"No matter at all; you may take your ease upon that vessel, while I and the elephant stand guard outside. You're free to go once you've rested."

The prince took the swaying woman's hand and guided her gently towards the ship, almost holding her close—and saw that her strength truly was spent. Her legs trembled as they walked and she could barely stay conscious, making her way almost by sheer will. Ah, could there ever be any power in the world—in all fourteen worlds—that might equal her indomitable spirit, and love? The very thought made tears start to his eyes.

***

When they finally reached the mired ship, both were startled to see smoke spiralling from behind it. Perhaps—perhaps those originally aboard had gone elsewhere and now returned? If that were the case, who could predict the effect of the prince and Poonguzhali's sudden appearance upon the scene? Anything might happen.

With this in mind, the two late-arrivals decided that stealth was the order of the moment, and tiptoed forward ... but not a sound, no voice could be heard, even when they were in close proximity. Neither had any idea about how many were gathered, or their identity. And then—a most wonderful scent assailed their nostrils: the tantalizing aroma of roasting sweet-potatoes. The prince, who'd gauged Poonguzhali's state to a nicety by now, decided that assuaging her hunger was his first priority. This was no time to hesitate; he took the plunge, circled the ship, and saw that preparations were in progress for a cook-fire—by a woman. The next instant, he recognized her.

Said elderly woman, on the other hand, didn't seem fazed in the slightest at their sudden appearance but seemed, instead, to have expected them. She welcomed the duo without the assistance of speech and within a short while, provided them with a meal. To the prince, after a day's exertions, her simple offering of piping-hot, fluffy *varagu* rice and roasted *vallikkizhangu* seemed more mouth-wateringly delicious than all the delicately flavoured, sumptuous feasts of the Pazhaiyarai royal palace.

They retired to the upper decks, once the meal was at an end. The moon had risen fully now, sailing high in the sky, and they could see a good deal beyond the ship in its pearly light—to where the Thondaiman River met the vast sea. Its flat surface which had glowed a greenish bronze as twilight set in, now shone a dazzling gold under the moon's lustrous rays.

The sweltering heat dotted their bodies with perspiration, despite being in an open space surrounded by water. There was not the slightest breath of wind, and the prince mentioned this astonishing fact to Poonguzhali. The elderly lady who seemed, somehow, to have understood the gist of his remarks, pointed at the moon which sported a grey, ash-coloured halo.

"That's usually a sign of thunderstorms," explained Poonguzhali.

"Storms can make their much-vaunted appearance when they want," groaned the prince. "All I wish right now is just a little breeze!" Then, he wondered about the speed with which the lady had accomplished her journey to the place, and how on earth had it been done?

"That's hardly anything to be wondered at. My *athai* has done this and a great many more wondrous deeds," Poonguzhali announced with not inconsiderable pride. "Besides, there's no limit to her love for you—and is there anything that true, boundless love cannot accomplish?"

The lady seemed to divine this speech too, for she touched Poonguzhali's face and turned it towards a certain direction. There lounged the elephant on which they'd journeyed—and beside it stood a majestic, well-bred stallion, the sight of which surprised them considerably.

"Is this how she came here?" marveled the prince. "She possesses the skill of horse-riding, does she?"

"Riding horses or elephants; there's nothing my *athai* doesn't know. She can row boats and sometimes, her speed in reaching destinations might make us wonder if she perhaps rode the very wind!"

The prince, however, had found another reason to sink into a sea of astonishment—namely, the undoubted pedigree of the stallion currently standing bored, elegantly swishing its tail.

"Surely this is the best among the mostly purely-bred Arabian horses," he murmured to himself. "How on earth did it get here and more importantly—into the hands of this old lady?"

Poonguzhali turned promptly to Oomai Rani (ah yes, surely we may call the lady thus, henceforth?), and gestured the question.

The horse had climbed ashore in the vicinity of *Yaanai Iravu Thurai*, the lady signed in answer. Once on land, it had plunged about here and there, unsure of itself, before standing in one spot, petrified. Oomai Rani had stepped softly up to the fleet-footed animal, patted and crooned a great many sweet-nothings, brought it under her control and ridden over here. The prince's astonishment grew by leaps and bounds upon listening to this extraordinary tale.

Fascinated by the old lady he might be, but all his pre-occupation with her did not render him blind to the fact that Poonguzhali's eyes were closing all by themselves. "You said you were drowsy a long time ago, didn't you? Lie down, then."

She moved a little away from him, lay down the next instant, and spread over herself a torn section of the ship's sail. That she was fast asleep within moments was evident from the change in her breathing pattern. And yet ... her lips murmured a song, even within the clasp of slumber.

Why anguish, my soul,

When tumbling seas lie smooth?

Ah—surely this was a snatch of the song Vandhiyathevan had been murmuring all of yesterday? He must have learnt it off this girl, then. Another time, when she was awake, the prince decided he would ask Samudhra Kumari to sing it in its entirety. The next moment, his attention had turned once again to Oomai Rani. Aha, there were times in every mortal being's life when the soul anguished, and the heart heaved with emotion, but what of the tortuous feelings of a woman such as this, deaf and mute? Could anything equal the enormity of her heartache? How many months and years had she spent alone, unable to express even a fraction of her joys, sorrows, the yearnings—anger and annoyance and affection and the pangs of a family life—so many, many such emotions, all bottled up, without a means of showing them to the world ...

Said lady moved now, and made herself a seat beside the prince. Her hands crept towards him; her fingers caressed his hair. She pressed her strong, calloused palms upon the prince's face and touched his cheeks gently, like the breeze kissing the soft petals of a flower.

He sat still, unaware of what to do. Then, he touched her feet and pressed his hands to his eyes. She clasped them and held them to her face; soon his hands were drenched with her tears.

She signed to him to take a respite and assured him of standing guard; he could rest in peace. He wasn't sure that he could sleep a wink in such strange circumstances but lay down all the same, to please her. Storm-tossed waves churned the sea that was his heart; he shifted restlessly. And then, soon enough, a pleasant breeze crept around the ship. The heart cooled and so did the body; sleep embraced him lightly.

***

For all the semblance of peace, however, the prince's rest was devoid of ease. Strange, uneasy dreams clouded his consciousness; he climbed onto a well-bred Arabian stallion and rode swiftly even unto the skies; he galloped swift as the wind through the clouds and entered heaven! Devendran himself, Lord of the Gods, welcomed him astride his celestial mount the Iravatham with pomp, and bade him take a seat upon his own, jewel-studded throne.

Ah no, I cannot, refused the prince. *I should like to place my step-mother Oomai Rani upon this lavish seat,* to which Devendran laughed with great good-humour. *We shall see when she arrives.*

Then, the Lord of the Devas offered the gift of divine nectar *Devamirtham* and the prince, after a taste, twisted his lips. *Oh, this isn't nearly as sweet as the waters of Kaveri, is it?*

Lost at this comment, Devendran finally escorted the prince to his own royal apartments, where were gathered a great many lovely *apsaras*; Indrani, Devendran's consort, appeared and guided the prince towards them. *You may choose the most beautiful among these celestial maidens and wed her, Prince.* He, however, took one look at those angels and turned away. *None of these girls can even hold a candle to Poonguzhali's fresh, exquisite beauty,* he spurned them.

Abruptly, the face and form of Indrani transformed into that of Ilaiya Piratti. *Have you forgotten Vanathi, then, my brother?*

Akka, pleaded the prince. *Akka, how much longer must I lie in chains, slave to your every whim? Surely a life in the Pazhuvettarayars' gloomy dungeons would be a far better fate than a lifetime imprisoned in your heart, bound by your stifling affection. Release me—or treat me like that hapless coward of a prince Utharakumaran, Virada Rajan's son, who led a life of dissipation, drowned in song, dance and a host of women. Confine me to the palace and let me know nothing except a decadent existence!*

Kundhavai Piratti stared at him, her lovely eyes wide with astonishment, and placed a finger slender and graceful as a *kaandhal* flower upon her coral-red lips. *Pray, what's this you say, Arulmozhi? Why have you changed thus? Whose evil hand has destroyed your mind? Why yes, Thambi—love is indeed a form of imprisonment, and you can do nothing but submit to its tyranny.*

No, Akka, not at all, protested Ponniyin Selvar. *You're wrong—there is love in this world—love that demands and expects nothing. Pure, and worthy*

of worship. May I show you? Wait a moment—Poonguzhali, Poonguzhali!
He called out. *Come here!*

***

Poonguzhali awoke with a start, at the clip-clop of hooves. Dawn had broken over the skies, and she espied Oomai Rani galloping away on her steed. Before she could do her best to stop the older woman, however, her horse had vanished like the proverbial wind.

She shivered and stared around as the world awoke with her, fresh and delightful under the early morning sun. Dawn, that new day, was exhilarating and exquisite. Her heart was well-nigh bursting with a delight she was hard put to describe, and she craned her neck to peer at the upper deck of the ship. The prince was asleep still, and she decided to stroll along the riverbank, heart singing along with the birds. A large parrot rested for instance on a conveniently low, curved branch, and seemed completely unperturbed at her presence. Instead, it gazed at her out of beady eyes and cocked its head as if asking, *What on earth are you doing here?*

"The prince will leave very soon, pretty parrot and then, I shall be all alone," she crooned. "You'll stay with me and be company, won't you, my friend?"

From somewhere floated a low, sweet call. "Poonguzhali! Poonguzhali!"

For a moment she wondered if it was the parrot, and then realized that the voice came from the ship.

The next instant, she bounded over the banks and fairly leapt up to the vessel for it was the prince who had called out to her—but when she finally climbed to the upper decks, she saw that he was still fast asleep. She tiptoed up to him, and saw his lips move slightly.

"Poonguzhali ... Poonguzhali ..." he murmured, again, and her heart thrilled with ecstasy. She bent and touched his forehead very slightly, in a bid to wake him.

Dream and slumber at an end, the prince cast off the last wisps of sleeps and rose. The sun was making a slow majestic ascent in the east while Poonguzhali's rosy face glowed with a rivalling radiance. "Why did you call out to me?" she asked with a smile that bloomed like a red lotus.

"Did I mention your name? I must have been talking in my sleep," he answered. "If you could sing in slumber, why shouldn't I speak?"

He jumped up then, and stared around. "I seem to have slept for hours," he murmured. "Where's my stepmother?" Poonguzhali explained that the old lady had left on her horse at sunrise.

"And a good thing too," decided the prince. "Now, Samudhra Kumari, it seems to me that your fatigue has bidden good-bye—and so may you. I, on the other hand, will have to stay here until my friends catch up with me, and I've decided to search this ship while I can."

"Look! Over there!" Poonguzhali pointed, and when Arulmozhi Varmar followed her finger, he saw a large ship at quite a distance, upon the sea. Closer to shore was a small boat, carrying five or six people.

"Ah, the time of enlightenment draws near," muttered the prince. "Everything will make sense now, I hope."

And then, a worrying thought occurred to him: what if the boat swept away, ignoring land altogether, unaware of his presence by the wrecked ship? He leapt down from the upper deck at once, landed upon the river banks and began to stride towards the beach. Poonguzhali followed him, and so did the elephant.

***

Upon reaching the seashore, the prince perceived that the large ship was drifting further away, while the boat was drawing nearer with each second.

Poonguzhali, who had fallen behind, hesitant at putting herself forward, was now so driven by curiosity that she edged up little by little, and was now standing a little in front of him.

Even amidst all his worry, her eagerness tickled him a little; the sight of her peering across the ocean to gauge the newcomers brought a slight, amused smile to his lips.

For it wasn't as though there wasn't reason enough to worry: instinct gnawed at him that somehow, he ought to have been on the ship that was now moving beyond his reach—and that was not all: there seemed to be someone missing amongst the people crowding into the little boat. Someone who ought to be there—yes, he could see the Senathipathi; Thirumalaiyappar, and there were the soldiers who had formed the escort and even the boatmen ... but no scion of the Vaanar clan. Where was Vallavarayan? Where was that fearless warrior; the man who could laugh at death itself; who made rib-tickling jokes in the worst of situations; the confidant of Ilaiya Piratti herself, sent on highly secretive missions—where was he? The prince might have known Vandhiyathevan for only the space of two days, but the bond between them had already strengthened to that of lifelong friendship; such had been Vallavarayan's sparkling personality that it had endeared him to the prince almost at once. His absence in the boat—an arrival the prince had looked forward to almost without his knowledge—was distressing; Arulmozhi Varmar was conscious of a pit of dismay and intense disappointment.

The Senathipathi and the rest of his party waited only until the boat scraped the shallows, and promptly leapt ashore; Boodhi Vikrama Kesari almost forgot himself as he bounded forward and engulfed the prince in a hearty hug.

"What a thing to do, *Ayya*—how could you terrorize us, thus? And how did that elephant calm down—ah, look at how placid it is now, lounging about, the wicked beast ... your highness, when did you come here? Did you manage to catch sight of the Pazhuvettarayars' ships?" Questions shot out from him. "Where are they?"

"All will be made known in due course Senathipathi, but tell me this, first: Where on earth is Vandhiyathevar?"

"Ah, that impetuous brat ..." the commander turned and pointed towards the vessel in the far distance. " ... is upon that ship!"

"What? Why? Whose ship is that?" demanded the prince. "And why is he on it?"

"Forgive me, your highness, but I find myself quite in a muddle," apologized the Senathipathi. "The Vaishnavite here seems acquainted with all your dealings and that boy's temperament; perhaps you would do well to ask him?"

"Thirumalai," the prince turned to Azhwarkkadiyaan. "Tell me this quickly: why is Vandhiyathevar aboard that ship?"

47

GHOULISH LAUGHTER

We're obliged to make known to our readers the fate of those left behind, post the precipitate exit of the prince and Poonguzhali atop their conveniently mad mount.

At first the others, upon whom the Senathipathi's screams of "The elephant has run mad!" wrought powerfully, believed it to be true and rode hard in the elephant's wake, following its path of destruction. This, however, was easier said than done and became well-nigh impossible once they reached *Yaanai Iravu Thurai*—in fact, Vandhiyathevan, who, in characteristic fashion had driven his steed furiously ahead of the posse, promptly found himself mired in the swampy mess of the strait and consequently, had to expend a good deal of energy in dragging himself and his horse onto dry land.

The Senathipathi slapped his forehead, having given up all attempts to retain even a shred of composure. "Never—*never* have I committed such a grievous mistake in my life!" He cried out, wringing his hands.

"You—all of you, why do you stand here like rocks? What can be done, now? Tell me," he implored, unaware of what to do next. "How do we save his highness?"

Azhwarkkadiyaan judged this the right moment to step forward. "Something has just occurred to me, Commander," he said. "If I might be permitted to divulge ...?"

"What are you waiting for—an auspicious moment when the planets align in the heavens?" spat the Senathipathi. "Get going, man!"

"The prince's elephant hasn't, in truth, run mad—"

"Balderdash! Who else then—you?"

"No, and no one else here, as far as I know. If you wish to know the truth, Senathipathi—the prince rather suspected that you were doing everything in your power to stall the journey ... and roused his mount into a fever pitch so it would race through the forest and leave us all behind. After all, it's no secret to any of us is it, that his highness is well-versed in the art of training elephants, and can make them do just as he wishes?"

This, to the over-wrought Senathipathi, seemed to make some sort of sense and his heart, until then skipping several beats in panic, calmed down just a little.

"That may well be," he conceded, finally. "But we ought to make our way to the Thondaiman River's mouth to ensure we know what goes down, oughtn't we?"

"Certainly we ought—and that might be accomplished by journeying along the sea-canal, finding a boat and getting across, if possible. Failing that, we wait until Parthibendrar's ship arrives."

"Of all the unscrupulous ... you made sure to share this ruse with the prince, didn't you, wily Vaishnavite?"

"Not a single world have I spoken to his highness, for the duration of this journey."

They took his advice and began to travel along the banks of the canal, continuing the journey east.

***

Our esteemed readers would have formed an idea about the topography of northern Ilankai from the maps supplied in the previous chapter; the northern-most point was named Naaga Dhweepam in those days, for the rest of the island was separated from this area by a long canal, into which the sea had entered from both sides. *Yaanai Iravu Thurai*, so named because elephants crossed at this site—and where, in ancient times, it is said, they were even exported to foreign countries—was the point where the strait was at its narrowest and at low tide, often easy to ford by foot. At others, it was impossible, and could be crossed only by boat.

Almost all the crafts alongside those coasts at that time had made their way to Maathottam or Thirikonamalai; the Senathipathi and his party entertained hopes that one or two might still be moored thereabouts, and kept their eyes peeled. Their vigilance paid off, for they stumbled upon a *valaignan's* small fishing boat. More importantly, it possessed a boatman—but here, they hit an unexpected snag: said boatman proved recalcitrant. When he discovered, however, that it was the Chozha Senathipathi standing in front of him, he acquiesced.

They climbed into the boat and made their ponderous way to the canal—but how were they to reach the mouth of the Thondaiman River? It would not be feasible to tramp through the forest, not to mention time-consuming. And so, it was decided that they would retain the boat, paddle along the east coast and thus, reach the point where the Thondaiman River met the sea.

The boatman obliged by rowing indefatigably until midnight; by then, his strength was spent and he could go no further. He refused the assistance of the others however, by pointing out that from hereon the way was treacherous, requiring careful navigation between boulders under the surface, around unexpected twists and turns. "If the boat should crash into one of those rocks, it would splinter into pieces," he pointed out. "We can do nothing but wait until morning." The Senathipathi and the others, exhausted on their own account, accepted, and made their beds in a grove, nearby.

Vandhiyathevan, who had conceived a hearty disgust at the proceedings, made sure to let Azhwarkkadiyaan know his sentiments. "You—this is all your fault, Vaishnavite!"

"What on earth did *I* do?" Azhwarkkadiyaan demanded.

"Everything! Never, *never* do you reveal what's on your mind—don't think I haven't noticed you do this right from Kadambur. You'd start the conversation as though you were about to tell me something earth-shattering, but you'd swallow the rest and keep it a secret. You knew the reason for the prince's elephant ride—so why couldn't you have told me? I'd have gotten on, too ... and now we've lost the man we went to such trouble to find," Vandhiyathevan lamented. "What on earth am I supposed to tell Ilaiya Piratti when I get to Pazhaiyarai?"

"Your job was done when you delivered the *olai* into his hands," Azhwarkkadiyaan pointed out. "What's your problem?"

"That's where you're out. My job, as you so casually mention, ends only when I deliver the prince himself safe into Ilaiya Piratti's hands—and now, you've utterly ruined the chances of all that. You're happy now, I hope."

"Not at all, *Appane*. Let it not be said that I stood an obstacle to any of your marvelous schemes. I shall take my leave of the Senathipathi as early as tomorrow, and make my own way. There—*you're* happy now, I hope?"

"Ha—making your escape, more like, now that the prince is firmly snared in your net. I've always thought you were up to several tricks, Vaishnavite, and now ... my suspicions are confirmed."

They squabbled a little this way, scratching each others' faces, metaphorically speaking, until they fell asleep—and sleep they did deeply, after the day's exhausting alarms and exertions.

***

Azhwarkkadiyaan awoke with a start at daybreak—to the sound of oars splashing. The sight that met his vision when he sat up, rubbing his eyes, was startling: a ship lay a little out to the sea, its sails fully unfurled, seemingly ready to start its journey. Even more interesting—a boat was making its way towards the ship from shore. Three men occupied it besides the boatman, and Azhwarkkadiyaan realized that it was the very same craft that had ferried himself and his party the day before.

It did not take many minutes for the clever Vaishnavite to guess the erstwhile hiding-place of such a large ship, or how it had suddenly and inexplicably appeared, either: the sea had wormed its way through a canal a little behind their resting-place and this passage was shrouded by thick trees. The ship must have lain hidden in these waters and started out at day-break.

But whose was it? Where had it come from, and where was it now going? Why was the boat rowing towards the ship—and who were the men in it?

Thoughts flickered and cut through the skies of Azhwarkkadiyaan's mind with the speed of summer lightning. "Senathipathi, wake up," he called out, suddenly. "*Senathipathi!*"

The commander, Vandhiyathevan and two soldiers awoke, startled, and rose with a babble of questions—and the first sight that met their eyes was the ship, its sails unfurled.

"Ah, that's a Chozha vessel—perhaps one of those sent by the Pazhuvettarayars!" exclaimed the Senathipathi. "Is the prince upon it even now—*ayyo*, we've been asleep all this while!" He wrung his hands. "Now what do we do?" Then, he stared wildly around. "The boat—where is the boat? We could still manage to reach the ship—" which was the precise moment he caught sight of the little craft, bobbing upon the sea. "*Adede*, is that the boat we traveled in yesterday? Who are the men in it? *Adei*, get the boatman!" he shouted. "You—halt! Halt this instant!"

Whether the boatman actually heard the screams and shrieks from land is debatable, but he did not pause for a moment and rowed on.

***

Vandhiyathevan had been standing apart all this while, mute observer to his party's frenzied activity—but amidst all the frantic exclamations, one managed to pierce his stupor: the Senathipathi's remark. *Perhaps the prince is upon the ship even now ...*

The words wrought upon him powerfully, creeping through his ears and searing themselves into his brain—and then, there was nothing else. Not another thought managed to wrestle itself into his mind, for was there any further need to waste time plotting his next move? Or any point in commanding his legs to go forward? No, never!

He was in the ocean the next moment, cleaving the waves as strongly as his arms could manage and thankfully, it was rather shallow at that spot and he had crossed a good distance within a short space of time, even managing to approach the boat—when suddenly, the depth increased and he was left floundering in deep sea.

"*Ayyo!*" Vandhiyathevan screamed. "*Ayyo*, I'm drowning! Save me— save me please!"

The sound of laughter floated from the boat, and then, a confused babble of voices. The craft bobbed to a stop; the boatman leaned over and stretched out a hand to the thrashing Vandhiyathevan, who promptly climbed in.

The boat moved on.

Vandhiyathevan now bent his scrutiny upon the other occupants and realized that one wasn't even Thamizh but apparently an Arab, of all things. The Vaanar warrior stared at him in considerable surprise, wondering how such a one had even gotten here, and then took in the other two. Cloths covered the lower halves of their faces, but it seemed obvious that they were Thamizh—but that was not all; their features struck a chord in his memory. Now, where—*where* had he seen them and how—ah, yes! *I remember now—weren't these the men returning from Thampallai in the company of Parthibendra Pallavan? In that case, these must be the ones Azhwarkkadiyaan accused of trying to murder the prince ... and now that I think of it, I seem to have seen one of them somewhere else too, haven't I? Isn't this one Ravidasan, the mandhiravadhi? The one who'd hooted like an owl and arrived for a meeting with the Rani of Pazhuvoor? So that's why they're all making towards the ship—likely, they know of the prince's presence aboard! Aha, here was another peril in the prince's way—what an excellent thing that I braved the choppy seas and clambered into this boat ...*

The craft bobbed on, inching towards the ship.

Its occupants preserved a stony silence; not so Vandhiyathevan, a gregarious soul as a rule. He opened the gambit, unable to bear the stifling quiet.

"So, where are you all going?"

"I suppose it escaped your notice," muttered the magician, his muffled voice sounding ghoulish from within his face-coverings. "But we're on our way to that ship."

"So where's the ship going?" Vandhiyathevan persisted.

"That will be known only when we reach it," was Ravidasan's laconic answer.

Silence descended like a heavy blanket within the boat once more while the sea murmured uproariously, without.

This time, when the silence broke, it was due to the efforts of Ravidasan himself. "And where do *you* go, *Appa*?"

"Oh, I'm on my way to the ship as well," was Vandhiyathevan's cheery answer.

"And where else, once aboard the ship?"

"That," Vandhiyathevan replied blandly, "will be known only when I reach it."

***

The boat approached the large vessel; a ladder descended from the latter and everyone climbed up. Vandhiyathevan managed to hold on to the flimsy contraption before it could be raised. Some snatches of talk floated down the ship's deck, and it seemed to be in a language he couldn't understand. Decidedly, there was no more time to be wasted; Vandhiyathevan fairly slithered up the ladder, clambered over the edge and jumped onto the deck. "Where?" He yelled, at once, staring around the ship. "Where's his highness?"

And then, the sight that met his eyes almost froze even his steely heart. Huge, swarthy Arabs whose very appearance struck terror into the bravest warrior, stood upon the deck, each resembling a demon in dimension. All stared at him, eyes bulging out of their sockets; none answered.

For the first time since his mad dash from shore to ship, a pit opened up within Vandhiyathevan's stomach. *Something's really wrong here,* whispered his brain, for this was no Chozha ship at all, and its sailors were certainly not Thamizh. They were, in fact, Arab traders, bent upon selling their horses—huge lusty beasts—upon these shores.

No, the prince certainly couldn't be aboard this ship. *I've made a mistake—a huge mistake in coming here but now ... how am I supposed to escape?*

He turned towards the edge of the ship and peered down; the boat was moving away."*Dei,* stop!" He cried out and was about to jump back into the sea—when an arm as strong as *vajram* gripped his throat. A pull, and then a push, and Vandhiyathevan found himself on his back in the middle of the deck.

Nothing could rouse him like unprovoked violence; fury clouded his mind and Vandhiyathevan jumped up, shaking with wrath. He bunched his fists and aimed a punch at the chin of the one that had knocked him down; the Arab, taken unawares, staggered backwards, taking another man with him.

A low, terrible growl from behind alerted Vandhiyathevan in the nick of time; he turned and swiftly bounded away from a knife that would surely have plunged into his unprotected back. As it was, he knocked the blade away with the force of his twirl; it fell to the deck with a *danaar!*, clanged against the edge and disappeared into the sea.

Battle, now, was fairly joined; several men surrounded Vandhiyathevan all at once and began a rumbling speech in a language unknown to him. Then, one who seemed to be their leader barked a sharp command. A slender rope was brought; his limbs were swiftly bound and hands tied to his back.

Four men hoisted up and carried him downstairs like a sack of flour within a few minutes, the entire duration of which Vandhiyathevan spent kicking and squirming in a bid to escape. His efforts yielded absolutely no result, for they finally brought him to a lower deck, and deposited him with a *padaar!* on top of a pile of lumber. It was only after they had tied him up securely to a log that they finally left.

It was easy to guess from the way the ship swayed, Vandhiyathevan mused , that it had begun its journey. Some of the logs on which he had been thrown rolled away and fell upon him; he could do nothing to escape, as his hands were tied. Literally.

No more madcap enterprises, he swore to himself, as he was tossed about. *No more half-baked adventures or wild-goose chases—no more running off half-cocked at anything! No; henceforth, I will think, and think carefully, analyze and look at any situation like Azhwarkkadiyaan before I ...*

The sound of a raucous, ghoulish laugh from somewhere very near, startled him. He turned his head with great difficulty, and caught sight of the *mandhiravadhi* leaning nonchalantly against the door. It was easier than ever to recognize him now, as the cloth covering his face was gone.

"You know, I came here for a Chozha tiger, but couldn't get my hands on it. Instead, I've ended up with a Vaanar fox and to tell the truth, *Appane*," he said, with a maniacal grin. "That might not be a bad exchange after all!"

***

Of the stirring events above, those on the beach, watching Vandhiyathevan's progress knew of only what had happened until he boarded the ship; not even the boatman knew the rest for he had turned almost right away and soon, reached shore.

The Senathipathi and the rest of his party climbed into the boat, having convinced themselves, by now, that there was nothing to be accomplished by chasing after the ship. They might as well paddle around to the mouth of the Thondaiman River. The other ship might be anchored there still, and the prince too, perhaps. In any case, they might be able to glean some speck of information—anything that might lead them somewhere.

As for the boatman, a careful interrogation yielded no results. "I was sleeping blamelessly in my boat, when someone tapped me, woke me up and promised a great deal of money if I would take them to the ship," he mumbled. "I accepted and rowed them over, hoping to get back before you awakened. I swear I know nothing else."

***

Azhwarkkadiyaan came to the end of his recital, having retailed everything he knew, to the prince. "My first instinct, when Vandhiyathevan jumped into the sea and went after the boat, was to follow him, your highness," he continued. "But the truth, you see, is that I've always nursed a rather healthy fear of the sea. I cannot swim well ... and there was another reason: the ship that goes over there—well, I felt quite doubtful about it. I began to entertain the gravest suspicions about your presence on board—in fact, I even began to wonder if it *was*, indeed, a Chozha ship at all. I confided my fears to the Senathipathi and it seemed prudent to us to come here, see the lay of the land for ourselves, and arrive at any conclusion. And in truth, your highness, our hearts are at peace only after having set eyes on you—"

"All very well, Thirumalai, but *mine* isn't," voiced Arulmozhi Varmar, who had been listening to this account carefully. "Vandhiyathevan is on that ship—and that's a recipe for disaster; the Pazhuvettarayars will throw him into their dungeons!"

"Pray, why must we—or anyone, for that matter—put up with those rogues and their pestilent authority, your highness?" The Senathipathi barged in at this opportune moment. "Say the word, Sire; those wretched Pazhuvettarayars shall be wrested from their posts, and I shall take great pleasure in personally bundling them into their own gloomy dungeons!"

"Do not even presume to think, Senathipathi," came the prince's crisp response. "That I shall act in contravention of my father's express commands."

The sound of a galloping horse attracted their attention and they turned as one man. The horse stopped at some distance, and the whole party gaped to see that the one who rode it—without the necessary accoutrements of saddle, stirrup or even reins—was a woman.

48

DEATH OF A KALAPATHI

The prince recognized the lady on the steed at a glance and hastened towards her; the others hung back a little, obviously hesitant, and advanced by slow steps.

By this time, Oomai Rani had descended from her horse. She glanced at the posse behind the prince, rather concerned, and held a silent conversation with Poonguzhali. "Your *periyamma* has seen something strange, she says," the young woman interpreted. "She'd like us to accompany her." The prince had no hesitation in acquiescing at once, and wondered if the others might be allowed to as well. Oomai Rani bent her thoughts towards this knotty problem and then nodded in agreement.

The prince's party could talk of nothing but her wonderful steed on their way, for it was a marvelous, pure-bred Arabian stallion, and how on earth had this old woman ended up with such a one? After all, this area had seen no major warfare in recent times—not even the advent of a massive army—and so, a horse in the hands of this jungle woman was the subject of much astonished speculation.

We saw, some time ago, that a Chozha ship had been wrecked on the shores in the vicinity of the Thondaiman River mouth. The Ilankai coast meandered in the south-eastern direction for some distance from this point; the sea had broken in often along the curving shoreline, establishing miniature lakes and larger water-bodies. Indeed, it was from one such lagoon that Vandhiyathevan and the rest had seen the ship appear and put out to sea, that very morning.

It was in this same direction that Oomai Rani escorted them now, and through a jungle that grew increasingly dense. The prince's curiosity grew by leaps and bounds with each passing moment, for surely something extraordinary must have occurred to make the lady guide them so far, and through such thick forest. And then, abruptly—that very scene spread out in front of their amazed eyes!

The forest cleared a little and amidst the steadily widening path could be glimpsed a small lake. Several men lay on its banks, clearly dead; the smell of their decomposing corpses mingled with that of dried, dark blood. None of the newly arrived party, veterans as they were of a great many battlefields and so, accustomed to dead bodies and rivers of blood, were overpowered by loathing—but that something of great magnitude had occurred there—something catastrophically horrible—was apparent, making them approach the area with not just trepidation but disgust as well.

One look at the many bodies and it was clear that the sailors were Thamizh. The prince was galvanized into action. "Quick—check if any of them are alive—come on!" His men immediately bent over each of the scattered bodies, verifying proof of life.

Oomai Rani signed to the prince once again, escorting him to a tree slightly apart from the scene of the massacre, where a truly gory spectacle met their eyes. The figure that lay against the trunk might have been reasonably supposed to be human—not that this was an easy conclusion, for every inch of his body was bruised, while a large gash on his head was bleeding so much that dark blood coated his face almost completely, disfiguring it. Awaiting death at any moment, his marred countenance brightened just a smidgeon at the sight of the prince. He tried to speak but blood in his mouth made speech impossible, turning his expression even more grotesque, if possible.

"Bring me some water—quick!" snapped the prince, hurrying to his side at once.

"No, your highness," stammered the man. "This lady—gave me some, just a while ago. If she had not, my life would have departed ere now. *Ayya*, I have suffered enough in this lifetime for having betrayed you … God shall not punish me for this grievous transgression in the next."

His voice stirred a chord in the prince's memory, who stared at him keenly. "Ah, Kalapathi!" He exclaimed suddenly. "What sort of talk is this? What did happen here? As for believing you capable of treason—perish the thought!"

"Your compassion towards your fellowmen is well-known, Sire, and I doubt not that it is that which makes you speak so—but I did come here with intent to imprison you, upon the Pazhuvettarayars' command," the Kalapathi said, and with the waning strength of a man staring at death, prised an *olai* from his waistband and handed it to the prince.

"I see nothing here that implies treason on your part," the prince skimmed the proffered palm-leaf within a matter of moments. "You arrived in pursuance of the Chakravarthy's express commands—which is why I hurried here, myself. But tell me—quickly—what lies behind such a disaster?"

"Indeed, I shall have to tell you all I know soon, or I might never speak again," murmured the Kalapathi. Then, he began to retail his adventures haltingly, as follows:

The ship's captain received the Chakravarthy's commands with all due respect and departed, accordingly, from the port of Nagapattinam in two vessels. His heart quailed at the very idea, and nothing could have been more repugnant—but such was the order of his sovereign, and carrying it out was his bounden duty. This was not all, however: the Pazhuvettarayars had taken him aside and for their part, impressed upon him certain stipulations: once in Ilankai, he was to anchor his ships in an isolated spot and discover the prince's current whereabouts. Then, he was to seek an audience with him and deliver the Chakravarthy's orders into his hands. On no account was even a breath of all that had transpired to reach Senathipathi Periya Velaar. As for the prince, far better for him to accompany the Kalapathi of his own free will, but should he refuse, no matter; he ought to be imprisoned and brought to the anchored ships by force.

Such were the Pazhuvettarayars' covert commands and they sent a small contingent of their men, with the intention of assisting the captain on his mission.

It was not to be expected that the Kalapathi, a loyal Chozha citizen and a royalist to boot, would accept his commission with equanimity but he did so anyway, albeit with a heavy heart. Most of the sailors under his command were unaware of the purpose of their journey to Ilankai, and this made things even worse, in the Kalapathi's opinion, for he had no idea how he was to disclose it. When he finally made it to the mouth of the Thondaiman River, he took a few men as escort and journeyed to the port of Kangesan, to enquire as to the whereabouts of the prince. Here, he learnt that Arulmozhi Varmar was travelling somewhere deep within southern Ilankai, and returned.

By this time, of course, those of the Pazhuvettarayars' men who had been left behind had made known the true purpose of their journey to the rest of the Kalapathi's men, and upon the latter's return, most of them surrounded him in a quest for the truth. "Are we here to imprison Ponniyin Selvar?" They demanded hotly.

The Kalapathi had no choice but to admit that this was, indeed, the case. "We are in royal service," he tried to pacify them. "We are duty-bound to carry out the Chakravarthy's orders, whatever they might be."

"No!" chorused the rest of his men, incensed. "These are not his commands, but the Pazhuvettarayars'!"

"What *do* you mean to do, then?"

"Go to Maathottam and join the prince's forces."

"But he isn't there."

"Senathipathi Kodumbaloor Periya Velaar's men, then."

No argument that the Kalapathi advanced swerved their decision; only around ten men—and this included Pazhuvettarayars' loyalists, naturally—stood by him ... but how could ten possibly stand against two hundred?

"Get lost then, and good riddance to you!" thundered the Kalapathi in the end. "And when you come by your just desserts, I hope you'll learn your lesson—but I shall certainly carry out my duty to the best of my ability!"

Most of the defecting sailors then huddled in conference, debating if one of the two vessels could be commandeered to sail towards Maathottam; others objected. In the end, it was decided that the ship would be abandoned and the journey made on foot instead. Disembarking in a tearing hurry, they forgot to drop anchor; the ship drifted gradually in the tumbling waters until it breached shore and was promptly wrecked.

***

The Kalapathi, for his part, did not wish to stay in company of a wrecked ship. Moreover, another piece of news had fallen on his ears in Kangesan port; an Arab vessel had been wrecked in the vicinity of Mullai Theevu a few days ago, and several rather bloodthirsty Arabs who had managed to escape were even now wandering those parts. The Kalapathi had no wish, therefore, to anchor his own seaworthy ship near the wrecked vessel and took it further out; soon, he navigated his way to another concealed lagoon and dropped anchor. Next, he disembarked and began to discuss a course of action with his sailors. He would go alone to the prince and deliver the command; the rest ought to stay on ship and keep safe, he instructed them.

The sailors, already nervous at these turn of events confided their fears to him; the Kalapathi was on the point of soothing them when the most terrifying howls and yells smote their ears, and several men surrounded them. It became apparent that these were the Arabs and also, that the Thamizh sailors were taken completely unawares. Unarmed and unprepared for combat, they yet showed considerable courage and consummate skill but in the end, sheer numbers overwhelmed them and all to a man died a valiant death.

"I was the only one to hide away, despite my fatal injuries," the Kalapathi's voice was very faint. "I wanted to tell someone, you see, about the fate that had befallen us—and now I have been blessed beyond my wildest dreams, for I have had the great good fortune to meet you, Sire. I have been punished well for even entertaining the thought of betraying you," stammered the Captain. "Ponniyin Selva, forgive me ..."

"You don't require my forgiveness, faithful captain—for if there's a heaven for those who embrace an honourable death on the battlefield, be assured that you shall find a place there," murmured the prince, placing a soothing palm on the dying man's burning forehead.

Tears rolled down the Kalapathi's wan cheeks, mingling with the blood on his ravaged countenance. With the last of his swiftly fading strength, he raised his arms, caught at the prince's hands, and managed to place them on his eyes.

The captain's tears splashed onto the prince's hands; Arulmozhi Varmar's eyes were moist with unshed tears.

Within moments, the Kalapathi's breathing ceased; his soul departed his ruined, battered body, finally at peace.

49

THE SHIP HUNT

Dried sticks were gathered and weathered planks; the dead Kalapathi and his band of sailors were duly cremated.

Senathipathi Boodhi Vikrama Kesari, shaking his head over the whole business as the pyre began to burn bright, caught sight of the tears streaming down the prince's cheeks.

"Why waste emotion on these corpses, *Ayya*—rogues that came here to imprison you! Ah, God has truly given these treacherous wretches the deaths they deserve," he said, with a good deal of relish. "Why must you bemoan their demise?"

"Not traitors, Senathipathi and neither do I regret their deaths," Arulmozhi Varmar's expression was bleak. "If there's anything I lament, it is that the fate of Chozha Nadu has come to this."

"The times soured and turned against us with the advent of the Pazhuvettarayars; this is nothing new, after all."

"But it *is*, Senathipathi. To hear of sailors mutinying against their captain, defying their superiors—what worse fate could befall a *rajyam*? This is just the beginning, a small sign that rot has begun to set in and I shudder to think of how many other terrible omens might appear ... because if so, then the empire built stone by stone, the *samrajyam* almost single-handedly erected by the great Vijayalaya Chozhar would splinter into pieces! Must I be the cause of such wholesale destruction? I've heard tales from the Mahabharatham that wolves and jackals howled horribly when Duryodhanan was born, and I can't help but think that such a terrible portent must have occurred at mine too—"

"Every sign of prosperity, every good omen that has ever been recorded in this world were observed at the auspicious moment of your birth, *Ayya*! The astrologers who divined your blessed horoscope—"

"Oh enough, for God's sake, *enough*! My ears are numb listening to endless tales of my tremendously marvellous horoscope, so let us leave it be. The time has truly come for us to bid farewell to each other and here, I must beg of you a favour: should the defecting sailors ever return to you, do not receive them. Imprison every last one at once and despatch them to Thanjai."

"We certainly heard the Kalapathi's story, your highness, but as to sailors' side of the tale—how may we come to a decision based on one faction's account? No, no, that would hardly be in the interests of justice. If you will indulge me, I have a better notion: you shall accompany me and together, we shall listen to the sailors and determine the truth or otherwise of—"

"Beg pardon, *Ayya*, but that really is not possible at this time. Use your discretion, for I can't stay here another moment ..." the prince stared around him. "Where on earth is that boatman?"

"Whatever for?" demanded the Senathipathi. "Pray, where do you wish to go in such hurry, your highness?"

"Must you even ask? The ship that's carrying Vandhiyathevan, of course—hasn't that lion, that warrior among warriors risked his life and limb and found himself in the grasp of those demonic Arabs, just because he believed himself to be going to my rescue? How could you even think that I would leave him to his fate? As if my crimes until now haven't been enough, you wish me to crumple under the weight of betraying a friend as well, do you?"

"You have committed no crime that I know of, *Ayya*, and no matter what your explanation, the world certainly would not believe you. And then, Vandhiyathevan—an unprincipled brat, your highness, and a ruffian who does not believe in forethought in the slightest. How could you consider yourself responsible for the result of his idiotic, brash actions? As for all this soaring talk of betrayal … forgive me, but I must reveal my extreme aversion at your even befriending a loathsome youth such as this—without name or clan, and certainly not the status that would allow intimacy … surely only those of the same rank may maintain even a semblance of friendship?"

"I've no patience for idle talk, Senathipathi. Even if there's no question of friendship, there *is* such a thing as gratitude, and haven't we all heard Valluvar's couplets about that particular emotion? Not to mention a host of other great men … no; I cannot and will *not* allow such a slur cast upon the Chozha name on that account. I shall leave at once and hunt down that ship—"

"By what means, my prince? And how, pray, do you intend to conduct this much-vaunted hunt?"

"I shall have to commandeer your boat, of course …"

"Now here's a pretty tale: whoever heard of hunting a tiger with a hare? Running down a ship of the high seas with a puny boat such as this, fit only for paddling in shallow waters? And what do you intend to do when you do capture it, I wonder?"

"I don't care. I shall take that boat—and if it splinters, I shall clamber on to some plank and make my way. I shall find Vandhiyathevan's ship even if it carries him across the seven seas—and if I cannot save him after all this, then I shall die with him … *where* is that dratted boatman?"

The prince walked forward as he said this, staring all around him and discovered said boatman deep in conversation with Poonguzhali at some distance. Beside them stood Oomai Rani, and the prince hurried towards them.

***

Drawing close, he saw that Poonguzhali was arguing furiously—and that her eyes were glistening with unshed tears. "Good God, what's this?" the words burst out from him. "Not another mutiny?"

Abruptly, the boatman flung himself at the prince's feet, like a felled tree. "Forgive me, your highness—I was blinded by my desire for wealth—forgive this rash fool for his treachery!" He sobbed.

"What on earth ..." Ponniyin Selvar blinked. "Are you bent on driving me completely out of my senses, all of you? Couldn't *you* enlighten me, Poonguzhali?"

"I kept this from you because I was ashamed, your highness—but this boatman is my elder brother. And he—this wretch was the one who ferried the two murderous rogues burning to kill you, from Kodikkarai to Ilankai. What's worse—he's been waiting here all this while in obedience to their instructions and when he saw them, ferried them across to that ship we saw this morning!" she gasped. "And that's the one your friend boarded—"

"Kill me, *Prabhu*—cut me into pieces this very instant!" The boatman shrieked in anguish. "I did not know—I did not know they were such scoundrels or I would not have done it! Take my life with your own hands!"

"Your life is invaluable to me at the moment, *Appane*. Take me as well to that ship, and it shall be reparation for all the wrongs you've done me," answered the prince calmly. "Come; get up, now, and let's leave."

***

They hastened to the shore, where the boatman dragged his craft from the beach into the water. The prince, meanwhile, scrutinized the sea carefully, shading his eyes. "There—I can see the ship still!" He exclaimed. "We can get to them."

The Senathipathi stared at the vessel in the distance as well. "Good lord," he snapped, suddenly. "The fruit has slipped into the milk, as the saying goes ..."

"Has it, now?" The prince looked bemused. "And why would such auspicious words come from you?"

"The ship that is still in our line of sight isn't the one Vandhiyathevan boarded, but rather, the one belonging to Parthibendran. Trace the direction—it is sailing from Thirikonamalai, can you not see?"

"I can," said the prince slowly. "And if that's the case—excellent. Parthibendrar's motive in coming here might be unclear, but he's certainly chosen the right moment to do so ... fair enough, I shall hunt the leopard with a lion—but I'm not going to wait until the ship reaches us; I shall be ferried halfway, I think—"

"If I may accompany your highness—"

"Not at all, Senathipathi; I shall consider it a service beyond par, should you remain here ... and that goes for you too, Thirumalai. Besides, you're afraid of the sea, aren't you?"

"It's true that we don't quite see eye to eye, your highness; besides, I intend to stay behind, for my orders to keep you under observation hold only as long as you stay in Ilankai. Chief Minister Aniruddhar is in Madurai, as well, and I must apprise him of all that has transpired ..."

"Do so. I understand you ought to remain here ... and so must you, Poonguzhali. Don't worry about your brother; he's my responsibility, now. You mentioned that you'd left your boat tied up somewhere hereabouts, didn't you? Well, you may find it and go your own way. I shall never forget your aid ... *cheche*, dry your eyes, my girl! What will the people here think to see you shedding tears?"

The prince approached Oomai Rani now and bent, in a bid to touch her feet. The lady stopped him, raised him by the shoulders and gave her benediction with a loving embrace.

He leapt into the boat the next instant.

Those left on shore gazed at the small craft, bobbing away.

The prince turned to stare at them as well—and although his gaze took in all of them, it was drawn to one in particular: the lovely, tear-drenched eyes of Poonguzhali. And—ah, how surprising! Instead of growing smaller with distance as was the law of nature ... her face grew larger, for some reason. Larger and larger—and coming close, so close to him with every instant ...

He shook himself and turned away. Something rose to the surface from within the depths of his memory—a fragment of his dream from the night before—and spread before his mind's eye.

Thambi, whispered Ilaiya Piratti Kundhavai. *Don't forget that Vanathi awaits you here ...*

The low words reverberated in his ears, drowning out even the thunderous roar of the choppy sea waves.

ஐ

50

THE SWORN GUARDIANS

It would be impossible to describe Parthibendran's astonishment at the sight of the prince, in the boat. Wasn't it almost a case of God intercepting you on the way to worship, and asking your preference in boons? And yet … why was he alone? What of the Pazhuvettarayars' ships—wait, was he rowing here furiously under the mistaken impression that *this* was the ship sent to imprison him and therefore, the one he ought to be on?

It soon became apparent that the prince was under no such misapprehension, for he began to retail the events as they had happened without Parthibendran's asking, once he had come aboard. "Vandhiyathevan is on the Arab ship, so you see why it's important that he should be rescued, don't you?" he finished.

"But this is excellent—excellent indeed," Parthibendran's enthusiasm at this news was obvious. "Well, it would have been much better, I dare say, if that impulsive rogue hadn't thrown himself headlong into—but we oughtn't to leave him in the clutches of foreigners, of course. That ship couldn't have gone far; we'll be able to pursue and catch up to them easily enough," he assured. Next, he called up the Kalapathi and delivered to him the pertinent details.

"As to that, should the wind stay thus, in the right quarter, there ought to be no difficulty at all in tracing the ship by evening," promised the captain. "It isn't as if they can escape us; once they hit Kodikkarai, they shall have to hug the shoreline after all."

***

It seemed, however, that the divine intent of Vayu Bhagavan, Lord of the Winds, was otherwise: the speed dropped steadily and by mid-noon the winds had died down completely, leaving the sea with a surface like glass, calm and unbroken. Humidity stifled them; perspiration dripped upon their bodies as Surya Bhagavan decided to play accomplice to his divine peer in punishing the puny humans, by raining down scorching rays. Likely, it would not have burned to touch the water but the murky sea, thick and steaming, made one think that the Gods had poured down a veritable ocean of oil onto earth. Where the sun touched the waters, the seas seemed to froth and boil like molten gold.

The ship lay still. Every single sail onboard had been unfurled completely to catch the slightest hint of a wind—but what was the use? They hung limp and silent just as the waters below were quiet; not even the usual sounds that accompanied life on a ship—the crackling, rumbling noise of beams, rafters and masts—could be heard now, nor the hiss of the ship cleaving the waters. In truth, this horrible, stifling silence was more than aggravating—it was agonizing.

The prince's hands clenched and unclenched as worry about Vandhiyathevan's fate churned his mind. "When will the wind pick up? How long will it take before we move?" he demanded, more concerned than ever. "Won't that dratted ship have scurried away?"

Parthibendran directed a mute query at the ship's Kalapathi.

"It is not possible for the wind to stay thus, your highness. This weather can only mean that a gale is forming somewhere else. It might come upon us quickly—or ignore us entirely and wreck its havoc on some other location. Regardless, it is clear to me that the sea is about to turn choppy very soon. You see the surface now, my liege? Well, these calm waters will turn into heaving mountains; this very night, you will witness waves that throw us high into the heavens one moment, and dash us to the underworld the next!" The captain pronounced, not without some relish.

"But—wouldn't that be dangerous?"

"Extremely so, your highness; our fate rests now in the great God's hands!"

"We can't hope to reach the other ship, then."

"The seas and gales favour no man, your highness. It is likely in the same state—staying still, upon the ocean."

"But if the ship's already strayed towards the shore ...?" The prince asked, cautiously.

"The men aboard could clamber down and escape by swimming to land, I suppose—but the ship itself is done for," the Kalapathi shook his head.

"No matter the danger, it would be an immense relief if our nearest and dearest were by our side," the prince murmured. Vandhiyathevan's mischievous face, eyes glinting with spirit, and Poonguzhali's alarmed expression flitted across his mind's eye often. Where were they at this very moment, he wondered. What were they doing—and more importantly, what thoughts were running through their minds?

***

And now, without further ado, let us return to Vandhiyathevan, who was left behind in a truly precarious situation.

He was trussed up and bound to a log besides, inside a dark, gloomy cabin filled with lumber, odds and ends, and various knotted bundles, on the lower deck of the huge ship sent to imprison the prince.

For a long time he lay in a sort of daze, writhing under the merciless lash of his conscience at having walked so thoughtlessly into such a simple trap. Nothing made any sense—*nothing*, as his tortured mind tried to piece together a complicated puzzle that involved this ship: what sort of a vessel was this in the first place, and whose was it? How on earth did it come into the possession of those rogue Arabs and Ravidasan? What was its destination and most important of all—what were they going to do to *him*? No, he really didn't know a thing and now, all his hopes and rosy dreams for his future would likely remain just those—dreams.

And yet … one never knew. He had been caught in much more treacherous situations before this and had made it out unscathed—and perhaps he would, this time too. The hope could not but rear its head inside him. *Let's see*, he mused. *As long as there's breath left in my body—as long as I possess even a hairsbreadth of intuition and intelligence, there's no need to despair.*

Once he had managed to reach thus far in his cogitations, he stared around, taking stock of his surroundings. The pitch darkness meant that nothing was visible right away but his vision cleared gradually, and he could dimly perceive a variety of weapons heaped, nearby. His body might have been bound up tight, but his hands weren't. It wouldn't be too difficult to loosen one, reach for a sword and cut the ropes that bound his arms and legs. But what then? The door to the cabin was shut and he knew of no way to get out. And even if he could, in some miraculous fashion, make his escape—what of the Arabs, Ravidasan and his friend? And even if he could kill them all in a fight, what then? Could Vallavarayan possibly handle a ship this size all by himself? It wasn't as if he was an expert in such things—he was blankly ignorant of anything, ship-wise.

No, he oughtn't to do anything in haste. *Wait, Vandhiyatheva. Think. The very fact that they've tied you up for the moment without trying to kill you is something to be grateful about ... let's see what they come up with, shall we?*

This, however, was easier thought than done for soon, his discomfort grew by leaps and bounds. His patience now began to face a bigger test: the cabin became as hot as an oven. Sweat snaked down his body in rivulets, and Vandhiyathevan soon began to feel as though he were being baked alive. Not in his wildest dreams had he ever imagined sea voyages to be so very humid, and he tried to remember his travel on Poonguzhali's boat on his way to Ilankai. Ah, how pleasant that had been, with a gentle breeze that soothed his body and senses! And how different had that been, to his present experience? *Ah, now I know what it feels like to be roasted alive within a roaring lime kiln ...*

Abruptly, he sensed a change—and yes, the ship's rocking motion had stopped. It seemed that they were staying still; not moving. The humidity increased; he was possessed of an unbearable thirst that parched his throat and tongue. *I can't last long at this rate; time to reach for that sword, cut my bonds, escape and see what's what. Wouldn't a ship as big as this store drinking-water somewhere?*

Vandhiyathevan peered into the gloom again; this time, his sharp eyes caught sight of a few coconuts heaped into a corner. Aha, why would anyone hunt for *nei* with butter in their hands? Both thirst and hunger could be quenched with the help of these coconuts. It took only a matter of moments to loosen his bonds; he had even stretched out his hand to grab the sword when—

—footsteps. Followed by the sound of an opening door.

He shrank back the next instant, and tucked his hands away.

***

It was Ravidasan again this time, accompanied by a friend, who stalked in, both parking themselves on either side of Vandhiyathevan.

"And how do you find travel aboard a ship, *Thambi?*" smirked Ravidasan. "All to your exquisite taste, I expect?"

"Water—just a little," Vandhiyathevan's voice was scratchy. "I'm dying of thirst—"

"Aren't we all," Ravidasan nodded in commiseration. "But those rogues didn't think to store drinking-water anywhere aboard ship."

"Devi Kali is the thirstiest of us all," suddenly intoned the companion. "But hers is a terrible thirst for blood!"

Vandhiyathevan turned and stared at the man.

"Ah, don't remember me, do you? You have forgotten, *Thambi*— forgotten the Devaralan who danced such a storm of fury after the *Kuravai Koothu* in the Kadambur Palace—forgotten the man who was possessed of the divine will of Magnificent Kali, asking, demanding the blood of an ancient dynasty, a thousand years old—"

"Ah, yes," Vandhiyathevan mumbled. "You're the Devaralan."

"Indeed it is, boy," the Devaralan revealed, barely able to conceal his glee. "And though we did journey to Ilankai with the intent of delivering a pure-blooded prince of powerful lineage to Kali—and a certain pesky Vaishnavite to Vaikundam—neither happened. You, on the other hand, fairly walked into our arms, much to our delight," the Devaralan grinned. "The most divine Goddess will have to be satisfied with the weaker blood of puny local chieftains for now."

"Why wait, then?" Vandhiyathevan croaked.

"Ah, the sacrifice of your valorous life is no simple matter, boy; it shall have to be done once we land ashore, amidst truly glorious festivities and *urchavams* conducted by our own battalion of priests—not to mention the most important of them all, the great grand priestess herself."

"And who might be this august personage?"

"Come, come, *Thambi*. Surely you must know that it can be none other than the Pazhuvoor Ilaiya Rani?"

Vandhiyathevan mulled over these words for a moment. "If this really is your intention," he ventured, finally. "You'd better give me some water before I die of thirst here and now."

"But there isn't any to be had for love or money, *Thambi.*"

"Well, you're a *mandhiravadhi,* aren't you?"

"Ah, well said, boy. So I am, and I've cast a splendid spell too—notice that the ship hasn't moved an inch? By night, we shall be in the midst of a gale—and rain as well!"

"That might be very well for you on the upper deck, but what of my poor self, down here—"

"So may you, *Thambi*: get above stairs, stretch out your tongue and drink all the water you want—as long as you obey our commands implicitly ..."

"What's that supposed to mean?"

"In plain language, boy—your instructions are to sacrifice those demonic Arab scoundrels to the most illustrious Samudhra Rajan, Lord of the Oceans."

"Why?"

"They wish to steer this ship to the Kalinga kingdom, while our earnest desire is to disembark either at Kodikkarai or Nagapattinam."

"But there're six of them—huge armed thugs, into the bargain."

"Three are fast asleep and the rest are almost there. Once we dispatch the snoring trio, surely it ought to be work of moments to take on one each, of the rest?"

Vandhiyathevan stayed silent.

"Well? What do you say? Submit to us, and we'll cut your ropes straight away."

The prince's features swam before Vandhiyathevan's mind's eye for a moment. No, he wouldn't—the prince certainly wouldn't condone the idea of murdering sleeping men in cold blood; not for any price.

"That's the act of cowards; I won't do something as dishonourable as killing men who're asleep."

"Those Arab rogues attacked and killed Chozha sailors while they were snoring away, you petty fool."

"Their shameful act doesn't give me an excuse to follow their terrible example."

"As you please, then," shrugged Ravidasan, and bent to pick up a sharp broadsword from the heap of weapons lying in a corner. The Devaralan, for his part, chose a small, hefty staff molded with iron on one end. They left the room—but didn't, Vandhiyathevan noticed, close the door and latch it from the outside.

The next instant he reached a hand, caught up a sword and cut loose the ropes that bound him. He jumped up, strode over to the coconut heap, broke one open and slaked his thirst. Then, he drew a sack over the rest and concealed them from view.

He chose a sword that seemed perfect for battle and hefted it, testing its strength. Now he waited, ready to spring out any moment, and join the battle.

Within a very short while could be heard two separate 'thuds' from outside, and he guessed that two bodies had been thrown into the sea. The next instant, the upper deck exploded into a fury of shouts, screams and swords clanging against each other: *Danaar! Danaar!*

Vandhiyathevan needed no more persuasion: he bounded outside, sword in hand, to see Ravidasan and the Devaralan being assaulted by the remaining four Arabs in good earnest—and it was obvious that the two were on the losing end.

With a resounding battle cry, Vallavarayan leapt into the fray and was promptly rewarded by the sight of an Arab who turned around to attack him. Vandhiyathevan's sword knocked his neatly, flicking it into the ocean, and inflicted a long, bloody cut in his face into the bargain. The humiliated Arab, roaring in combined pain and fury, barreled towards Vandhiyathevan, fingers closed into a massive fist aiming for his chest. Vallavarayan stepped aside slightly; the assailant promptly fell flat on his face and one of the cross beams of the mast, upended by the force of his fall, smacked his head smartly.

Our hero turned his attention next to another Arab who, after a brief altercation, soon found his way into the sea.

***

Neither Ravidasan nor the Devaralan were accomplished warriors, which meant that handling an Arab each was a Herculean task for them— not to mention that they were tiring with every moment. Fortunately, fate itself seemed on their side: sounds of men thudding into the sea caught the attention of the Arabs at a crucial moment and the men turned, wondering about the fate of their compatriots. The distraction was enough; magician and companion finished them.

Their task done, all three collapsed on the deck, chest heaving but triumphant.

"At a good moment, *Appane*," Ravidasan gasped. "What made you change your mind?"

"You must have cast some sort of spell, I think," Vandhiyathevan said flippantly. "Witness my surprise when the ropes binding me fell apart all by themselves—and this sword practically jumped into my hands!"

"Indeed." Ravidasan raised his eyebrows. "And—what of your unbearable thirst?"

"A coconut floated up to me," Vandhiyathevan's voice was gently mocking. "It broke its head all by itself, and poured some of its sweet water into my mouth."

"Why, you wicked rogue, you," the Devaralan crowed, and the two men collapsed anew into laughter.

"We wished to test you, *Thambi*," said Ravidasan finally, wiping away tears of merriment. "We left the ropes loose and a heap of weapons conveniently nearby. And, of course, the coconuts within your line of sight."

Was all this true? Or just an elaborate ruse designed to stitch together random events? Vandhiyathevan, who could not distinguish between either, paused.

"Now think again, boy, and think well," Ravidasan counseled. "Do you wish to stay alive? See your near and dear ones again in this lifetime? Attain wealth no mortal could ever dream of—a great position, authority, and the obeisance of all? You may join us if you wish—and you will be the recipient of everything I mentioned and more!"

"And yet, you had no compunction in killing sleeping men," Vandhiyathevan countered.

"Only two—the third awoke. If you had joined us a little earlier, matters would have been resolved just a shade easily."

"I simply can't justify killing men who were asleep. How could you even consider doing something against *dharmam*?"

"Really, if swallowing these tiny mustard seeds makes you whimper, I wonder how you will manage large pumpkins, especially if you are going to join us—"

"All this talk of *us*—who exactly are you all?"

"Well ..." Ravidasan flicked a glance at his companion. "It makes no difference what we tell him: either he joins our cause, or the sea—neither of which compromises us. Why not reveal everything?"

"By all means," assented the Devaralan.

"Now listen very well, *Thambi*, for we are ..." Ravidasan paused impressively. "We are Emperor Veera Pandiyar's *Abathudhavis*; his sworn guardians, pledged to keep him safe at all costs—"

"But you failed, didn't you? For it was Aditha Karikalar who won ..."

"And how? Only by the incredible stupidity of a woman who over-estimated her charms—who believed that the net of her extraordinary beauty would reel him in, bring him to her feet, and make that poisonous snake dance to her whims. Well, it did—but not without sinking in its wretched fangs as well. Our beloved Emperor's head rolled onto the ground. They carried it all the way to Thanjavur and paraded it in the streets, in a palanquin ...ah, Thanjavur—Thanjavur! Wait, just wait, *Thambi*, and you shall witness that precious city's terrible fate soon ..."

Ravidasan's eyes, already huge and bloodshot, now widened, spitting sparks of sheer fury. His body trembled and the *nara-nara* sound of his teeth grinding in the grip of unimaginable wrath was audible and simultaneously, horrifying. The Devaralan presented a similarly terrifying spectacle.

"What's done is done," Vandhiyathevan said, noncommittally. "Why concern yourself with the past? You can't bring Veera Pandiyan to life, after all—"

"No; not even my spells are powerful enough to raise the dead—but we can and will take vengeance on those responsible for his death, and tear them by their very roots. We shall rout out those poisonous snakes, right down to their children and their mewling, flailing infants—now, will you join us? Answer, quick!"

"And—what're your plans, once you've finished decimating the Chozha dynasty?"

"Crown the one chosen by our Maharani ..."

"Maharani?"

"Ah, come now, *Thambi*. The one currently posing as the Pazhuvoor Ilaiya Rani, of course."

"What about Madhuranthakar, then?"

"Well, he's a little snake too, isn't he?"

"And Pazhuvettarayar ...?"

"Surely you cannot accuse us of the unpardonable crime of wishing to set *him* on the throne? Ah, no, we simply seek to relieve him of his riches and numerous resources, you understand ..."

"Which is why your Maharani resides in his home, I suppose."

"How very perceptive of you, *Thambi*! Really, such astuteness is beyond compare, you know."

"Wait—you said that a woman was the cause of Veera Pandiyan's death."

"Ah, that was her, again—the young queen of Pazhuvoor. She swore that she would care for our king, wounded in battle—but did she keep her word? No. We were about to burn her alive for betrayal but decided not to, when she pledged herself to our cause alongside us. And she has kept her side of the bargain until now, I must admit. We could not have accomplished all that we have without her immense aid, you see."

"But you haven't done much, have you?"

"Just you wait, *Appane*," Ravidasan said, with some relish. "Patience is a virtue."

"This one's certainly gotten everything from us," interrupted the Devaralan. "But we haven't learnt his decision yet."

"Well, *Thambi*—what is it to be? Join us? Who knows, fortune may favour you, and you may well be the one to ascend the valorous throne that reigns all over southern Thamizhagam. What do you say?"

***

Had it been a short while ago, Vandhiyathevan would have felt no compunction in throwing in his lot with these men: "Of course, where do I go and what do I do?" would have been his enthusiastic answer. Three days in the prince's company, however, had produced a phenomenal change in his temperament, and perception. Now, he discovered that the very thing he had valued best, thus far—his devious ruses, scheming strategies and instinctive predilection for hoodwinking others—seemed the most detestable.

"How did you end up capturing this ship?" he asked, in a swift move to change the subject. "And those Arabs we just dispatched to Yama's abode—how did you manage to gain their friendship?"

"All the result of my fabulous magical spells, *Appane*," Ravidasan said with a flourish. "These were the very foreigners from whom we'd purchased horses upon which we followed you, back and forth, in Ilankai. We saw the prince descend into *Yaanai Iravu Thurai*, and decided to come here hotfoot before he could. And we did, too, through a short-cut—only to see that our old friends, those Arabs, had commandeered this ship. Their own vessel had drifted too close to shore in the vicinity of Mullai Theevu and wrecked itself, they explained. They'd hidden themselves in the area and captured this one. They wanted to know if we could accompany them as guides and we accepted—it was as though the fruit had slipped into milk, as the saying goes."

"Does it, now? How?"

"We overheard that little Chozha snake in conversation with his Senathipathi, and understood that he would make his way to Chozha Nadu on his own—and that was not all, *Thambi*. There is a ferocious female demon on Ilankai that seemed well-versed in the magical arts, for it dueled with me, spell for spell, and kept Arulmozhi Varman safe — but it will not set foot on Chozha soil …"

The events that had transpired in Anuradhapuram flitted through Vandhiyathevan's mind.

Abruptly, Ravidasan began to laugh.

"What on earth are you cackling at?" Vandhiyathevan demanded. "What's so amusing?"

"Oh, nothing, *Thambi*, nothing at all—it is just that I was thinking of those Arabs, and their character and I could not help laughing. You saw their ruffianly side, didn't you? Killing men is as easy as lopping off plantains, for them—and yet, there is one thing that holds their complete attention and affection: a horse. No Arab rode his steeds, they told us, without supplying each hoof with an iron shoe. Whereas we, barbarians that we were, rode them bare-hoofed—and so were the most cold-hearted, merciless, uncivilized brutes in creation! It was a crime, they mourned, to even sell us stallions—do you know what happened this morning, *Thambi*?"

"Tell me."

"We boarded the ship and unfurled the sails. The vessel began its journey. There came the sound of horse-hooves from land—and that was it. Suspicions began to float around that it might be one of theirs from the ship wrecked on the coast of Mullai Theevu! They sent a man to shore, and us too, for company ..."

"And then?"

"There was no horse to be found, of course—just you, *Thambi*, and how convenient, to be sure! You made an excellent weapon with which to decimate these horse-lovers, didn't you?"

"This convivial conversation is all very well, but the boy has not given us an answer yet," reminded the Devaralan.

"So I shall, *Ayya*, so I shall," Vandhiyathevan began, elaborately. "And here is my decision: as someone sworn to serve the Chozhas, I will never, ever join you ..."

"Are you a part of the *Velakkara* Regiment, by any chance? Pledged your life in their service, or some such thing?"

"Not at all."

"Why the hesitation, then? You are a warrior, *Thambi*, and ought to join whichever faction benefits you the most."

It did not seem appropriate to Vandhiyathevan to mention that there were motives that tied him securely to the Chozhas—reasons more compelling, more resolutely binding than any rigid warrior-pledge or a so-called sworn promise: just a single glance of Ilaiya Piratti's exquisite eyes, or her lovely smile unfurling gently like a *mullai* bloom—could there be a more powerful motivator to sacrifice himself in Chozha service? And then, there was the prince's companionship—ah, could any man blessed with the good fortune of calling himself his friend, ever consider transferring his allegiance?

"Whatever the reason, I can't imagine joining your murderous crowd under any circumstances," Vandhiyathevan shook his head firmly.

"In that case, boy," Ravidasan's eyes glinted. "Prepare to pledge your life to the sacred service of Samudhra Rajan!"

ஜ

51

WHIRLWINDS

No breath of wind. Not a stir in the sea. No budging the ship, either. Vandhiyathevan sat silent, staring at the calm, smooth surface, still as an eternal lake. His heart, though, was anything but, heaved and tossed by massive waves. The next instant, he stretched both hands towards the ocean. "*Om hreem hraam vashat!*" he shrieked. Then, he snatched up his sword with lightning speed and twirled it around twice, like a discus. "Yes, indeed, you speak the truth!" He yelled. "Samudhra Rajan is ravenous and seeks appeasement—twice. He asks, in fact, for the lives of the great warriors who would fall upon sleeping men—and will not let the ship pass without this sacred offering!" He turned towards his stupefied audience of two. "Now, why don't you line up like the good, obedient sacrifices you are, and stretch out your necks? Come, now—let's honour the Gods—quick!"

Ravidasan stared at the man for a moment, astonished. Abruptly, he dissolved into peals of ghostly laughter again. "Ha—ha—ha!" He gazed at Vandhiyathevan, still grinning. "What on earth are you playing at, *Thambi*?"

"Not at all, most revered elder brothers. This is no play but your past, come to haunt you in the most horrendous way possible. Hark, you—I fell asleep some time ago, when you both tied me up and left me most obligingly below-stairs. And … I had a dream. A huge demon rose and stood in front of me—blue, blue like the sea and sky combined. Words spilled out of its mouth—words that made no sense to me then … but they do now! Samudhra Rajan bade me deliver the lives of two Kali devotees well-versed in the magical arts—and if I failed, he will not let this ship pass. His celestial soul is not satisfied, see you, with the unworthy lives of six Arab ruffians; he craves more! Come, come quickly, you!" And Vandhiyathevan twirled his sword, raising it to the heavens.

Ravidasan and the Devaralan traded glances.

"You know, I've never seen your equal when it came to spinning fantastic tales, *Thambi*," Ravidasan shook his head, not without some admiration.

"You accuse me of spinning tales?" Vandhiyathevan demanded, outraged. "You refuse to credit me with the truth? Ah, that such a thing should come to pass—Samudhra Raja—Emperor of the Oceans!" he screamed suddenly, and turned towards the sea. "Answer these ignorant scoundrels yourself!"

Perhaps his vociferous demands to Samudhra Rajan had reached the hallowed ears of that celestial being; perhaps the Emperor of the Oceans decided that such an insistent call deserved to be answered.

***

A rather extraordinary scene unfolded then. The sea seemed to quiver in all four directions as far as their eyes could see, and—there was no other word for it—*bristled*. A thousand tiny waves rose and fell; miniature waves that rolled out perfectly in tune, everywhere. This lasted only a moment, though: the next instant, they had broken and subsided into frothy, foamy droplets. Ah, the sight of those white beads tumbling and glinting all over the massive surface of the sea seemed like dainty, little *thumbai* flowers rollicking in a pleasant breeze all over a vast, grassy plain—such was its quicksilver beauty, now catching the eye; disappearing the next. Such a scene did the sea present, at this moment.

Then, a slow, pleasant breeze—cool and inviting—arose, caressed the vessel for a moment, and faded away. The ship seemed to quiver in ecstasy, as did Vandhiyathevan's tired body, wracked by heat and dehydration.

"Ha—ha!" Ravidasan and the Devaralan roared with laughter.

"Why, it seems the Lord of the Oceans wished to answer you Himself, *Thambi*," Ravidasan chuckled in great good humour. "Almost you make us believe that we ought to prepare ourselves for a divine sacrifice!"

Vandhiyathevan's heart, however, was in turmoil. That sudden, minute shiver in the sea and its subsequent change had rather shaken him.

Why, what on earth had happened to the thousand white waves, and the frothy flecks of foam that followed? Where had they disappeared? Like magic, they had vanished into thin air—and now the sea lay calm again like a flat, alluring emerald plate. Had those waves been real—or just a figment of his tortured imagination? Wait—was this all the work of Ravidasan, perhaps? Had he produced some sort of marvelous spell and made the ocean shift?

"Would you look at that, *Thambi*?" The *mandhiravadhi* flung a hand towards the southwest. "Even the sky would seem to agree with the sea."

Where he pointed—at the exact point the emerald sea and azure sky met and mingled as one—rose a small, nay, almost miniscule fluff of a black cloud about the span of a hand. Most astonishing was the top of this black cloud, which was anointed with red—a glowing, blazing red that took everyone aback.

It is highly doubtful if Vandhiyathevan would have even noticed such a thing at any other time—of what conceivable interest could a black cloud be? Clouds, upon the horizon! There was nothing to surprise one in these things, after all. But now—even such a minor occurrence as this served to fret our hero.

Vandhiyathevan took hold of himself the next instant. *Not for anything*, he counseled himself, *must you fall for this petty magician's sleight of hand*. He steadied himself and stared pointedly at Ravidasan and the Devaralan. "No reason to tarry then," he said in a resolute voice, and twirled his sword again.

"We should like to pay our obeisance one last time to our patron goddess, *Appane*, before travelling to the next world," Ravidasan petitioned devoutly. "Grant us this last boon, I beg of you."

"As you please," Vandhiyathevan waved them away, grandiloquently. "Carry out whatever *prarthanai* you please and get back here. Don't waste your spells or magic arts on me, for they won't work!"

"Dare we, *Thambi*? Of course not," promised Ravidasan. "We're even leaving behind our weapons in good faith—look." True to their word, both men dropped their staff and sword respectively and made their way to another part of the ship.

Truth be told, Vandhiyathevan was badly in need of at least half a *naazhigai*'s respite now, for the changes happening upon both sea and in the sky were rapidly becoming a source of anxiety. His body was trembling a little with weakness. He had been prepared to despatch both men with a single stroke of his trusty sword—but doubted, rather, if his arms had the strength to accomplish such a thing. Their removal at this point was very welcome, as he steadied himself in both body and mind, preparing for the task at hand.

He gazed at the southwest corner of the sky again almost despite himself. The black cloud of miniscule dimensions just moments ago, had now grown in height. In addition, the red that had blazed at the top had dimmed a little. To the already concerned Vandhiyathevan, it seemed that the dark mass was rapidly increasing in size.

The wind that had died down after that one pleasant breeze now began to rise steadily; the sea lost its glassy, unnatural calm and began to stir. Small waves began to dance upon its restless surface.

The single cloud now seemed to have multiplied, spreading all over the sky.

The wind appeared to have picked up. The ship began a gentle, rocking motion.

His sharp ears, however, registered something amidst the wind's endless swishing and the ceaselessly murmuring waves—the sound of something falling into the sea.

Vandhiyathevan turned, but failed to see either Ravidasan or the Devaralan. This, he mused, was not surprising; they would likely be on the other side of the ship and the welter of masts, sails and the platform in the middle of the upper deck screened them from his eyes.

But—stay! His ears pricked up again—was that, or was that not the plash-plash of oars ...?

Vandhiyathevan dashed over to the opposite side of the ship at once, and peered down. The sight that met his eyes almost unmanned him. No suspicion of what was occurring now had ever crossed his mind; he had, in fact, been confident that magician and companion had simply made up a ruse to draw apart and discuss a strategy to reach, perhaps, a compromise with the Vaanar warrior.

But they had simply made their way to the other side, cut down the ropes that tethered a small boat to its side, sent it to the surface, and had clambered into it. Why—why, they were rowing away, at this very moment!

***

Ravidasan laughed out loud when he raised his head and caught sight of Vandhiyathevan's confounded expression. "You see, *Thambi*," he called out gleefully. "We have really no wish to sacrifice our glorious lives to Samudhra Rajan!"

In an instant, his predicament revealed itself to Vandhiyathevan. They were leaving—leaving him alone on that large vessel. As for him— Vallavarayan knew nothing about steering ships; the science was a sealed book to him. His knowledge of these large crafts—his present direction, possible sea-routes; the ways and means of operating the wheel to reach any destination—was non-existent. And now, these men were leaving him all alone to battle a choppy sea and an unknown ship—good God, they were *leaving* him …

"You—you scoundrels! Couldn't you have taken me with you?" He shrieked helplessly.

"Ah, do but consider the plight of Samudhra Rajan, *Thambi*," Ravidasan cackled. "So unfair to deprive him of even a single sacrifice, don't you think?"

Meanwhile, the boat bobbed further and further away, from the ship.

For a brief moment, a wild idea flashed across Vandhiyathevan's mind: could he possibly jump into the sea and reach the craft? The next instant, he discarded it. His swimming skills were not exactly accommodating of a dive into deep sea; he didn't even know if he *dared* to dive, let alone swim. And even if he should screw up his courage, flounder across and reach the boat— there was no saying what those scheming rogues might do. They had, after all, revealed to him their most dangerous secret— not to mention that they knew, now, that nothing would persuade him to join their cause. What was the guarantee that they might not try to belabour him with their oars? There was no way he could fight them, flailing all over the sea.

No, let them go—go and get lost! Far, far better to be all alone in this vast ship than in the company of those foul, murdering rogues in their small boat. Hadn't he walked out safe and unscathed from far more precarious situations? Such an escape might be possible this time too, and the good God might find a way to extricate him out of this toil.

And yet … had it been the right thing to let them flee? There was no saying where they might climb ashore, after all; as to what further schemes and plots they might spin, and whose downfall they might actively plan—no one knew. Well, those and other affairs were now, indeed, on the knees of the Gods for what could he, a puny human, hope to accomplish? But if he could only meet the prince again … *all said and done, he oughtn't to have left me alone that way—why couldn't he have taken me atop the elephant with Poonguzhali? I shall argue with him about that, when next I see him: "And are these the manners and morals of the ancient Chozha clan, your highness? To treat your friends thus …" But will I ever get such an opportunity again? To even catch a glimpse of him … well, why not? The Senathipathi and Azhwarkkadiyaan saw me get into his hobble, after all; couldn't they be depended on to mount a rescue? They'd have informed the prince of my plight, at the very least …*

Even as he was ruminating upon this, his eyes noted, rather dispassionately, that the boat had gone quite a fair distance upon the sea—too far, in fact. His eyes sharpened, and he wondered how they had accomplished this is in such a short time.

And then, realization struck him: it had not just been the boat; the ship had been moving away steadily as well—and hence the vast distance. Vandhiyathevan noticed something else: the size of the waves had increased—but was this all? No, no … why, why was a section of the sky darkening at midday?

Vandhiyathevan stared at the southwest. The black cloud that hadn't been more than a hand span had now grown monumentally, he noticed, and almost filled the entirety of the western sky. Not content with this, more were blotting out the blue in large, unruly patches; even as he watched, dark clouds scurried across the vast expanse, fairly swallowed the sun, hanging midway in the heavens. Now, both western and southern skies were darkening simultaneously; the sea reflected their somber grey-black, turning into a murky mass black as ink. Vandhiyathevan could no longer distinguish between either, for everywhere was just blackish, gloomy darkness.

Soon enough, that self-same darkness coalesced into roiling clouds that swam over Vandhiyathevan's head, descending swiftly into the eastern sky.

He turned towards where he'd last seen the boat, and made a discovery: it had vanished. Likely, it had moved beyond the horizon and therefore, his line of sight.

The wind's buzzing, which had been a low reverberation until now, suddenly swung into a roaring "*Ho!*" which drummed unpleasantly in his ears. The waves, now growing larger with every moment upon the choppy sea, added to the steadily growing clamour.

Sadapada—Sadapada! The ship's unfurled sails fluttered and flapped furiously against the mast in a vain bid to free themselves. Rafters and wooden beams rustled and rubbed against one another, unable to resist the steadily rising winds, sounding like a thousand doors banging open and shut all at once.

Peering at the madly twirling sails above, Vandhiyathevan guessed that the ship, far from moving in a certain direction, was corkscrewing round and round.

Ah, much had he heard about the famed whirlwinds upon the seas— well, this must be it, then, Vandhiyathevan gasped. He was about to experience one, firsthand.

It occurred to him, dimly, that a whirlwind wasn't really an ideal situation to have huge sails fluttering high above; he ought to unhook and wrap them up neatly. On the other hand, such a monumental task could hardly be accomplished by him alone—it needed at least ten or fifteen men, didn't it? Well, if not ten, four at least. Nothing could be done by him alone; no, he would have to trust to God and leave the ship to its fate.

Considering how quickly events escalated, Vandhiyathevan had no doubt, soon, what this was likely to be.

The ship would be pulled this way and that and finally, flounder in the treacherous waters and sink! And likely, it would splinter into smithereens before it did—but whatever this massive ship's untimely fate, there was never going to be any doubt about Vandhiyathevan's own.

Death in the high seas!

Drat that Kudanthai *jothidar*—wretched man hadn't even breathed a word about any of this. What sort of a stupid astrologer simply forgot to mention something as monumental as a whirlwind—*just you wait, you ruffian—just you wait until I get my hands on you—what absolute nonsense! I'm never going to see him again ...*

Vandhiyathevan jumped as a hard object struck his shoulder. He turned and saw something that made his eyes widen in astonishment: small pebbles were raining down all over the ship: *Sadapada—Sadapada!* They fell with stunning speed and in great quantities upon the deck; many dropped into the sea as well. But—why did they sparkle and gleam so?

Two or three more fell upon his head, back and shoulders. There was a sharp sense of hurt; then cold ... struck by an idea, Vandhiyathevan stared at the pebbles upon the deck. Wait—they were melting away—ah, these were chips of ice!

Never before had Vandhiyathevan seen a hailstorm; certainly never experienced the novelty of ice upon his body. A sort of euphoria filled him at that moment: ah, wasn't it fortunate that he'd managed to see something as unique as this before death claimed him!

He plunked himself down on the deck promptly, stretched out a hesitant hand, and felt one of the rapidly dissolving chunks of ice. It stung. He snatched his hand back, ecstatic. *Appappa*—how cold it was—and how it tingled when you touched it—like a flick of fire! But it didn't burn like flame and soon, the feeling of being scorched evaporated, leaving behind only a fascinating coolness.

The hailstorm stopped as abruptly as it had begun—indeed, it was doubtful if it could have lasted for more than a few minutes.

***

Then the rain began—of the common and garden variety—and Vandhiyathevan now had the opportunity to witness and marvel the consummate skill of the Chozha naval artisans who had designed and built a ship such as this: no matter the deluge upon the decks, or the waves crashing over the ship, it all slithered down and back to the sea; there was no way of sinking this vessel unless the decks below were ruined, and water entered.

This last thought made him take heart a little—and reminded him of something, as well. Should the cabin below deck, where he'd lain tied up be open, water might pour in and present a very real threat. He scrambled downstairs the moment this thought occurred and entered the cabin, to find his worst fears confirmed—the door was wide open, and banging in the wind, to boot. Thankfully, it was still not too late; he shut it tight, locked and latched it for good measure.

It occurred to him then, that if the wind and rain grew to unbearable proportions above, he could seek refuge in this room, barricade himself against the elements, and then trust his fate to God. For a moment, he pitied the lunatics that had actually left the safety of this ship and taken to their heels in a petty boat. On the other hand, that little craft was no ordinary one either; it was a hardy little thing, designed to withstand gales and hurricanes; it would take a great deal to render it useless. And even if, by some unforeseen circumstance, the boat did smash, those within could easily save themselves by holding on to the planks lashed to the sides of the boat for this very eventuality. Those deadly assassins might easily climb ashore and make their escape—likely in the vicinity of Kodikkarai, even …

From that little port to Pazhaiyarai was a mental leap easily accomplished, and Vandhiyathevan found himself wondering about the lovely princess in residence there. Would the Chakravarthy's beloved daughter know the fate that had befallen him? Ah, but how would she, indeed? Who would inform her of the hapless warrior who had met death in the high seas, all in a vain effort to carry out her task? The sea, perhaps? Or even these winds? *Oh God, oh God, why couldn't I have died before I met her, that maatharasi, that epitome of exquisite womanhood? Why couldn't glorious death on a battlefield have been my fate? To die now, and this way—is to have a taste of heavenly bliss, and then be pushed into the roaring, scorching inferno of the netherworld ...!*

The wind's speed was rising to gale proportions; the sea heaved and sank, its aggression growing steadily. The ship's sails fluttered and rustled madly, mimicking the insane gyrations of ghouls and ghosts in a lost world.

Darkness now surrounded the sea—and it seemed as though the gloom was even blacker than pitch. Could there ever be black that was darker than even, well ... blackness? Such a thing ought not to be possible but somehow, it seemed to be happening, now.

Lightning lit up the sky in a jagged line.

The darkness that followed this brief flash seemed even terrible than before; darker than the darkest pitch.

Thunder followed lightning; crashing across the heavens, reverberating through the sky and sea in a way that made the ship, water and the very directions throb in an uneasy beat.

Another flash of lightning! This one tore through the sky from end to end, stretching its ready claws, tearing through the sky, branching in every direction, sending out tendrils of light that transformed the heavens and ocean into a magical world lit with leaping curls of fire—and disappeared the next instant.

Thunder followed. *Ammamma*! Could there be any doubt that all the worlds in the universe were crashing down, drowning the earth in their everlasting din?

Lightning flashed again; thunder roared. Ah, how was it, Vandhiyathevan wondered, that the skies had not smashed into smithereens and fallen upon his hapless head?

His wish was granted, it seemed; the heavens cracked and with an almighty heave, shattered.

A deluge—the kind that destroyed whole worlds—fell through.

Indeed, this could not be called rain; rather, a veritable ocean ought to have been churning and roaring above the clouds; now that the sky had broken, it was simply pouring through the crack. At least, that was how it seemed.

Huge waves tossed the ship every which way. To his horrified eyes, mountains seemed to rise all around the vessel; a brilliant flash of lightning showed them heaving and swaying in a mad, mad dance lasting through the aeons.

The wind touched heights of fury; Vayu Bhagavan seemed to have transformed into a whirling dervish, uprooting and flinging whole peaks of water down into hell one moment; up heaven the next. And some of those selfsame mountains also crashed upon Vandhiyathevan's ship.

Rain thundered down from above; the sea hauled and crashed walls of water around him—and as for the sails, words cannot describe the agony of those fluttering, frail scraps upon the masts. The miracle, however, was the Chozha vessel itself—righting after a particularly murderous wave, screaming wind, or ravenous rain. Against all these attacks it stood; still it bobbed and corkscrewed madly; fragile, but valiant.

But there was a limit to battle, of course; a limit to protest, to withstand the greatest powers on earth, to fight against the five great demons that empowered earth—no, no, soon, this ship was bound to crack, to break, to splinter into pieces, to give up against the elements and so too, would Vandhiyathevan, going down with the ship.

But now, there was a subtle shift in his perspective: now, he felt no distress. There was no sadness, no grief—for the death that met him now, the end that stared him in the face would be magnificent, unrivalled by any that man had ever seen.

His heart leapt and sang, bounding with the humongous waves that climbed and crashed the seas. His spirit soared; abruptly, his laughter rang out. "Ha-ha-ha!" roared Vandhiyathevan; his uproarious mirth competing with the screaming gale; the thunderous sea-waves and rumbling, reverberating thunder.

Why, was it not for this—was it not to see and revel in nature's awe-inspiring performance had he lashed himself securely to the lowest part of the mast, under the sails?

The ship spun in the churning seas; the masts spun and so did he.

There was no saying how long they had all been whirling together like this: sea, ship, masts and Vandhiyathevan—it could have been as long as several aeons, or short as just a handful of moments. Vandhiyathevan himself, was now far beyond the time and space of mere mortals; he had ascended to a fantastic plane of existence, the abode of the Gods itself, where nothing of the earth could touch him, anymore. Or so it felt.

The wind dropped; even the torrential rain seemed to seek some relief, and mellowed to a drizzle.

Lightning and thunder stopped; the sea seemed a brackish murk of black pitch.

For at least a while Vandhiyathevan had screwed his eyes shut against the flickering, dazzling lightning, and covered his ears to protect them from the roaring, blasting thunder. Now, he opened his eyes, and released his ears from the protection of his palms.

Aha—have I really escaped the horrors of a whirlwind? Have I truly made it alive out of this disaster? Has God truly seen fit to save me? Then— then shall I have the great good fortune of meeting the lovely princess of Pazhaiyarai again in this birth? And the prince—shall I meet him again, partake in all his adventures ...

Wait, no, let's not get ahead of ourselves, he thought, prudently. *There's no saying where this ship might be, at this moment—and where's the assurance that it will even reach shore safe? And even if it should, by some unnatural chance reach shore, there's no guarantee that mine will be a similar, secure fate ...*

Who knew the perils that still awaited him?

It was as though nature wished to answer his question right away: a jagged flash of lightning lit up the sky, its dazzling brilliance searing his eyes with the ferocity of a hundred suns. Before now, he could have boasted of feeling his way through the darkness, but this blinding incandescence made any sight impossible. For a moment he was terrified, wondering if the lightning had snatched his eyesight, and screwed his burning eyes shut.

His ears came under assault, the next instant.

Vandhiyathevan had experienced thunder in plenty before this; why, he had heard much this very night—but the crash now, this almighty roar! *Che*, was it even thunder? He hadn't heard anything like this at all so far—this was not thunder; this was Indiran's *vajrayudham* itself, ploughing into his very brain through sensitive ears and reverberating unpleasantly.

He couldn't open his eyes for a while; as for his ears, an incessant whining noise—"*Oi!*" kept thrumming endlessly, making it impossible to even hear anything.

But then—there was something else, something new—a light of some sort that pierced even closed lids. And he could finally hear something past the whining in his ears—something very peculiar. The sound of forest wildfires, trees burning and crackling …

Vandhiyathevan's eyes snapped open in horror. High above, the masts of his ship had caught fire.

Aha … now he understood why that flash of lightning had been so dazzlingly bright—why that last clap of thunder had been particularly deafening …

Thunder must have struck either the ship, or somewhere very close—which explained why the mast had burst into flames …

Two out of the five elements had tried, so far, to destroy that Chozha ship; wind and rain had done their damndest and failed. Now, it seemed that another divine element had arrived to try its hand.

Agni Bhagavan, God of fire, had come to take the place of Varunan and Vayu.

52

THE WRECKED BOAT

Vandhiyathevan realized one fact with absolute certainty, the moment the top of the mast caught fire: this ship would not survive. And if it was doomed—then so was he.

For some very strange reason, however, this prospect did not overpower him at all; his heart felt light and his spirits soared. His laughter rang out with enthusiasm and in a swift stroke, he untied the ropes that had bound him, hitherto, with the mast. What was the point in being roasted alive in a raging inferno? One might as well sink into the cool waters of the sea to its very depths and there, give up life in the most peaceful fashion.

With this in mind, he decided that his last few hours were not to be spent mourning over circumstances he could not change; rather, he sought to fill his hungering eyes and heart with the wild, tumultuous beauty of the raging sea, in the dazzling light of the burning mast. It wouldn't be a bad idea, it occurred to him, to take a good, long look at his final resting place. Hadn't he heard spine-chilling stories about the ghosts of people who'd met a gory end before their time, circling the place of their death? Would *his* spirit float above these very waters, long after his demise? Would he glide with the breeze, or hover above the waves? Or would his hapless ghost swirl and twirl with the whirlwinds lashing at the sea?

Aha, someday, perhaps, the princess of his dreams might sail along these very oceans upon a ship. Her sailors would point out this spot and murmur: "This was where Vandhiyathevan met his end, your highness," and then—ah! Tears, like translucent pearls would spill from those exquisitely beautiful eyes, long and piercing like lances and roll down her face, dazzling as the full moon. And if he should happen to see her misery, hovering about as a spirit, would he be able to wipe them away?

The ship climbed laboriously upon a mountain of a wave; Vandhiyathevan could see for a great distance, in the burning brilliance of the mast's fire. The sea, writhing like a monster, looked like a vast slab of black marble—but where the light touched it, the surface turned to molten gold. However, there was no time for him to admire and exult in this, nature's spectacle—for something else caught and held his attention.

A ship, in the distance. A ship—sporting a tiger flag.

Good God in heaven, is there no end to your divine miracles! There could be no doubt that Arulmozhi Varmar was upon that ship … and a small voice whispered into his heart: *He's come in search of you.*

***

Parthibendran's ship had found itself in the same dire straits as Vandhiyathevan's own, courtesy the whirlwinds—but unlike the latter, the former was well-stocked with experienced sailors and seaworthy men; men who knew the characteristics of a temperamental gale extremely well, and were more than capable of dealing with its vagaries. Within moments, the sails were furled and brought down; the wheel was manipulated expertly, so that the ship need not battle the considerable winds with all its might. The vessel would ascend huge peaks on one hand, making those within think they were about to topple over; the next second, it would right itself, somehow.

No matter the force of those huge, thundering waves; no matter the endless battering and smashing waters—did the boards and planks budge? Not a smidgeon! The Lord of the Oceans picked up and tossed the little ship in his massive hands like a ball; the whirlwind spun the ship like a tiny top, twirling this way and that. A veritable cataract poured from the skies, trying its very best to drown the vessel. But none of nature's very formidable forces could beat that ship, designed by the cream of Chozha artisans—and manned by the Chozha naval elite; not a dent could they make in its well-stocked armour.

"I have seen and battled far, far worse, your highness," assured the Kalapathi. "Whirlwinds a thousand times more ferocious and *sandamaruthams* that would beat this one to flinders!" There *was* one factor which worried him though—and this, he confided to the prince and Parthibendran.

Dark, gloomy clouds had scurried over the sky, plunging them all into pitch blackness; rain poured down, determined to flood the whole world, it seemed, not to mention the sea, which rose in massive waves that heaved and danced, shutting out what little light remained with watery curtains. This lack of sight meant a very dangerous situation: the ship they were hunting was likely in the same position—even in close proximity, perhaps ... but they might never catch sight of it. The other ship might well be corkscrewing just like their own; should the two crash into each other, both would splinter into smithereens and sink! As for the fate of those aboard ...

"Now you see what I fear the most, Sire," explained the Kalapathi. "Not the whirlwind or the sea or even the rain—but pitch darkness which destroys vision completely."

The captain's concern was not exactly unknown to the prince, who placed himself in sentry position in a corner of the ship, standing rigidly in the tearing wind and stinging rain, braving all the elements. His piercing eyes stared through the darkness, taking desperate advantage of each brief flash of lightning. As for his heart ... words cannot describe the incredible turmoil that churned within, laying it open to all sorts of fears.

His beloved sister's confidential envoy was even now in the hands of rogue Arabs and a murderous *mandhiravadhi* and as if all this was not enough, a treacherous whirlwind had been added to an already volatile situation. What if—what if the ship carrying the brave Vaanar warrior was never to be found? And even if, by supreme good fortune, it was, there could be no guarantee that the man himself might be alive—what if the Kalapathi's worst fears were realized and the two ships collided? That would be hilarious, wouldn't it, if both sank without a trace—no, wait, who on earth could deliver a certain important message to the Emperor? Well-nigh impossible to trust Parthibendran with the task; the prince could not consider him worthy of the undertaking and even if it came to that, as a last resort, the Pallava scion would likely mock it. Certainly, there was no saying that he might take such a mission seriously.

The prince felt his spirits sink a little. Thus far, no enterprise of his had ever failed; would this be the first? No, no—certainly not: Samudhra Rajan would not—*could* not stand by and watch Ponni's beloved son suffer defeat, subject to evil plots of enemies, or even nature's malicious machinations.

He'd been peering through the gloom all this while, staring into the darkness resolutely, ignoring the brief flashes of lightning—but even he had to screw his eyes shut against this, the latest and most brilliant jagged line that cut across the sky. His eardrums protested the harsh, deafening roar of thunder ... but when he opened his eyes again, it was to light—a new source of light that owed nothing to lightning. And then, his eyes widened.

For he saw a ship—a ship, its sails unfurled fully, dancing wildly amidst the mountainous waves!

The top of its mast had caught fire and in its raging, flickering light, the prince caught sight of a man standing close by. Good God—could such miracles even occur? For he had no doubt that it was Vandhiyathevan himself, in the flesh, the brave, brave warrior ... but wait, why was he alone? Where were the others? But no, now was not the time to waste wondering about such things.

The prince knew his next course of action in an instant.

Not unnaturally, others had seen everything as well and set up shouts. "There—look!" Their raucous yells made themselves heard over even the roaring thunder.

The prince strode towards one of the small boats lashed to the sides of the ship, and turned purposefully towards the sailors. "Which of you will come with me?" He asked in a firm, loud tone.

His intentions burst upon the awareness of those who stood near; stunned dismay and alarm were writ large on many faces. Despite these emotions, many fell over themselves, eager to assist in his quest.

"What sort of madness is this, your highness?" Parthibendran and the Kalapathi hurried forward, remonstrating with him. "What are the odds of sailing a little boat upon these murderous waves—and even if you found a way to steer it, how could you hope to save a man from a burning ship? True, one cannot help but try," Parthibendran changed tack, once he took a look at the prince's grim face. "And should this really be your wish, Sire, there are others, much better qualified; you need not be the one to go—" He paused suddenly.

"Never, *never* shall I forgive those who try to stop me at this time," Ponniyin Selvar fairly hissed. "Is that quite understood?" His authoritative voice cut through the deck like whiplash. He drew himself up to his full height; his audience was in no doubt that they stood in the presence of a prince, descended from an ancient race of emperors. "No more than two men, thank you," he assured, cutting the ropes and freeing the craft in an instant.

***

The boat dropped into the ocean; the prince and two men gauged the depth, and jumped in.

The small craft bobbed away from the ship within a matter of moments, dancing and spinning like a mad, mad cork; the prince and his cohorts had the devil's own work to do, paddling and plying the oars with all their strength.

Inch by inch, it seemed, the boat crept towards the burning ship. By now, the fire had steadily burnt down to the middle of the mast—but Vandhiyathevan stayed exactly where he was.

The bright glare of fire meant that he'd seen the approaching ship; seen the boat drop down to sea ... but such was his astonishment at the sight that he'd simply stayed rooted to the spot, stunned. It hadn't even occurred to him that some action was required now, on his part.

"Jump!" screamed the prince, from below. "Jump into the sea!"

Not a sound registered in Vandhiyathevan's ears; he stood like one turned to stone, amazed and perplexed.

No, there was no time to be wasted. The fire was shredding the ship with its toxic fingers with unimaginable speed; soon, it would reach the lower decks and that would be it. It would sink. And then, there could be no hope of saving Vandhiyathevan.

Once again, the prince came to a decision about his course of action within a moment; he unwound the rope lashed to the side of the lifeboat just for such an eventuality, and tied one end firmly around his waist. A word of swift warning to the two sailors and he jumped into the sea.

The waves that had hitherto tossed the boat around like a plaything, now decided to extend the same courtesy to the prince—and yet, for all their cruel play, for all their wretched flips that raised him to heaven and dropped him to the netherworlds, the ilango swam resolutely towards the ship, never losing sight of it for even an instant, and certainly without straying off-course.

Then there came a wave—bigger than all that he had seen so far; the size of a mammoth; no, several mammoths, looming terrifyingly, like a giant about to fling him down, down to the very depths of the ocean; the prince certainly could not have survived a fall such as that—but no, the wave seemed to possess an instinct for benevolence; a most compassionate wave, this one, for it swept him up, bore him on its head and deposited him neatly onto the upper deck of the burning ship.

Vandhiyathevan, already engaged in untying the ropes that bound him, caught sight of the bedraggled figure flung into the vessel. *The prince*, his mind whispered to him, amazed. "*Oh!*" He shrieked, and bounded forward to help him up.

The prince saw his chance and flung his hands around the other man's neck in a crushing embrace. "Just hold onto me and walk," he whispered hurriedly into Vandhiyathevan's ears. "Whatever you do—don't let go!"

The next instant, they'd jumped off the ship, into the sea—and were promptly buffeted by the waves.

The sailors stopped rowing and began to reel in the rope frantically.

The prince—and Vandhiyathevan, who'd stuck to him like a limpet— began to inch towards the boat.

It was no easy task to clamber into the craft amidst such heaving, choppy waves—especially with Vandhiyathevan firmly hanging on to his shoulders; every minute seemed like an aeon.

It would seem like the boat was within reach for a moment; the next, it was whisked away, and they were left to be engulfed by the merciless sea.

In the end, another compassionate wave decided that the two puny humans had suffered enough; took matters into its own watery hands and gathered them into its arms. They rode upon it and with the help of the sailors, fairly fell into the boat.

"Row quickly," the prince gasped. "*Now!*"

There was reason enough for his order; the burning ship was about to sink, and the resultant churning might well upend the frail boat back into the frothing sea. And this was not all: with the ship down, the flames would be extinguished, making it impossible for them to navigate their way towards the other ship.

Aha—there! The Arab ship had begun to submerge ... and how bewitchingly beautiful was the sight of that huge vessel descending gradually into the vast, black sea, its masts burning merrily right to the end?

Not that those on the boat had much leisure to observe and relish that breath-taking sight ... for the sea began to heave and toss to the very skies as the ship sank, transforming the waters into a roiling, frothing mass—exactly as the prince had predicted.

Surprisingly, the fragile little boat managed to right itself; a testament to the consummate skills of Chozha craftsmen—but now, they were beset by another, worrying problem: the sinking of the burning ship had extinguished all light; they could no longer pin-point the location of the other ship. Visibility was non-existent; none of them had the faintest idea about their position, or direction.

Were they approaching the ship? Or drifting further and further away? There was no way of divining either possibility.

Both were dangerous, of course.

Were they in close proximity, larger vessel and smaller craft would collide and there could be no doubt about the outcome of that eventuality.

As for drifting away—why, what on earth could such a small boat accomplish, bobbing helplessly, endlessly, in the black, black sea, with no means of navigation?

Ah, Samudhra Raja, Lord of the Oceans! You and you alone can save the beloved son of your adored, cherished River Ponni!

***

The many vagaries of Vayu Bhagavan, most illustrious Lord of the Winds are indistinguishable indeed, and astonishing—for those whirlwinds ceased just as abruptly and surprisingly as they had burst upon the sea. The devastation left in their perilous wake, though—that was something else altogether.

The gale-force winds might have dropped, but the lesser said of the churning seas the better, for the waters do not subside easily, often choppy for a day and a night—and the effects of such a massive upheaval is usually felt for long distances. Kodikkarai itself would prove no exception; its long, sandy beaches would be swamped by the sea; Nagappattinam's famed harbour will likely be pounded relentlessly by a furious, wrathful sea, waves the height of palm-trees, and even ports as far as Kangesan *Thurai* and Thirikonamalai would be affected. Not even Maathottam and Rameswaram would escape the fury of a whirlwind.

Meanwhile, the boat on which the prince and his men huddled bobbed upon the sea, buffeted by the waves. Soon after, the sailors stopped rowing for frankly, there didn't seem to be any point—who knew the position of the ship, after all? Where would they go?

The wind had dropped completely; rain had ceased to deluge them long since; even lightning had stopped assaulting their sight; thunder had died away.

And yet ... the waves remained furious and massive. Their anger seemed not to have abated one jot; the boat weaved, tossed and turned.

But now, something else was approaching them swiftly—a hitherto unknown danger. There, it was almost upon them!

Remember the burning ship that sank? Well, one of the masts that had not quite been reduced to cinders broke away from the vessel, and began to drift upon the sea. Closer and closer to the boat it bobbed—and no one aboard noticed; it was pitch dark, after all.

"Oars!" It was no surprise that the prince caught sight of it first, and registered the peril. "Row now—row quickly!" He screamed.

The breeze drew his words away; the half-burnt mast smashed underneath just as he stopped.

Padaar! The boat splintered within moments. It broke into two first, and then, into smaller planks; the mast completely disintegrating the craft.

"Fear not, my friend!" The prince raised his voice. "That mast is a far safer bet than the boat's planks. Grab hold of it—and *don't let go!*"

౧௯

53

SONG OF A SAVIOUR

The party at the mouth of the Thondaiman River stood watching as prince Arulmozhi Varmar was rowed in the small boat, right until he climbed aboard Parthibendran's ship. Once its precious cargo was safely delivered into the hands of the Pallava scion, the craft turned around at once.

That Senathipathi Boodhi Vikrama Kesari was in fine fettle was patently obvious, from his thrilled expression. "Ah, there can be no doubt that the good God is on our side. After all, the divine signs of the conch and discus on the prince's blessed palms—could they possibly let us down?" He rubbed his hands in delight. "Parthibendran shall deliver him safe to Kanchi; I may rest assured of that. Now," mumbled Kodumbalur Velaar to himself—although in an audible tone certainly meant to reach others—about his plan of action. "All that needs to be done is take myself and my armies back to Thanjai ..." His gaze fell upon Azhwarkkadiyaan and he jumped a little. "Still here, are you? Well, that matters little, I suppose; there can be nothing that the Chief Minister's most confidential aide cannot know ..." his voice trailed away. "And what of your own plans, Vaishnavite? Will you be joining my train to Maathottam?"

"I'm afraid I must decline your offer, *Ayya*; I have yet to perform one other commission kindly entrusted to me by the Mudhanmandhiri."

"And what might that be, *Appane*?"

Azhwarkkadiyaan directed a thoughtful glance at Poonguzhali and Oomai Rani, standing a little apart.

"Something to do with those women?" hazarded the commander.

"One of them, certainly," Azhwarkkadiyaan admitted. "If I ever stumbled across a certain mute woman in Ilankai, it was my master's command to bring her hotfoot to Thanjavur by any means possible."

"Upon my word, Vaishnavite—! He might as well have ordered you to stuff a whirlwind inside a pot and deliver it to the capital; getting hold of that speechless woman will certainly prove to be impossible. No idea who she is, of course—although she certainly seems to cherish a wonderful regard for our prince," the commander paused, and eyed the spy. "You wouldn't happen to know anything about her, would you?"

"Only that she has been mute and deaf from birth, and that stuffing a whirlwind into a pot would be great deal easier than trying to bring her to Thanjai. And yet—my master's wishes are paramount and I shall have to do the best I can."

"As for this boat-girl ... she and that woman seem to be on excellent terms; witness their silent communication! And that reminds me: get her here, will you? There is a warning I ought to deliver ..."

Azhwarkkadiyaan departed at once, and made known the Senathipathi's command to the young girl. Poonguzhali left Oomai Rani's side and walked towards the older man.

"Now look here, my girl," the Senathipathi began, portentously. "There is no doubt that you have your wits about you; you brought us valuable news in the nick of time, and have been of immense service to the Chozha dynasty. Never let it be said that I forgot such loyalty as yours; rest assured that I shall confer a fitting reward when the time is right."

"My thanks, *Ayya*," Poonguzhali answered politely. "But I require no repayment."

"Ah, let me not have these coy refusals, girl. Just you wait until affairs have settled down somewhat, and then—then ... well, I shall bestow a warrior among Chozha warriors upon you in marriage! He certainly ought to be a champion; a very giant of a Bheemasenan at any rate, who can curb your exuberant spirits—else you will lead him a very pretty dance, won't you, girl?" And the commander grinned, pleased at his own wit, and his masterful reading of her character.

Poonguzhali made sure to keep her face lowered; had she met his glance, the wrath that churned her heart would have been obvious in her sparkling, glinting eyes—but she chose not to reveal her feelings. There was no point in wrangling with this rogue of an old man, after all; she stayed silent, curbing her tongue and mind.

"Now, to come to something important: I warn you young woman— do not imagine that your signal service might have some claim on the prince, or that you have a right to his affections," the commander's iron voice was coarse with severity. "Reserve your nets for fish in the sea, do you hear me? Indulge the slightest hope of reeling in the prince on one of your fishing expeditions ... and you will regret it. Careful, girl, and keep away. Should you try to approach him in the slightest, the consequences will be ... dire."

Each of these words seared Poonguzhali's ears like molten drops of lead. Her lips quivered with the need to fling a vicious rebuttal at his every accusation—but the words died upon her tongue. A lump rose in her throat making speech impossible; the molten lead in her heart made its way somehow to her eyes, transforming into hot, stinging tears that trembled upon the lids, making them burn.

She turned without raising her head, and began to walk in a direction opposite the sea. Her gait, slow and unsteady at first, gained momentum. She darted a glance at Oomai Rani; Azhwarkkadiyaan stood beside her, trying to impress something upon the mute lady and abruptly, it occurred to Poonguzhali that she detested humans. Her legs refused to stand even a moment in the presence of these horrible beings; she could not stomach a human voice—ah! Cruel, hateful things; how could they speak so—utter such awful words? How wonderful it would be if every single human also happened to be mute?

She plunged through the forest for a while and appeared, finally, on the banks of the Thondaiman River, following the river further inland. Her instincts tracked a route unerringly, towards her boat; yes, she must reach it soon—soon, and get into it; climb into her beloved boat and paddle out to sea all alone—row right out to the open, where she could hear human voices no more. And then she would rest her oars. Cradled by the sea, her faithful boat would bob further and further—and so would she. On and on she would drift in the endless waters and find solace, perhaps, in its vast emptiness; receive some balm for her wounded, churning heart upon the lap of the one she had known all her life—her best and most understanding of friends; the ocean. And then, perhaps, the searing ache of the Senathipathi's pitiless words might ease; her flaming anger might abate somewhat, and tranquility restored.

Ah, what was it that that wretched old ruffian said? Something about reserving my nets for fish ... "Don't dream of reeling in the prince on one of your fishing expeditions!"

Chee, dreadful, terrible rogue, to insinuate that *I* could fish—that I could even dream of—how could he? *How could he*? Was I trying to draw the prince in—good God, fish in the sea are far, far worthier creatures than petty humans on land; they do not spend their time speaking such treacherous words; rather, their lives are spent swimming contentedly in the depths of the ocean. They worry about nothing and care for no one. Neither sorrow nor anxiety is part of their lives. Ah, why couldn't I have been born one, swimming at leisure where and when I chose! I needn't experience the grief, hatred, desires and deep dislikes, anger, frustration and despair of this human world, but may swim lazily, uncaring and unconcerned, enjoying nothing but the deep sea. There would be no one to speak of me and the prince this way—no one to separate us by dark and devious means; no one to spill such malicious threats, such poison into the ears of others ... no, no! There was no saying that it might be so; these petty, vindictive idiots might trawl the sea and reel us in their nets—or even worse, trap just one and leave the other—those wretched scoundrels ...!

Turmoil churning her heart like a rumbling volcano spurred her legs into action; such was her speed that she reached her boat by the time the sun rode high in the sky and thank the heavens; it lay exactly where she had left it. That little boat was her dearest friend; her sole refuge; the only, tiny space that afforded her relief and happiness in a malicious world filled with deep sorrow and betrayal. It was her great good fortune, she supposed, that no one had tried to steal it away.

Nothing mattered now; in fact, the whole world might just go to hell with her great goodwill. That old bat of a Senathipathi might guard the prince like a demon hoarding treasure; Arulmozhi Varmar might wed that precious Kodumbalur cat as he pleased—what did it matter? *What does all this have to do with me, anyway? I have everything I need: my beloved boat; my precious oars; strength in my hands to ply it and best of all, this vast, endless sea—I can go where I please. Ah, Samudhra Raja, Lord of the Oceans—you'll never let your precious daughter down, no matter who else does, will you? You won't let the prince's own name for me, the best of them all—Daughter of the Oceans—rot to nothing, will you?*

Poonguzhali climbed into her boat and began to paddle in the direction of the ocean; following the river's current made her task easy, for she reached the mouth of the Thondaiman River soon, and was out in the open sea in no time at all.

Years of experience in reading the weather now stood her in good stead; nowhere was she more at home than at sea—and her senses now foretold a whirlwind. She had no difficulty in gauging the winds and sky; the moon had been shrouded by an ash-coloured halo the night before and the day had been sweltering hot. Not a leaf had quivered on trees and—there! Dark, roiling clouds had begun to gather in the southwest; a cyclone was certainly in the offing. The sea would be a marvelous mass of seething, heaving fury—but it wouldn't augur well to be caught on it during one. She'd do far better to row to Bhoodha Theevu, where she could beach her boat and enjoy Samudhra Rajan's outrageous tantrum to the fullest. Once the furious winds had died down, and the ocean had ceased to tumble and churn, she could row over to Kodikkarai. Ah, surely there was no need to hurry; that ship would have reached the tiny port by now. A relief indeed, to know that it wouldn't have stayed, to be caught in the approaching whirlwind. The prince ought to have disembarked at Kodikkarai, or even Maamallapuram, if he so pleased. *Chee*, what did his destination matter, after all? He would have escaped this blasted hurricane, and that was the important issue.

She had no inkling of the true state of affairs; that the ships, despite fully unfurled sails had not moved an inch, as the wind had dropped completely. She was not to know, therefore, that they had not reached their destination.

Do not dare to reel in the prince … The Senathipathi's cruel words tormented her wretched heart often; it might not be a bad idea, she decided, if she didn't go to Kodikkarai just then. Her mind was made up about her own destination: Bhoodha Theevu it would be, where she would take her ease, enjoy the wonderful, breathtaking fury of the whirlwind and leave at leisure. As the island lay not so very far from the Thondaiman River, she reached its shores within a *naazhigai*—and in the nick of time, to boot: the hurricane began its reign just as she leapt onto the beach.

She dragged her boat onto land, upended and secured it with rope against a tree, and retreated to the safety of a small *stupam* on the island, hunkering down in a cavernous, underground room to wait out the wind and stormy rain. Not that she could stay there for long: Vayu Bhagavan's glorious, reckless play drew her like a magnet; she crawled out and climbed the steps to the top of the *stupam*.

Her surroundings, she thought, echoed her heart's tumult to a nicety. She could see around her to a great distance and observed, with satisfaction, that the numerous coconut trees around were heaving and tossing with abandon, like the *boodha ganams* dancing around Siva Peruman in his incarnation as the Samhara Moorthy, Lord of Destruction, wreaking the end of the world. Waves rose as high as those trees, resembling the snowy heights of the Imayam, and broke down into hundreds of thousands of foam-flecked droplets. The rousing, shrieking winds that tore through the skies; the scores of trees that rustled and rasped in those self-same winds and the roar of the heaving seas, not to mention the deafening peals of thunder, made it seem like the very cosmos was crumbling, ripped apart by forces beyond control; the world was tumbling down around her. Jagged shards of lightning torched pitch-black skies at intervals, branching off here and there, throwing the seething seas and madly waving trees into relief—and vanished, plunging the world once more into darkness.

Poonguzhali stood rooted to the spot for what seemed like hours. Her body swayed and danced like the trees around her, seized as though by insanity; her long, luxurious locks ripped free of their braids and flew about her lovely face; the rain drenched her lithe figure; thunder deafened her ears and lightning nearly blinded her eyes. She heeded them not and continued to stand like a rock, feeling the rain and wind batter her. Nature, it seemed, was simply giving form to the frustration and hapless fury that raged in her own heart; she grinned, very sure that the skies and seas had put on this abandoned, reckless display for her sole entertainment, and was determined to wring every single drop of enjoyment from their inspired performance.

Thoughts of Prince Arulmozhi Varmar could not but intrude; she mused that he'd have certainly reached Kodikkarai by now and was safely ashore; he might even have decided to stay in her own parents' home. Or the elaborate royal palace in the port of Nagapattinam, perhaps.

But—could he have stayed on board the ship? On the sea? Well, and what if he had? What could all of nature's forces do to a marvelous, massive vessel such as his? No whirlwind could touch it; there were hordes of men around him too, eager to defend his person. What had he to do with her—why must she intrude upon his thoughts? Would he ever bend his mind towards her, wondering where that silly young woman Poonguzhali was, at this moment? No, he certainly wouldn't. Likely, he'd spend his time worrying about Vandhiyathevan, sent by his sister. And that precious Kodumbalur queen-in-waiting, probably. Yes, that was very possible. There was no reason to expect him to indulge in even a moment's reflection about a poor little *karaiyar* girl. Why indeed?

She stayed atop the *stupam* for hours that night, giving herself up to the complete enjoyment of the whirlwind's mad, mad dance, descending to the cavern at the base only much later for some desperately needed sleep. Not that her slumber was peaceful; vague, chaotic dreams insisted on invading her subconscious; once, she even dreamt that she tossed a net into the sea, capturing the prince himself. Another time, she and the prince had transformed into fishes, swimming side by side in the ocean— and she awoke, each time, wondering at the insanity of her own mind that conjured up such impossible eventualities. "This is sheer madness," she murmured to herself, and tried to wipe away their remnants, clearing them away for sleep.

By the time she woke up fully, day had broken. The whirlwind had ceased to torment sea and land: both lightning and thunder had died down; so had the rain, more or less. She strolled towards the beach and noticed that the waves were no longer as high as the evening before—but the sea did remain choppy. The bright, unforgiving light of day showed clearly the havoc wreaked upon the island; in every direction could be seen trees entirely uprooted or, in the case of old gnarly giants, crowns bowed down, almost to the ground.

Even as she stood there, drinking all this in, her sharp eyes caught sight of something entirely unexpected: a catamaran—or what looked like one—bobbing on the sea. Buffeted this way and that by playful waves, it managed to stumble onto the shore, finally—and it was then that Poonguzhali noticed the man within.

She leapt across the sand to him like a hare, and discovered that he was almost at the end of his tether, hanging onto life by a thin thread. Poonguzhali untied the ropes that bound him to the small craft, and soothed him a little, whereupon he divulged details about himself: a *valaignar* fisherman from one of the hamlets that dotted Ilankai's coast, he'd been caught in the hurricane on one of his fishing expeditions. The sea had claimed his companion; the very fact that he'd escaped and was now speaking to her was proof of his rebirth.

And then, he told her something else.

"The whirlwind had been blowing fiercely and dropped for a while, before midnight," he informed her haltingly. "We were surrounded by pitch blackness. And then, thunder roared deafeningly. Lightning flashed, and that was when I caught sight of two ships upon the sea. One of them was on fire. We simply sat in the catamaran, watching it burn. No one seemed to be upon it. We saw another ship a little way off, and this one seemed to have plenty of men scurrying about. The burning ship sank after a while ..." the man stammered, gasping. "And the other ship vanished in the darkness."

It flashed across Poonguzhali's mind that the vessel bearing the prince might have been one of these—and then, she convinced herself that it couldn't really have been. Dozens of ships passed each other upon sea routes; what did they all matter to her? And yet ... some of those on the burning ship might well have fallen into sea; they may have clutched some plank or the other and even now be drifting helplessly, just like this half-dead fisherman. Surely she could lend them a helping hand? It would be well within her power to row across the sea, take them into her boat and bring them safely ashore. After all, what else was the point of this pitiful life?

To think was to act; Poonguzhali bounded to the boat the moment this idea occurred, turned it over, untied the binding ropes and pushed it into sea. She clambered in, used the full and considerable strength of her iron arms, and began to row. It was an incredibly difficult task, battling the waves close to shore, combating the choppiness of the tricky sea—but once she was beyond the first, risky barrier, paddling became easy; her hands plied the oars like a well-oiled machine and the boat cut through the waters like a hot knife through butter. On and on it went, bobbing enthusiastically; its progress slow but steady.

Her earlier depression vanished; Poonguzhali's heart lifted and with it burst out the old, familiar song that habitually found itself on her lips. Her lovely voice, possessing a deep, pleasing timbre, rose above the clamouring seas, wafting in all four directions, commanding the silence of the elements.

Why anguish, my soul,
When tumbling seas lie smooth?
Why rage, dear heart,
When Lady Earth sleeps, soothed?
When thunder and lightning
Trample the very cosmos
Why spin and twirl in madness
Like dancers, so true?

The prince and Vandhiyathevan drifted upon the sea, buffeted by the choppy waves endlessly, clutching the wrecked mast with a deathly grip all the while. Their ordeal had lasted only a night—but it seemed an aeon to the exhausted Vallavarayan, in whom all hopes of reaching shore and safety soon evaporated.

His customary optimism had deserted him; he no longer even toyed with the idea of survival. Each time a massive wave dragged him right to the top, it occurred to him that he was drawing his last breath: "I'll die soon," he would tell himself—and then, he would look down at his bedraggled body and wonder that he still drew breath.

His thoughts turned often to the prince, and he would glance at the man beside him, mourning his crass stupidity that had flung them both into chaos. "Ah, it was my haste that dragged you down into danger," he rasped, and the prince tried to offer comfort.

"I've known men who've survived three or four days upon the open sea," he murmured often in a voice that rang with conviction and assurance.

"How many days has it been since we fell in?" Vandhiyathevan's voice shook.

"Not even a night yet," soothed Ponniyin Selvar.

"Liar," Vandhiyathevan quavered. "It must've been days—*liar*!"

And then, something happened that drove all thoughts of the prince and peril from his mind: thirst. His throat grew parched; a deadly, all-compassing thirst invaded him—but alas! There was no water to be had. Here he was, drifting in a whole sea of water—but with not a drop to drink. This, he decided, was worse than all the torment he'd undergone and he said so, to the prince.

"Patience," counselled Arulmozhi Varmar. "The sun will rise soon, and we're bound to reach shore at some point."

Vandhiyathevan tried to follow the prince's advice; he really did but it was too much—too much and he really could not bear it anymore and he wished he could die and his mouth was blubbering the words before he could stop himself. "Cut the ropes that bind me, your highness," he begged. "I can't—I can't do this—I cannot bear—cut me away, and let the sea take me!"

This, for some very strange reason, the prince would not do, but his calm words counselling courage failed; he'd reckoned without the desperation that was swiftly overtaking his companion. Vandhiyathevan's tattered composure deserted him completely; he raved, ranted and in a fit of utter insanity tried ripping the cords himself.

The prince ran experienced eyes over him, took stock of the

situation, crept closer and delivered two smart, sharp blows to his head. Vandhiyathevan lost consciousness.

By the time he clawed his way to awareness, it was light. Day seemed to have broken; the sun had undoubtedly risen somewhere—but where exactly, Vandhiyathevan seemed unable to decipher. He blinked away the mists of oblivion to notice the prince gazing at him with deep, if exhausted affection. "Land must be close, my friend," he murmured. "I glimpsed the top of a coconut tree just now. Patience—just a while more!"

"You ought to leave me to my fate, your highness," Vandhiyathevan pleaded, again. "Let me go—save yourself—"

"Don't—don't say that. You ought to know by now that I'd never give you up—ah, was that a voice?" The prince raised a head that seemed unaccountably heavy, and peered across the water. "Someone singing ..."

Indeed, it was Poonguzhali's glorious voice that was washing over them, now.

Why anguish, my soul, When tumbling seas lie smooth?

Her melodious song fell upon their fatigued ears like the clarion call of a blessed saviour; even Vandhiyathevan, more than three quarters dead from mental depression and physical weariness, perked up a little. A tiny burst of enthusiasm shot through him.

"That's—that's Poonguzhali's voice, your highness," he gasped with all his strength. "She's probably rowing her boat—oh, we're saved!"

And a boat did appear in their line of sight within a while. It drifted in their direction bit by agonizing bit, until Poonguzhali herself caught sight of them.

Astonishment paralyzed her. *I'm not seeing things, am I*, she wondered. *Is this really happening?*

The prince cut the ropes that bound Vandhiyathevan in one stroke, and leapt into the boat first. Then, he gave a hand to his companion, who clambered in heavily.

Poonguzhali stood gaping at them, oars clutched in her nerveless hands, like a maiden carved from stone.

BOOK 2 CONCLUDED.

ABOUT KALKI R KRISHNAMURTHY

Most men manage to embrace a single vocation in their lifetime—but very few are successful in what they have chosen to do with their life. Even among these, Kalki Ra Krishnamurthy was something of a rarity, for he managed to be a freedom-fighter, a talented writer, traveller, poet, journalist and a veritable connoisseur of the fine arts. He formed a part of the elite breed of writers who could churn their reader's emotions with their passionate words, or rouse them to wrath with powerful expressions.

Born on September 9, 1899 in the village Buddhamangalam, in the Thanjavur District, to Ramaswamy Iyer and Thaiyal Nayaki, Krishnamurthy, as he was named, began his earliest studies in the local school, later pursuing his education in the Hindu Higher secondary school. His thirst for literature became evident at this stage, for he began to write short stories and essays, under the able tutelage of his Thamizh professor, Periyasamy Pillai.

1921 saw the launch of the Non-Cooperation Movement by Mahatma Gandhi, to which Krishnamurthy, like thousands of other students, responded in earnest by giving up his education and participating in the fight for freedom from the British Raj. In 1922, he was awarded the sentence of one year in prison, during which time he met two people who would provide him with encouragement and enthusiasm all his life: T. Sadasivam and C. Rajagopalachari (Rajaji). It was during his imprisonment that he produced his first novel, *Vimala*.

During October, 1923, he ascended to the post of Sub-editor in a Thamizh periodical, *Navasakthi*, edited by eminent Thamizh scholar and veteran freedom-fighter, Thiru. Vi. Kalyanasundaram, otherwise known as Thiru. Vi. Ka. The next year saw his marriage to Rukmini, while he translated Gandhiji's *My Experiments with Truth* into the famed *Sathya Sothanai*. He also published his first collection of short stories, titled *Sarathaiyin Thanthiram* (Saratha's Strategy). In 1928, he walked out of *Navasakthi*, and engaged in the freedom movement in earnest. Living for the next three and a half years in Gandhiji's Ashram, he was a part of the magazine *Vimochanam* (Release) edited by Rajaji, and it was from this period that his writing skills began to come to the fore. With Rajaji banished to prison, Krishnamurthy wrote rousing essays and short pieces in the magazine, for which he paid the price—another term of imprisonment for six months in September, 1930. Released on March 19th the next year, he took over the editorship of *Ananda Vikatan*, a humour weekly which was swiftly ascending to popularity. From this period, his fame increased phenomenally.

Writing under the pen-names 'Kalki,' 'Thamizh Theni,' 'Karnatakam' etc. his witty, precise and impartial essays attracted readers of all walks. His novels and short stories appeared as serialized versions in the magazine, among them, notably *Kalvanin Kadhali* (The Bandit's Beloved) in 1937, which happened to be his first novel, followed by *Thyaga Bhoomi* (The Land of Sacrifice), both of which were made into movies. In 1941, he left Ananda Vikatan to start his own magazine, *Kalki*, in which T. Sadasivam was instrumental.

He wrote *Parthiban Kanavu* (Parthiban's Dream) during this period, one of his first forays into novels based on a historical setting, with members of the Pallava and Chozha Dynasty as its principal characters. In 1944, *Sivakamiyin Sabadham*, one of the best historical novels ever to have been written in Thamizh was produced, for which Kalki (by which name he styled himself) journeyed to Ajantha and Ellora, so as to add the touch of realism and precision. He also wrote the screen-play for the hit-movie *Meera* starring M.S. Subbulakshmi, the legendary Carnatic singer. 1948 saw the start of *Alai Osai*, a novel set in the era of freedom-fighters, discussing the then political and social situation, and was considered by Kalki to be his best. It won for him the Sahitya Academy Award, posthumously. In 1950, he journeyed to Sri Lanka, which formed the base for his magnum opus, *Ponniyin Selvan*, which, according to many, has none to equal its stature as a superb historical novel till date.

Kalki performed many roles with consummate ease during his lifetime; he wrote stirring novels which explored human relationships and social conditions, subjects considered largely taboo in those days for society was, in general, above criticism and history largely confined to schoolrooms. His writings were in simplified chaste Thamizh, so that they would reach a multitude. He was one of the first writers to add a large humour quotient in his writings—at a time when many authors considered humour beneath their dignity or were unable to project it into their works, Kalki used wit to deliver his sharpest snubs and most pointed criticisms. The effort, not unnaturally, made friends for him even among those who sought to criticise him. At a point when the self-esteem of the Thamizh population was at its lowest ebb and honour, to most, consisted of identification with the British regime, Kalki strove to bring Thamizh Nadu's rich history and culture into focus—he was largely responsible for tearing away the cloak of convention, the stigma around Bharathanatyam, and made it accessible to the common public. Until that time, it had largely been left to the devices of courtesans, and learning it was not considered proper by the general public. Kalki brought the understanding that the Thamizh population had plenty to be proud of.

Kalki relished travelling; his love for the Thamizh countryside, its people, the language and their customs can be found in abundance in almost all his works. He was one of the first authors to promote research and precision in writing, for he actually visited many of the places mentioned in his novels and short stories.

As a freedom-fighter, he was among the most respected in the country—he did much to rouse the people from their self-imposed lethargy and diffidence. Occasional periods of imprisonment did nothing to extinguish his fervour; he made more friends who were willing to join hands in his quest, and his popularity increased.

Small wonder, then, that he is revered by many to be a veritable Leonardo Da Vinci of Thamizh Nadu—for he managed to accomplish much with little.

TRANSLATOR'S NOTE

My father never quite approved of travel, for women. According to him, women could go to temples, perhaps and that, close to home. Any place beyond two kms from our residence was off limits. And it was easy to enforce these constraints as well: living in a (then) suburb roughly 15 kms from the city, we depended on him for conveyance.

And I—well, I'd first read Ponniyin Selvan when I was 12. To my housebound mind, thirsting for new places, Vandhiyathevan's journey to Kodikkarai, abounding in deer, quagmires and mysterious mandapams was fraught with excitement; his midnight ferry to Ilankai made me catch my breath, while his further adventures in that land of lush beauty and intriguing people was beyond even my fertile imagination. The only way I could expand my young mind was to experience Vandhiyathevan's own journey vicariously, and I did.

To this day, I trace my love for travel from Vandhiyathevan, Poonguzhali, Arulmozhi Varmar and Ilaiya Piratti. Years later, I would begin my own pilgrimage—as every loyal PonniyinSelvanist does—to all the historical places mentioned in the novel. I encountered Thamizh Nadu's pretty, down-to-earth and sometimes dangerous, always interesting villages, temples, ruined mandapams and lotus-filled ponds. My interest in History grew—grew beyond the Chozhas and Pandiyas, to Nayaks, Marathas, the British Raj and eventually, Mongolia, Scotland, Wounded Knee, Leeds, Hiroshima … and although I'm yet to visit these story-laden places, like Arulmozhi Varmar, I hope I will, someday.

I dreamt of visiting Thanjavur when I was 12. I ended up marveling at the Brihadeeswarar Temple in my twenties. The experience was richer, more meaningful because Ponniyin Selvan had given me a deep and profound connection to it. I have hopes that someday, I will visit a great many other heritage sites. Because Ponniyin Selvan taught me to see and admire. Look beyond the written word; push away the veil. And in later years, to never give up hope.

I'm sure it's the same for each reader of Ponniyin Selvan, old or new.

Pavithra Srinivasan
August 2019,
Chennai.

Pavithra Srinivasan is a writer, journalist, artist, translator, columnist and editor – not necessarily in that order. She is fascinated with History, and writes children's fiction in The Hindu. She's also an organic farmer and lives in her farm in Thiruvannamalai District, Tamil Nadu, where taps are still seen as luxury items. She has to her credit two collection of historical short-stories for young adults, *Yestertales* (Vishwakarma Publications, 2017); *Little-Known Tales from Well-Known Times: Back to the BCs,* (Helios Books, 2012); two historical novellas *Swords and Shadows* and *I, Harshavardhana* (Pustaka Digital Media, 2016); the translation of Kalki's epic historicals, *SivakamiyinSabadham* (Helios Books, 2012, Tranquebar Press, 2015) and *PonniyinSelvan,* (Tranquebar Press, 2014); *Lock-up: Jottings of an Ordinary Man* (Tranquebar Press, 2017) – the novel on which the National Award winning movie *Visaranai* was based. She has translated Jeffrey Archer's short-story collection into Tamil, *MudiviloruThiruppam* (Westland, 2009) as also Amish Tripathi's acclaimed *Shiva Trilogy* (Westland, 2014, 2015), and *Scion of Ikshvaku* (Westland, 2016). Book 2, *Sita: Warrior of Mithila* (Westland, 2018) is currently under production.

Pavithra is a miniaturist – an artist who draws miniatures. Her work has been featured in The Hindu, Deccan Chronicle, and AvalVikatan. To get regular updates about her work, check out her Facebook page: https://www.facebook.com/pavithra.srinivasan

9 789388 860093